Timeless Lust
in the Ancient World

edited by D.M Atkins

I0553851

ForbiddenFiction
www.forbiddenfiction.com

an imprint of

Fantastic Fiction Publishing
www.fantasticfictionpublishing.com

TIMELESS LUST IN THE ANCIENT WORLD
A ForbiddenFiction book

Fantastic Fiction Publishing
Hayward, California

© D.M. Atkins, 2016

CREDITS
Authors: Elly Green, Konrad Hartmann, Mina Kelly, Jess Lea, Annabeth Leong, Slave Nano, Natasha Neil, Murín Piper
Anthology Editor: D. M. Atkins
Story Editors: Lon Sarver, James L. Wolf, T. J. Alden
Cover Design: Siolnatine
Cover Art: Collage by Siolnatine, adapted from photos © Luislouro and Captblack76 at Dreamstime.com, and various public domain sources.
Internal cover art: Original art and design by Siolnatine with photos by Ron Chapple and Les3photo8 at Dreamstime.com, and adapted from paintings by William Adolphe Bouguereau, Frans Kristoph Janneck, Charles François Jalabert, and Lord Frederick Leighton Production Editor: Erika L Firanc
Proofreading: Aislinn, Derrick N. Davidson, Jae Knight, Todd Michaels, Kailin Morgan

SKU: SPC-100015-02 FFP
ISBN: 978-1-62234-293-8

Published in the United States of America

"You helped me."

His voice was wistful, as his mind returned to the past. She had given Glaucus an herbal concoction that had changed him back into a man, in exchange for some hard labor on her cottage. She had made him promise to stay for a year in payment. He did the best he could regarding the repairs, considering he was a fisherman by trade. She was pleased nevertheless. In fact, toward the end of the contract, he had begun to realize she hadn't cared a bit what he did, as long as he was near her.

He shook his head to clear the memories, his final understanding hanging in the air between them. Standing opposite each other, silence filled the house. Was that the source of the tension he always felt between them? Did she love him? It was difficult to believe. He was, after all, a monster. And if she did — despite his monstrosity — there was now a greater obstacle.

"I need some more help. Again."

If you enjoy this collection, you can sign up for a free membership at ForbiddenFiction and discuss it with other readers and the authors at the *Timeless Lust in the Ancient World* story page at http://forbiddenfiction.com/anthology/SPC-1.100015.
We do our best to proof all our work, but if you spot a text error we missed, please let us know via our website Contact Form at http://forbiddenfiction.com/contact.

Also recommended...

You may also enjoy these other ForbiddenFiction collections:

<u>Divine Desire</u> — **Erotic stories of sacred sexuality**
There's a reason people often cry, "Oh, God," in the throes of passion. God is the only concept big enough to hold all the pleasure they're feeling; pleasure that is as close to beatific grace as any mortal comes. This collection explores the connection between sex and divinity, the mix of temporal and transcendent passions. These ten stories of erotic encounters with the divine invite the reader to witness mortals who crave an immortal touch, deities whose anger with one another is matched only by their lust for one another, and the fate of those tempted by gods of the grave.
http://forbiddenfiction.com/anthology/SPC-1.100011

Liquid Longing by Annabeth Leong
From Annabeth Leong's penetrating view of the sensual, the sacred, and the profane comes an anthology of erotic tales of wonder. Passion flows, mercurial, through these eleven tales of sex, death, and rebirth. Curiosity mingles with shame, anger revels in worship, exploring desire of all types. Here are dead gods, undead starlets, and immortal creatures hungry for connection — a collection of love letters to human nature, with no easy answers among them.
http://forbiddenfiction.com/anthology/AL1-1.100010

DISCLAIMER

This book is a work of fiction which contains explicit erotic content; it is intended for mature readers. Do not read this if it's not legal for you.

All the characters, locations and events herein are fictional. While elements of existing locations or historical characters or events may be used fictitiously, any resemblance to actual people, places or events is coincidental.

This book depicts fictional BDSM; it is not intended to be used as an instruction manual. It contains descriptions of erotic acts that may be immoral, illegal, or unsafe. The characters are not models for the Safe, Sane and Consensual forms embraced by most current practitioners of BDSM. The authors take license with the use of BDSM for dramatic effect. Do not take the events in this story as proof of the plausibility or safety of any particular practice.

Contents

Keeper of the Bedchamber

Jess Lea

Jess Lea first fell in love with the ancient Mediterranean world during school trips to the museum and library. In shadowy rooms, Jess found a wealth of secrets and treasures: tomb paintings of dancing girls, erotic poems to beautiful boys and ruthless women, folk stories of hermaphrodites and shape-changing eunuchs, and 2000-year-old hauntingly lifelike portraits. Later, Jess became fascinated by the silences in most accounts of history. Where were the lives of women? Of people whose genders and sexualities had made them outlaws? Writing the queer past through fiction came to seem difficult, necessary, and irresistible.

Keeper of the Bed Chamber

"Half man! Half man!" The children squeal and stumble backwards as I turn around, their side locks flapping on their shaved skulls. One of my venomous glares is enough to send them hurtling back to their mothers, scarab-charms bobbing and bare feet kicking up the dust. Turning back to the market stall, I can hear them being scolded: "Don't you go near him! You never know..."

No, there are many things you never know, here in this little village south of Thebes. Like what pronouns my neighbours will use for me today. Like whether they will spit and clutch their Evil Eye charms as I walk by, or wish me good morning, or ask my help reading legal documents or learning Greek or lifting a curse. Like whether the soldiers of the new emperor will kick down my door tonight, tomorrow, or next year.

I can't even be certain what they think I am—eunuch, tribade, hermaphrodite? Or maybe just a funny foreigner, with my Alexandrian accent and Arab features, a shade lighter than these native Egyptians but a good deal swarthier. If I think about it I get quite doleful, for in my old life I was used to being admired. I could scarcely leave the house without feeling the sweep of greedy eyes along my bare limbs, tanned and curling with soft, dark hair, and my craggy face framed by thick black curls, not to mention the view from behind.... But standards of beauty are different out here. My eyebrows alone must appal them.

This isn't an easy place for an outsider to settle. Cobbling together a living writing letters for farmers, giving lessons to their spotty sons, and fixing up the ledger-books for the owners of granaries and breweries whose own slaves are too dopey or too honest. If anyone asks, I used to travel with an acting troupe, but was thrown out when they found somebody younger and prettier to play the female roles. It piques me that no one, so far, has questioned this tale. I could live better in a city, but I daren't take the risk of being recognised.

When the Romans invaded and I fled the capital, I thought of changing myself entirely. Plenty of Cleopatra's followers did — astrologers and acrobats turning overnight into respectable scribes and bakers, or vice versa. But I was too proud for that, and besides I doubt I'd have been convincing in another part. I'd lived as a male, although not as a man, for most of my life. Ever since I was a child, and our village was attacked and my mother dressed me in my dead brother's clothes for protection. A fat slave trader counted my teeth, looked in my ears, then prodded my loincloth.

"*Eunochos?*" I'd never heard the word before. Later, I discovered it meant "keeper of the bed chamber," for our role in guarding the women of the palace. He raised one bushy eyebrow. "Well, why not? They sell for more. Smarter than girls, and just as pretty." He gave a phlegmy laugh — "I won't tell if you don't, eh?" — and shoved me into line.

It didn't always protect me, and I never saw my mother again. But life in Alexandria gave opportunities to eunuchs, chances at wealth, learning and political power that few slave women could have dreamed of. And besides, by then it was what I knew.

I'd like to think I still cut a dash, even in this tattered finery, the bright silk and linen robes that were the height of fashion five years ago. Their swirling colours above the clump of my hefty boots gave me just the right gait, a feminine swagger that was utterly male. No one did elegance like the royal eunuchs of Alexandria, and the people who sneered insults after us — *gelding, catamite, dancing boy, freak* — wanted us most of all. With my ebony walking stick, tasselled turbans and jewellery that could take your eye out, I was a sight to behold. The queen herself put this chunk of turquoise and silver on my little finger.

Not that I've told anyone the circumstances under which she gave it. I may have been outrageous, but for those I loved I could be very discreet.

Ten years ago, if you were young and energetic with a smart mouth, sharp looks and big plans, Alexandria was the place to be. Cleopatra's alliance with Marc Antony, her canny governance, and her ruthless skill at squashing her rivals meant that Egypt held vast, wealthy territories through Asia Minor and the Levant, all the way to Libya. Trade was buzzing—olive oil, balsam, timber, silks, ivory, spices and wine—and temples and public buildings were springing up in great hefts of marble, speckled granite and deep red porphyry. Athletes, artists, courtesans, merchants, mystics and criminals flocked to the city from as far as India, Spain, and Babylon; there were parades with giraffes, cheetahs, and elephants, and no one had had the plague for ages.

I'd had two years of freedom and a budding career as a trader of rare books, thanks to my old master, a scholar and antiquarian with a kind nature and bad eyesight, both of which proved lucky for me. I spoke high class Greek, fluent Aramaic and passable Latin; I had two gold earrings, a shepherd-boy haircut and the sort of legs that made priests and ambassadors walk into walls. I knew how to spot a valuable manuscript from across a market stall or beneath a rubbish midden, how to haggle and flatter, and how to make the women of the court giggle and blush from behind their veils. In short, I was an irksome, strutting little pest, but I like to think I was kind to most people, and life in the palace didn't exactly encourage modesty. You only had to look at our queen—which I did, as much as I could.

The first time I saw Cleopatra, she was seated in a litter painted in gold leaf, carried on the oiled shoulders of a dozen guards. Incense burners swung before them, trailing plumes of scented smoke. Her features were like those of the women in my old village: long black eyes ringed with kohl, a swooping nose, thick dark slashes of eyebrows and hair like black snakes. She wore great silver earrings in the shape of cymbals, her sandals were painted with the figures of her enemies to be trodden underfoot, and she was talking about tax reform in a way that made you actually want to listen. Musicians were playing at a wedding nearby: *"With her hair she ensnares me, with her eyes she fetters me, with her thighs she binds me fast, with her seal she burns the brand...*" The queen smacked a mosquito dead with her peacock-fan and swore in Egyptian. I fell in love on the spot.

I couldn't have called myself innocent. Handsome eunuchs got plenty of attention, from older men who wanted a boyish young beloved, softened by the blade, and from their bored, restless wives, who weren't averse to the idea of a lover who could linger in women's quarters without gossip, and without leaving a bastard behind. *"Who wouldn't have it that way?"* one of them whispered, her lips nuzzling my ear, her manicured fingers nipping at my ass. *"The flowers of love without the fruits..."* I avoided the first group of suitors as graciously as I could, although I admit I didn't always send back their presents — well, I had a lifestyle to maintain. As for the second group — ah, let's say not all my Alexandrian education took place in the Great Library. Although there was one occasion with a certain Olympia in the mathematics section — her red hair spread across the scroll rack, her creamy breasts in my hands, her tongue in my mouth...

Looking back, it seems insanely risky, but none of those women, whose duty meant bearing children and tolerating their husbands, ever complained when I didn't need to be caressed in return, or when I kept my clothing on. Perhaps they imagined my body as so shamefully mangled that it was a relief to leave it private. Or perhaps they just liked my tailored tunics in Chinese silk as much as I did.

The queen was a different matter. Lucky for me she was of a literary bent.

"I don't know how you do it, Ariston." It had taken me two rare editions and a promise of dinner with the chief librarian, but I'd wrangled an introduction at last. The queen liked my conversation and my opening gift, a volume of the poetry of Nossis of Locri: *"Nothing is sweeter than love, all other riches second..."* I had taste, she said, as I kissed her hand; I should come back. Which I did, so many times that her guards threatened to charge me rent.

I can't pretend I was discreet in my crush, laughing too hard at her jokes and loitering outside the most tedious diplomatic functions in the hope of winning a smile. And I daresay a few eyebrows were raised when she had me sit by her at dinner, where she could flick me with her fly-switch and pop olives into my mouth, while I fought back the urge to lick the salty juice from her fingers. Ridiculous, people sniffed, but what objection could they make? Everyone knew eunuchs were made to be harmless.

It was the evening meetings I especially longed for, when she would call me in to advise on the acquisition of some document or other for the Great Library, and regale me with stories of how her ancestors had filled the place to begin with. One dastardly old king wrote to all the world's sovereigns asking to borrow their most treasured books for copying, only to keep them for himself; another sent his soldiers to storm foreign ships in the harbour and seize every volume on board. The curtains rippling in the breeze, the crisp smell of the scrolls in their leather casings, the thought of piracy... my imagination never needed much encouragement to run wild. Still, I never dared to hope for more than her conversation, which was worldly but never indecent, and the warmth of her hand against my lips as I said good night. Not until one very particular evening.

That night she received me alone. It was late, the vast marble chamber all shadows and jumping lamplight. I'd sent word that I'd brought something special.

"Alchemy?" she exclaimed. "Wherever do you find these things?" I unravelled the scroll and she leaned forward in her chair. Its arms were carved with the heads of lions; its legs ended in ivory claws. The queen's hair was loose and drops of rose oil sparkled in it, making me breathe in deep. She crossed her legs and I heard the swish of silk.

"A rare specimen, majesty. Unearthed from a library vault in Memphis, and at least three centuries old."

"You could say the same thing about your colleagues, Ariston. You do know these theories are impossible?" But she was smiling as she bent her head over the mystic symbols and the recipes for melding copper, zinc and mercury into gold. Cleopatra liked peculiar old volumes as much as I did, and could read them in nine languages. Her hair fell forward, caressing the back of my hand.

"Ah, but there's more, majesty. Inside the scroll, we found this." I unwound it carefully, a smaller, crumbling parchment. "An essay in the Platonic style. It explains that the four elements of life are in a constant state of transformation: water, condensed, becomes earth; wind compressed into clouds becomes water; fire burns itself out into air..." The queen nodded and I continued. "All living things are just imperfect copies of an ideal that exists only in the world of the imagination. Why, therefore, should artists think their creations inferior to nature? Why should we not seek to improve upon it?" I realised the queen had stopped tracing the letters. The tip of her forefinger had come to rest against mine.

"Well," she said quietly, "you must know about that, Ariston."

"The curious thing is, majesty, we think the document's province is Athenian—around four hundred years old." I grinned. "When word gets out..."

But if I'd thought the possibility of a real Platonic manuscript would please her, I was mistaken. She sat back with a sigh, her hands withdrawing to the arms of her chair, the smell of roses fading.

"Ingenious, Ariston. No doubt you'll want to get it catalogued."

I blinked in dismay: "Your majesty does not wish to read further?"

"Of course, but as you see..." She gestured towards the avalanche of letters and petitions across her desk. "Besides, I shouldn't like to keep you. I'm sure you have plans." Her tired movements and the edge in her voice surprised me; only then did I realise my error. I'd thought to impress her, but Cleopatra was weary of presents. How many nights had she passed alone in here? Her children's father preferred spending his evenings in dice games and the bodies of courtesans, a thing I suspected the queen of encouraging, for apart from world domination they had few passions in common. And as for her other admirers—the poets and princes who rhapsodised about her beauty, getting the colour of her eyes wrong and vowing to die for her, should the occasion arise—none of them ever got close. Cleopatra had created a legend for herself that was splendid enough to scorch anyone who touched it, and she preferred it that way... but perhaps not all the time.

I bowed over her hand in farewell, and from habit she extended it to me to kiss. Silver and turquoise glowed on her little finger. I kissed her ring as I had done on our first meeting, but this time I made my lips soft enough to fit right around it, feeling the swell of the stone, the metal band growing warm as it pressed a ridge into my lip. Cradling her hand between both of mine, I let my lips wander higher, tracing with my mouth the tendons pulled like bow-strings beneath her skin, marvelling at the softness of a woman's flesh when she has never had to work, before turning it over to inhale the scent of spikenard and cinnamon oil on the inside of her wrist, where the veins throbbed. When my kisses reached the warm hollow of her palm, the queen stifled a sigh—"Oh, you are such a flatterer"—but she did not draw away. She stroked my face instead, and traced my lips with the salty ball of her thumb. It was only when I caught it lightly between my teeth and made as if to take her inside me that she pulled back and slapped me a little.

"What foolishness is this?" I had never heard her voice tremble before. "You don't get enough kisses already? Enough rich widows and randy old men chasing you around the court?"

"Too many, majesty, but I've never wanted them. I've kept my honour." She rolled her eyes, and I insisted, "Truly, I am not nearly as corrupt as you imagine."

"What corruption do you think me capable of imagining, Ariston?" She arched an eyebrow and I blushed.

"People have strange ideas about our sort, majesty, but I've only ever wanted... kindness. Someone to respect."

"And you went looking for it here?" She laughed, a hint of sadness in her voice. "Still, it must be lonely, knowing you can never marry or have children." She regarded me for a moment, then reached out to touch my hair. "You're not from here, are you, Ariston? Do you remember your own family? Your mother?"

I shook my head; it seemed simpler that way. Cleopatra sighed in pity, hesitated, then beckoned me with her chin. She was not a depraved woman, whatever her enemies said, but she was a lonely one, and like many powerful people she liked to feel generous sometimes. Fighting a rush of shyness, I leaned down and kissed her.

Our kisses were slow at first, exploratory. Her head tilted back towards mine, her fingers lacing their way through my hair. I tasted wine and the slippery sheen of her lip paint, and felt those lips of hers yield to the pressure of my tongue.

"Kindness, he says..." But she was smiling. She pushed back her chair and rose halfway, drawing me up against her.

At the warm press of her body, I forgot about being shy. I kissed her all over her face—eyelids, cheeks, the ridge of her nose—while she laughed in a whisper and scolded me for my craziness, and held me tight until I found my way back to her mouth. How long since she had been kissed by someone who meant it? And really, how long since I had been?

My hands settled around her sash, then began to loosen it, as a man does with his bride on their wedding night. She nudged them away, but higher, towards her breasts. Through her clothing I could feel the soft contours pushing forward to fill out my palms, her back arching, her nipples tightening between my fingers. I worked them back and forth, timing each gentle pull to her indrawn breaths, the layers of silk in between us serving only to heighten the sensation.

"Darling boy... oh, that's enough..." Each word was punctuated by further kisses, but still I took her at her word, releasing her and dropping to my knees on the marble.

"Forgive me, your majesty." She sat back in her chair too quickly, as if unable to trust her legs. "I know it is forbidden, even for one such as me. But you've no idea how I've struggled, trying to contain my love." Bowing further I touched my forehead to her big toe, then kissed it, feeling the strap of her sandal along my cheek, smelling rosewater, leather and sweat.

"You are a silly one..." She gave a faint laugh that caught halfway, as my mouth traced her instep, the fine bones on the inside of her ankle.

Her gown was made of layers of filmy silk, its hems embroidered with arching peacocks and phoenixes rising. It brushed against my cheeks, then the back of my neck, forming a scented tent around me as I kissed my way higher.

"Ariston..." From underneath the fabric, the lamplight was muted; everything seemed a dim shade of amber, warm and intimate. She let me coax her knees apart. "Oh, my boy, you mustn't degrade yourself."

"Majesty, it's an honour." The flesh was tender on the inside of her thighs; I nipped it playfully, then with firmer force, letting her feel the ridge of my teeth and the pull of my tongue. She was moving by then, and trying not to; I could feel the muscles tensing along her legs as she fought to contain herself, could hear the soft scrabbling of her toes inside her sandals, and her nails as they gripped the arms of her chair, with the lion's head carvings. Did she prefer to think this was all a whim, an act of kindness towards me in my sad condition? Did she fear losing control even now? I couldn't help pushing my luck by teasing her further, running my fingertips up and down her calves and caressing the ticklish backs of her knees, until she squirmed and cried out loud. The next cry was muffled — she must have bitten her hand — but deeper and impossible to disguise, as I nuzzled my way through the downy fuzz between her thighs to the place that was waiting for me.

Her lips were full and slick with need, parting to the sweep of my tongue. I breathed in the scent of her and thought of sea-sprites, of Nereids. Sliding my hands up to hold her steady, I flickered and strummed and played, feeling as if I'd stolen into a temple and was plucking out tunes on some sacred instrument, half-expecting to be hauled out and beaten at any moment. But instead there was only music: soft, incoherent murmurs that might have been admonitions, and which soon gave way to sighs and moans and rough little gasps. She was moving freely now, all pretence gone, as I grasped her tighter and drew her sweet, swollen bud into my mouth. I felt her strain and rock against me, felt my knees screaming in protest against the marble and the chair scraping on its lion's claw feet — until she yielded on a long, shuddering breath, anointing me deliciously.

Despite the pain in my legs, I took care not to hurry away. I kissed my way down the same route that I had come, finally lingering over her big toe and nibbling it until she laughed and kicked me weakly backwards.

"Crazy boy." She smoothed down her skirts, the movement almost shy. Then she nudged me. "Time you were on your feet, Ariston."

"Your majesty is weary?" Not for anything would I have admitted how much that stung me. Still, I could feel my face darkening as I stood up. I'd known this was madness, never to be repeated or spoken of afterwards, but I had not thought she would be so cold, so soon. Then to my surprise, she rose up too.

"What's that face for?" the queen asked. Her smile widened. "Ariston. Do you think me so ungallant?" I looked down to find her fingers hooked in my belt.

Cleopatra eased me back a step, until I felt the edge of the table behind me. She drew my face to hers and let our foreheads rest together, her long fingers teasing the whorl of my ear, the back of my neck where the street barber had shaved my hair down to bristles.

"Look at you..." Her cheekbone rubbed against mine, her lips brushing the line of my jaw. "Smooth as a peach. Are you like this all over?"

"Majesty — " With the table at my back I'd nowhere to go; her belly was pressing into mine. Ripples of sensation were spreading through me once more, and I hardly knew whether to be frightened, moved, or astonished. All those wealthy women who never gave my hidden, unspeakable body a second thought — and the only one who did was *this* woman? The queen traced my thigh along the hem of my tunic, then slid her hand up underneath.

Feeling me tense, she kissed me and whispered "Don't be shy. What did they leave you with?" Some eunuchs had their parts crushed or twisted instead of being cut away; some, it was rumoured, could perform all the functions of a natural man. In a panic, feeling her reach my loincloth, I blurted "Nothing, majesty."

But if I'd thought that would make her stop in disgust, I was wrong again. Instead she loosened the twist of my loincloth with deft fingers, and slipped her hand inside.

My eyes had shut tight, my body rigid with nerves. I could feel the heat hammering behind my face and prickling beneath my clothing. She plunged her fingers deeper, through the springing curls, lusher than our kind were supposed to have, until she reached —

"Oh — " The queen's body grew still. I waited for her to withdraw, braced myself for insults, banishment, even cruelty.

Instead she turned her head slowly, until her eyelashes tickled my cheek. In the same growl she used for the dawn prayers in the temple, Cleopatra said, "It doesn't feel like nothing to me."

Now, as I reach my house and cross the threshold, here in this village so far from Alexandria, the memory goes melting through me, making my eyelids flutter closed and my hand grasp the doorframe. How the thought of her stirs me, still. How I miss her, still.

There is little left of her in Egypt now. The agents of the new emperor have toppled her statues, burned her documents, melted her coins and chipped her name from temple walls. But they can't destroy a memory: the rasp of her laughter, her husky voice reading from some philosopher's riddle or traveller's tale, the purple trail of her gown along the marble—or her hand between my legs that night, bringing me to a helpless, adoring climax.

Opening my eyes again, I venture forward into the courtyard, regarding the whitewashed walls, the blue mosaic tiles and the little fishpond, as if it has been years, not hours, since I saw them last. It isn't Alexandria, this place, but here and there it is beautiful. It occurs to me that maybe the soldiers won't come, not tonight, not ever.

"Ariston?" Neferne's voice reaches me before she does: calm and lilting, with that accent I couldn't understand at first and now couldn't do without. "Is that you?"

Letting the memory go with a sigh, I don't answer straight away. Instead, I look around to find her leaning in the doorway, her bracelets clattering along one slim brown arm, that quizzical smile on her lips. We haven't known each other long, but I think we will.

"Yes. I'm home."

Andromache's Prize

Annabeth Leong

Annabeth Leong has written erotica of many flavors. She loves shoes, stockings, cooking, and excellent bass lines. Forbidden Fiction publishes many of her dark erotica titles.

Find her online at annabethleong.blogspot.com
or on Twitter @AnnabethLeong.

Chapter 1

Remembering Achilles

The men came back from raiding too loud, too drunk, with sheepish grins on their faces. Briseis sat outside the tent she shared with Calygdus, repairing the bronze belt that Achilles had given her when she had still been innocent enough to love a man.

The day faded. That's what things did in Briseis' world. Once, there had been glory in this place—the great city of Troy, and the great army of the Achaians. Once, there had been Achilles, and Hector, and good, sweet Patroclus—heroes worthy of the name. Now, the city had fallen, the heroes had died, and yet she remained, drinking up the bitter dregs of war in the chariot-rutted meadow where she had lived ever since being taken from her home. The fight had finished, and yet people could not seem to leave. She sometimes thought nothing remained in the world but this.

The beauty of her face had faded, the strength of her passion had faded. Hope had faded.

She sighed at the men's unsteady gait across the worn and trampled meadow. Calygdus, to whom she now belonged, was impotent, a fact for which she thanked Zeus every day. Tonight he would at least want to pretend. If he was drunk enough, he might want to actually try.

Maybe tonight she could finally stab him in the heart and run away. She did want to be free. And failing that, she could stab herself in the heart, if she had the courage.

Courage, unfortunately, was what she had always lacked. Briseis never had a fighter's spirit. She was cursed with the gift of making do.

Briseis ducked into the tent and put away the belt, combed out her long, fair hair, and changed into clothes she didn't care about. The men's conversation came closer and wafted through the thin material of the tent.

"Can you believe what that bitch said to me?" Calygdus' voice would have stood out anywhere, high and nasal, trailing off into a gurgle when he paused. His voice went even higher as he mimicked a woman: "'Watch your backs tonight, boys. We'll be coming for your women.' She couldn't really have been Andromache. I'd think Hector would have married a bitch with at least a few of Aphrodite's blessings. Still..."

He must have gestured, because a moment later a round of raucous laughter burst from the men. After the laughter subsided, a young man's voice spoke up. "Why didn't you take her and her band right there in the road?"

Briseis rolled her eyes and stepped out of the tent, in time to get a good view of Calygdus' jaw working as he tried to come up with a response. A cruel light came into his eyes when he saw her. He reached for her hair and jerked Briseis to her knees on the ground beside him. He pulled her face against his crotch, and she knew to kiss at the limp mass under his tunic. Shame still stabbed through her heart at the act, though Calygdus had shown her off this way ever since he'd captured her. Achilles had never used her so callously, and before being taken by that powerful warrior, she had been the daughter of a king.

"Take this one," Calygdus said. "She's getting a little ugly now that she's used up and worn, but you can still see what Achilles must have liked about her. Look at those lips. And it doesn't hurt to know you're plowing the field in the footsteps of a great man."

Briseis bit back her retorts and kept her eyes on the ground. The gods had always hated her, and Calygdus was her latest proof. She had dared to attempt escape from the Achaians, but instead of finding a way to sail home, she found this oaf and his degradations.

"What's all this?" The old man joined their group. He'd once been a warrior among the Achaians, but the departing kings had sailed away in their treasure-laden black ships, leaving him behind with the rest of the dross.

Briseis liked him. He called himself No Name, did not delight in telling endless stories of his past exploits, and participated in the looting and general mayhem as little as possible. He remained at the tents with the women often, and she talked with him sometimes. He favored grim pronouncements about the end of the world and the sad state of the race of men, but this echoed the thoughts in her own head. She didn't mind.

"Stay to your knitting, old man," Calygdus said, to a reward of guffaws.

"Andromache says she's coming for your women? How can that be? Neoptolemus, son of god-like Achilles, made her his concubine during the sacking of Troy." Confusion trembled on the old man's lips. Despite her own humiliation, still trapped against the stinking balls of Calygdus, Briseis pitied No Name.

"Your stories are out of date, old man," Calygdus sneered. "The whore shanked Achilles' whelp in the thigh with his own weapon, dove out of his ship, and swam back to Troy, screaming about her dead son the whole way. Crazy bitch. What's she looking for back here? She'd have been better off laying back and taking it like a good slut should."

Briseis' heart pounded. Achilles had spoken often of the nobility of Andromache, and there could be no better proof of it. Andromache must possess honor and dignity that Briseis could only imagine. "Maybe she didn't want to leave her home," Briseis whispered, too moved to remember to keep her mouth shut.

Calygdus dropped a thudding blow on her ear. "Don't you have enough work for that mouth?" He lifted his tunic and pulled her under it more completely, yanking her hair until she opened her lips and took in one of his balls.

No Name's confusion persisted. "Andromache says she's coming for your women?"

"It's not going to happen," Calygdus laughed. "If Andromache tries anything, she'll be warming my bed tonight. If she displeases me, perhaps I'll send her to warm yours!"

The old man shook his head, not seeming to hear the bursts of laughter from the others. "She should be the wife of Neoptolemus, or ruling in Epirus beside Helenus. She should not be free."

"No, the bitch should not be free! What do you think I'm trying to say?" Calygdus released his grip on Briseis to make shooing gestures at the old man. She seized the opportunity to get away from him.

Briseis leapt to her feet and ran to No Name's side. "Old man," she said kindly, taking his arm. "Let me show you back to your tent."

Her grandfather had been confused this way before the end of his life. No Name's features resembled a child's, his skin too soft for the harsh winds that buffeted the ruins of Troy. His eyes, pale as the sky, watered and wavered when he tried to fix them on her.

"Wash off that old man's come before you crawl back to my bed, whore," Calygdus mocked Briseis. She ignored him and coaxed No Name to walk with her.

"You shouldn't be here either, girl," he said, shaking his head. "This has gone all wrong."

"Did he fuck you?" Calygdus growled when Briseis returned to him. He rubbed a meaty hand through his loose, greasy hair.

"Of course not." She would have found something to do on the opposite side of the tent, but he grabbed her by the wrist and yanked her to the ground beside him. She planted one shoulder hard in the dirt, grunting at the shock to her bones.

"Don't tell me you're not getting it from somewhere. A beautiful little thing like you." He traced the line of her cheekbone. His finger dug into her flesh. Briseis closed her eyes and turned her head away. He gripped her chin and forced her to face him.

Her heart pounded with the habit of fear, but more than that, Briseis felt tired of him. "What do you want?" The words came out with a sigh.

Calygdus buried his face in Briseis' hair. He rolled onto her, crushing her with his weight. Rancid smells left over from dinner stung her nose. She wanted to get this over with. If it went on too long, she might have to feel a bit of the old pain.

He stroked one of her breasts with ominous reverence and kissed the side of her face. "Tell me you want me."

"Please," Briseis said. "I want you." Acting came easily with long practice. She moaned when he undid the laces on her dress. She forced herself to purr and arch toward him when his hand slipped under the material, squeezing and groping at her bare flesh. She even spread for him when he reached between her legs.

"Say it again."

"I want you," she repeated, her nervousness increasing. The bruises from the last time he'd tried to take her and been unable had lingered.

He forced his body between her thighs. She closed her legs around his waist obediently, as if she wanted him, her stomach turning at the idea even as she stretched her face into a smile for him.

Calygdus fumbled, lining his half-hard cock up with her cunt.

"I want you," Briseis said again, hoping to encourage the reluctant tool as he worked to stuff it into her. She rolled her hips and tugged at her nipples. He'd forced her to put on lewd shows for him in the past. She forced down her pride and performed for him voluntarily, still looking to make the night pass more easily.

Calygdus groaned. "That's the way. Show me what you want." His fingers groped between her legs, blunt and blind.

She tried to remember Achilles' face. She used to get wet for him. Sometimes, she would come around his cock the moment he shoved it into her. That had happened the first time, despite her terror and her efforts to fight him off.

Heat flushed through her at the memory, and she moaned sincerely. "That's the way," Calygdus said. But his cock did not cooperate. It slipped to one side or another, soft and shrinking now. He growled with frustration and banged his pelvis against hers like a little boy having a temper tantrum.

"Fucking slut," he said. He slapped Briseis' face. She yelped with shock and outrage, then bit her lip and forced the sound down. Now, he would spend the night beating her. She'd taken it before, and she could do it again. She did her best to meet his eyes as the blows continued. Her lip split and filled her mouth with the flavor of metal. She retreated into her mind.

"Who is it?" he demanded. He'd been asking for a while, she realized. She just hadn't heard him.

"What are you talking about?"

"A hot slut like you can't live without it. I know it. Someone is spearing you."

"No!" Briseis said, truthfully, not liking the direction his drunken suspicions were heading.

He shoved one finger into her cunt, but wasted no time escalating it to three. Her memories of Achilles had not aroused her enough to prepare her for this. Briseis winced and tried to squirm away. He pinned her by sinking a knee deep into the flesh of her thigh. Briseis shoved at the limb helplessly, but his weight easily overmatched her attempt. He slammed his hand in and out of her until she cried out from the pain of it.

"If it's not me," Calygdus spat, "it's got to be someone. Who is it? Who is it?" Blows rained down on her face in time with the fingers driving into her cunt.

Briseis raised her arms to shield her face. This was routine, she told herself, not even worth noticing. Still, she trembled violently.

After a few minutes, she realized that the sounds of his flesh crashing against her body weren't the only noises breaking the night. The thunder of horses' hooves shook the ground. A woman's voice rose in a wild whoop unlike any sound Briseis had ever heard.

A piece of her heart followed the sound. Joy rose in her chest as long as the noise lasted, and the feeling made Calygdus fade.

Calygdus stiffened above her, something like shame flickering across his cruel features. "Andromache."

"You're afraid," Briseis murmured, in wonderment. What would it be like to be a woman and yet wield such power over men?

He looked down at her, curling his lip. "She's just a woman," he said. "If she hasn't had enough of war, I'll remind her of its ways."

He eased himself off her, joints cracking. He armed himself and slipped outside. Briseis hauled herself upright. She'd ache something awful in the morning, but the pain hadn't really set in yet. She'd had enough of war, long ago, even if it seemed no one else ever tired of it. She struggled to her feet, found her dagger, and stepped outside the tent in time to see a woman bury a spear between Calygdus's ribs.

The woman jerked her spear free and kicked the man away. Briseis stared at her. She held the reigns of a lovely black horse. The animal dwarfed her, but her small stature didn't lessen the power of her stance. All over the camp, women swooped down on fast horses, torching tents and leaving carnage in their wake.

The woman before Briseis tossed her hair back, fires from behind her giving the brown mass of curls a bright red corona. She wore very little—her breasts were bound tightly against her chest with strips of cloth and a garment around her waist seemed more a place to attach her weapons and tools than an effort to cover the cleft between her legs. An improbably large bronze shield was strapped to her left forearm, but she showed no strain from holding it.

"Andromache?" Briseis said, awed. This was the first time since the death of Achilles that a warrior's ferocity had stirred her.

The woman grinned. Even her teeth seemed sharp. "Daughter of Lyrnessus," she said, "what a shame it is that weak men continue to hold you by the chains the mighty used to bind you." She stowed her spear across her back and held out her hand. "Come with me. We'll travel together to build the City of Women."

"The City of Women?"

"We will carve out a place in this broken world. We need somewhere to start again, a place where the war stops outside the walls. Come, sister, and I will show you."

Briseis took Andromache's hand. Her bones were delicate, made for sewing tapestries, but calluses studded the skin of her palm. Briseis shivered and let Andromache lift her onto the horse.

Her brain pounded with one thought: *Not since Achilles.*

But before the warrior queen could race them both out of the ruined camp, she thought of No Name. "There's one other who shouldn't be put to the spear," Briseis said. "An old man. He's confused. Even if your women don't kill him, I don't think he can survive on his own."

Andromache fixed her with darkly burning eyes. Finally, she nodded, and they went into the camp together to retrieve him.

Chapter 2

The City of Women

Briseis' hands were torn and bleeding, and she didn't think she could lift her arms to pull her hair out of her eyes, much less to drive a spear into a wooden target. "Andromache," she said. "You've got to have mercy. I'll train again tomorrow."

The warrior woman turned, scowling. "Is mercy what you've been getting out of life, Briseis? Did your Calygdus have mercy on you? Did Agamemnon, King of the Greeks, when he stole you to his bed just to make a point? How about great Achilles, murderer of my husband and killer of your father and brothers?"

Briseis threw down her spear and put both hands on her hips. "No, Andromache, they didn't have mercy on me. But I'm not here to live the same life I had with them. You told me we're headed for a city that stops war outside its walls. I'll believe it when I see it, and when I meet someone who's not completely addled by battle lust and bloody honor."

A heavy silence surrounded her. Briseis glanced around and saw the other women in the camp watching her and Andromache with a combination of fear and envy. She ignored them and turned back to the fiery woman. Briseis displayed her bloody palms. "I'm going to go and wrap these in leather. I'll train again with you tomorrow, and I'll give you everything I've got but no more. I'm done giving more than that."

She turned her back and stalked away; half fearing that Andromache would cut her down for her insolence. When no one stopped her, she walked to the outskirts of the camp, where No Name had his tent.

The old man sat in the brittle grass just outside it. "Hello, Grandfather," Briseis said.

He looked up at her, his face at first suspicious, then changing to warm. "It's easy to see why Achilles loved you."

Briseis stopped, taken by a wave of bitterness. "And how do you know that he loved me? He never told me so himself."

"He defied the Atreidai for your sake. He punished Agamemnon with his bitter refusal. He stood aside from battle, heartbroken by the loss of you."

"That was about glory, old man. I was only an excuse."

No Name caught a flea with his thumbnail against the skin of his arm. "Not even the architects of this world could have suspected what you would become."

"A whore?"

He shook his head gravely and touched the side of her face. "You will bring the end of war."

Briseis laughed. "Are you a prophet now? Has Apollo visited you?"

"I am old. I am allowed to make no sense." They both cracked smiles at that one.

Briseis pressed his hand and left him. Soon, she strolled beyond the perimeter of the camp, sniffing at the few flowers that remained, splashing through the big puddles left in the chariot-rutted ground. When she tired of moving, she found a place to lie on the earth. She stared up at the sky and thought about how the soil beneath her had soaked up the blood of so many men and women. She supposed she could remember a time before the war, before the pillaging, before she was taken for the first time, but those few images of her family and home seemed colorless as a stone carving.

A footfall in the grass a short distance away brought her rolling to her feet.

"Your instincts are good, anyway," Andromache said. A sheen of sweat covered her bronzed skin and her hair was tangled from training. Every time she saw Hector's former bride, Briseis could barely breathe from awe at her strength. How could a woman transform herself so thoroughly, going from helpless prize of war to living imitation of Athena?

"Why are you looking at me like that?" Andromache asked.

"You don't look like a woman who ever belonged to a man."

"I never did," Andromache said, tossing her head. "Hector was my lover, my friend, my husband, the father of my poor lost child. He never owned me."

Briseis bowed her head.

"Daughter of Lyrnessus," Andromache said. "I am no better than you. I came to say that you were right."

"About what?"

"If we can't be different from the rest of them, what's the point of fighting them at all? You know that better than me."

Briseis smiled gratefully, and Andromache stepped closer. "What I learned," Briseis said, "is that you can always make your own life, no matter what's happening to you. There's a corner of your mind that belongs only to you. I didn't know that when Achilles first took me, and so I fell in love with him. But after that, I walled off a part of myself, and I always knew that I didn't have to open the gates to that place to anyone."

Andromache reached for her hand and guided them both down to sit in the weeds. "That's what I hope the City of Women is like," she said quietly. "That's what I want it to be. I've heard about a clutch of ships Achilles' Myrmidons left behind. We will go to them, kill any men who defend them, and sail over the ocean to find a place for ourselves."

"Andromache, how did you become this way? I don't imagine Hector taught you to fight, and yet you saved yourself. You didn't let yourself become a thing like..."

"Like you? You're not a thing."

"How did you find the courage to fight?"

Andromache was silent for a long time. She sat close enough that their bodies pressed together, and Briseis could feel her blood pounding through her veins and her breath coming fast and hard. "I used to be just a woman," Andromache said finally. "I loved my husband. I raised my son." Her hand squeezed Briseis' hard enough to grind the bones together. "When Achilles cut down my dear husband and the men brought his body back to me, something died inside me forever. Then, Troy fell. Neoptolemus flung my son Astyanax over the city wall, then raped me. A dark and terrible thing grew in me then. It replaced my love for Hector, for my home, and for my son. It makes me strong, and I can pretend the joy I feel at pressing a spear into a man's breast resembles the joy I used to feel at pressing my breast to Astyanax's lips to feed him my milk. Zeus has turned me to stone."

"I pray to Hera, and she has taught me the way of being softer than water," Briseis said.

"Show me," Andromache murmured.

Briseis lowered her eyes from the other woman's fiery gaze and pressed her mouth forward. The famed "white-armed Andromache" had been baked dark by sun and hardship, but her skin smelled fresh.

Their lips met. Andromache's wind-chapped mouth scraped against Briseis'. Briseis embraced her, finding her body taut everywhere except for the soft, tender skin of her scars. Briseis slipped her hand under Andromache's leather shirt and felt her breasts, fascinated by the pliant, supple flesh surrounded by so much muscle. Briseis continued her exploration by running her hands down Andromache's sides. For all her strength, she had a woman's shape—a narrow waist and generous hips. Briseis stroked them, then worked around to Andromache's lower belly. She found the signs of her pregnancy there, differently textured skin streaked like the marks of a tiger's claws.

The honor of a noble husband's children had never come to Briseis, and she had been spared the shame of bearing the whelp of an unworthy man. She caressed Andromache's scars with delicate fingertips.

The other woman moaned and seized Briseis, rolling her onto her back in the weeds. Briseis yielded, opening her mouth to Andromache's tongue. A thousand differences made themselves known to her. Andromache held herself over Briseis lightly even as she asserted dominance. Rather than forcing a path to Briseis' center, Andromache's legs found a comfortable, intimate way to entwine. She forced nothing, kissing patiently until Briseis parted her legs and clasped the back of her neck with both hands.

It felt strange for the gestures of desire to be true, but Briseis' body had never lied to her. Her cunt moistened, her nipples hardened, and her thighs trembled. She wanted Andromache, even if she could not be sure what that would mean. She wanted this for herself. "Undress me," she whispered.

Andromache undid Brises' robes as efficiently as if she had sliced them off with a knife. Briseis' stomach looked pale, weak, and soft beside Andromache's tan, muscled skin. She flushed with shame. "This is the beauty they always spoke of," Andromache breathed. "You and Helen. The kind of women who could start wars between kings."

Andromache's admiration only increased her discomfort. "Please don't compare me to Helen," Briseis said. "Any woman has been cursed by Aphrodite—me, you, or the old woman who carries water. Besides that, I'm nothing like Helen." She did not know, but she hoped. Briseis could not stand the idea that Andromache had once looked at Helen with this same expression of lust and wonder.

Andromache shook her head. "Of course you're right. Feeling a man's desire seems to have changed my eyesight as well."

"A good man appreciates each woman for what she is." Achilles had. Briseis bit back the comparison.

Andromache pressed a kiss of apology to the side of Briseis' face. "Helen used her beauty as a weapon. She did not wear it so well as you. And she had long, dark hair, which she curled each morning."

This speech did not help Briseis' rising irritation. "No more about Helen."

Andromache laughed, wrinkling her nose. "I have no skill at this, I fear. It makes me feel pity for poor Hector, when he fumbled with his tongue in our youth."

Briseis cupped the side of Andromache's face, fingers gripping harder than she intended. She had never felt this way before, but more than that, she had never been free to feel this way. "I don't want to think about the past."

Andromache's eyes slipped down Briseis' body, her expression carrying more meaning than her words had managed. "I swear by Athena, the past is not what commands my attention at the moment."

Briseis relaxed. Her grip became a caress. Andromache's eyes searched hers for a long moment, then she, too, loosened her posture. She joined Briseis in a kiss that began slow but built again into the fire of genuine desire.

Andromache lowered her lips to Briseis' right breast. She bit the nipple lightly, then sucked. Her lips nursed softly at first, then grew harder. Briseis spread her legs and arched her back. "Please," she said. "Make me come for real. It's been so long."

She found Andromache's hand and guided it between her legs. Still suckling, Andromache slipped a finger into Briseis' cunt, stroking the inside wall in a way that made ticklish shivers spasm up and down Briseis' body.

Andromache's finger teased and slid through Briseis' growing wetness. She moved her mouth to the cleft between Briseis' legs. Her tongue could have been a sword that pierced Briseis through. Briseis cried out and grabbed Andromache by the hair, pulling her tight against her body. She spasmed under that tongue, around Andromache's finger. The sensation felt too strong, but she couldn't let go of Andromache, and the other woman's tongue never stopped moving.

Finally, Andromache released Briseis. The fair-haired woman lay gasping, color-spots obscuring her vision of her new warrior lover. "If we're cursed by Aphrodite," Andromache said, "it's past time we learned to make our own luck."

"Which of the gods is responsible for this ruined place?" No Name wailed. Briseis walked beside the horse he rode, holding its lead and paying only half her attention to him. She glanced at Andromache, at the head of the party, her body thrilling at the memory of the other woman's touch and tongue.

"Do you hear me?" the old man demanded.

Briseis glanced up at his face, blinking in the noon light. She surveyed the blasted, war-torn landscape. "Whichever it is," she said finally, "is not doing a very good job."

"The ships of the Myrmidons will be just ahead," Andromache cried to the group. The mass of women behind her could have been those great warriors themselves, resplendent in gleaming bronze armor. "Beyond that hill!" called the warrior woman. "My sisters, we will sail away from this place and be free."

No Name shook his head. He whispered to Briseis. "Child, there will be no ships beyond the hill. There's no grace in this world anymore. There can be no hope. No City of Women. It's just a story Andromache likes to tell."

Briseis expelled an exasperated breath. "Who do you think you are, old man? I've had it with your drivel."

"There will be no City of Women. The only things beyond that hill are a twisted olive tree and a dying stream."

Briseis' heart felt cold in her chest. "You're not Zeus," she said.

They went on in silence toward the crest of the hill, Briseis stumbling occasionally on the pitted earth. Her heart pounded harder the closer they got, and it irritated her that part of her believed the old man's prophecy.

Andromache was first to reach the place from which the Myrmidons' ships should have been visible. She approached with a triumphant gait, but froze. Briseis could tell from the way she held the muscles of her back that all was not as it should be.

She avoided No Name's eyes until they got close enough that she could see for herself. When they stepped forward and she saw the tree and the trickle of water just as he had described, she couldn't help glancing up at him. He shrugged apologetically, just as Andromache's shoulders shook and the warrior woman began to cry.

Briseis slipped into Andromache's tent through one of the back flaps, after managing to avoid the guards posted on each side. In the center of the tent, she saw a lump wrapped in blankets and heard breathy, voiceless sobs. "Andromache," she murmured.

"By Ares, Eris, and Hades, woman. Leave me alone."

Briseis moved closer, easing herself down to the earth beside Andromache's shivering body, which seemed even smaller than usual now. Briseis didn't know what to say, and so she just reached inside the pile of blankets and stroked her hand down Andromache's back. The other woman sobbed harder, and Briseis' heart hurt for her.

Briseis had seen Achilles, too, mourning and aching and crying, but he had never let her close to him when he was in such a state. Andromache's wordless acceptance of Briseis left her uncertain. How could she behave as a person, rather than as a possession? What would she do for Andromache if left free to decide?

She worked her way into the blankets beside Andromache and clasped the warrior woman to her chest. "Softer than water," she murmured, and Andromache's body slackened in her arms, surrendering to her touch.

Briseis petted Andromache's hair, then loosened the leather shirt she still wore and pulled it away from her. She undressed Andromache completely, slowly, shadows flickering over the other woman's skin. Fierce enjoyment bloomed in Briseis' heart. This body belonged to her, as much as hers belonged to Andromache. Perhaps this went even beyond bodies, to the hearts within.

Then, because she still hadn't found the right words, she trailed her fingers up and down Andromache's body — over her breasts, still full and motherly; over her scarred and well-muscled arms; over her taut belly and the shiny stretch marks there left by the birth of Astyanax; over her short, thick thighs; and over her surprisingly delicate feet.

Andromache started to say something, but Briseis laid a finger over her lips. She let her mouth follow where her fingers had been, until Andromache's sobs turned to soft moans. Briseis rubbed at the tears at the corners of Andromache's eyes. Finally, she knew what she wanted to express. "You don't have to be so hard," she said. "You have me now, and I'll never leave you. Mourn for Troy and Hector and Astyanax and all of us, and I can take it in for you and keep it somewhere safe."

She guided Andromache's hand between her legs, and slipped her own fingers inside the warrior woman's cunt. Andromache snorted. "Is that what it's for?" she said. "To take in all the pain in the world?"

Briseis colored in embarrassment. She had thought of it that way sometimes while she lay beneath Achilles. Naive girl that she had been, she had thought that his joy in being between her legs might take away the pain of his dark fate, might make him love her the way that she loved him. Now, she arranged her fingers in the shape of a spear and stabbed them into Andromache so they would hurt a little. The other woman grunted and arched her back, moving her fingers inside Briseis as well. "Maybe we turn pain to pleasure," Briseis ventured.

Andromache's juices soaked Briseis's hand. She began to give quick little gasps, which Briseis drowned in a deep kiss. The scent of their arousal rose sharp and pungent, filling the tent. Their tongues did battle. Briseis encouraged Andromache to ride her hand, to use it for her pleasure, but she also did not stint from doing the same in return. Briseis worked her fingers deeper and deeper into Andromache, the flesh she found seeming ever softer, smoother, and wetter. She wanted to get even deeper. For the first time, she understood the desire of a man.

Sweeping Andromache's hand out of her own cunt, Briseis knelt between the other woman's legs. She retreated her fingers and set about opening Andromache afresh. She wanted to possess her more thoroughly than any other, even Hector.

She began with patient licks to Andromache's bud, but soon her tongue grew more warlike. It roamed and claimed. She drooled all over the space between Andromache's legs, her saliva dripping clear from the top to the bottom of her slit, mingling with her juices, and spreading over Andromache's inner thighs and Briseis' chin. Andromache might have come, but Briseis wasn't looking for that at the moment. She wanted her lover to *open*. She leaned back and examined Andromache's opening.

Briseis tested Andromache first with two fingers slipped inside her, then spread apart. She kissed the top of her slit and resumed her tongue's attention, probing to feel whether this pleasure encouraged Andromache's body to let her in.

"Briseis, what are you—"

"Sh. Take me into you." Briseis shaped her hand into a spear again. She positioned at the heated, soaking entrance to Andromache's body. Her fingertips went in easily, but then Briseis encountered resistance. She persuaded with her tongue while persisting with inexorable pressure. Her hand slid in deeper. Andromache's body gripped her now, sucking her in past the resistance with almost terrifying force.

Andromache sobbed a little as she began to open to Briseis' fist. Then something cracked in her voice and her body jerked as her legs spread wide and Briseis' hand sank in wrist-deep. Briseis wriggled her fingers, and Andromache growled low in the back of her throat. She shoved her own fist into her mouth and screamed into it as her body clenched and released in a spasm that radiated from Briseis' hand.

The power of it shot up Briseis' arm and into her own body. She wished she could continue reaching up and into Andromache. Her insides quivered with sympathetic tremors. Briseis straddled Andromache's knee, imagining she could take that in along with Andromache's leg. She imagined Andromache filling her more utterly than she had ever been filled before. Briseis bucked against Andromache's knee until she joined the other woman in orgasm.

Briseis pressed her face to the spot where her arm met Andromache's body. She touched her tongue down tenderly, now, as if licking a wound. Softly, slowly, she eased her hand out of Andromache as gently as she could. "What do you think?" she whispered. "Pleasure or pain."

"Both," Andromache gasped.

"That's the point," Briseis said, climbing up Andromache's body to lie beside her. "I think it's always both." She stroked Andromache's hair again, cradling her like the children she'd never had. Men had satisfied themselves with her, but they had never allowed her to care for them. She had never taken their burdens on as her own.

Andromache began to speak a few times, but drifted off in little groans. They began sated, but soon became anguished. Briseis' forehead wrinkled with concern. "What is it?"

"What do I do about having led us all to nonexistent ships, so we can sail to a place I don't know, where we will build a city that can't exist?"

Briseis kissed the top of her head. "We build that city anyway," she said. "Maybe right here. Achilles and Hector were the greatest warriors of our age, but they both let fate lead them around by the nose. You can be a better warrior than both of them if you take the future in your own hands."

Andromache kissed Briseis long and passionately. "You should have been a queen, not a slave."

Briseis shrugged, but she noticed the way her heart warmed in her chest until it burned. "I can be your queen," she said.

"What are you doing?" No Name said. The old man was doubled over in the mid-day sun. He sounded angry.

Briseis let go of the shovel she held, wiping her bleeding palms on her shirt. All around her, women dug the foundations for the wall surrounding the City of Women. The stream and olive tree would be in the center of the courtyard of Andromache's house, and the rest of the city would radiate from there. "We're tired of the Trojan War, Grandfather. We're tired of raids. We're tired of all the stories that men tell. I'm declaring the end of war." She glanced at Andromache, who was coming toward them. "We're telling our own stories from here on out," Briseis said. "We're making our own world."

Then Andromache was in her arms, and for a moment there was nothing else in the world for Briseis but the other woman's soft mouth and warm skin.

If you enjoyed this story, you can sign up for a free membership at ForbiddenFiction and discuss it with other readers and the author at the Andromache's Prize story page at http://forbiddenfiction.com/library/story/AL1-1.000123.

FORBIDDENFICTION
SHORT STORY

The Nemesis Bird
by Slave Nano

The Nemesis Bird

Slave Nano

Slave Nano is an author of erotica drawing on the themes of female supremacy, BDSM, and fetish. His short stories and novellas have been published by ForbiddenFiction, Xcite Books, House of Erotica, Coming Together, and Greenwoman Publishing. His novel *Adventures in Fetishland* has been published by Xcite Books. He is a member of Leodis Pagan Group and has also had work published in the Pagan e-magazine *Eternal Haunted Summer*. You can find out more about his writing on his website: www.slavenano.co.uk.

Chapter 1

The Caliph Spies a Wondrous Bird

Scheherazade took up a golden jug and poured a goblet of wine out for King Shahryar.

"Tell me, my Queen, what tale do you have to entertain me tonight?" he asked.

"O King, if it pleaseth Allah, let me tell you the tale of the Caliph of Ishfahan, the slave girl Sofia-al-Din Hasan and the Nemesis Bird."

"I trust, for your sake, it will be as captivating as your other stories, Scheherazade. Did you know that before I married you, I wedded a virgin every day and had them beheaded the next morning? I executed 1,000 virgins in this way as revenge on your sex because my first wife was unfaithful."

Scheherazade smiled. Of course, she had heard the tale. She was the daughter of the Sultan's vizier, his most trusted adviser. How could she not know that? Yet she trusted in her ability to use her wits to bewitch the King with her beguiling tongue.

She had perused history and legend. She studied philosophy and the sciences, and she was well versed in the arts... including the erotic arts. She had a magnificent library of thousands of books and, from them, she could draw on tales of love and loss of incredible adventures and of genies and magical beasts. And there was a large section dedicated to erotica. She studiously examined these books, became absorbed in their pictures and read the advice offered by courtesans in their texts. Through them, she had learnt how to give oral, as well as aural, stimulation to the Sultan.

As he reclined on the divan bed, taking a sip of wine, she slid a hand into the gap in his silk robe. She brushed her fingers tantalizingly against his cock and felt it twitch with arousal. The Sultan let out the slightest moan of pleasure.

"You are wise, O mighty Sultan," she said, as she wrapped her fingers around his hardening cock. "not to trust the fairer sex. For it is true, we are wily and not to be trusted."

The Sultan let out a gasp as Scheherazade tightened her fingers around his erection and pulled on its shaft.

"You did well to treat those virgins so. And how many tales will it take before you release your wife and Queen from the threat of the scimitar's sword?" she asked as her hand tugged at his member with vigorous strokes to the sound of his groans.

"Oh... 1001, my queen," he gasped.

"1001 tales of love and magic... 1001 nights of passion!" she laughed.

Scheherazade removed her fingers from his cock and untied the cord around the Sultan's robe. She parted it to expose the smooth, brown skin of his chest and drew her painted fingernails across his flesh. She bent over him to take his engorged penis into her mouth and ran her lips up and down its shaft. His body twisted and jerked in ecstasy at the soft touch of her lips on his hard cock.

She removed her lips from his penis and let her silk gown slide onto the floor. Naked, she crouched over him, her cunt hovering invitingly over his crotch as the delicious orbs of her breasts hung over his face. She lowered herself onto him, taking the full length of his rod into her. She sat up and rotated her hips around his member, gradually bringing him to his climax. He moaned in pleasure as he came inside her.

She would seduce him and leave him begging for more. Every night he would crave to hear her mellifluous tones as they drew him into the web woven by her magical and erotic stories. Every night he would desire her touch and crave to have his cock swallowed up in her flesh.

She lay on the divan, her head resting on his chest, as she fondled his now flaccid, cock.

A few months of nights like these, with bewitching tales and seductive sex, and he was already captivated by her. She knew. She would avoid the executioner's sword. Yes, she would rule as his Queen. She would make herself indispensable to him and then, un like those innocent virgins, not only would she avoid death, but she would live to control him. She could see it already... it would take much less than 1001 nights before he belonged to her.

"The story, my Sultan?" Scheherazade murmured in the soft tones of post-coital bliss.

"Yes, my love. You must start your tale."

She cupped his face in her hands and kissed him.

"Then I shall begin. If your highness will indulge me, I believe you will find the story of The Nemesis Bird instructive... and arousing. Listen to my tale and then, O mighty Sultan, pass your judgement on whether your humble wife and servant should die an unworthy wretch at the hand of the executioner's sword or live to entertain your majesty another night."

King Shahryar raised his hand and bid Scheherazade to begin her story.

O auspicious Lord, long ago, there was once a proud and cruel Caliph who ruled over the city of Ishfahan, and his name was Harim-al-Rashid. One morning he emerged from his Hamman bath draped in his silk robe and, as was his wont, went out onto the balcony of his palace to look over his domain. Now, Caliph Harim was powerful and vain. It gave him pleasure to survey his dominions and indulge himself in the knowledge that he ruled with absolute power. No resident of this rich city, from humble porter to wealthy wazir, would dare question his command.

And what he saw from the balcony of his palace pleased him. He could see he ruled a city that was thriving and wealthy. He observed the caravans of camels entering the city gates laden with silks from the Orient. He looked out on the busy market place with its mounds of brightly coloured spices, exotic fruits, copper pans, and embroidered slippers. He could hear the sound of the imam's call from Ishfahan's minarets over the bartering of the merchants.

As he surveyed this scene, his eyes were drawn to one small courtyard garden below the palace balcony. It was a sight so beautiful and wondrous that it amazed the Caliph. Now, he possessed all manner of precious objects: rubies the size of rocks, luminous pearls from the depths of the Arabian seas, and exotic beasts from Barbary Africa, but he had never seen the like of this before.

It was a bird. But this was no ordinary bird. Its plumage was magnificent to behold. Its tail and wing feathers spread like an ornate canopy over the small courtyard. Around its neck was a huge tufted crest. But, even more wondrous than this fantastical display was the miraculous quality of the colouring of the bird's feathers. For, as the Caliph gazed down in amazement, the creature constantly shifted its colours. His first view was of a bird with carnelian body, tail feathers of sapphire blue and a bright green crest, and before his very eyes, the hues of the feathers changed to violet, cerulean, and orange and again to aquamarine, copper, and stone grey. Harim-al-Rashid observed in astonishment as the colours of the bird's feathers constantly changed their hue.

Even more miraculous was that the Caliph felt his emotions shifting with the changing colours, from great joy to fear and trepidation.

The Caliph resolved this magnificent beast should belong to him. How dare any of his subjects possess such a marvellous creature and not surrender it to him? Whatever he desired he was determined to possess, and nothing would stand in his way. And now, having been captivated by the magnificent colours of this fantastical bird, he knew it must be his.

Now, there was a servant girl serving in the Caliph's household who had attracted his attention. He recalled her being taken into his service when she was a young girl after he had cause to execute her mother for blasphemy. She was a pretty girl all those years ago, and now she had blossomed into a beautiful young woman. Her name was Sofia-al-din Hasan, and she was most wondrously fair. Her cheeks were the colour of sun kissed peaches in the dawn light. Her lips were the colour of red coral glowing in the clear waters of the Arabian Sea. Her body was soft and voluptuous as if the delicate rippling sands of the desert had been brought to life.

He had long admired her beauty from afar and desired to have this servant girl to add to his harem, so he could have her in his bed every night to service his sexual needs. He remembered fondly ravishing her mother prior to her be-heading, and it would amuse him to have her daughter in his bed chamber. He could have her now if he so desired, but he sought to test her trustworthiness first by setting a special task for her. If she performed it to his satisfaction, he would elevate her from the position of servant girl into a respected one in his harem.

After several days observing the bird, the Caliph summoned Sofia-al-din Hasan into his presence and pronounced, "Hearken to me, my girl. I have a task I desire you to carry out. If you succeed, then you will be given the honour of being summoned into my harem. You will be allowed into my bed where your beautiful body can be offered to your glorious master... just as your mother's was," he added with a malevolent grin.

"From my palace balcony, I have spied a courtyard garden. In that garden is a bird so marvellous it must be one of the living wonders of the world. You will sneak through the lanes of Ishfahan town, climb the wall into the garden, capture this magnificent bird, and return to me where I will keep it in my private chambers for all time to admire. I have fashioned a cage for the bird for this purpose."

The Caliph snapped his fingers, and a pot-bellied eunuch entered carrying a cage. It was not any cage. This had been fashioned by the Caliph's own goldsmiths. It was a beautiful piece of craftsmanship, decorated with motifs of half-moons and scimitars in fine gold leaf. It was a thing of beauty, fitting for the object for which it had been designed.

Now, Sofia was full of foreboding and with good reason. The memories of that fateful day were still raw. Her mother had been a priestess of a secret cult dedicated to the ancient deity, Goddess Inanna. Of course her beliefs were blasphemy to the word of Allah, so when the cult was exposed, she was brought before the ruler of Ishfahan. Sofia's recollections were vivid. Her mother had been dragged before the Caliph and, whilst Sofia was forced to gaze on, her mother was treated barbarically and be-headed before her very eyes. She had been a young girl and did not fully understand what was being done to her mother, but she did now. She remembered the determined defiance her mother demonstrated right until the final moment when the scimitar sliced through her neck.

Sofia was taken into the Caliph's household and was raised by the

Caliph's wives in his harem. She was a servant girl and tried to make herself anonymous as she floated through the marble halls of the palace like an invisible djinn serving the imperial household. But she had never forgotten. She hoped she was nothing, yet now it was clear the Caliph remembered who she was and how she had been brought into his household.

Thus, Sofia had good reason to be full of apprehension at this task, and the supposed reward the powerful and vain Caliph was offering. She foresaw how her body would be his to use how her life would be spent in his harem amongst the petty rivalries and jealousies of his courtesans. She still harboured hatred at the trauma she had experienced of having her mother raped and executed in front of her very eyes.

But what could she do? The Caliph's power was absolute, and there was nothing she could say to contradict him. She had witnessed the terrifying punishments the Caliph meted out to those who defied him.

"My will is yours to command, O master," she replied, but her heart was filled with a simmering resentment.

Sofia set off through the streets of Ishfahan with the golden cage, covered in a silk cloth, in her hand. She reached the walls of the courtyard garden where the Caliph had directed her and clambered over the wall, lowering herself down into the secret garden. She descended into a cool and tranquil place shaded by the four walls of the courtyard.

She was not prepared for the sight that befell her there. The Caliph had told her of the wondrous beauty of the bird he wanted captured, but the creature before her was magnificent beyond her wildest imaginings.

Her tail feathers — and Sofia felt certain the bird was female — were a stunning cerulean, her breast a bright lime green, and her body a glowing fuchsia. As she watched entranced, the bird gradually transformed herself to shades of dusky salmon, burnt sienna, and violet. Sofia was overwhelmed with great joy at the sight, then with feelings of quiet meditation and, finally, as the colours changed to charcoal, indigo, and magenta to emotions of foreboding and fear.

The bird fixed her tiny obsidian eyes onto Sofia's. They pierced into her very soul. They hypnotised her, luring her into a reverie that was both euphoric and joyous and dark and threatening all at the same time. Sofia felt her heart torn asunder as she became captivated by the spell of the wondrous bird.

How could she allow the Caliph to imprison such a beautiful creature? His selfish nature would keep the bird as his possession, hidden in a secret place where only he would see her until eventually her golden lustre would diminish, and she would expire, a prisoner in Harim-al-Rashid's gilded cage.

"Come to me," she called as she knelt down with her hand held out, beckoning the bird to fly on to it.

The magical bird swooped up into the air, circled around the garden three times, and alighted onto Sofia's waiting hand. She cocked her head, with its brightly coloured tuft, to one side and gazed up expectantly at Sofia.

Now, her mother had brought Sofia up to revere Inanna, the Sumerian Goddess from ancient Babylon, and the lovely walled garden reminded her of a story from her childhood. The beauty of this place where she sat reminded her of the sacred garden of Inanna from a tale her mother had related when she was a girl.

She turned to the bird, "Let me tell you of the tale of Inanna and the Huluppu tree," she said, as much to bring solace to herself as she reflected on her decision, though the bird looked back at Sofia with understanding as if she was listening.

"There was once a magical and beautiful tree on the banks of the Euphrates, called the Huluppu Tree. One day the tree was swept away by the force of the river. But the tree was rescued by the Goddess Inanna, the Queen of Heaven and Earth, who took it away and planted it in her sacred garden in Uruk, planning to make a throne in its trunk and a bed to lie in.

"Whilst she was waiting for the tree to grow large enough, it became occupied by three creatures. Its roots were taken up by a snake, which feared no spells. Its trunk was lived in by Lilith, the female storm demon, who coveted the tree for herself. And in its branches, the Anzu bird, the lion-headed eagle and servant of the sky god, made its home. Inanna was unable to rid the tree of these intruders and, tearful, she sought the help of her brother Utu, the sun god, but he refused her.

"But Gilgamesh, the warrior king of Uruk came to her aid. He smote the snake and drove Lilith and the Anzu bird out. And so it was that Inanna carved her throne out of the Huluppu Tree and ruled as the Queen of Heaven and Earth."

Sofia sighed. She was saddened by the bird's fate if she delivered her to the Caliph. She knew she would face his wrath if she returned without the bird and was aware from how her mother had been treated of how vengeful and cruel he was. In her heart, she wanted to free the bird, but where would a mere servant girl find the bravery to resist the all-powerful ruler of Ishfahan? And how could she endure the punishment she knew would befall her if she did not do his bidding? And yet had not an opportunity presented itself to extract some revenge on the Caliph by denying him something he so sorely desired.

With the bird perched on her hand, Sofia sat in the shade of a juniper tree in the courtyard and reflected on her dilemma. She stroked the bird's feathers with her finger and gazed into her beady eyes admiring her vibrant colouring.

She spoke to the bird, "I know what's right, but do I have the courage to follow my convictions? If I run off, the Caliph will pursue me, and my punishment will likely be worse. If I return, I have the chance to explain myself and plead for pity. What should I do?"

The magical bird stared back at her. Her feathers transformed into scarlet red. To Sofia, this was a sign. The bird was telling her to show courage and, as she sat there, she felt strength surge through her.

"Inanna was a goddess of love," she reflected, "but she was also a warrior, she was brave and fearless. I will learn from her."

Whatever power the Caliph might wield, Sofia would do what she felt was right. And, although she would manifest contrition, in her heart, she would take great pleasure in spiting him. At that moment, Sofia decided she would not return to the Caliph with the bird. She knew she would face his wrath but resolved that she would rather endure punishment, whatever that might be, than see the wonderful creature imprisoned forever in the palace.

She took up the bird. Its beauty and constant shifting of colouring mesmerised her. She could not resist the temptation to pluck a solitary feather from her tail as a remembrance of her encounter. Then she held the bird to her breasts and whispered in her ear.

"Fly my beauty. Don't linger here. Spread your wings, and take to the sky."

The bird gave Sofia a meaningful look. Her colour transformed into an amalgam of glittering gold and silver. She spread her wings and soared into the air, a dazzling jewel against the azure sky.

Sofia was overjoyed at the sight. She felt sure she had done the right thing but knew now she had to return to the palace and make her report to the Caliph as to the failure of her task. She hoped he would understand why she had let the bird go but knew, in her heart, that such hope would likely be in vain.

Chapter 2
Sofia's Punishment

Sofia-al-din-Hasan returned to the palace and related to the Caliph what had befallen her. She told of how she had been captivated by the bird's presence. She spoke movingly of her feelings that this object of beauty should be served and worshipped. She described how she had released the bird and pleaded with the Caliph to show mercy.

Harim-al-Rashid flew into an extreme rage. Denied possession of the fantastical bird and affronted by the disobedience of a mere servant girl, his temper was beyond reckoning. It swept through the chamber like a fierce sandstorm summoned by a powerful genie. The Caliph berated her and invoked the name of Allah to bring curses down on her. He accused Sofia of possessing the same disloyalty and irreverence as her mother who had been justly punished. Then he struck Sofia across her face. She fell to her knees, tears streaming down her cheeks from the force of the blow. She had prayed for compassion, but all of her worst fears had been realised.

"You dare to return here empty handed? You dare to defy your Caliph's command? I will make you understand, it is no bird that you serve but me, your master, and through me, Allah the great. Sofia-al-din-Hasan, when I have finished with you, you will kneel before me abused and disgraced."

He summoned his imperial guard, twelve of his most entrusted warriors, to his chamber and pronounced Sofia's fate.

"To all these present, hearken to the judgement of the Caliph of Ishfahan. This servant girl before you has willfully disobeyed my orders and displeased me beyond measure. She has invoked the wrath of her lord and master, and her punishment will be severe.

"She was meant to present me with a wondrous bird in a cage but has returned empty handed, so it is just and fitting she should be put in a cage. But this will be no golden cage where she will be admired for her beauty. This will be an iron cage. She will be chained into it and raised into the rafters of my dungeon where she will become an object of disdain. Then, after evening prayers, she will be lowered and released only for my personal body guard to use her. Since she has denied my pleasure, I will turn her into a captive and an object for other people's pleasure. This ordeal will continue for forty days and forty nights after which she will be brought before me and beheaded. Now take her away."

Sofia was dragged down to the dungeon and stripped naked. Her clothes were strewn across the floor, and the single feather, which Sofia had plucked from the bird just hours ago, had turned a dusty grey and lay hidden and ignored against the stone flags of the dungeon.

The guards roughly attached iron shackles onto her ankles and wrists. Then she heard the sound of a winch and the crank of chains as a cage was lowered from the roof of the dungeon. She watched in trepidation as it slowly descended to the floor. It was a body cage, made of cold forbidding iron, ingeniously designed so that a body would fit tightly inside it whilst still permitting the occupant to sit on its base. The front of the cage was opened, and the Caliph's cruel guards pushed her in. The door was closed on her. The cold metal pressed against her naked flesh. The shackles on her ankles and wrists were secured to the metal frame. She was encaged, and there was no escape for her.

She heard the rattle of chains again. The cage was slowly raised. Sofia could feel herself being lifted from the ground, and as the cage was pulled higher, she felt herself suspended and swaying in the gloomy dungeon light. The experience was disorientating. She felt her pulse racing and her head spinning. The cage was raised higher and higher to the sound of the guards' jeers and laughs until eventually, she was hanging from the rafters of the roof.

Sofia's fear began to overwhelm her. She began to wish the Caliph had just beheaded her and spared her the torment of this cage and the abuse she knew she would face from the guards. Yet this was her fate. She had exchanged the liberty of the wondrous bird for her own captivity. But, in her heart, she had no regrets over the choice she made. The beautiful bird deserved to be free for others to admire and worship and not subjected to Caliph Harim's imprisonment. Gazing down from on high, she caught a glimpse of the single feather and believed she saw an indigo glow on its tip.

Sofia hung in the iron cage awaiting her fate at the hands of the Caliph's Imperial Guard. She was lonely and fearful. She never expected the Caliph to relent, but, nonetheless, felt she hoped for some justice at letting the magical bird have its freedom. Now she faced punishment at the hands of his hand-picked bodyguard, renowned for their cruelty. She was in despair, deserted, and surrendered up to unmentionable abuse. In a strange way, she even felt betrayed by the beautiful bird, which had accepted her freedom in exchange for Sofia's imprisonment.

After evening prayers, the twelve members of the Caliph's Imperial Guard entered the dungeon in a raucous mood, ready for some sport. They looked fearsome in their sleeveless tabards, displaying their muscular arms and scimitars tied around their pantaloons.

On the evening of the first day Sofia was lowered to the floor and pulled out of the cage by the guards. They jeered and taunted her, but their captain, Umar Malik, took the lead, commanding them to exercise some discipline. He was known by Sofia because his reputation for sadistic cruelty was renowned amongst the Caliph's servants.

He knelt over her as she crouched on all fours on the stone flags, tipping her face towards his with his finger, "You heard the judgement of the Caliph. For the next forty nights, you are ours," he whispered, "We will use you in whatever way I command. Do not look for pity, for there will be none; you will not be spared, and your body will be abused by me and my men until your spirit is broken, and you descend into despair. You will crave for your death and wish you'd never been born. That is your fate for disobeying the almighty ruler of Ishfahan."

Sofia trembled with fear and foreboding at the captain's vicious words.

Malik stood up, and pushing the others aside, he made it clear he was in charge and was going to take her first. He gestured for the other men to hold her down. Sofia's resistance was half-hearted. She knew there was no point struggling against the strongest of the Caliph's warriors.

Despite her submission, they were unnecessarily harsh, pinning her wrists and ankles down hard on the stone floor, so she could not move. Malik dropped his pantaloons to reveal his raging erection; his cock was long and its girth broad. Sofia was frightened at the sight of his ruddy engorged member and its fearsome hardness. She was still a virgin, and though she had heard other servants talk of sex, Sofia had never been with a man before. Perhaps for the first time, Sofia truly understood the fear her mother must have felt when the Caliph took her as her daughter looked on helplessly.

He knelt between her spread-eagled legs and forced himself into her. Sofia screamed out. It was a searing pain as the guard's hard cock pushed into her. She sobbed as he thrust inside her with powerful strokes until he grunted, and his body shook as he released his come inside her.

"Your ripe pomegranate has been split... and now it's open for all to enter it," he hissed.

Sofia could only whimper in pain and fear, knowing that her punishment had only just started. Whilst being held down by the muscular arms of the guards, they each took it in turns to penetrate her. Her ordeal did not finish until all twelve of the imperial guard raped her, and she was left in a daze. After they had all taken their turn, they merely laughed with disdain at her predicament.

"And that's just the start, disloyal whore. You have forty nights of this," Malik threatened, "and I have some cruel punishments planned. You will be abused until you learn the lesson of complete obedience to your masters."

After that, Sofia was returned to her cold iron prison. She curled up into a ball on the base of the cage and cried. She felt sore all over. Her crotch was throbbing with the pain of the relentless abuse by the guards.

It was only the first day, and she already doubted how she could endure this ordeal. She was desperate and fearful. Where would she find the strength to survive this? And then, for what, to still be executed by the Caliph. Her tormentor would be proved right. She already wished she could be put to death now rather than face another thirty-nine nights of torment like this.

As Sofia sat in the cage, limbs aching and mind full of dark dreams, her gaze drifted down to the dungeon floor. She noticed the feather had changed colour. It was now amber. Did that signify anything?

On the evening of the second day, Sofia was hauled down from the roofs again and dragged out of the cage. This time, the Caliph's imperial guards were ready for her, their cocks already pulled out.

As she stood silently before him, Malik ran his fingers across her breasts and down to the bush above her vulva. Sofia drew in a gasp of breath. He was teasing her.

"The Caliph chose you for your beauty. Yes, I can see why he would want you in his harem to de-flower you. But he'll not recognise you once I've finished with you. And today you are going to be subjected to such a humiliation."

Malik grasped Sofia and pushed her onto the floor.

The Imperial Guards stood over her, pricks in hand, and one by one, pissed all over her. She was humiliated by the streams of hot piss in her beautiful fair hair, her face, and all over her naked body. When she tried to cover her head in her arms one of the guards pulled her hands away leaving her face exposed. The golden waters gushed over, and Sofia could not avoid drops falling on her lips and into her mouth. It had a salty, alkaline taste. She felt so degraded. And then each of the guards penetrated her mercilessly again, with the same savagery as the night before. That night she was returned to her cage, a sodden and forlorn figure.

On this occasion, as she swung high in the rafters sobbing at her humiliation, she noticed the hue of the feather had changed again, to a dusky pink. Her curiosity was aroused now. Was the feather still a living thing?

It was the evening of the tenth day, and the cage was hauled down from the rafters again. By now she had gotten used to the incessant fucking and was resigned to it. But this time the guards had a new game.

Umar Malik studied with a sadistic glint in his eye, "I think you've been getting too comfortable of late, so I've a new punishment for you today."

The captain had become Sofia's main tormentor. She was treated cruelly by them all, but the others — with their beards and turbans — blurred into one. It was Malik who commanded them, devised her punishments, and taunted her with them, and stood out for his fearsome muscular presence and malevolence.

This night, the guards were issued with whips. On Malik's order, they rained the wicked cords down on her. They struck her on the arse, back, and tits, whipping her until she screamed out in pain. He urged them on. When their sadistic pleasure had been satiated, her skin was beaten red and raw. She was taken again by all twelve before being imprisoned in her cage and raised up to the ceiling again. Sofia reached a new low of despondency as she huddled down in the bottom of the cage, her body aching and throbbing in pain.

Each night she sought out the feather to see what colour it had transformed into. It was now a subtle shade of silvery grey. And that night, despite being in a pit of despair at her plight, she felt the power of the feather for the first time. Just as in the garden, what seemed like many moons ago, her emotions shifted with the changing hue of the bird, the same influence emanated from this single feather. And she was reminded of the bravery of her mother as she faced her fate with quiet, determined dignity. She felt a wave of steely determination wash over her. The feather was telling her not to give in. The feather was helping her dig deep into her inner strength.

It was the evening of the fifteenth day. She had been subjected to more corporal punishment, and of course, each night, all twelve of the imperial guards raped her before she was returned to the cage. But the power of the feather had changed her and had given her greater resolve. It was an ordeal, of course, a painful and savage one, but she no longer cowered or tried to protect herself. Before, she often tried to scramble away from her punishments, much to the amusement of the guards as they roughly pulled her back and pinned her down.

Malik noted this change in Sofia's response over the last few nights and taunted her with further threats.

"There will be no escape for you. I will find new torments to break your spirit. By the fortieth night, I promise you will be returned to the Caliph in a state of shame and contrition to face your execution."

Sofia was tied, spread-eagled, onto links in the dungeon floor and left. When the imperial guards returned they brought with them huge candles from the Caliph's personal mosque. They dripped burning wax over her exposed tits and cunt. Sofia squirmed with the pain of the hot wax and watched in fear as the burning flames were held over her naked body. It was a different kind of ordeal for her, scarier than the beatings inflicted on her over previous nights. She was hard pressed to use her new courage and determination to accept this new form of pain. Needless to say, her hornet's nest was penetrated by the guards before she was returned to the cage.

Strangely, that night she felt as strong as she had ever done during her ordeal. She recalled the tales of Inanna from her childhood. The goddess had descended into the underworld to save her husband, Tammuz. She surrendered everything as she passed into the land of darkness and endured. Sofia couldn't save herself from the tortures, but she could draw strength from Inanna's story.

When she observed the feather from on high, it had turned a rusty brown.

It was the evening of the twentieth day, the halfway point in her forty day punishment. She was dragged before Malik, the Captain of the Guard. He observed how Sofia had grown in spirit lately. She accepted her punishments in resigned silence, never responding to his sadistic threats or to the more raucous jeers of his men, but recently he noted a hint of determination in her eyes. He resolved to find a new torment to bring her back under his control. He ran his hands across her crotch and nipped her vulva between his fingers causing her to squeal and squirm.

"Your hushed sesame has been split so much I think you've got used to it. I think you've even started to enjoy it. I will break you," he gloated, "and tonight, I've devised a special punishment for you."

Chapter 3
The Nemesis Bird's Judgement

Sofia dreaded the threat of this new challenge, whatever it might be. She soon found out. She was strapped onto a bench with her backside exposed invitingly in the air, and each of the Imperial Guard forced themselves up her arse. They thrust their hard cocks into her, filling her back passage with their length and girth. Her back-side throbbed with the pain of being penetrated so roughly. Tears ran down her cheeks from the pain and humiliation and — seeing how she had been affected by the anal fucking — Malik mocked her in front of the other men to add to her misery.

When she was returned to the cage, the feather had turned an olive green. But on that night the feather failed to provide her with any succour. She felt dirty and sordid, and her miserable mood returned.

It was the evening of the twenty-fifth day. Seeing how effectively the repeated anal penetrations had quelled Sofia's spirit, Malik introduced it into her daily punishment. But on this day, Malik had also devised another torment to add to her humiliation. When she was let out of her cage, the Imperial Guard did not fuck her, but they stood and masturbated over her, covering her in their thick spunk. Sofia felt disgusted and degraded. She was left a sticky mess with spunk, not only over her body, but also in her hair and face.

The feather was now a saffron colour. She'd survived twenty-five days of the ordeal. That night, she meditated on the feather. There was no question that the colours had grown deeper over the course of her imprisonment. Again, Sofia took strength from that. Over the course of the next day, she tried to recover some of the resolve she had lost. She drew on the feather's power and the memory of her mother, feeling some of her determination to face the last stages of her punishment return.

It was noted by Malik that Sofia's steely acceptance had come back. So, on the evening of the twenty-eighth day he introduced another ordeal. She was forced to kneel before him with her arms tied behind her back.

He lifted her chin up with his finger, "Tonight," he pronounced, "you'll be made to suck on cock and feast on the come of the Imperial Guard."

The erect penises of each of the guards were forced, in turn, into her mouth. They were rammed down her throat until she gagged on them. Sofia was made to suck on the cocks until the hot sticky come emptied into her mouth or dribbled down her chin. Malik smiled malevolently as she was forced to swallow the seed of his men. He went last, forcing his member into her mouth until she choked, and groaning with pleasure, he emptied himself into her.

Far from being cowed by this latest humiliation, Sofia felt the feather radiate an air of calm. She had survived so long now, and this contributed to her endurance and growing confidence.

Strangely, through all those twenty-eight days, the feather had remained ignored. It was a constant presence and had even been trampled and sat on by the guards. Sofia was anxious that they would discover it and remove her source of succour, but they never took any notice of it. Tonight, the feather turned a shade of cerulean blue. The colour was luminously bright and shone like the sun reflecting off the tiles on the façade of Ishfahan's most magnificent mosque, yet the guards were still oblivious to it. Sofia wondered if only she could see the feather and whether it was invisible to the guards.

On the evening of the thirtieth day, she was lowered down but not let out of the cage. The guards reached inside and stroked her tits and pubic hair. Her nipples were squeezed and tormented with rough fingers until she squealed in pain. Her flesh was left with reddened blotches and bloodied marks at the rough treatment meted out by the guards. She suffered all this before being dragged out and taken by the guards.

As the cold metal of the cage dug into her flesh that night the feather had transformed itself into jade green.

On the evening of the thirty-fifth day, Malik ordered the cage to be lowered just a fraction above the ground and placed candles under the cage so its metal base became red hot and burnt the soles of her feet, forcing her to jig from foot to foot to the great mirth of the guards.

"Look how you dance at my command," laughed Malik at the sight of Sofia hopping around on the base of the cage.

After they had got their amusement from this game, she was removed from the cage and fucked again.

The feather was now light beige. Only five more nights, and her ordeal would be over. She faced death, of course, but at least her torment would be over. Yet, another thought occurred to her. The feather had been her companion throughout. She could not help but wonder if its shifting colour signified a purpose?

Over the last five nights, the savagery of her fucking became frenetic as Malik tried to break Sofia's will. But she remained stoic and silent in the face of rape and relentless beatings. Throughout the punishment, she never uttered a word to her tormentors, and she maintained her steely silence to the very end. But whereas, at the start, it was out of fear, it was now an unspoken defiance of the kind she had seen in her mother. Over these last nights, she would fix her gaze on Malik, challenge him to do his worst, and accept it in resilient silence. He had become more and more frustrated seeing that Sofia's will had not been broken as he resorted to shouting at her and hectoring his men to more severe levels of cruelty. But this had no impact on Sofia. So it was that, approaching the end of her ordeal, Sofia felt she had gotten the upper hand over him, and this showed in his desperate brutality.

On the evening of the fortieth and last night, when she had been hauled from the cage for the last time, a metal collar was put around her neck and a chain lead attached to it.

"On this, your last night before your execution, I have a special treat for you," announced Malik, "you will be treated like the bitch that you are and taken for a walk around the streets of Ishfahan."

Malik led the way as the guards took turns to walk her along the streets of the town like a dog. The Captain of the Guard looked smug and triumphant as he pronounced to the crowds that lined the streets, "See what happens to those who challenge the authority the Caliph of Ishfahan."

Yet the crowds remained silent. Sofia was not subjected to the taunts and jeers she expected, and when she looked up, what she saw in the eyes of the people was pity and disgust at her treatment.

She had been imprisoned for forty days. In that time, rumours had spread about the servant girl, Sofia, who had defied the Caliph, and her punishment. Rumours had also spread about the magical bird in the courtyard garden and how Sofia had set her free. Many people had witnessed the bird whilst it paraded around the courtyard, and tales of its beauty and magnificence had reached all that had not. There were those who believed the bird was a gift to them from the Goddess Inanna of old, and they were saddened that she had flown away to save herself from the Caliph's cage. And there were many more who hated the vain and cruel Caliph.

So, when Sofia was taken to the main square of Ishfahan and each of the guards mounted her in turn to take her like a bitch in heat in full view of the crowd, her ordeal was met with a stony silence. The guards drew their scimitars and yelled, trying to rouse the people, but to no avail. Then, somewhere from the back of the crowd, a mouldy tomato was thrown at the guard who mounted Sofia. It was followed by a couple more and a rotten cabbage. Some of the guards broke off and charged into the crowd. The culprits disappeared into the winding lanes of Ishfahan, but one young lad was caught and be-headed in front of the crowd to set an example.

Umar Malik did not expect this turn of events and immediately ordered the guards to lead Sofia back to the dungeon. They continued to take their turns at fucking her for the last time, but their efforts were now half-hearted. And Sofia saw all that had happened in the town's square. She'd thought she was alone. During all her incarceration, she had no idea the rumours of her unjust ordeals had spread throughout Ishfahan.

On the fortieth and final night, as Sofia stood defiantly before a subdued Malik, her spirit remained indomitable. She had endured. The order was given to put her back in the cage for the last time.

As she sat there, the cold iron pressed against her sore tits and aching cunt. Her body showed all the signs of the abuse she had received. Her arse and back were covered in welt marks and her body in bruises. Her hair was a bedraggled mess. She was in a sorry state, but in a strange way she felt triumphant.

The thing that kept Sofia's spirits raised and enabled her to endure the ordeal was looking out for the single feather every night when she was returned to her cage and discovering what new hue it had morphed into. The change was subtle, but it seemed to her that with every passing night, the colours became bolder and brighter. By the evening of the fortieth day, the feather glowed a dazzling crimson. Seeing the feather reminded her of the fateful day when she looked into the eyes of the bird and chose this suffering over surrendering her to the Caliph. She drew strength from the magical power of the feather, which for forty days and forty nights sought to transfer some of its magical powers to Sofia. Reflecting on this gave Sofia the strength to endure her ordeal.

The final day loomed, and Sofia resigned herself to her fate. She was ready to welcome death as a release from the abuse she suffered, but she would do so with quiet resilience and as much dignity as it was possible for her to muster, her spirit unbroken by her terrifying treatment.

On the morning of the fortieth day, Sofia was released from the body cage for the last time. Her wrists were bound behind her back, and she was led to the Caliph's throne room to face her fate. The black hooded executioner awaited her, his scimitar whetted and razor sharp.

Sofia was brought to her knees before the Caliph, who pronounced, "My wrath remains undiminished, and now you must face the ultimate penalty for your crime. Has your punishment made you repent of your disobedience to me?"

Sofia looked up. She remained a stunning figure despite the ravages of the Caliph's guards. Her fair hair was disheveled, and her body bore the marks of her abuse, but her beauty still shone through in her shapely figure and alert eyes. She contemplated the single feather on the dungeon floor and drew courage from its power. Then, she fixed the Caliph with a defiant gaze.

"O ruler of Ishfahan, symbol of Allah's power on earth, yes, I have learnt a valuable lesson." Sofia paused for effect. "Yes, for if I had to face another forty days and forty nights locked in the cage and was fucked another thousand times by your guards, I would still never surrender the wondrous bird into your cruel hands."

The Caliph's wrath knew no bounds now. He was enraged beyond reckoning by her insolence.

"Then, by the will of Allah, Sofia al-din-Hassan, you will pay for your willfulness with your life. You will be beheaded, and your abused body will hang in the cage from the palace walls so all can see what happens to those who defy the authority of the Caliph of Ishfahan."

The Caliph raised his hand to signal to the executioner to carry out the punishment. Sofia's neck was forced down. The silver scimitar was raised high above the executioner's head ready for the Caliph's command and the final, fatal, blow.

And then, with this scene set, it was as if time stood still for a moment. There was the sound of gentle fluttering at the arched window of the Caliph's throne room. Perched on the balcony, where the Caliph had stood when he originally spied her, sat the wondrous bird. The colours rippled through her feathers, first black and red, then black and purple. Her eyes, now blue, surveyed the scene before her with a knowing perspicacity. It was as if she had returned to witness the resolution of the poor servant girl's ordeal and pass her judgement on it.

"See, how high the moon is in the sky. The night is late. I am tired now your majesty, and the completion of my tale can surely wait until another night. I have left everything so finally balanced. It is such a good moment to pause and take some rest."

Scheherazade stretched her slender arms and yawned as she laid her head back on the silk cushions. Yet, her eyes did not look tired, they were bright and knowing.

King Shahryar jolted out of a reverie. He was entranced by Scheherazade's sweet voice. His mind was full of images of the beautiful bird and the fair servant girl in the cage and enflamed by the sexual acts forced on her. He waited expectantly for the final denouement of the tale.

"No, my Queen," he said, "you must continue now, I desire to hear how the story ends, I cannot wait another night."

Scheherazade smiled inwardly. She noted the growing tumescence of the King's cock as she described Sofia's ordeal. She would tease him a little before she completed her story. She reached out and touched his erection.

"So, my King, you are hard again. Did the abuse of Sofia arouse you? Did you enjoy listening to how she was chained up, beaten, humiliated and fucked? Did it turn you on?"

The hard object in her hand and the droplets of spunk on its tip provided the answer to her questions. "Would you like to fuck me like the Caliph's guards fucked Sofia?" Scheherazade taunted. "You see, O auspicious King, I would continue my story, but I am fearful of my fate. If only your majesty would promise to spare me when dawn breaks and listen to another story tomorrow night, then I would willingly continue. And then, after you have heard the end of my story, you can enter me again, and as you ram your cock into my cunt, you can imagine you are the guard fucking me like he took Sofia."

Scheherazade felt the pulsing in his aroused cock. She knew he wanted to fuck her, but how much did he want to hear the climax of the story?

King Shahryar waved his hand.

"Yes, my Queen, of course, you must complete the story, and then we can make love again. Now, tell me, what befell Sofia-al-din-Hasan and the wondrous bird?"

"O fair and just ruler, the scene is so delicately balanced. Hear now how fate dealt with the characters in my tale."

Scheherazade continued her story.

The bird swooped across the throne room and alighted on the Caliph's outstretched hand. The Caliph was full of great joy that the bird had returned. He was overwhelmed with yearning desire and happiness that the wondrous bird would finally be his. He called out to one of his guards.

"Quickly, bring my gilded cage."

He lifted his hand up to his face to take an admiring look at the wonderful creature close up. The bird cocked its crested head and fixed her gaze on the Caliph.

Sofia looked up and observed the scene in awe. Her heart was filled with great foreboding. Had the bird really returned to surrender herself to the Caliph?

No longer was the bird constantly shifting colour. She had transformed herself black, and her eyes were like two stones fashioned out of jet. She fixed the Caliph's gaze.

Peck. With one swift movement her beak had pulled out one of the Caliph's eyes.

Then, before he could even call out in pain and shock.

Peck. With another deft movement the beak penetrated his other eye and plucked it out of its socket.

The two bloodied orbs were left on the chamber floor. The Caliph was on his knees howling in agony and the guards were stunned into silence and inaction. The executioner had dropped his sword in horror at the scene that unfolded before him.

Sofia seized her moment. She felt a surge of strength burst through her as she tugged at her wrists and broke free of the leather ties around them. Now Sofia understood. The magical bird was the instrument of Inanna and had returned to dispense justice. Throughout her ordeal, the goddess's influence was present through the feather, trying to protect Sofia for this moment. She grasped the executioner's sword. Sofia realised she had been chosen as a tool for divine retribution... but she also had her personal subjects for revenge.

Fearlessly, she strode up to Umar Malik.

"You claimed you would break my spirit, yet here I stand undaunted. Now is the time to pass my judgement."

Umar Malik, seeing how events had turned so unexpectedly, was frozen into inaction. Gazing upon the scene of carnage around him and the look of grim determination in Sofia's eyes, he was full of trepidation.

With one swish of the razor sharp sword Sofia cut through his pantaloons and sliced his penis off. As he screamed out in agony, the severed member dropped onto the floor alongside the bleeding eyeballs. The rest of the Imperial Guard gazed on the scene, awe-struck. What powers did this girl command that she could survive her tormentors and emerge to deliver such decisive retribution to their captain?

Sofia marched towards the miserable Caliph and held the scimitar to his neck. The bird, now a mixture of fiery reds, bright oranges and glowing yellows, perched on Sofia's naked shoulder, her presence filling the room. All the assembled guards and servants of the Caliph surveyed the scene of bloodied horror around them and looked upon the lowly servant girl with new found reverence.

"Now hear this," pronounced Sofia. "A just punishment has been delivered here. Cruelty, vanity and selfishness have met their just reward. I will set the bird free, and I will rule in your stead."

The Caliph was a broken man. He recognised now that the bird had been sent as a test for him to judge if he could rule wisely. He had failed. He should not have coveted the magical bird, and he should have shown Sofia compassion. He was filled with remorse and finally recognised the error of his ways.

He confessed before all his advisors and guards present in his chamber, "Fate has delivered a just judgement on me. I will submit to the will of Sofia-al-din-Hasan, pass my power to her, and retire to nurse my wounded body and pride. There is a power in her and her benefactor that is beyond my understanding."

Sofia took the bird in her hands and stood on the balcony of the palace. She looked down upon a huge crowd that had gathered, angered by the summary execution of the young lad. They gazed up in surprise when they saw that it was Sofia on the balcony high above them.

And there, she whispered into the bird's ear, "I will name you, The Nemesis Bird."

And then she released the bird for a second time and watched her soar over the rooftops to the sound of cheers of joy from the people of Ishfahan.

Scheherazade brought her story to its end, "And that, O auspicious King, is how the servant girl Sofia-al-din-Hasan came to be the Caliph of Ishfahan. Did you find the tale instructive?" she asked.

She noticed how shocked King Shahryar looked.

"The ending is so savage, my Queen; to witness the cock of the

Captain of the Imperial Guard being severed so savagely, and to see the great ruler of Ishfahan blinded, reduced to nothing, and surrendering his kingdom to a servant girl. How can that be just?"

"But my King, divine retribution does not follow the laws of men, even the most powerful of men. And if the Caliph had been wise and shown poor Sofia compassion, then his fate would have been different, don't you think?"

"The punishment was so harsh. Surely, the fates are not so cruel?"

"Indeed, they are," she replied, looking down upon his still rampant erection. "Come, let us not argue over the moral of the tale whilst my King's cannon is ready to fire. Come, enter my fortress, and let me relieve you of your shot.

If you enjoyed this story, you can sign up for a free membership at ForbiddenFiction and discuss it with other readers and the author at *The Nemesis Bird* story page at http://forbiddenfiction.com/story/SN1-1.000258.

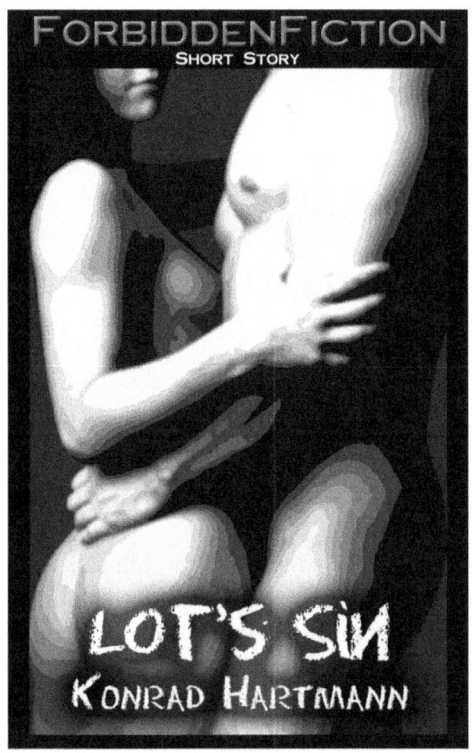

Lot's Sin

Konrad Hartmann

Konrad Hartmann writes action-oriented erotica and a bit of horror, seeking to offer exciting, cross-genre stories. Drawing on mythology, dreams, and the oddities of human experience, he explores the fringes of the imaginative world. Hartmann believes that we all have stories, and that the world will be better for the telling of them. Find his work in Forbidden Fiction's catalog, and scattered across the Web.

Chapter 1

Insurrection

Lot swallowed the scream before it could escape his lips. The ground hardened his feet, sent tendrils of stone up his legs, rooted him to the spot where he peered over the boulder in front of the cave, hiding in the shadows of the night.

Punish them. Punish them, now! he told himself.

Within the cave, illuminated in orange from the fire, two naked forms writhed together on the makeshift bed. His younger daughter, Thamma, lay on the bed, naked with legs spread shamelessly, the fingers of one hand moving against her vagina. Sitting on Thamma's face, her back turned to Lot, Pheine quivered, lustrous black curls hanging down her bare back. Her full buttocks clenched and unclenched as she rhythmically rode her sister's face. The women glistened with sweat, reflecting the firelight. Thamma's slender body contrasted with Pheine's more voluptuous form.

Lot tried to speak, but no voice found its way from him. Was this a vision? Was this his wife, committing this sin with another woman? Was this Ado? The fine curve of the back, the narrow waist, and the perfect moons of the rear looked exactly like Ado; at least, how Ado looked when she was young.

No, he reminded himself, *that is Pheine, and she is shaming herself with her sister.* Lot suspected this, but the shock of seeing it overwhelmed him. His head throbbed and sweat appeared on his brow as his erection grew.

He touched his curved penis, knowing he shouldn't. Pulling his coarse robe aside, he stroked his erection. *What is happening?* He'd become impotent in the last years before fleeing Sodom, before Ado met her end.

And now this? Now? He realized he was pumping his fist up and down, unable to stop, watching as Pheine wriggled her hips. When she moved, he saw Thamma's tongue wiggling like a little snake against her sister's twat. Or was it in fact a small viper now, its diamond-banded scales wet with spit and slit-slime? The viper shot into Pheine and she moaned.

The surge shot through Lot's cock and he watched the seed spatter on the stone before him. Thick and viscous, the fluid slowly trickled into a narrow crack in the rock. He wondered how deep the fissure traveled. He shuddered, feeling linked to the spot now, his shame irretrievably embedded. He imagined a reptilian beast far below in a hollow space, catching his semen as it trickled down. What would it do with the fluid?

Burn, Lot, he heard a voice say, and he trembled, for it was the voice of an angel.

But still he watched Thamma fingering herself. Soon she stopped her licking and turned her face. She cried out, arching her back. As she relaxed, Pheine turned Thamma's face back to her vagina, easing herself down again on the smaller woman's face. Thamma held Pheine's ass cheeks, kneading them as she licked, until the older sister mewled and dropped forward, exposing asshole and cunt to Lot. The orifices seemed to stare mockingly at him.

His fluid spent, hot indignation now flooded his cheeks. Pulling his robe into place, he stormed into the cave, the ceiling just high enough for him to stand. He grabbed a switch from where it lay propped against the wall. He found himself using it more and more on his daughters, and, occasionally, on himself.

"Sinners!" he barked, charging the girls. He held the switch high, scraping the ceiling, a thunderbolt ready to fall.

Pheine and Thamma disentangled from each other and cowered against the wall of the cave, each women awkwardly trying to find a space between the stones. Pheine covered her full breasts with her hands, but Thamma squatted and held onto the wall behind her, too full of fear to cover her long-nippled teats.

"What I will now give you is only mercy! Did you learn nothing from Sodom? Lie on your bellies like the serpents you are!"

The girls scrambled to lay on their stomachs, both of them tucking their arms underneath their bodies and staring down at the bed.

"Not on the bed! You've soiled that enough with your sin! On the floor!" he shouted.

The girls slithered off the soft sheepskins and onto the cold stone of the floor. Lot watched as goose bumps broke out on their thighs and bottoms. He was grateful that his daughters could not see him, for he was already aroused again.

"Keep your brows pressed to the floor, or it will be worse!" he yelled. *What is happening to me?* Why, now, after all that happened in Sodom, should this monstrous urge rack him?

Without warning, Lot brought the switch down, the rod whistling through the air, then landing with a crackling sound across Thamma's ass. The girl yelped and shook, the branch leaving a neat red stripe across her buttocks, the cheeks clenching with the stroke. He would scourge this sin away from his daughters, and then he would punish himself with the lash. He brought the switch down on the tuck of her buttocks and she recoiled, as if to push herself through the floor. Again Lot lashed her. The sin had to be purged. He gritted his teeth and raised his arm high.

With the fourth stroke, Thamma broke and lurched to her feet. She turned to look at her father, crouching like a whipped dog. Her large, dark eyes fell on the bulge of his groin. Her lips quivered, as though about to ask the question, *Why?* Tears of humiliation stung Lot's eyes, though his penis remained erect under his robe.

"Pheine! Hold her down!" Lot yelled.

Pheine grabbed her sister by the arms and tried to pull her down. Thamma squealed and pulled toward the far end of the cave. Pheine was larger, but Lot knew Thamma had a wiry strength. He wanted Pheine to subdue not only Thamma's body, but also the unspoken accusation on the younger sister's face.

"Now, Pheine! Or you will take both yours and your sister's share!" Lot said, grabbing Pheine's hand and thrusting the switch into it.

Pheine glanced at him, a flicker of confusion in her eyes as they too passed over Lot's unabated swelling. But she did not hesitate, grabbing a fistful of Thamma's hair and pushing her younger sister face down on the floor. Pheine straddled Thamma to restrain her, and the position reminded Lot once again of the scene he witnessed. Facing Thamma's ass, Pheine placed one knee into her sister's back. Pheine braced herself with the other leg, leaving her legs open, her hairy vulva exposed to Lot's view.

Again and again, Pheine striped the pale flesh of Thamma's rounded bottom. It was smaller than Pheine's, Lot noticed, but no less shapely. Perhaps if he went to the entrance, he wondered, he could touch himself again and watch in concealment. *No!* he told himself.

Urine ran from beneath Thamma's legs, flowing across the uneven stone floor. A trickle ran towards the fire, as though seeking the flame, the fire sputtering on contact with the liquid. Lot stared at the flames reflected in the puddle, and saw a conflagration within that liquid mirror, people burning, screaming. He smelled the smoke of death, the acrid taste of burning human flesh in his mouth. Other things moved within the fire, things that were not people. He saw Ado, transformed in her final moment into that shape–

"Now, you lay on the floor, Pheine!" Lot gasped, stifling a scream as a fever burned in his brain.

Shaking, Pheine rolled off Thamma and lay face down on the floor, her forehead resting on the back of one hand. Thamma rose, her legs wobbling. Pee ran down her smooth thighs and tears streaked the dust on her face. Shame and humiliation darkened her face. Was there something else? Anger? *She wouldn't dare defy me again*, Lot thought.

"Punish your sister!" Lot said, and pointed to the switch still clutched in Pheine's hand.

Sobbing, Thamma grabbed the switch and began lashing Pheine's plump bottom. The younger sister swung the stick like a warrior in battle, her teeth clenched. *Perhaps that is also sin, if she enjoys this,* Lot thought. *As I enjoy this. No! I must not give in. Pain will cleanse. I will scourge myself tonight.* Thamma's hair whipped around as she punished her sister, her firm breasts swinging as she moved.

Lot collapsed on the bed, noting the scent of the womens' juices on the bedding. He had to find something to deaden the longing, for what he wanted brought tears to his eyes. He grabbed the large wine jug by the bed and drank deeply.

Lot heard Pheine screaming. He looked to see Thamma, her face contorted, landing a frenzy of strokes across her sister's thighs and ass. She looked inhuman, a mad look in her eyes, sweat plastering hair to her face. Blood beaded on the welts and Lot suddenly feared Thamma.

"Enough!" he shouted. "Cover yourselves now!"

Thamma staggered to her part of the cave and pulled on a short shift. The fabric covered her buttocks, but left the red welts on her slender thighs exposed.

Pheine slowly pulled herself to her feet, eyes vacant as she silently cried. Thamma helped Pheine slip on a long white shift. Lines of blood soaked through the linen that covered the swell of her ass.

Lot swallowed the wine as fast as he could. *It is shameful to drink in this way, but the sin is less than that which it restrains,* he reasoned. *God gives us the wine so we may subdue the beast within. The fire must not come here. It must not. I will stop it from coming here. We shall not turn into — what Ado became. I told the girls she turned into a pillar of salt. It was not salt. I cannot think of that now. Drink.*

The girls cowered against the wall, silent, not looking up. The fire burned lower now, allowing shadows to creep over the sisters. Their hair hung forward, obscuring their faces. *They do not even pull back their hair, but let it hang like whores do,* Lot thought. *What have they become? What have I let happen?*

By the time Lot set down the empty jug, he saw double. The girls now sat closer to him, and he did not like the way they stared at him. He would beat them in a moment, only now he felt so tired. He would rest his eyes for just a moment, and then he would find his switch.

"You cannot hide. We descend from the Heavenly Father Himself," he man said, grinning. "Would you have Zoar destroyed as well?" Taller than Lot by at least a foot, the man stared down at him from a face worthy of the finest sculptor. Lot recognized him immediately as a Nephilim, the bastard offspring of an angel and a woman.

Lot turned away from him. He was in Zoar again, the town spared from God's annihilation. Surrounded by a now scorched plain, the city suffered from its isolation. Lot tried to keep his daughters and himself inconspicuous, but every day, he found himself stared at more often, the citizens sneering, whispering, spitting on the ground. But now, he feared something worse than scorn.

"How much more will our Creator scorch, just to end our bloodline?" the man called out, following Lot.

He is not a man, Lot thought. *He is an abomination, a living violation of the Almighty's will.* Lot walked on through the twisting corridors which Zoar called streets.

"How long before he judges you and your people as unclean?" the thing continued behind Lot. "How long before you fail Him, and He commands your destruction? Your life has been a series of atrocities in the name of good. How will it feel when our Father tires of the sport you offer?"

"My God will stop you and your perverted race from poisoning the Earth," Lot shouted, spinning on his heel and shaking his fists at the Nephilim. "By whatever means necessary!" Lot shouted.

"Our Father may send flood after flood, firestorm after firestorm," the Nephilim said. "But He will never eradicate us. He may thin our ranks, but somewhere, in some part of the Earth, we will survive. And we will be fruitful and multiply."

"Abomination!" Lot shouted.

"Abomination? Perhaps we should look at what forms the Almighty chooses to create," the Nephilim said, pointing behind Lot. "Would you like to see the necessity of your wife's new form? Look at Ado, and explain to her the wisdom of Jehovah!"

Lot watched as a shadow loomed next to his on the dusty ground before him, a black bulk with writhing forms. He wanted to run, but his limbs could not move.

"Tell her, Lot, why you remained human and she did not!" the Nephilim said, laughing.

Lot screamed, then sobbed with relief as he woke from the dream to see the rough ceiling of the cave.

But something pulled against his wrist. He tried to pull away but the grip was too strong, and now it held his other wrist as well. The room spun as he screamed again, hoping to awaken from this new dream. He tried to get to his feet, but something gripped his ankles. If Ado came here, he would not be able to look or run away.

He cried out and willed the cave to stop spinning. Bound. His hands and wrists were bound with leather thongs, which were tied to ropes that wound around the heavy boulders in the cave. It was no dream.

And now his daughters stood before him, impudent, smiling. Lot couldn't stop shaking.

"Father," Pheine said, stepping up to stand over him, her hands on her hips. "Why do you scream so? Would you suffer your daughters to live to the end of their days in this cave? We will grow old and gray. No bees will visit these blossoms, and our wombs will bear no fruit."

"Untie me! Untie me or I will punish you in ways you've not imagined! We will not bring the fire here!" Lot howled, feeling his face grow purple. *Is there no escape from torment?* He asked himself.

"Punish us?" Thamma moved to stand on his other side. She ran the delicate toes of her bare foot along his thigh, but the touch only stoked his rage. "Is it not punishment to live year after year without love? We shall grow old, Father, and grow barren, never knowing the touch of a man. Stealing furtive pleasures from each other's tongues when you are gone, my own sister as my only lover. Is this the fate you wish for us?"

Lot listened, too angry to speak, too furious to form words.

"Would you have your line end now, Father?" Pheine asked. "Do you wish no offspring should come forth from us? That Lot should have no descendants to speak his name? Do you wish to simply become an old man, ending his life in a bleak cave, forgotten by the world?" She tucked her hair behind one ear, and let the shoulder of her garment fall low, exposing her neck and shoulder.

"How dare you question me!" Lot said. "What is God's will is His! He did not destroy us in Sodom because He did not wish it so. But to live in filth is to die in flames! It is not for me to question Him on the fate of my offspring, corrupted as they may be!"

"But Father," Thamma said, frowning. "We must question you, for you seem to defy the Almighty. God did not allow us to be soiled by the Sodomites, though *you* were willing for it to be so. But it was not us the people wanted, but the angels. And the angels did not desire the Sodomites. They desired us, Pheine and I!"

"Silence!" Lot screamed. He could not bear her voice, her words making real all that he refused to recall.

"And we desired them, Father," Pheine said. "As all desire to know the angels, the very Children of God himself."

"God would cleanse the Earth of the blasphemies produced by such union!" Lot shouted, his voice hoarse. "Be it with flood, or be it with flame!"

"But was it not you who brought the fire to Sodom, Father?" Thamma asked. "The angels came, and asked us to join with them of our own free will. You refused it, and Sodom burned. You sacrificed a city, only for the sake of denying our union with the Children of Heaven."

"Lies! Lies!" Lot shouted. "It is forbidden! It cannot be done! I will not allow you to create evil spawn this way, no matter how many sinners must perish!"

"Why do you hate the Nephilim so, Father?" Pheine asked.

"Speak not of them!" Lot screamed.

"Was Mother as evil as the Sodomites?" Thamma asked.

Lot choked on his response, clenching his fists, imagining choking a daughter with each hand.

"We fled to Zoar," Pheine said, "but that was not safe enough for you, Father. Who do you fear will come for us? What weight bears on your soul? Where will we hide next? A hole in the ground?"

"Perhaps our destiny is written," Thamma said. "You did not object to the Sodomites violating us; yea, you even offered us to them. Yet it was not God's will that it should happen. He would allow our bloodline to be pure. The angels sought to know us. It was not your will that it should happen, though the angels could have taken us at any moment. And so, it was God's will to allow you your choice, as he allowed the Sodomites to choose. And now, all paths are closed to us but one. No one remains to give us children, except for one man. God's choice clearly lies before us. He has chosen for Pheine and I. And He has chosen for you."

"What blasphemy do you speak of, sinner?" Lot gasped.

"Father," Pheine said, "was it blasphemy when you conceived us with our mother? Your wife? When you put your seed into her womb, was it wrong? Would it be wrong to love us the way you loved Mother?

Give us children, Father, children of the purest blood."

"We must not!" Lot hissed. "I shall not join your transgressions, harlot!"

Pheine grabbed the hem of her shift and slowly lifted it, exposing the dark curls of her pubic hair. A tuck formed between her pubic mound and her thigh, her skin soft and creamy. Lot longed to touch her, to taste her.

"Does my sex look so different from that of our mother, Ado?" Pheine asked. She stood over him, one foot on either side of his head. "We are our mother, and we are you. What sin would you commit with us? We are of Ado, and we are not so different from your wife. Tell me. Do you not feel the same urges Mother once brought you? Do you not long to put your root inside of us?"

Lot stared up at her as she spread her labia, the moisture glistening in the fire light. Pheine slipped her shift off and threw it aside, standing naked above him now, the swell of her breasts jutting out beneath her face. She stood above him, a statue of sculpted flesh.

"I must shut my eyes! I must not look," Lot muttered to himself, but he could no more force himself to turn away than he could break his bonds, no more than he could save the cities as they burned. *Hopeless. Helpless. I fail you now, God. As Ado failed you. As Sodom and Gomorrah failed you. We all turn to ash before your burning splendor.*

He watched as the labia parted, but now they did so without Pheine touching them, and he heard a wet sucking sound. The sound became speech, the lips moving like a mouth speaking,

"Would you save us again, Lot? Would you build our tribe? We are in you. Ado was impure, but you are of the flesh, and you are our flesh, and you must come into this flesh so we may continue to live, Lot. God has only burned the dross. Come into me, Lot, that I may swallow your seed, and with it create life. With it, I will create a new people, a people of strength and virtue, purified by flame and destruction. We have been burned clean. Cleansed, untainted by forbidden unions. Come into me, and we shall live forever."

Lot felt his robe being lifted as the voice stopped. He looked down to see Thamma pushing the garment up over his stomach. Her soft hand caressed his scrotum, lifting it, rolling it gently as his penis swelled with blood, becoming almost painfully rigid. *The flesh of my body betrays me,* Lot thought. *And my offspring betray their father. I can-*

not resist what happens next, anymore than I could resist what happened in Sodom. Could I have done differently? Could I have permitted the angels to know my daughters? The Sodomites knew the angels often, without calamity, until I rebelled against the act in my own house. I have lived as a pious man, but have I ever had a choice? Perhaps I have, only to fail. This is my punishment, to succumb to my own flesh and blood.

Chapter 2
The Plot Betrayed

"This is how we see your member more often, Father," Thamma said. "Long and hard, like we saw on the men of Sodom. We are virgins between our legs, Father, but not in the back."

"What do you mean?" Lot sputtered.

"Sometimes," Thamma said, kneeling beside him, "the men would take their cocks, hard and be-veined like yours, and they would thrust them into our rear." She wrapped one hand around his shaft and slowly stroked him, cupping his scrotum with the other hand. "They would fuck us in the anus, Father." Thamma lifted her hips, slowly wiggling her bottom in the air.

Lot's cock grew even harder. He stared at Thamma as Pheine stroked her hair.

"But we don't want that with you," Pheine said. She gently pushed Thamma's head down, until Thamma's lips wrapped around Lot's purple cock, slobbering. Her sucking mouth pulled and pulled at him, her tongue rubbing against the underside of his shaft. Thamma's hand gripped the base of his root, pumping him as she worked. Lot thought of the little viper again. He imagined it inside Thamma's mouth, wrapping around his penis, probing the hole. The pressure built inside, his head grew light—

And then he lost himself, feeling nothing but the pure energy of his sperm squirting into Thamma's mouth. He looked down to see her frowning, her lips locked tight around the head of his cock. When the last drop of come had coursed out, Thamma sat up, not opening her mouth. She took her hand, then, and let the white slime flow out of her mouth and into her cupped palm.

"Quickly, help me, Pheine," Thamma said, laying on her back and spreading her legs.

Lot stared, puzzled.

Pheine knelt down between her sister's legs and spread the smooth petals of Thamma's cunt lips. Carefully, Thamma trickled the sperm from her hand into her vagina.

Thamma cried out as Pheine quickly thrust her fingers into her, pushing the seed in as far as she could reach. The younger sister clenched her teeth and gripped the sheepskin as, Lot realized, she lost her maidenhead to her sister's hand. But as Lot watched, Thamma's labia quivered, mouth-like, as though sucking at the fingers. He half expected the vagina to devour Pheine's hand, pulling her into her sister. Lot heard wet sounds, like a beast feeding.

He closed his eyes, afraid to open them again for a long moment. When he did, he saw the girls reclining. It was done now, he realized. They had crossed a boundary, and could never return.

The girls rested for a moment, and then Pheine held a wineskin to Lot's lips, letting him drink. Thamma crawled on top of him and laid her slender body on top of him, gently fondling his flaccid penis. Lot despised how good her body felt, and stared at the ceiling. That they physically forced him to carnal actions enraged him. But the fact that his inner being so badly desired this congress sickened him. There could be no redemption for his soul's collaboration with this plot.

"Show me," Thamma whispered in his ear, "how you licked Mother." Thamma slid herself up Lot's sweaty body and climbed up, sitting on his face.

Thamma's pubic hair pressed into his nose, her curly hairs wet. She rubbed her cunt against his lips. Her musky scent made something rage inside himself, and Lot stuck out his tongue, tasting pussy juice, blood, and his own seed in Thamma's slit. He could no more resist the act, than could a starving man turn away from food.

Thamma moaned and ground down, taking his tongue inside her pussy as his nostrils filled with her aroma. She slid back and forth, fucking herself with his tongue. How long had it been since he last enjoyed the silken taste of a woman? Lot wondered. Thamma wiggled back, using her fingers to expose the bump of her clitoris. Lot's tongue darted against the bump, remembering the taste of Ado so long ago.

He sucked hard at her clit, angry that it was not his wife. Thamma clutched his head as she yelped and came, shivering and trickling juices into his beard.

"Now, Thamma," he heard Pheine say. Thamma lifted herself and slid down his body, straddling his hips and rubbing her oozing cunt against his cock. As his member swelled again, he realized with a shock his daughter was about to mount him. *The sucking hole will take my seed directly*, he thought.

Pheine knelt between Lot's legs and grasped his penis, pressing the crown between Thamma's labia. Lot grunted at the tight resistance of Thamma's cunt as she slowly moved her hips, whimpering as the rigid shaft forced its way into her flesh. She rested her cheek on his shoulder, gently rolling her hips and taking him in and out of her slit. He wanted to be repulsed, but could not resist the pleasure, the terrible hunger for release, gnawing at his innards.

"Come inside me, Father," Thamma whispered into his ear. "Come inside me." More words spilled out of her mouth, and these words Lot did not recognize. As she whispered her voice changed, becoming strange, and the voice of another whispered in his ear,

"All of the tribe lies within the wombs of the daughters of Lot. Feed your people with the screams and the blood of the outsiders. Let this cunt be an engine of war, destroying the enemies of your children with its power," the voice said.

As her muscles loosened slightly, she held onto his shoulders and fucked him harder, smacking her bottom against his hips.

"I feel you deep inside me!" Thamma grunted. "Let it come, Father, do not resist."

Lot thrust to meet her rhythm. Nothing mattered then, not that it was Thamma, not that it was sin. There was only the ecstasy of the flesh, the perfect feel of her pussy sliding up and down on his cock. He wanted this now and forever, even if it destroyed him.

Thamma moved as she had moved when whipping Pheine, driven, pumping up and down hard enough to hurt Lot's hips. Her face shone, livid, leering. Lot cried out as his fluid erupted, his daughter suddenly still, holding him. She stared into his eyes as she took his come. When Lot no longer twitched, and his member softened, she rolled off of him.

Lot stared at the ceiling of the cave and wept.

Thamma watched her father wake the next morning, groaning as he tested the restraints. She wondered if they should unbind him, but she knew he was still too wrathful. Moreover, Pheine had yet to lift her share of the burden.

"Wine," was the only word Lot spoke, not even looking at her or at Pheine. Thamma tended to him that day, massaging his sore body, feeding him, and helping him to relieve himself. Lot accepted her help in silence. And she gave him wine, not too much, but more as the day faded.

"Sister, I dreamed of Sodom and Gomorrah last night," Pheine said to Thamma, as dusk approached. Pheine had grown pensive and quiet.

"And?" Thamma said, glancing up from her chores.

"I saw the people burning. I saw the things that moved through the streets and the desert. I saw angels," Pheine said. "And they reminded me what happens to those who anger our God."

"And what, my sister, does that portend?" Thamma asked, stopping and staring at Pheine. Pheine worried the edge of her shift, averting her eyes from her sister's gaze. *Look at me, damn it,* Thamma thought. Thamma continued her work, staring at her sister.

"Perhaps we need to stop what we are doing. Perhaps we should not force this sin upon our father," Pheine said.

"Strange," Thamma said, her face growing hot. "Very strange they would speak to you last night, and not the night before. Do they think that perhaps it suffices that your younger sister should bear the guilt? That your younger sister should bear the offspring of our father while you remain a virgin for your husband?" Thamma swore a silent oath such would never happen.

"I can only tell you of what I dream," Pheine said, her face placid.

"Do you think God is not guiding us now? What we do is holy, my sister. Remember that," Thamma said. "That which is chosen cannot be

unchosen." *You will not leave me alone with this,* Thamma thought.
Pheine stared blankly and returned to her chores.

That night, Thamma fed her father much wine. Lot accepted the drink
passively, and reflected on how much Pheine resembled Ado. Pheine
would not tend to him — only Thamma. And Pheine — was this truly
his daughter? How could it be his daughter when she looked exactly
like Ado? He listened to them talk.

"Pheine. My sister. Dusk has fallen. It seems it is your turn with
Father tonight," Thamma said.

"But, Thamma, what of my dream? Dare I ignore it? Dare *we* ignore it?" Pheine answered, her voice grown high-pitched.

"Whatever sin has occurred has already stained you, my older
sister, who I might have depended on for guidance from the very beginning," Thamma said. Lot watched her fists clench as she spoke.

"I am sorry, my sister. I can only follow the wisdom granted me
by God," Pheine said, turning away. Pheine? Or was it Ado, afflicted
with some kind of madness? She must be Ado, Lot thought.

Lot felt fingers moving against his wrist, and looked up to see
Thamma untying the bonds. She stood, walking toward Ado.

Lot did not understand why his wife was not tending to him.
Why did Ado stand with her back turned toward him? Why should
it fall upon his very daughter to rescue him? His hand was free now,
though. Pain shot through it as the blood flow resumed. He glanced
at the woman Thamma had her arm around — was it really Ado? Had
she not been turned into a pillar of salt? She must have survived. But
what was she doing? *She did not live, Lot. She is salt. She is gone. She was
not worth saving,* he heard the voice say.

"But she was good," Lot spit the words out. "What did you make
her into? You made her into a monster. And you let her live still out
in the desert!"

Quickly he untied his other hand. The young woman turned
around, and recoiled as she faced him.

This was not Ado! Lot was stung, infuriated. Thamma grabbed
Pheine, as Lot growled and untied the bonds around his ankles.

Thamma stepped behind Pheine and hooked her arms under her older sister's shoulders. The younger woman let herself fall backward onto the bed, grunting as Pheine's weight fell upon her. Still, Thamma maintained her grip, and wrapped her legs around to trap Pheine's soft limbs.

"You!" Lot roared, pointing at Pheine, "You who would pretend to be my daughter, and then pretend to be my wife! You will *serve* as my wife now!"

His penis pointed at the girl like an angry spear. Pheine kicked and writhed, trying to free herself from Thamma, but the younger one only tightened her grip.

Lot pushed himself between the grappling legs of the girls. He clutched Pheine's shift with both hands and tore it open. Her full breasts swayed and moved in the struggle. *This will be magnificent. Mine to enjoy. Mine to punish for her insult,* he thought. He mashed her breasts in his hands, relishing the soft warmth. He grasped her dark nipples, pinching them, watching her squirm as they hardened against her will.

"So, you would be my wife, would you?" Lot said, taking his cock in hand, pressing against the fleshy folds of Pheine's cunt. "Then so be it!" He felt her wetness on his glans, the moisture only confirming in his mind the sinfulness of this deceiver.

Lot thrust forward, pushing into the girl's hole. He wanted it to hurt. Pheine gasped and arched her back.

"You call this suffering?" Lot asked. He savored the warmth and tightness of Pheine's cunt, sinking his shaft deeper and deeper into her, holding onto her breasts as he thrust into her tender hole. There was nothing else as he pounded into her, just the gripping flesh and the pleasure. They were one and he was three. Why should his wife be salt and he be alive? Why should this harlot bite her lip and grimace at him so? What wrong was there in putting his seed into the girls? Were they not almost the same as his wife? Were they not his wife? Was it not his right and duty? God would punish him, as he punished all, and how should he defy the will of the almighty? He would sin now, and invite the inevitability of destruction, as God desired, as it must be written.

The false-Ado, the fight fading from her, quit her struggle as she lay trapped between Lot and Thamma. Lot listened to the younger one cooing in the pretender's ear. She relaxed her grip on the woman and reached around, sliding her hand in to rub her captive's fleshy clitoris while Lot pounded into her.

"We must do this, sister," he heard Thamma whispering into the False-Ado's ear. "We must build the tribe."

Lot's anger dissipated as Pheine moved beneath him, moaning, the skin of her chest and face blushing. He felt her cunt tightening around his shaft, and she cried out, shaking.

"Who is this woman who maddens my flesh so?" Lot whispered.

"You do not recognize your daughter?" Thamma asked, smiling at him. She slid her fingers along the woman's slit, touching Lot's thrusting penis for a moment before reaching to slide two fingers into Lot's mouth. He sucked them, tasting the woman's juices. "Do you not recognize Pheine?"

The woman blinked at him. Lot gasped, recognizing Pheine, but unwilling to stop, the pleasure irresistible.

"Come inside her, Father," Thamma said. "Plant your seed in her womb."

"No!" Pheine said, her eyes widening. She pushed at Lot's chest.

"Now, Father!" Thamma cried out. Her arm locked around Pheine's throat, holding her in place. "Do what you must!"

The pressure inside overwhelmed Lot and he let himself go, sinking deeper and deeper inside the writhing Pheine. A warm rush crashed in his ears and the clutched Pheine as tight as he could, spending himself inside of her. He saw Pheine's wincing face next to the laughing visage of Thamma.

The world spun before his eyes. He saw Ado and his daughters and the angels, as the city of Sodom sought them out. The crowd screamed and writhed before him, and he smelled fire and choked on smoke and heard the screams. When he could see again, the girls were staring at the mouth of the cave. *The people of Sodom and Gomorrah were evil and God destroyed them. But God did not destroy me,* Lot thought. *What I do cannot be evil. But what of Ado? Was she evil? She did not obey God, so she was transformed. And yet, I fornicate with my daughters, and I live.*

Lot looked at the mouth of the cave. They were there. Not Nephilim, no hybrid spawn these, but the angels from Sodom. They stood, gleaming against the ink-black night. Lot recognized them in his heart, though they no longer wore the guise of man. Their skin rippled and changed, sometimes the palest white, sometimes the color of smoke, but always flickered over their hides what looked like threads of lightning to Lot. Their faces looked only vaguely human, skin stretched tight over wolf-like, hairless heads. Their bodies surpassed any warrior Lot ever saw, muscles flexing asymmetrically on their limbs, enormous turgid members jutting into the air. The air tasted like a massive storm approached. Lot heard his daughters weeping. A hum filled the air like the buzzing of bees.

The flesh of one angel unfolded at its stomach, the skin opening like a box. Long white worms wriggled within the cavity. The worms lifted themselves and stretched forward, their heads expanding into round knobs, the round knobs of glistening tissue opening to form mouths.

And the mouths spoke as one, and they sang songs to Lot in words that he did not understand, but the sounds touched him inside his skull. White liquid dribbled from the mouth of each worm as it spoke.

We speak the seed of the tribe, Lot. Your daughters will know us tonight. We are the tribe and the tribe is you, and we shall all dwell together forever.

Behind the angels, a shadowy mass lurched into the mouth of the cave. Lot refused to look at it, and let the angels hold his gaze.

"Ado," he wept.

Never Before Touched by Cupid

Mina Kelly

Mina Kelly lives in one of England's most historic cities. During the day she cooks from Roman recipes and swings medieval swords, trying to convince the tourists that history is more than just a pretty background to a photograph. From this she draws inspiration for her mixed up myths and flirtatious fairy tales, and has an especial fondness for things that go bump in the night.

Never Before Touched by Cupid

Quintus Horatius Flaccus—Horace to his critics, Quintus to his friends—keeps a straight face while Publius talks about Sextus. Publius talks about Sextus a lot. It's not that Quintus can't see why; Sextus Propertius is tall and broad and really does not so much wear his toga as drape it enticingly about himself. It's just that Quintus doesn't want Publius to talk about Sextus.

Maecenas is holding one of his little house parties. It's a nice night, if a little muggy, so the couches have been set out in the garden. Three stand empty in a small tent; the Emperor popped by earlier but couldn't stay and no one is willing to claim the now-abandoned dais set up for him. The Egyptian dancers Maecenas hired for the Emperor's visit huddle together in a corner of the garden, unsure whether they're still expected to perform. Quintus hopes they don't; the slaves would stop serving while they performed, and any table in front of Quintus is in constant danger of running out of food.

Publius eats well too, of course, but the blame is always laid at Quintus's chubby feet. Publius Vergilius Maro—Virgil to his fans, since he has no critics to speak of thanks to Augustus's favour—is skinny, balding and harried looking. He's terrified of women. He's not much better with men, but Quintus has always been able to warm him up a little. Publius never really expresses attraction towards anyone; he barely manages to express liking. When he does fall for someone he writes poems that allude to it, that have someone a little like Publius addressing someone a little like the object of his affection. After reading the Eclogues, Quintus had demanded to at least be shown the boy, and Publius had reluctantly agreed. Quintus now knows that Publius has a *type*, but Sextus isn't it.

Sextus isn't Quintus's type, either. Like any good Roman man, Quintus demands superiority in sexual relations, and he suspects he wouldn't get it with Sextus. And that he'd like not having it.

Quintus is short and round, with a hairy belly and jowly neck and a great many laughter lines. He doesn't really mind — it would be against his philosophy to, after all — since it's his poetry that gets him laid. Pretty girls and boys are so easily swayed by a silver tongue. Other poets, though, not so much.

And this is why Publius's little crush on Sextus is wearing so very hard. Publius is tall and thin and Quintus is short and fat and they have been best friends for most of their lives now (or the important parts thereof), and Quintus can't remember a time when he wasn't in love with Publius. Skinny, neurotic Publius, who writes like Apollo himself is dictating. Quintus is more of a Bacchus man, all things considered.

Sextus writes like Callimachus, who Quintus despises. He informs Publius of this.

"Youth," Publius says. "He'll grow out of it. We all went through a phase like that."

"And *she's* a prostitute," Quintus adds. "I mean, if Augustus disapproved of Catullus mooning over his very-much-married Lesbia, I doubt he looks kindly on Sextus choosing a whore for his muse."

Publius frowns. "You consider it an excess?" he asks.

"I consider it a good way to catch something nasty, and pretty vulgar to boot," Quintus says.

"It's not like you to get so worked up," Publius chides him. Quintus curses himself for making a philosophy out of such things, and craves a few extremes every now and then.

Maecenas wanders over to see how his guests are doing and is pleased to learn how keen Publius is to 'take young Sextus under his wing'. Maecenas's words, of course, not Publius's.

"No, I, um. He's very. Um." Publius blushes and stammers.

"And you call yourself a poet," Maecenas teases.

Sextus, talking to Maecenas's wife in a way that Quintus thinks the man ought to pay more attention to, looks over and winks at them. Publius falls silent and fixes his eyes on the floor but Maecenas notices his wife's blush more than the direction of Sextus's smile.

"That whore-loving son of a—" Maecenas says. "In my own house!" Quintus glares at Sextus until Maecenas blocks his view, ushering his wife away from the party.

Publius offers Quintus a sad, apologetic smile, and takes a grape from the table between the U of couches. The third is unoccupied, and it is perhaps this that prompts Publius to be a little more honest. "I am not even going to attempt to woo him," he says. "Look at him. He looks like Aeneas or one of those men of old. He could be a gladiator with that physique."

"And you would be at the stadium with all the wives, dirtying your toga for him," Quintus observes cruelly.

Publius nods. "Worse than those whores," he says. "My tits sag worse than theirs and my pubes are greyer. My eyesight has been wrecked since I started the Aeneid. He wants some lithe slave boy, some star of one of your odes. I wouldn't even have the nerve to assert my authority over someone so virile."

"If your eyesight is so bad, how can you tell?" Quintus can't resist a joke at his friend's expense, but it makes Publius smile a little. "Give him five years, my dear. He will hunch like the rest of us, with no voice from dictating and eyesight like a blind beggar. He will have my belly from Maecenas's exquisite catering. Not to mention everything his pretty Cynthia will gift him with."

Publius laughs a little. "Yes, there is definitely something worth saying about that."

Quintus reaches over and takes Publius's hand. "We must go to my little farm," he says. "Get you away from our plague-ridden Eros and back where you belong." He pauses, and adds, "I recently purchased some bee hives."

Publius grins. "For me?" he asks.

"Of course, my dear," Quintus says. "I was hoping that you would observe them at work with me, and explain their behaviours."

"You know me too well," Publius says.

"You're referencing book four of *The Georgics*, am I right?" An unwanted voice interrupts. "'The qualities Jupiter himself gave bees'."

"They're such fascinating animals," Publius says, smiling up at Sextus.

Quintus hates Sextus's accent. Umbria always grates on him;

harsh and brash and earthy. No wonder his poetry is so... How did Publius put it? Bold. Everything the man does is 'bold'. He wears a toga like a savage, but those tantalising glimpses of flesh seem all the more deliberate for it. His taste in food is bizarre, and when Sextus reclines it looks more like a sexual invitation than the proper way to eat dinner.

Sextus takes the couch opposite Quintus, and Publius, to his friend's fury, switches so that his head is next to Sextus and Quintus must talk to his feet. They are apologetic feet, though, and Quintus finds it hard to stay angry with them.

"I love being alive right now, don't you?" Sextus says, swirling his wine around in Maecenas's imported cup.

"Yes, I particularly enjoyed the civil war," Quintus says nastily.

"Well, if you will choose the wrong side," Publius says.

"It's all over now," Sextus says. He spread his hands expansively. "And look what peace brings us."

"You?" Quintus snarls. "Mars, send me soldiers again."

Sextus laughs at him, not improving Quintus's mood at all. "You are nothing like I imagined you," he says. "I was expecting some old stoic. It's good to know you're a little human. Well, in stature if not in girth, am I right?"

This does little to mollify Quintus.

"You've not read much of his poetry, have you?" Publius says, tossing a smile at his friend. "Or you have not read it well."

Sextus laughs again, this time at himself. "You've caught me," he says. "It's not to say I haven't *tried*. It's just too evocative. You write about some beautiful girl or boy, and, well, I have to go out and find one. You write about your farm and I just have to have a holiday."

"You write about Cynthia and I have to visit a doctor," Quintus says.

Publius looks embarrassed, but Sextus just keeps chuckling. "If you knew her," he says. "Oh, Cleopatra and Lesbia and all the mortal women in the world could not compare."

"At least you are not invoking Venus," Publius says.

"You should never tell a lover that another is more beautiful than they," Sextus says, "and that goes doubly so for a god. Greater men than I have suffered all kinds of fates."

Quintus looks up and meets Sextus's eyes. It's entirely unexpected and sends a bolt of lightning all the way down to his groin. Sextus grins. There is a cleft in that square jaw and dimples in his cheeks and that shit-eating smile would seduce a Vestal Virgin, and probably has. Sextus knows exactly what he's doing.

"Priapus preserve us," Quintus murmurs.

"I want you both," Sextus says in a low, rough voice. "I want you both at once, and one after the other, and to watch you together."

Publius moans and bites his lip. Quintus pulls his gaze from Sextus's and looks at his dear friend. He wants that moan for himself. He wants that skinny body with its folds of skin and greying hair; its wrinkled, tired phallus and its bony, sagging buttocks. He wants that man's poetry to be about him, surround him, inside of him. He wants to compose couplets in bed together. He wants to show him how to seduce the boys and girls he's bought for just that purpose, how to spend a whole day having nothing but sex with one beautiful person after another, because he has a beautiful mind. He doesn't want the bronzed Adonis before him, with its square shoulders and flat stomach and tight buttocks. Well, he does, but he does not think he could stand to write couplets with the elegaic little slut. He can't admire the man, or respect him like he does Publius. He just feels... threatened.

"I'll leave," Sextus promises. "I'll leave you together. I just want to *hear* you."

"Hear us?" Publius asks, voice trembling.

"Poets," Sextus says, "aeon-defying, epoch-defining poets. I want to hear you throw poetry at each other in the throes of passion. I want—"

"You want a better teacher," Quintus says. "And I suppose we will have to do. Honestly, what drivel you speak, my dear boy." The drivel is comforting; at least Quintus is his verbal superior, and he knows that that is what Publius will love him for, in the end. Sextus's looks are fleeting, but Quintus's poetry will last past his death (he hopes).

"Maecenas has loaned me his brother's room for the evening," Publius says.

Quintus adores him for the first romantic bravery he has ever shown. He loves him all the more, because Publius is looking at Quintus, not Sextus.

Publius's borrowed room is gaudy and overfurnished, draped with silk like a matron's boudoir. Sextus likes it, but then, he loves a prostitute and writes elegies, so what does he know about good taste? Publius is clearly uncomfortable with the ornate furniture; he circles the room, peeking behind each decorative curtain to make sure it conceals no spies or unexpected windows. He is on his second lap when Quintus takes his hand and leads him back to the bed, where Sextus is waiting.

Sextus has already unwound his toga, laying it across the bed as though he's concerned with protecting the sheets.

"I thought you were going to watch?" Quintus says, eyeing Sextus's already erect cock. It bobs against Sextus's stomach as he shifts slightly.

"That's up to you two."

Publius looks at Sextus. "I don't know," he says. "I don't know which is worse."

"We should have had more wine before we started," Quintus says. "Come on."

He sits on Sextus's feet, forcing the other man to move up the bed. Publius sits beside him. Quintus cups the back of his head gently, his thinning hair silky against Quintus's fingers, and pulls him in for a gentle kiss. They've done this before; Publius relaxes against him, into the familiar pleasure. He allows Quintus to slide his toga down his shoulder as long as their lips don't part. Quintus runs his free hand over Publius's exposed nipples, tangling in the wiry hairs growing around them. Publius might mock himself, but his lean body looks now much as it did twenty years ago, the first time Quintus got this far with him.

Behind them Sextus groans.

Quintus ignores him, putting everything he knows into the kiss, inching Publius's toga lower and lower. Finally he frees Publius's half-hard cock, something Publius rarely lets him do. He breaks the kiss to admire it.

"I want that in me," Sextus says.

Publius jerks away from Quintus, scrabbling for his toga. Quintus sighs, shoulders slumping forwards.

"What's wrong with you?" he mutters.

"Sorry," Publius says stiffly, not realising Quintus had meant Sextus. "I'd rather not do it than do it badly."

"You mean you've never done it at all?" Sextus asks, honest surprise lacing his voice. "But... the way you write..."

"I have a good imagination," Publius says. Too good, to Quintus's mind; it always works too fast for reality to keep up, and he knows his friend well enough to know he has considered every possible end to this night and is coming to the conclusion it's not worth risking the bad ones. "I've never had a Cynthia of my own."

"But you have Quintus."

"I have myself, and Quintus has his self."

"Have you ever had each other?"

"May your mouth be stopped with Priapus's cock," Quintus swears at him. "Shut up!"

Publius snorts. "Is that what you meant about poetry and passion?" he asks Sextus.

"I suppose so, though I'd rather my mouth be stopped by your cock than Priapus's. I know I have a reputation, but even my lips can't stretch that wide."

Publius tilts his head to one side, considering. His cock, which had wilted under Sextus's barrage of questions, stirs.

"What would I have to do?" he asks.

"You? Nothing. Just let me suckle it."

Publius frowns, considering.

"And what of Quintus?"

"What would you like Quintus to do?"

Quintus knows what he'd like to do. He hopes Publius knows it too.

Sextus crawls up the bed and puts his hands on Publius's hips. He turns Publius around, forcing him to stand as he does so. Publius's toga falls to the floor. Feeling overdressed, Quintus sheds his as well, though it doesn't seem to matter whether he's clothed or not right now. Quintus's cock is unsure of itself, half hard but wanting an invitation to truly join in.

Sextus rolls onto his back, head hanging over the edge of the bed, and pulls Publius's hips over his face. Publius bends over him at a near ninety degree angle, putting his hands on the bed either side of Sextus's hips to brace himself. Being the tallest of them all, Publius's face isn't quite square with Sextus's cock, but it brushes against his adam's apple and Publius swallows nervously. He looks behind him at Quintus for reassurance.

"What do you want?" Publius asks.

"I want to fuck you."

He's always wanted to fuck him.

Publius looks down at the cock bobbing below him. "I want that too," Publius says. His voice stutters; Sextus has gone to work on him. Cynthia must have taught him a few tricks.

Quintus sidles up behind Publius. His arse is all bones; the bulge of Quintus's stomach rests comfortably on top of his pelvis. He rubs against Publius's crease; it's sweaty, but not slick enough for Quintus to enter him.

Sextus groans around Publius's cock, and slides his mouth from it with a wet pop.

"I have some oil," he says. "Search my toga."

"Confident," Quintus says.

"It pays off." Sextus grins up at him from under Publius, and returns his attentions to Publius's cock.

Quintus forces himself to leave Publius, watching the other man's arse goosepimple as the cold air hits it, and roots through the bedclothes for Sextus's oil. He eventually uncovers a discreet pouch, cut from the same cloth as his toga, and finds within a delicate glass bottle. He uncorks it; the oil does not smell strongly, but there's something bitter about it that catches the back of his throat. It isn't olive oil, that's certain.

Well, it isn't like he's dipping bread in it anyway.

He pours a little into the palm of one hand and replaces the cork as best he can before his fingers get too slippery. He puts the bottle to one side, balancing it next to a bust of Pallas Minerva, may she appreciate his wisdom in not entering his friend dry. Virgins usually appreciate a little lubricant, he finds.

He warms the oil between his hands. He feels awkward slicking his cock, a cross between soaping himself and masturbation. Sextus can't see him from where he lays, and when Publius looks up he is almost cross-eyed with pleasure. Sweat drips from the lines on his forehead, sticking down his greying hair.

"Quintus," he moans.

Quintus positions himself behind Publius, sad to lose eye-contact but driven by lust now. He teases Publius's entrance open with his stubby fingers, years of practice on virginal boys and girls paying off now. Publius groans and thrusts down into Sextus's mouth, fingers clenching in the layers of togas that now adorn the bed. Sextus is jerking his own cock, as is only appropriate in the company of men so much more important than himself.

Quintus lines himself up and slips into Publius. Publius's head drops to Sextus's thighs and he stills, breathing heavily.

"You trust me, friend?"

"I trust you."

It isn't the poetry Sextus claimed to expect of them, but Quintus likes the simplicity of it. It's a chiasm; what it really wants is another word, maybe 'lover', in front of—Publius thrust back against him and the train of thought is lost. He clutches at Publius's hips, fingers curling around the jutting bones of his pelvis, and sees the tension in his friend's shoulders.

He returns the thrust and a rhythm begins between them, iambic trimeter; they even fuck like poetry. Longum, brevis, longum brevis, longum brevis. But Sextus sucks like he writes, elegaic, and it throws their epic couplets off. Publius comes into Sextus's mouth, gasping for air like a just-landed fish, the least eloquent Quintus has ever known him.

Sextus comes next, spilling his seed under Publius's slack jaw. He slumps against the mattress and Publius slumps on top of him, but Quintus keeps pounding until his balls ache with the need to come. He doesn't know why he can't until Publius lifts his head to look at him.

It's not poetry. They're not friends.

"Cupid," Publius gasps, "Never been touched like this before!"

And Quintus comes.

Later, when they've ceased to be a sticky pile of poets and become a sticky row instead, Sextus folds his hands behind his head and says, "I wonder if I've screwed a little lyricism out of you?"

"Sextus Propertius, your tongue, may it be renowned for centuries to come," Quintus says, "is in danger of being ripped from your mouth and fed to the emperor as a delicacy. Do you ever shut up?"

If you enjoyed this story, you can sign up for a free membership at
ForbiddenFiction and discuss it with other readers
and the author at the *Never Before Touched by Cupid* story page
at http://forbiddenfiction.com/story/MK1-1.000126

The Snake and the Lyre

Annabeth Leong

Annabeth Leong has written erotica of many flavors. She loves shoes, stockings, cooking, and excellent bass lines. Forbidden Fiction publishes many of her dark erotica titles.

Find her online at annabethleong.blogspot.com
or on Twitter @AnnabethLeong.

The Snake and the Lyre

Eurydice rested her cheek against Orpheus's thigh. His rich voice tingled in her ears, its timbre sweet as a persimmon. His foot tapped slowly as he plucked his lyre, rocking Eurydice's head with the ancient rhythm of the ocean.

The strings of the lyre—they trembled and thrilled beneath his fingertips. They exulted and crooned. Eurydice would have responded just that way had he thought to draw his music from her body rather than the instrument.

She didn't mind the rocks on the hill where they sat, and yet she recrossed her ankles under her body, fidgeting. Her heel pressed between her legs, sinking slightly into her cunt. Safely hidden by her skirt, Eurydice rocked on it in time with Orpheus's song.

She closed her eyes and pretended that the notes slipping into the wind around them were his hands slipping into her clothes. Her inner thighs shivered. His tongue could leave wet trails there. He could find his way to the juncture of her legs and sing only to her, his full lips and white teeth forming private poetry. Eurydice imagined his eyes, the shade of grapes in the vineyard, gazing up along her belly and between the peaks of her breasts. She would grip hunks of his black hair and pull his face tight to her. She would lock her ankles at the base of his spine and refuse to let go until she tired of finding release against his beautiful mouth.

"My love?" Orpheus's song had ended. He stroked her hair—too gently. "Eurydice, my love? What did you think of that Hypophrygian setting? I might compose in that mode for our wedding. It speaks so delicately, expressing the yearning of youth joined with the peaceable accord of family life."

Eurydice made the effort to smile. She kissed the top of his thigh through his tunic. "Your music would make the gods ache. It will be lovely." She inhaled his sharp, male scent, lifted from his body by the heat of the day. She pressed her lips to his leg again, a little higher up.

Orpheus frowned, adjusting his grip on his lyre. "The Lydian mode might be more traditionally appropriate. Simple happiness — that's a good atmosphere for a wedding." He scratched absently behind Eurydice's ear. "I think I can transpose this, so you can hear them one after the other."

She sighed and touched his ankle, just above the strap of his sandal. She angled her body to emphasize the swell of her breasts and lifted her eyes to his through the veil of her curling dark hair. "Orpheus...."

"Yes, love?"

"Perhaps you could lay aside the lyre for a little while?" Eurydice moved her hand up past the hem of his tunic. The muscles of his thigh twitched as she approached his cock.

Orpheus's indulgent smile dashed her hopes against the rocks of his perfect cheekbones. He retrieved her hand from beneath his clothes and returned it to her. "The wedding will come before you know it, my dear. We'll spend all night making love and singing to the stars."

Eurydice folded her hands in her lap, unable to resist pressing them against her crotch. "Of course," she said. "You want to try the Lydian mode, you said?"

"Go down and bathe in the spring below the juniper tree," whispered Eurydice's friend Apollonia on the day of the wedding. "Invite the Naiads to come and dance to your betrothed's lyre."

Eurydice giggled. "Does he need more recognition? The sun stands still in the sky to listen to him."

"You'll be the only woman in Thrace to have Naiads honor your wedding."

"Aren't they dangerous?"

"Playful," Apollonia said. "Beautiful. Sensual. People will talk about your wedding for years. It will be worth it."

Light splashed onto the hills like the water of the clearest stream. Apollonia grinned and waggled her eyebrows. Drunk on the promise of the day, Eurydice allowed her friend to coax her out of her clothes and point her toward the juniper.

Warm mud caressed her bare feet and tickled her naked calves. Eurydice ran her hands down the sides of her body. Now, the breeze teased her nipples. Tonight, it would be handsome Orpheus, her husband at last.

Eurydice dipped a foot into the sun-warm spring. "Sweet ladies of the water," she called. "Would you like to dance at my wedding? Silver-tongued Orpheus will play and sing for his esteemed guests."

"Or-phe-us," the water sighed, its surface rippling. The silt at the bottom bubbled. A pale arm emerged, as strong and slender as a young tree.

"Yes, Orpheus! He will be my husband!" Eurydice dove eagerly into the water and took hold of the hand, helping the Naiad out of the sucking sand.

The nymph clasped the offered hand and crawled up Eurydice, her skin cold and slippery. She darted between Eurydice's legs, her moss-green hair tickling her thighs. She wrapped her arms around the young woman's stomach and surged up to break the surface, her pebbled nipples scraping Eurydice's.

Eurydice gasped, her lungs suddenly tight.

"The wife of Orpheus," the Naiad purred. "We have heard him sing. Is his tongue worth the silver of its sound?" She winked. A clever hand darted between Eurydice's legs, parted her folds.

Eurydice jumped back, covering her cunt protectively. The nymph laughed, the water of the spring quivering with her merriment. "So shy." She placed a hand on Eurydice's waist and idly dragged a lily pad toward them. "Tell me, how does he play his instrument?"

The Naiad's lips nuzzled the young woman's ear. "Does godlike Orpheus know where to place his hands along the neck to draw the loveliest tunes?"

Eurydice realized with a shock that the Naiad's fingers followed her words, caressing up and down her throat. She knew she should make her excuses and escape the spring, but the thought of Orpheus's hands doing the same held her in place. The calluses from playing the lyre would feel rough against her skin. He could reach into her cunt and strum to his heart's content.

The Naiad pressed her slick lips to the base of Eurydice's throat. The young woman moaned. "Does Apollo's favorite musician know which touches produce which notes?" She nipped the same spot with her teeth, eliciting a shriek, then licked with her rough tongue, making Eurydice sigh.

"I long to know," the Naiad whispered. "Does our handsome player prefer his rhythms fast or slow?" Her hand returned to Eurydice's cunt, and this time the woman did not resist or pull away. The nymph's finger wriggled inside. Eurydice unconsciously spread her legs wider to accommodate the invasion. The finger stroked lazily at first, then accelerated to a pounding crescendo that made the young woman lose her feet and fall into the water, still wound around the nymph.

They floated there, Eurydice staring nervously into eyes the pale gray of river stones. "Speak, girl," the nymph demanded.

"Orpheus," she began, then trailed off and cleared her throat. Her pulse pounded everywhere the Naiad had touched her, but most strongly between her legs. She tried to disguise her longing. "Orpheus plays on his instrument, not his betrothed."

"Ah. Not a very giving lover, then, if he's left you virgin."

Eurydice bit her lip. She didn't wish to speak ill of her future husband. "He wants to share his love with me when the time is right. He says it's worth waiting for the perfect night."

"And what do you say?" The Naiad cupped Eurydice's breast, rolling her nipple between her long fingers. "Do you cherish a little girl's romantic dreams? Or a woman's desires?" At this last, she pulled Eurydice onto her thigh, driving hard against the center of her need. "I think you need more than Orpheus can offer you," said the nymph.

A whimper escaped Eurydice. She rode the nymph's leg helplessly, their hands tightly clasped together. The Naiad guided Eurydice's arms back so that her breasts thrust forward. She lifted her head from the water and flicked her tongue up and down on Eurydice's nipples.

Orpheus's bride-to-be arched into the nymph's mouth, her hips rocking in the water. She strained and reached for the pleasure that seemed just a breath away, thinking still of Orpheus's strong jaw and knowing fingers. She paid no attention to the water lapping first at her armpits, then just below her chin.

Eyes squeezed shut, Eurydice came against the Naiad's leg, the name of her betrothed on her lips. The word trailed off in a gurgle, triggering a panicked attempt to breathe.

Eurydice thrashed in the water, but the nymph's grip had tightened like a noose. She could not lift her head to the air above.

Through the wavering depths of the Naiad's spring, Eurydice saw a collection of water snakes swimming toward them, their bodies writhing and twisting. Her attempt to scream filled her lungs with water. The Naiad smiled and made a pacifying gesture.

The first snake coiled around Eurydice's ankle, weighing her down even more, holding her to the bottom of the spring. She struggled to shake it off, but before she could make headway, another twined itself around her breast. Its body squeezed the sensitive flesh, and then its head drew back. Eurydice watched in horror as its mouth opened wide enough to span a man's thigh. It's thin, sharp fangs embedded themselves in her breast, above and below the nipple.

The nymph held Eurydice in place, stroking the viper's head affectionately. The bite hurt less than Eurydice expected. Ecstatic warmth spread through her body, starting at her nipple but quickly rushing down to her cunt and up to her head.

Looking down her body, Eurydice saw another viper wending its way up her thigh. Its head probed between her legs. She would have panted if she'd been able to breathe. The snake penetrated her just as another bit her neck where it joined her shoulder.

Eurydice's body shuddered, tensing and relaxing while blackness bubbled in her mind. Would her husband have felt like this inside her? "Orpheus," she whispered, slipping entirely into the vipers' underwater nest.

Vipers wrapped Eurydice's neck and filled her mouth, smooth muscles pressing against the insides of her cheeks. Aching pressure between her legs revealed their presence there as well. Snakes around her ankles held her legs apart. Others stroked her nether lips with their bodies as they squirmed into her cunt, traveled deep inside, then out again.

Sensual heat enveloped her, sliding over, around, above, and below her. She lay comfortably, her body held and supported. Silky scales rasped gently over her skin, leaving her shivering in their wake.

Eurydice trembled. The water had gone. Instead, she and the snakes occupied a dark room, its features difficult to determine. She could not have guessed how long she had lain that way, her body being plundered by the snakes. She slid her hands carefully down her body, avoiding contact with the vipers.

Sticky residue covered her inner thighs. It felt like her own dried juices. How many times had she come? Eurydice tried to get to her feet, but the snakes resisted, suddenly binding where they had caressed.

They held her in place at dozens of points—her neck, her shoulders, her elbows, her wrists, her waist, her knees, her ankles. From the press of them, one viper rose, its body twice as thick as any of the others. Eurydice whimpered into the mass of snakes that filled her mouth.

A snake slithered out of her cunt, followed by another and then another. She wondered how many had been inside her. The massive viper found her opening and easily slid its head inside. It struggled to get in deeper, its muscles whipping its body back and forth between her thighs.

The snakes must have broken through her hymen while she'd lain unconscious. Her body slowly stretched open to allow the enormous viper room within her. The pressure of the snake's diamond-shaped head against the walls of her cunt matched a building inner tension.

Another viper, still slick with the juices of her cunt, worked its way between the cheeks of her buttocks and prodded at her other hole. Eurydice shook and poured herself into muffled screaming.

She didn't think she could come. Her body felt too full to ripple and spasm. And yet, as the thin viper pushed tentatively into her ass, Eurydice's cunt clenched almost unbearably around the thick snake inside it. Sweat trickled between her breasts. Her hips worked uncontrollably. Her tongue worked against the vipers in her mouth.

She could have remained in that blissful oblivion forever except that familiar tones came faintly to her ears, echoing strangely as if traveling a great distance. That cursed Hypophrygian mode—she heard it clearly. *Orpheus?* Now frantic, Eurydice struggled against the vipers, shame replacing her pleasure.

A heavy foot trod outside the room where she lay. She could already envision the disappointment and contempt in Orpheus's violet eyes when he looked upon her, writhing and spreading herself like a whore. Her face and neck burned.

But the man who appeared in the doorway seemed neither surprised nor disdainful. His thick, black eyebrows knitted as he studied her. He had a broad face, as ominous as storm clouds. "Eurydice," he said slowly. "Your husband is here for you."

The man clearly expected a reply. The vipers seemed to understand. They removed themselves from her mouth. Her distended cheeks relaxed. Eurydice sighed with animal relief before she could summon words for the man. When she did, her voice did not sound like her own. "Who are you? Where am I?"

"I am Hades," he replied. "You are in my domain."

Eurydice shuddered. Dead on her wedding day, bitten by a viper while held in a Naiad's embrace. What must Orpheus think of her? "Please don't let him see me," she whispered. She smelled her sex heavy on the air.

"He has convinced me to release you to the land of the living. I came to bring you out to him."

A viper slid over her belly, and Eurydice could not suppress a moan. Could she truly return to Orpheus? Would he want her if she did? Her body now seemed a mockery to his love of beauty, his perfect intentions. She hesitated.

Hades smiled kindly, holding out a hand. Eurydice managed to stand and go to him, her knees still weak from her long stretch of rapture. "Child, don't look so fearful," said the Lord of the Underworld. "This place differs from the land under the sun. We do not flinch from our desires here, but we keep our secrets with the most sacred respect."

He tugged her to the door. When Eurydice still resisted, he sighed. "If Demeter saw the forms her daughter Persephone takes with me in this place, she would blight the earth in eternal cold fury. What you have found here will await your return, and no living soul shall learn of it."

Eurydice swallowed. "Please, Lord. Swear that Orpheus will not see me until we return to the world above."

Orpheus and his ever-present lyre walked ten steps before Eurydice. She sighed with longing. Every line of his body spoke of perfection. She admired his powerful calves, tight buttocks, strong shoulders. She wished she could see his face, but she still stumbled naked and shamed through the halls of the Underworld. Eurydice could not bear the thought of meeting his gaze while in this place, the truth of her desires crusted on her thighs for all to see.

What other man would brave the Underworld and drag his love from the grip of Lord Hades himself? Eurydice's breath caught at the romance of it all.

"My love, are you still behind me?" Orpheus said, his voice low and anxious.

"I'm here, my Lord," Eurydice replied. Creatures of the Underworld lined the passage where they walked on either side, their forms grotesque and suggestive. She tore her eyes from a woman with a face between her legs, and then from a man who opened his mouth to reveal three flicking tongues.

"How do I know you are not an apparition of my Eurydice, meant to deceive me into leaving this place without my wife?"

Eurydice swallowed. "Test me, my Lord." A snake dropped from the stone ceiling of the passageway. She jumped to avoid it, but could not help wondering if this was one of the snakes that had been inside her.

"Sing me our wedding song in the Aeolian mode."

"The mode of mourning, my Lord?"

"Indeed, this is the way I sang it when I found my love had drowned in the spring at the base of the juniper."

Eurydice thought hard. He had made her listen to this composition in so many different forms, indifferent all the while to her panting after his body. Hesitantly, Eurydice sang the first notes.

Before she found her footing in the melody, Orpheus took over, accompanying himself with his lyre and improvising dramatic variations that made her lose her place in the song. Eurydice frowned, struggling to pass her test while also keeping up the pace through the passageway.

A man with a thick horn in the middle of his forehead threw a handful of snakes at her. One landed in her hair, slithered down her throat, and fastened its fangs around her still-bare nipple, suckling at her like a babe. Eurydice gasped at the sexual surge that passed through her body, faltering.

"Eurydice?" Orpheus asked, halting his steps. "Are you quite well?"

"Yes, my Lord." Another viper copied the first, so that a snake hung from each of her nipples. Eurydice ached between her legs, their poison making her limbs languorous and slow.

"Please continue the song. I need to know you're still following me."

Eurydice closed her eyes. She felt feverish. She struggled to force notes past her thickening tongue. Vipers crawled over the stone floor toward her in an undulating wave. They wound over her feet and worked their way up her body.

A snake with the thickest body she'd seen lifted its patterned coral head, separating itself from the others on the floor. Eurydice's body remembered the ache of the vipers' insertion and longed for it. She wanted to pierce herself on that hard, triangular head.

"My love? Will you sing?"

Eurydice managed a few half-hearted notes, but desire for the viper dominated her attention. Up ahead, Orpheus sighed and stopped walking.

"Eurydice, please."

She stole toward the snake. It knew what she wanted, arching its body up to her and shaping itself into the most pleasing curve. Eurydice stood above it, her legs spread wide. She tugged on the snakes at her breasts, her cunt clenching tightly in response to the sharp sensation. She leaned down and stroked the snake's head, then guided it toward her trembling cunt.

"My love? Did I lose you?"

The viper's forked tongue flicked over her cunt, raking over her bud just before it buried its head inside her. Eurydice sucked her breath in through her teeth and plunged onto it. The flood of vipers wrapped her and pulled her flat on the floor, but she felt held, not restrained. Eurydice worked her hips wildly, trying to force the thick viper deeper inside her. She groaned in a voice not her own.

"Eurydice? What have they done to you?"

Too late, she realized what would happen, but she could not extricate herself from the vipers before Orpheus turned. They engulfed her flailing body, but the ecstatic motion of her fingers against her cunt left no doubt of her feelings about the situation.

Orpheus's handsome face contorted with disgust and horror. "Eurydice? No! It can't be!"

She wanted to respond to him, to explain herself, but when she opened her mouth, a mess of snakes slipped in. She closed her eyes, another orgasm beginning to take her over.

Orpheus's wails shattered the passageway, but the vipers covered Eurydice's ears as they dragged her back into their underground nest forever.

If you enjoyed this story, you can sign up for a free membership at
ForbiddenFiction and discuss it with other readers
and the author at The Snake and the Lyre story page
at http://forbiddenfiction.com/library/story/AL1-1.000052.

Scylla's Pool

Elly Green

Elly Green spins tales of lust and love that re-imagine the ancient myths of the Greeks and Romans, weaving back into those old legends all the arousing and tragic eroticism that was originally present. When not writing, she loves to read about treasure hunting adventurers and watch every sort of dinosaur documentary available.

Chapter 1
Seeking Magic

Inside lives Scylla, yelping hideously; her voice is no deeper than a young puppy's but she herself is a fearsome monster; no one could see her and still be happy, not even a god if he went that way.

–Homer, *The Odyssey*

Glaucus grinned at the rare glimpse of a domestic Circe, hunched over her worktable, a sharp-bladed knife clutched in her hand. Her long, black hair was tied back with a scarf, her chiton unbelted and clasped loosely on her shoulders. She looked relaxed, comfortable, ordinary. With a quick glance out the window to her exotic and free-roaming menagerie, spread out in the garden beside her cottage, Glaucus reminded himself this was so very far from the truth.

He had been lucky when he washed up here, many years ago, that she hadn't turned him instantly. After all, he had already been half a monster. Since the moment he'd found refuge with her, the tales of her predilection towards changing men into animals had taken on a startling reality. He'd witnessed her anger many times while serving her that first year. No man except him had been safe.

His gaze caressed the home he had once shared with her. Not much had changed. The walls were still crowded with hanging herbs, in various stages of drying. The dirt floor still meticulously swept, hard-packed where she walked and worked the most. All manner of forged metal pots and pans, glass jars, and clay urns cluttered every flat surface. A variety of smells, both strange and familiar, assaulted his nostrils.

Stepping through the open door, a cool wind off the shore followed him. He could hear the creaking of his boat as it rocked in the rising tide. His splashing charge through the waves should have alerted her to his presence. She was obviously deep in her work, whatever it happened to be. With her, it was better not to guess.

She trembled as another gust of brine-scented wind washed across the threshold. She flicked her wrist, absently, toward the hearth at the back wall of the cottage and a fire roared suddenly to life, casting its glow and warmth everywhere.

Glaucus jumped at the burst of flames. "I see you haven't lost your touch, sorceress."

Circe froze at the sound of his voice, and his grin widened. Not many men could sneak up on her the way he could. With the knife still in her grip, a droplet of fresh blood falling from its edge, she turned around slowly to face him. He caught a glimpse of raw, crimson-edged meat behind her as she moved. Unusually human looking meat. Glaucus swallowed the sudden lump lodged in his throat.

Surely she hadn't progressed to eating the men...

He quickly looked into Circe's twinkling eyes. Her open mouth closed.

"That? Fire is simple magic. You could do the same with a bag of herbs." She was grinning. Her dimples — the ones he found so disconcerting in a woman like her — popped into life. In a moment, she appeared younger. Beautifully attractive.

Glaucus smiled wide in response. Stretching out his arms, he held his palms up in greeting. "You look divine!"

A moment passed between them, full of tension. Glaucus felt it in his soul and in his bones. Circe scared him. He took a deep breath and held his position, keeping the knife in his peripheral. One could never be sure of her emotions. She was a fickle woman. Finally, the knife clattered to the floor and Circe rushed to wrap her arms around his waist.

"It's been far too long! Welcome h — " she began, then clacked her teeth together. He arched an eyebrow at her started syllable, but then forgot as she clasped him tighter, locking her wrists behind his broad back.

He rocked them both side to side, hugging her back just as hard. He had missed her, despite his misgivings in coming to her now. Missed this house. It, and her, had been his saving grace, once upon a time, and the island still held a special, if terrifying, place in his heart. When he'd arrived the first time, he had been near death. He really shouldn't have eaten that magical herb. Sure, it had brought back the dead fish, but why he thought it would be safe for him to ingest, still boggled his mind.

Pushing her back a bit, he took her hands and examined her from head to toe.

"How do you do it, Circe? I swear you haven't changed a bit." His sparkling topaz eyes, stunning in his dark, sea-beaten face, met her gray ones. She batted her lashes in response and summoned a blush to her olive cheeks. Wrapping her fingers in his, he lifted one hand to kiss, then the other. Her hand trembled at the gentle press of his lips on her soft flesh and he searched her eyes for why. She appeared happy—no, thrilled. Leaning forward, she presented a cheek and he kissed her there, too. Her blush deepened. She smelled like amber and rose petals. The scent washed over him and his smile grew, exposing his teeth.

"You tease," she murmured. "Would you like something to drink? Eat?" Glaucus glanced at the meat still on her table, his previous thought returning, then back to her.

"Pork?" He prayed to the gods the guess what right. And that it was real pork and not once a man.

He watched as confusion scrunched her features as she answered, "Of course." Relaxing, he noticed Circe's eyes dart from him to the meat on the table and back. It took her a moment before she realized his reason for asking. "I'm not a monster."

She leaned back and her eyes gazed over his face and down his body. Not unlike his examination of her.

"Are you keeping up with the medicine I gave you?" Circe asked playfully, slapping his upper arm in the same manner.

He hesitated. "Why? Do you see any scales?" Their warm welcome forgotten, he took a stride away, spread his arms and legs, and spun in the middle of the floor. Beseeching her with a worried look, he encouraged her to examine him everywhere. "Please, do not say it is losing its effectiveness." His voice quivered with real fear.

The side effects of that herb had manifested slowly. At first, his skin itched. Then, it had begun flaking off. Underneath, hard, tooth-like scales had appeared. He hadn't worried. Sometimes the sun did strange things to a fisherman's skin. He had seen far worse in his years. Though, the blue-gray color was disconcerting. It was the webbing which had begun forming between his fingers and then over his fingers after the first week that had him panicking. That, and the slits behind his ears. When, two weeks after eating the herb, he'd suddenly toppled off the deck of his vessel and discovered his feet had fused together and the toes flattened out vertically, the fear had truly set in.

"No. It works. I promise." She grasped his wrists and pulled his arms down, wrapping her own around his back again.

Thrashing in the sea, he thought the end was near. He had no idea how to swim. Most fishermen didn't. There were monsters in the deep of the sea, and no one in his right mind chose to swim with monsters. Those terrifying creatures would grab a man and pull him under, never to be seen again.

He didn't drown. Instead, he swam, sort of, under the water. The waves carried him. Days later, he washed up on Circe's shore. He was almost completely transformed by that point. Only his head remained human, though his teeth were razor sharp. His body ached, his brain mush. He wanted to die, had crawled up higher on the shore in order to do just that. Fish could not live outside the water. Yet he survived.

"Thank the gods. I am enjoying my new-found immortality, but the fins and tail were a bit too much." He laughed, a little shakily, about it now.

"I remember. You washed up on my beach a wreck." Circe grinned, amused at the memory. He was less so.

It was Circe who identified the herb he'd eaten. She had pushed him back into the water and then sat down in the surf to cradle his head while she explained to him what had happened. She told him he was immortal, but cursed. He would never be fully shark or fully man. A hybrid, she'd called him.

Another word for monster, he had thought. *I am now what men fear. I am the monster who lives in the deep, ready to pounce and kill whoever falls beneath the surface.* The realization had been shocking. He was his own worst nightmare.

A god of the sea, she had amended, after studying his crestfallen face.

All he could see had been the horror of the ocean's depths. Blackness closing in on him, surrounding him, the press of the water from all sides. The screams of dying men and the roar of sinking ships echoing in the overwhelming silence. He didn't want to be like this. Even if it meant giving up immortality. His fear was too great, too ingrained. "You helped me." His voice was wistful, as his mind returned to the past. She had given Glaucus an herbal concoction that had changed him back into a man, in exchange for some hard labor on her cottage. She had made him promise to stay for a year in payment. He did the best he could regarding the repairs, considering he was a fisherman by trade. She was pleased nevertheless. In fact, toward the end of the contract, he had begun to realize she hadn't cared a bit what he did, as long as he was near her.

He shook his head to clear the memories, his final understanding hanging in the air between them. Standing opposite each other, silence filled the house. *Was that the source of the tension he always felt between them? Did she love him?* It was difficult to believe. He was, after all, a monster. And if she did — despite his monstrosity — there was now a greater obstacle.

"I need some more help. Again."

Her pupils widened briefly in shock and he recoiled, uncertain in his request. *Would she help him? Would she deny him? Should he have come back? What if she got angry? Could she reverse the magical herbs?*

"What kind of help?" Her voice came roughly, as though she choked on the words. Her hands fell to her hips and rested there, balled into fists. She cleared her throat and tried again. "What can I do for you this time? You didn't eat any more questionable herbs, did you?" He cocked his head at her curiously. Her words were lighthearted and silly, but he could still hear anger in her tone.

She waited for him to answer, a small smile softening as silence greeted her. Circe took a few deep breaths. Her body, which had stiffened at his question, relaxed. Her hands flexed and nervously smoothed the front of her chiton.

"What did you eat this time?" Laughter edged her words, now. She tossed her black hair back and fluttered her eyelashes.

His grin returned — she was a making a joke after all — making his whole face brighten. "I'm in love —"

Circe's scream sounded far more like the roar of a lioness than the shriek of a scorned woman. Not that Glaucus would remember. His body crumpled to the floor in a heap, unconscious. The arc of energy she had released sizzled in the air above him, the odor of sulfur filling the room.

Glaucus opened his eyes, well rested and rejuvenated, with a surprising energy that seemed to enliven his every action and thought. He hadn't realized he'd been so tired before. The rising sun was just peeking over the horizon, setting the sea awash in bright pinks and royal purples. *Morning? Had he slept here overnight?* He reconsidered how he felt. *More than one night?*

Sitting up, his gaze roamed over the interior of Circe's main room. Everything seemed as it always had. Embers crackled in the hearth and steaming water boiled in a cauldron hanging over the ashy logs. A caged bird chirped from the far corner. Circe was nowhere to be seen. Tilting his head to the side, he listened for sounds of her from the garden or from her menagerie behind the garden. Nothing.

He hauled himself to his feet and began to search the rest of the house for her. Perhaps she was asleep, though he had never known her to stay in bed past the sunrise. Checking a small bedroom and a then her well organized pantry — it was the only space left for her to be hiding — he returned to the hearth. She was gone.

Her absence made him wary. The island where she lived was vast for one person, with any number of dangers lurking about. Dangers not even a witch could magic her way free from.

Absently, he juggled two items he had found on a side table. A linen bag of scented herbs tied off with a leather band and an attached note, and a jar of creamy unguent, also with an attached note. Both notes bore his name.

He looked down as he toyed with the items. She must have made them while he slept, although he didn't think he'd told her what he had wanted before he'd gone to sleep. *Had she guessed?*

Glaucus read the notes. Apparently, she had. These were just what he had wanted. Special herbs and a potion to make Scylla fall in love with him. The nereid-queen was an obstinate beauty, demanding gifts, passionate words and his never-ending worship, but always holding back. She refused to return his love. Not any more, not with these. He lifted the gifts and inhaled the aroma. Circe had outdone herself; there was no way Scylla would refuse him this time!

Shaking his head, he still wavered. Should he stay or go? Glaucus looked down at the things in his hands again. Go. He should go. Scylla was waiting for him. No doubt, Circe was fine. She was probably off picking more herbs in the island's verdant jungle. Who knew when she'd be back? He knew from experience she could spend an entire day lost in her mind as she collected the herbs.

Having made up his mind, he shut the door behind him as he marched back down to his boat. It rocked gently in the waves.

Circe watched his departure from a behind a thick, moss covered tree. Swiping at the tears she couldn't control, she waited until the speck of his boat disappeared in the shimmering reflection of the sea, then slid to sit against the tangled roots. Dropping her head into her hands, the jungle's fauna quieted as her anguished sobs filled the air.

He had left. Again. And he was in love. With another woman. Her grief turned to self-pity, then anger. Hours passed, the sun high in the sky before she was too exhausted to continue on.

He would return, she knew it in her soul. Especially after those gifts she had left for him.

She lifted her hands and took a deep breath, smelling the strong odor of the herbs picked earlier. She really had outdone herself this time. Smiling inwardly she imagined the havoc the gifts would create. Glaucus would run from his love, whomever she was, and return here. Whether in joy, finally realizing at last Circe's power and her love for him, or in anger at this trick, she didn't know and honestly didn't care. She just wanted him.

Chapter 2

Scylla's Cave

Watching the ruffle and slap of the canvas sails, Glaucus' smile grew. The winds were in his favor this day. The splash of the waves rocked his boat as it sliced quickly through the water. He would be there soon. Back with his love. His heart raced with excitement. He couldn't wait to see her again.

Standing on the beach, looking up the sheer cliff face, he glanced back to make sure the boat was secured. Placing his hands on two rocks, he pulled himself hand-over-hand up to the cave. Hauling himself, at last, over the ledge, he lay there a moment collecting his breath.

"Lover, is that you?" Her dulcet tones struck his heart and plucked it like a harp. Closing his eyes, he savored the harmony of the sea mistress's words. A whiff of the scent of her sun-warmed skin flitted across his nostrils and he groaned. He had missed her so much.

"Yes, I've returned," he said softly, standing. "With gifts." He stepped inside the cave and Scylla's giddy grin greeted him as she rushed forward. Her honey-colored curls swung around her shoulders. Naked and unashamed, the nereid was the most beautiful woman he had ever laid sight on. "Oh, Scylla, you take my breath away." He sighed as his hungry gaze took her in. His heart skipped a beat.

Love. It had to be love.

"Where? Where do you have them hidden?" Scylla used her fingers to search within his limited clothes for her promised gifts. Reaching the border of his tunic, she dipped her fingertips under the hem. His breath caught in his throat and his vision narrowed, completely focused on the beauty kneeled before him. Pulling her bottom lip between her teeth, she flashed her long lashes.

One hand slid up and teased the very top of his thigh, stroking along the angle of his pelvic bone. Glaucus' eyes rolled back into his skull at the sensation of her warm palm so close to his cock. He was already hard. Uncomfortably hard.

She repeated her question. "Where?"

Slipping her hand back down, Scylla tugged at his tunic. He fumbled at his belt, suddenly in a hurry. Working the jar free from his pouch, he handed it to her.

Scylla settled back on her toes and looked at the gift. Tilting her head sideways, she flicked her gaze back to Glaucus'.

"Read the note."

She flipped the tag over and did as he suggested. "To awaken the senses?"

"I'll show you." He took the jar from Scylla and, though he hated himself for doing it, helped her to her feet and pointed her in the direction of the bed. "Lie down."

Before moving to the bed, Scylla turned in Glaucus' embrace and kissed him roughly, rubbing her lips across his with delicious friction. Lowering a hand to wrap her fist around his length, she stroked once through his tunic.

"I'm very happy you came back." Her purr followed her to the bed.

Stunned, Glaucus stood dumbly watching her arrange herself on the finely woven cloth covered straw bedding. Spreading her arms open wide, she kept her legs demurely closed. Squirming on the bed, she raised a knee.

He rolled the jar of unguent back and forth in his palms, warming the herbal paste. Taking long strides closer and closer to the bed, his face hardened and his attention fixated on the source of his growing arousal. Coming to stand at the end of the bed, he popped the cork from the mouth of the jar. The scent of spring blossoms, summer honey, and autumnal herbs filled the cavern. Both lovers moaned at the overwhelming odor. The muscles in his shoulders and back relaxed, his breathing slowed, and his mind succumbed to tender feelings.

"It smells divine." Scylla's full lips parted on the whisper. Glaucus rolled his head back across his shoulders. He felt both drowsy, and more awake than ever. It was a strange sensation.

Scylla shifted on the bed again, this time letting her legs fall open.

Her skin glowed with life, glowed with passion and he hadn't even touched her yet. Moisture seeped from between her legs. Glaucus yearned to settle between them and lap at her juice. Grasping her ankles roughly, he pulled her to the edge of the bed. He bent her knees back so she was spread open and available. Dipping three fingers into the cream, he started on her feet, and worked north.

He massaged her flesh, making sure no part of her body was left untouched. Pointedly ignoring the moist center at the crux of her thighs and her pert nipples, he swirled his fingertips through the cream and then across her skin in silky strokes. She began keening and wailing. Her breasts bounced and her hips rose and fell in not so subtle waves, urging him on and threatening to disturb his attention. He stopped, enjoying the view of her so close to the edge. Her eyes sprang open and she glared at him. Her mouth, so soft and pliable before, froze in an ugly line.

"Don't you stop, Glaucus. I will toss you from this cave into the treacherous waters below..." Her voice, pleasant so recently, was now harsh with denied ecstasy.

"I wouldn't dare. Turn over."

Immediately, her entire demeanor changed. Light as a feather, Scylla quickly flipped over. Her girlish giggle returned. She tucked her arms beneath her head.

"Go ahead. Do your worst."

Glaucus huffed at the order. He grinned. This was the woman he loved. Like the sea — the approach of a storm on calm waters was counted in breaths. Easy-going one moment, harsh and commanding the next.

There was only a little remaining unguent. Taking the last of the cream, he smoothed the soothing herbal tincture over her warm ass. She moaned and ground her clit into the sheets under his caresses.

He grabbed her hips in a rough hold and hauled her to him. She squealed in anticipation. Wrapping one arm around her waist, he knelt on the edge of the bed, and spread her thighs apart. The side of her arm caressed his, as she reached under her body and ran her fingers up and down her slit, preparing for his entrance. He watched, mesmerized by the scene. Her folds parted under the ministrations and he almost fainted at the heady odor of her heat.

Moving swiftly, he undressed. His cock was fully erect, purple, and aching. He joined Scylla's fingers with his own, coating his digits with her nectar. Nudging hers aside, he sought out her most sensitive clit and began to circle the flesh. He flicked her nub with his thumb, pressed upon it, then clasped it between his fingers and tugged. She arched at the feeling and whimpered in need, thrusting her hips back at him.

That was the cue he was waiting for. With the scent of her arousal strong, her noise making him crazy, her body laid out like a sumptuous banquet for the taking, and his need for her greater than his self-control, he let go.

Glaucus drove forward with a powerful thrust, entering her sheath halfway before retreating and plunging in again. Taking her without finesse, he slammed his cock into her tight passage over and over. She shook in his embrace. Her fists tangled in the sheet. Her head thrashed side to side, her sweat-soaked spirals tightening delicately. He reached up to run a hand over her scalp and down her curls. He tangled his fingers in her hair, pulled her head back and sunk even deeper into her core. Her inner walls squeezed his cock. The pulse of their heartbeats throbbed in unison. Their flesh seemed to melt together in the rising heat of their lovemaking.

"Faster, dear gods, faster. Move, bastard!"

Glaucus groaned. He didn't want to move. The feel of her impossible tightness was enlightening.

Scylla rotated her hips and bowed her back. The change in position sent him reeling. He was so damned close!

With his hand still caught in her locks, he shoved her forward, knocking her chest down to her elbows, forcing her to the sheets. She fought him but he didn't care. He stretched out on top of her, embedding himself between her folds. Cradling her to his chest, he rolled them over and let go of her hair. She lay atop him, breasts toward the craggy ceiling. Taking her breasts in hand, he kneaded the soft, ample flesh. Glaucus twisted and pulled on her nipples. She whimpered and moaned. Sitting up, she pushed down on his cock.

"Do it, then. Take me!" Scylla yelled.

Glaucus didn't hesitate. He lifted his hips, bent his knees and plunged his cock as deep as possible. She slammed her body onto his cock, meeting each of his thrusts. Racing him to the finish line, she set the punishing pace, pushing him further and further towards his completion.

"Now!" she screamed, the final vowel stretching into a shrill shriek of ecstasy. Glaucus closed his eyes, welcomed the blinding light of his orgasm, and let go. Scylla continued to move on top of his lap, but her motions were easy and languid. Opening his eyes, he could see her skin flush crimson—a full body blush.

"Oh, gods...that was amazing," she sighed. He couldn't agree more. Turning his head on the bed, he glanced at the floor and saw the empty jar. He would have to remember to ask Circe for more.

Side by side, the lovers struggled for breath and tried to calm their racing hearts. Their skin steamed in the cool air of the cavern.

"Do you feel like a bath?" Scylla asked, after a while. She rolled onto her side and propped her head with the palm of her hand. With her other hand, she traced the lines of his physique, wrapped a few strands of dark chest hair around her finger and pulled teasingly. The smile she wore was bliss, pure bliss. Half-lidded eyes, satisfaction gleaming in their depths, had trouble focusing on anything, darting here and there. Glaucus loved her like this. Sated. She was so beautiful.

"I would love one. With you."

She moved slowly, stretching her limbs like a cat as she stood from the bed and sashayed toward the back of the cave. A spring-filled basin was tucked into the corner behind a large stalactite.

Rolling off the side of the bed, he tripped over his tunic. Kicking it aside, he saw his belt and remembered the satchel of herbs. Circe's other gift to him. His other gift for Scylla. Glaucus retrieved the bag and, swinging it on one finger, sauntered back to join Scylla.

"Did you like the cream, my dear?"

Bent over at the waist, humming happily as she fiddled with the collection of combs and sponges she kept beside the bath, the first sight of her swaying ass froze him to the spot and awakened his cock anew.

"Why, do you have more?" She straightened and spun around, her gaze immediately locking on his quickly growing erection.

Glaucus shook his head, remembered the satchel, then answered,

"No, but I do have another gift."

Her features lit. "Please?" Scylla held out her hand and Glaucus dropped the bag into her open palm. She brought it to her nose and inhaled. The scent of plum, peach, orchid, wisteria, and amber all combined to have her on her knees. Weaving side to side, her lips serene, eyes closed, she moved as if in a trance. She drifted on a second sea of passion. All from one whiff.

He laughed at her reaction. "Let me have it back and I'll read the note for you." She handed the linen bag back absently, letting the waves of the aroma wash over her. "To awaken the animal within." Purring where she swooned, he reached down to tuck a stray strand of hair behind her ear. "Which seems to being working already." He grasped her beneath her arms and pulled her back to her feet.

She thanked him with a hug, her purr deepening to the yowl of a cat in heat. Letting her rest on his chest, he chuckled at her current state, already imagining the fun they would have in the bath.

Glaucus untied the bag of herbs behind her back, fiddling with the tiny knot Circe had secured. At last, the leather band undid and drifted to the ground. Dumping the herbal mixture into the bath water, he allowed himself a moment to pull the wonderful scent deep into his lungs. Unlike Scylla, he felt no more than a slight tingle in his cock and between his balls. Shrugging, he didn't think to panic. Perhaps he was stronger, more immune to Circe's magic, than Scylla.

Since they were still naked, he slowly maneuvered her into the bath—nothing more than a deep basin carved naturally from eons of underground water in the rocky cavern's back wall—and then slid down into the warm seawater across from her. Her head fell back and she slipped further into the bath, the water rising just below her heavy breasts. She closed her eyes and sighed, slow and deep. Glaucus eyes settled on her nipples. He hadn't gotten the chance to taste her there yet, and suddenly, he wanted nothing more.

Floating off the slight bench that formed midway in the basin, he slunk across the space between them. He kept low in the water, letting the herb-infused surface lap right above his pecs. Touching her nowhere except her breasts, he used his mouth to lick all around the voluptuous, perky globes. As he licked, he nipped gently on her sensitive skin, loving the savory saltiness of her sweaty flesh. Glaucus' eyes locked on her peak. He craved her dusky, pink tit.

He took it between his lips, rolling the peak back and forth, feeling the areole pebble. Sucking the nipple, peak and areole both, inside his warm mouth, he began to draw roughly, like a starving infant. His hair brushed across her collarbone. Lifting one hand from its purchase on the underwater bench she reclined on, he palmed her opposite breast. He seized her tit between the nails of his thumb and forefinger and pinched hard. Very hard.

Scylla's head whipped up and her hands found purchase in his hair, holding him tight to her bosom. "Gods!" Without consent, her hips gyrated, lifted and wiggled, begging Glaucus for his cock again. So soon after her first orgasm.

Though his scalp burned with the pain of her nails digging into his skin, he didn't let go. Dropping his other hand to her abdomen, he started at her navel and stroked purposefully down to sift through her nether curls. Finding her clit, he punished it as he did her nipple.

She wailed, shrieking unintelligible words.

"Let go," he growled, ripping his mouth from her breast. Delirious, she only pulled him closer. His fingers squeezed her clit and pulled. Scylla yelped and, tilting her head forward, glared at Glaucus.

"Ouch!" She growled.

"Let go," he repeated. They stared each other down, fighting the need for pain and the want for more pleasure. Both desiring, in that moment, domination.

She was the first to relent. Releasing her grip on his locks, she spread her knees and beckoned him with a curved finger. Instead of crawling in with his bobbing staff, ready and poised to enter her, he eased his hands under her ass and lifted her off the bench, holding her poised at the surface of the pool, and pressed his nose to her moist folds. He swooned at the scent. The sweet smelling aroma of the herbs only added to the sweetness of her feminine nectar. His nostrils flared at the overwhelming experience and he hurried to taste her fully. Kissing her with his lips open, he fed on her, slipping his tongue past her slit and, imitating the final act, thrust his tongue as far as he was able into her. He suckled her as though he could not live another day without her on him, in him, everywhere. Her purring resumed with interspersing yips as he happened upon a particular spot over and over again. The spot varied, but her body nonetheless responded. He tried to memorize his actions, but soon lost count and interest. He was too pleased by her burgeoning arousal to care.

Sliding her hands from his head, she caressed the shell of his ears, down to the lobe. Then, taking it between her fingers, she pinched hard with her nails. His head popped up. His shoulders followed, extending her thighs even wider. He dropped his hold on her and let her sink back to the bench.

Now it was his turn to complain. "Ouch!"

Wrapping her arms around his neck, she trailed them lower to his chest. He stared at her, confusion clear. Fingertips gliding along his wet skin, she tickled his ribs and dropped her hands to rest on his hipbones. She forced him to scoot closer so the head of his cock bumped against her slit. She moaned. He groaned.

"I want it slow." Scylla winked. Her eyebrow lifted and one corner of her lips tweaked in a smirk.

"Yes, mistress." He lowered his eyes in an act of modesty. Then, taking her hands in his, he pulled her up so they stood chest to chest. Reaching under the water, he caressed her thigh and lifted her knee, placing her foot on the bench. Crouching slightly, he took his cock in his fist, and lined himself up. His cock teased her folds. His breathing quickened as he watched the joining of their flesh for the second time, this time amplified by the water.

Slowly, bit by bit, ever so slowly, he sheathed his sword in her.

He filled her completely, her core muscles relaxing to ease his conquest. Once in place, his length deep inside her, the lovers released the breaths they held. With one of her legs draped around his back, the other supporting her weightless body, he held her in the perfect position for the long, slow, strong strokes of his staff.

Glaucus reveled in the feel of her tight on his width. He savored each plunge.

"You are divine, my love!"

"So are you..."

The two lovers moved together, lost in the moment. Around them time both seemed to stop and stretch out into eternity. Their climaxes approached quickly, but far too leisurely. He hung on the metaphorical edge, suspended, waiting intermittently for the fall.

"Your nails, dear," Glaucus grumbled, feeling a sharp pain bite at his inner thigh. He thrust forward forcefully, loving the sound of their bodies slapping together in rhythm. Loving the swells that rippled across the water from their union. "Oh, gods, Scylla, stop scratching me!" A white light sparked behind his eye as another stinging graze ripped the thin skin of his abdomen. The climax that seemed so close, was abandoned. Pleasure was gone, but the pain remained. "Oh, Hades..." he screeched as numerous pinpoints of pain erupted at once along his balls and cock. His nerves screamed in agony. He tried to pull free of her, but her legs remained around his waist.

"What? Don't stop." Her lashes fluttered at his sudden absence.

The splash of limbs — not any of theirs — tossed droplets in the air from behind Scylla's body. A drop of the water landed on Glaucus' hand. He eyed it curiously. What in Tartarus was going on? His gaze lowered and he sucked in a sharp breath. Creatures were thrashing beneath the surface of the bath water. Dark, writhing animals, alive, frenzied.

"Scylla?" His voice rose, shrill, as fear and adrenaline coursed in his veins. He lifted his eyes to hers and stared, terrified.

"Glaucus?" His finger pointed down. She looked.

Pulling her leg from behind him, she placed her feet on the bottom of the bath and stood tall. Suddenly nervous, Glaucus watched with her. *What were those things?* Creatures flailed, sending water everywhere. They shifted with Scylla, their snouts and white snarling teeth rising from the water as her midsection cleared the surface. The eyes of rabid dogs glowed in the cloudiness of the churned water. Too many to count. Foam gathered along fleshy lips raised in growls as their snouts broke free of the surface. Scylla scrambled to get away, but with every move, the strange dog heads followed — as though attached.

As she took a step toward him with arms outstretched, panic at the scene before him caused bile to rise in his throat. He could see the fear in her eyes. She was scared. Very scared. Her body vibrated with terror. She opened her mouth to scream. Closed it, then grabbed his arm. Her eyes watered and her lip quivered. She opened her mouth again, this time to beseech him for help. No words came. She was immobilized by fright.

He retreated, backing away slowly, all his attention focused on her transformed midsection. His body shuddered as more and more of the monster she'd become rose clear of the water. Every nightmare from childhood on came drastically to life.

Ears pinned back against their skulls, the doglike heads surrounding her waist began to sway to and fro, nostrils flaring. Like a pack of starving wolves, they were searching for prey. Searching for him. Newly born from her loins, they were very hungry. Locking on to his warmth, their heads swiveled on serpentine necks and lunged for Glaucus. The sharp snap of teeth made him jump and spurned him to swifter action.

He had to get away. She was going to grab him, pull him beneath the water and rip him to shreds. He'd drown in his own blood. He eyed the snarling dogs. Those creatures were hers to command.

Glaucus' calves bumped into the bench and, without glancing back, he climbed quickly over the edge. Crashing to the floor of the cave, he kept his eyes on her as he crawled away.

She found her voice. "Come back, love. Help me."

Tears streaked down her cheeks. Her bottom lip quivered as her pleading eyes dropped from his to stare at the abominations arising from her waist. He followed her gaze and felt his own lips curl in disgust and fear. The creatures' heads thrashed ever searching and their forelegs kicked and struggled. She looked up at him. Her brows were drawn, her forehead creased. Fear and worry marred her once beautiful features.

He looked away toward the basin. Herbs still floated, spinning lazily, on the surface. His gift. Circe's gift to him. It had changed her into this monster.

"Love?" he taunted. "Oh gods, no. You're a—" His voice wavered, but grew stronger with each backward step he took toward safety. "A monster." He shook his head and pointed his finger at her. The finger trembled slightly. "Look at you! A nightmare!" He spun on his heels, not even bothering to gather his clothes or belongings, and fled, leaping from the cave's entrance in his haste. Without a glance behind, he rushed to his boat and huddled, curled into a ball, beneath the wheelhouse.

A melancholy howl rang out from the cave, echoed by a dozen

more. The eerie noise sent shivers racing down his spine. Clutching his knees to his chest, he blubbered in fear.

Circe stared at the swirling cauldron of water. Scylla was no longer the sea goddess Glaucus had thought he loved.

She stood and stretched, a smile splitting her face. Her eyes roamed her tiny cottage, trying to decide how best to pass the time before he arrived. He would undoubtedly allow his body to revert to his transformed state to reach her fastest. Fear and anger were both powerful motivators.

With that decided, she burst into motion. A new batch of medicine for him was the first order of business. Humming, she pulled a cloak over her shoulders and hurried out into the jungle.

If you enjoyed this story, you can sign up for a free membership at
ForbiddenFiction.com and discuss it with other readers
and the author at the Scylla's Pool story page
at http://forbiddenfiction.com/story/EG1-1.000239.

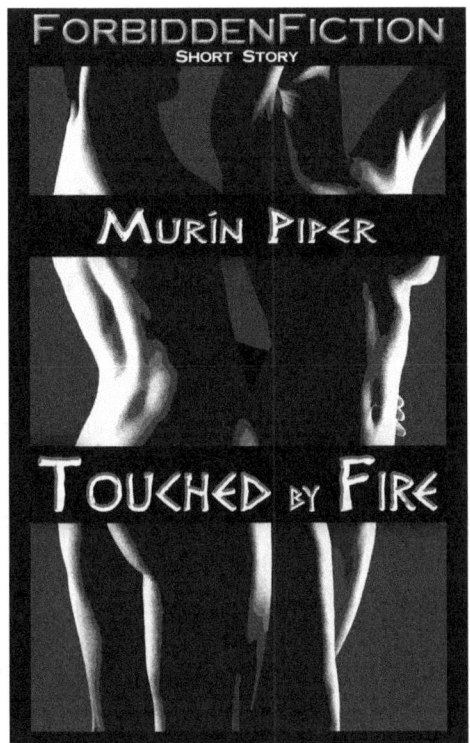

Touched by Fire

Murín Piper

Murín Piper is a British erotic fiction writer who has been writing since she can remember. Her first attempt at a novel was a "whodunit" she started at the age of seven. For the record, she still doesn't know who did it. Since then she has written for her enjoyment and over a variety of genres. She moved into erotic fiction while she was studying psychology and took an interest in psycho-sexual behaviour. The rest, as they say, is history.

Chapter 1
Vestales: Virgins of the Fire

Licinia watched as Aemilia, her Vestal sister, ran her fingers through her hair, untangling the plaits Vestal Virgins were made to wear. Aemilia's hair was a mass of raven curls, unruly and untamed. Licinia followed Aemilia's gaze as she glanced over to the window; the sun was starting to set, already dipping below the horizon. Turning to Licinia, Aemilia smiled.

"She is ready."

Licinia cast her eyes down. She didn't want to openly disagree with Aemilia but she had her doubts about involving Marcia. Theirs was already a delicate relationship, one balanced between the dangers of getting caught and the deep-seated need in both of them to be loved in a way most people wouldn't understand. Licinia doubted anyone, not even Vesta, could ever love her the way Aemilia did, even though such ungodly thoughts made her shiver in the cool breeze.

"Are you certain?" Licinia asked, approaching Aemilia at the window, despite her fears. Behind them were walls and more rooms dedicated to their goddess, the insides of Temple of Vesta. In one of the rooms was the hearth where Marcia would be sitting now, warmed by the fire, completely unaware of what awaited her.

But hidden away in the privacy of her room, Aemilia was looking out over the Palatine Hill, at the grass and dirt, the water trickling down the viaducts to the temples of the other gods. Not a single one of them had servants as devoted as they, the servants of Vesta. No man stayed up the whole night to ensure the fire was burning for the whole of Rome. No man chose to forsake marriage and love, pleasure and companionship.

Licinia pressed her cheek to Aemilia's back. No other servant of Vesta had found love in such a place, where the very idea was prohibited. No virgin gave herself to anyone other than Vesta, but for a goddess of fire, Licinia refused to believe she would be so cold as to deny them their love. Perhaps one day she would turn on them, reveal them for breaking the laws of *Nefas* and committing that which was impure, unchaste, but so long as her mercy lasted, so would her love for Aemilia.

Aemilia held out her hand and pulled Licinia in front of her, taking her by the waist. The night air chilled her skin further, and she longed to pull the shutter closed. Aemilia held her tight, her body warm.

"I was certain about you."

Licinia smiled, her heart rising again. She'd been twenty when she finally worked up the courage to ask why they must remain chaste, and why a goddess of family and home would care about purity. Aemilia had taken her aside and told her something very different than what their *Maxima* had. She said chastity was the idea of the priests, not of Vesta. Whether they feel her fire with their hands or with their whole bodies, they were still worshipping her. Aemilia believed that to feel Vesta's fire in their very hearts was the greatest worship of all, and to ignore such a fire would be as blasphemous as breaking their vows was supposed to be. When she said it like that, Licinia could see the truth in her words, but she wasn't sure Marcia would.

"She's young," Licinia pointed out, relaxing into Aemilia's arms.

Aemilia pulled back the golden strands of her hair, kissing her neck, whispering against it, "You were younger."

Licinia turned, staring into Aemilia's dark eyes, trying to fathom what exactly was going through her mind. Her stare was returned and Licinia broke first, looking away. She didn't mind the idea of sharing — the idea of them having another person to love made her belly do excited summersaults — but behind it all, she was scared.

They had sworn to Vesta they would never tell another soul, not ever, but Marcia asked all the same questions they had. She expressed the same curiosity and yearning they did. She was almost one of them already; she just didn't know it yet. But it could still go sour. She was unable to rid herself of the worry that Marcia, in her inexperience, would get them caught or say the wrong thing. Or worse, she wouldn't want to be a part of their relationship at all and she'd run to the authorities and tell the world their secret. To be found guilty of what they were undeniably guilty of—of loving each other, giving each other their bodies as well as their souls—they would be killed, as surely as if they'd had a tryst with a man, and Licinia was sure Vesta wouldn't be able to save them if that happened.

Licinia swallowed, forcing down all her doubts and her fears, and placing her trust in Aemilia's love and her faith Vesta's judgement. "I love you."

"I know. I love you, too," Aemilia said, stroking her cheek and bringing their lips together. She tasted of strong wine cut with thin water and Licinia clung to her, deepening the kiss until it wasn't enough on its own anymore.

Stumbling backwards, she sat down on Aemilia's bed, pulling at Aemilia's robe, her *infula*, until it fell gracefully from her shoulders, revealing plains of skin that rarely saw the sun. Licinia breathed in, like every time she saw her, she was taken aback by her beauty, overwhelmed by it. She'd never, before Aemilia, seen another woman laid bare but was certain they wouldn't be a match for her love. Even the stone carvings of Venus lacked the radiance of her skin and the glint of mischief in her eyes.

She ran her hands down Aemilia's sides, feeling the groove of each bone, each rib, the jut of her hip. She kissed her belly and turned her head, pressing her cheek against the soft flesh, feeling an echo of each rise and fall of Aemilia's chest, each breath soothing her. Wrapping her arm around Aemilia's back, she anchored herself against the other woman's body, her fingers finding her knee and creeping higher, the barest scratch of her nails sending shivers through them both as her hand climbed up her thigh, seeking out her cunt, finding her lips already wet.

Aemilia caught her hand before she could push deeper and breach her. "Not tonight, my love."

She kissed Licinia's fingers and folded her hand, placing it in her lap. Licinia frowned, a pit forming in her stomach, making it hurt. She was confused. Aemilia had never rejected her before, even when she told her the darkest desires of her heart, even when she realised she wanted Marcia as well.

"Why not?" Licinia asked, trying to keep the hurt feelings out of her voice, but failing. She opened her hand, wanting to reach out to Aemilia but when Licinia saw the heat in her eyes, she stopped in her tracks.

"I want to watch you," Aemilia started, moving to pull Licinia's *infula* over her head, leaving them both naked. "I want to tell you about what you have to look forward to tonight while you touch yourself. Will you do that for me?"

Licinia's breath caught in her throat, her insecurity melting like the night's frost into morning dew. "For you."

Licinia pushed back against the wall, drawing her feet onto the narrow bed. Spreading her knees, she opened herself for Aemilia to watch. Her fingers teased at her lips, at her clit until she started to feel the beginnings of pleasure washing over her like the pleasantly warm water in the baths.

"Tonight," Aemilia started, watching as one of Licinia's fingers slipped past her lips and into her cunt, returning shining wet and disappearing again. "Tonight we are going to take sweet little Marcia, like a luscious red apple, ripe for the picking."

Licinia closed her eyes, imagining the girl with her long, light brown hair, running straight down her back when she didn't have it in plaits. Keeping that in mind, she added another finger alongside the first, still too tight to be ready for it, feeling the burn like Vesta's fire blazing inside her.

"We are going to take her, both of us, and we are going to show Vesta what she's missing by only blessing the two of us in our love," Aemilia continued. "I'm going to show Marcia all the secret ways we worship, all the ways we show Vesta our love."

"Yes," Licinia gasped, her blue eyes opening wide again, needing to see Aemilia's face glow pink as she uttered such inflammatory words.

"Then upon seeing what she is missing, she will want you. She will beg to touch you like I touch you. She will beg to love you as I love you. She will want to feel Vesta's fire as you do and I will show her how."

Licinia curled her fingers, pressing down on the spot inside that shut the world off, leaving only Aemilia's voice, her promises. She could feel Vesta's fire in her veins now, churning inside her and raging like a beast in a cage.

"Doesn't that sound like fun?" Aemilia asked, leaning down and kissing her roughly.

Licinia nodded, gasping out half formed words as Aemilia bit down on her lip and reached down to stroke her clit, hard and fast, drawing Licinia over the edge, her pleasure exploding outwards into a thousand sparks before it all rushed back inside her, leaving her spent and whispering prayers of gratitude.

"Tonight, then?" Aemilia asked, sitting down beside her, pulling her down into her lap and stroking her hair.

"Tonight," Licinia agreed, closing her eyes even though it would be hours before she could sleep. "Tonight."

Licinia crept around a pillar, her heart beating wildly even though she had nothing to fear. The only thing she was guilty of in that moment was licentious thoughts, her mind aflame with them, but she knew Vesta would forgive. She'd been watching Marcia for a while now. She couldn't help it. She rarely saw anybody other than her Vestal sisters and their *Maxima*. The priests were of no interest to her and they rarely received visitors.

Marcia was kneeling, her long hair twisted into plaits and held against her head with ivory pins. Licinia had only caught sight of it free and flowing the once, when she'd woken Marcia from a dream, usually *Maxima's* task, but she would never forget it, thick and impossibly straight. She longed to touch it, run her fingers through it and feel it but Aemilia had come up behind her, as if she was a spirit, and held her back. That was the day Aemilia decided they would invite Marcia to join them. It had been nearly a year since that day and now it was here, now she had to do her part.

"Marcia," she whispered, stepping out from the shadows. Licinia was due to tend the hearth soon but not quite yet. It meant Marcia couldn't leave without hearing her out at least.

"Licinia?" Marcia turned, her big brown eyes searching her out and her lips widening into a smile. Her cheeks were red from the heat of the flames but they were beautifully rounded by her smile. Licinia couldn't help but grin back. "It is not yet your turn, surely."

"Not yet," Licinia admitted, kneeling down beside her. "I wanted to sit for a while. Perhaps we could pass the time by talking."

Marcia smiled again, shifting on her knees to be closer to her. "I'd like that."

Licinia tried to stop her mind from reeling; she tried to think about how Aemilia had talked to her that very first time. How she'd steered her gently away from *Maxima's* lectures and made her see anything was possible, there was nothing wrong with how she felt.

She took a deep breath and hoped it would all come out in the right way. "It's completely natural, how you're feeling."

Marcia was looking at her out of the corner of her eye, she could tell, but other than that gave nothing away. At twenty-two, she was a lot more confident and calm than Licinia had been before Aemilia saved her from the priest's lies about Vesta. But then, she had been younger, with nobody else to look up to besides a goddess she couldn't understand. Aemilia changed that.

"How am I feeling?" Marcia asked shrewdly, cocking her head to the side but not meeting her eyes.

"Confused, angry, afraid," Licinia answered honestly, recalling how she felt. "Like they have a hundred answers to your questions but not one of them is the right answer."

This time Marcia did look at her, the fire reflected in her eyes making her look like a goddess herself. "And what is the right answer?"

Licinia took her hand. Despite her calm complexion and her level tone, her palms were damp with sweat. "Whatever you want it to be. But if the question is 'why can't I love like everyone else?' I can tell you now — the answer is you can."

"But our vows, Vesta's vows?" Marcia asked, desperation starting to peek through her careful caution. She needed the truth, she needed to see the light.

"Vesta loves you," Licinia said simply. "She would not deny you the things you are made to worship. Family, love, her very fire. We are supposed to burn with it, not be left to the cold. She wants our love, Marcia, however we can give it to her."

Marcia bit her lip, staring down into the flames. "How do you love her?"

The air was heavy, hot and thick, like there might be a storm coming, but Licinia breathed it in all the same. Her heart was fit to burst. She was about to risk everything with one small gesture. What if Marcia didn't see things her way? What if she didn't want love? What if she couldn't love a woman? A thousand what-ifs circled through her mind.

Licinia held her breath, like she was about to sink under the waters of the Tiber or the Great Sea. Her lips felt cool against Marcia's, so hot like the rest of her skin. It was only a gentle, innocent kiss but neither could deny the meaning behind it, the question it held. Neither could ignore Vesta's presence igniting the air between them. Pulling back, Licinia held onto her breath until it made her dizzy. She couldn't breathe until she knew they would be safe.

Marcia put her fingers to her lips, as if she expected some lingering sign of the kiss that had passed between them to remain. "Now I just feel more confused."

Licinia let go, the air rushing out her lungs in relief. "I felt the same. It's nothing to be scared of, I promise."

"You've done that before?" Marcia asked sceptically.

"Every night, when I kiss my love goodbye. No bolt of lightning has struck me down yet," Licinia admitted before reaching out to pull Marcia close. "Go for now, *Maxima* is not yet asleep."

Marcia frowned, hesitating on her knees and Licinia couldn't resist reaching up and taking another kiss from her lips.

"Come back when the moon has risen, we will show you Vesta's love," Licinia promised.

She quickly turned to face the fire, putting her heart in Vesta's hands. She couldn't watch Marcia go in case she begged her to stay. She'd had so many fears about the girl and they weren't all settled yet, but something inside her knew it was all going the way Aemilia had promised. She loved Aemilia, with all her heart, but something baser drew her to Marcia. It was like a hunger she didn't want to feed but knew she must. She bowed her head and thanked Vesta for making Aemilia share in her desires and understand them. She thanked Vesta for what tonight might bring.

Chapter 2
Nefas: That Which is Forbidden

"You're certain she will come?" Aemilia asked, kissing behind Licinia's ear as she whispered the words, making her shiver despite Vesta's flames burning before them.

"Nothing is certain," Licinia said to avoid answering properly. She wasn't sure of anything. She couldn't promise Marcia would come, or that when she did, she wouldn't bring *Maxima* and the whole priesthood down on them. A part of her wasn't even sure this wasn't some trick of Aemilia's to test her loyalty.

Licinia took a calming breath, trying to remember they had carefully planned every detail to ensure they wouldn't get caught. Aemilia had taken care of it, like she always did, though she never said how.

"You are certain we won't be interrupted?" she asked, glancing away from the fires and into Aemilia's eyes.

"Nothing is certain," Aemilia echoed back at her, reaching to run her fingers over Licinia's lips, silencing anything she might say. "I think I hear a mouse creeping."

Licinia could feel a shiver up her back, like eyes boring into her from behind and she longed to turn her head and look but Aemilia held her chin, stopping her, kissing her to distract her. She knew what Aemilia was doing; putting on a show for the girl but her presence still lingered in the back of Licinia's mind. The idea of them being caught made her heart race; even if she could tell herself being seen in this instance might be a good thing.

Aemilia pulled away from her lips, leaving them red and tingling. Her hand descended to her throat, tilting her head to the side to expose her neck. Sweeping her light hair aside, Aemilia kissed her neck.

She knew Aemilia's eyes were staring out into the darkness behind the pillars, challenging Marcia to come out, daring her to join them while at the same time claiming Licinia as her own. And as if to remind Licinia of the same fact, she felt the hard press of teeth at her neck as Aemilia sucked the delicate flesh there until it went from a radiating pleasure to a sharp pain, leaving a purple bruise in its place, marking her. She'd have to make sure her neck was covered come morning.

Licinia heard the rustle of cloth against stone, her first sure sign Marcia was hiding behind the same pillar she had chosen earlier. She reached for the hem of her *infula* and slowly pulled it over head, giving Marcia plenty of time to choose to go back or to stay. The air turned hot by the fire prickled her skin like a slap but she didn't shrink away from it; they were her flames to tend tonight, her goddess to please. She would serve Vesta the best way she knew how, giving herself entirely to the fire ignited in her.

She felt Aemilia's teeth nip at her collarbone, her kisses dropping lower now; her robe had been cast away. She put her back to the dusty floor when Aemilia urged her down, her lips closing over each nipple in turn, tongue running circles around them until they peaked, worrying them with her teeth and sucking them until Licinia thought she couldn't take any more. Settling between Licinia's open knees, Aemilia leaned over her, kissing her way back to her mouth and down again over her chest and belly, waiting for Licinia to beg.

"Please, Aemilia," Licinia whispered, giving in. Aemilia looked up, hovering just over her navel. Her curls were more of an unruly mess than normal and her dark eyes were shining with glee. She loved to hear Licinia's voice, heavy with lust, plead with her. "Please stop teasing."

"You don't want me to tease?" Aemilia asked, idly drawing circles on Licinia's skin. "Then what do you want?"

Licinia stretched, arching up, pulling on every tense muscle in the hope it would give her some relief. It only served to make her feel tighter, more in need. "Please touch me."

Aemilia dug her fingernails into Licinia's hipbone, leaving pink and white half moons behind. "I am touching you."

She could hear the good natured laugh in Aemilia's voice, she was doing it on purpose, stringing her along until she could think of nothing else but how desperately she wanted her. She grabbed Aemilia's hand and dragged it lower, the nails scraping over her skin, making her stomach tense. She let go of her hand when it was laid over her cunt, fingers absently toying with her curls. She turned her eyes back to Aemilia's face. "For the love of Vesta, please."

"My sweet girl, did you really think I would deny you? Deny her?" Aemilia asked, fingers stroking downwards with a purpose, finding her clit and finally, finally touching her in the way she needed. "How rude would that be, to you and to Vesta, and especially to our guest."

Licinia breathed in sharply. She didn't think Aemilia would be bold enough to actually call Marcia out. She waited with bated breath, it was like watching a hunter raise a bow to a deer, her heart didn't even beat for fear it would scare her away.

But it didn't. The shadows moved and Marcia took a step forward, her hair had gently curled from where it had been in plaits all day, and she wore only her robe, despite the late hour. She openly stared at Licinia, making it seem like she hadn't stumbled upon something so private and forbidden. Their eyes connected just as Aemilia pushed two fingers inside her, thumb flicking over her clit, making her cry out in unexpected pleasure even though she knew by now they had to be quiet.

"Come, little Marcia," Aemilia said invitingly, beckoning her over. "Don't you want to taste her?"

Licinia could see the girl hesitate before she crossed that final line and approached them. From that moment on, she could never claim she wasn't interested, that it hadn't sparked something inside her.

Aemilia held out her hand, the firelight playing over her fingers, still shining with Licinia's wetness. Licinia watched, having to keep her own hand from straying and touching herself as Marcia knelt beside them and cautiously took one of Aemilia's fingers into her mouth.

"Good girl," Aemilia told her when her finger came back sucked clean before taking the other in her mouth herself.

Licinia let her head fall back, relief washing over her. She was still desperate to come but the axe she'd placed over all their heads by revealing their secret to Marcia had been lifted. She would be one of them now.

"Why don't you taste her properly?" Aemilia offered, moving back and letting Marcia take pride of place between Licinia's legs.

"I don't know how," Marcia admitted, showing uncertainty for the first time.

"Don't worry, sweetheart," Aemilia said soothingly, placing a hand on Marcia's back, pushing her forward so her head was low but her rear raised. She pushed up her robe, exposing her cunt at the same time. "I'll show you how, like the goddess taught me."

Licinia watched over Marcia's head as Aemilia buried her face in the other girl's cunt. She didn't expect to be jealous and it didn't surprise her when she wasn't at all. The idea of sharing had always appealed to her but the sight of it, the bounce of Aemilia's hair around the silhouette of Marcia's arse as she ate Marcia's cunt almost overwhelmed her with desire. She thought she could stand to never be touched again if only she could spend forever watching them. But Aemilia would see that she would not go forgotten for long.

"See, it's easy," she said, bringing her hand up to lightly spank Marcia's arse. "Now you try."

Marcia looked indignant that she'd been spanked but she didn't say a word against Aemilia and meeting Licinia's eyes, a blush came to her cheek that rather suggested she enjoyed it, even if she would never admit to it. Licinia kept her head raised; the sight of Marcia lowering her mouth down over her cunt was almost more thrilling than the feel of her hot breath against her clit or the experimental kitten licks she gave.

"I think we can do better than that," Aemilia muttered, brow furrowed in a frown. She slapped the other side of Marcia's arse, making the flesh pink and making the girl squeak before she renewed her efforts, licking Licinia properly, in long sweeping strokes of her tongue that ended just over her clit.

Licinia relaxed back onto the ground, letting the pleasure wash over her. Even if Marcia had never done it before, she was still hitting all the right spots and with Aemilia steering her with whispered words and gentle spanks when needed, she learned quickly.

"I think that will do," Aemilia decided, pulling Marcia back and kissing her, licking the wetness from Marcia's lips. "We don't want to spoil her."

Marcia nodded and sat back on her heels when Aemilia released her. Licinia waited, knowing Aemilia would have something more in mind than the little game they'd played so far. Sure enough, Aemilia pulled out a ribbon from her robe. It was almost identical one of the ones they used to tie off their plaits, but longer.

"Your wrists, Licinia," Aemilia commanded, taking them before they were even offered and placing them above her head. There was nothing for her to tie them to so she merely bound them together, pulling the ribbon tight so it wouldn't slip off.

Licinia squirmed, testing her bonds. She could move her arms if she wanted to, she could even roll over or get up if she needed to but she knew Aemilia would want her to keep still and in place.

"Knees up and spread wide," she continued, nudging Licinia's thighs apart. The cold air made her cunt tingle where she was still wet and she longed to press her thighs together again but she knew better than to disobey Aemilia.

"Try touching her with your hands now," Aemilia suggested to Marcia, noticing the girl still hadn't taken her eyes off Licinia's naked body, her soft curves and sharp edges.

Aemilia took her hand and pressed it to Licinia's clit, guiding her fingers to stroke in slow, wide circles and when Aemilia pulled away, Marcia kept on with a gentler pressure than Licinia was used to. A small part of her missed the heat of her mouth.

Aemilia lazily ran her hand over Licinia's chest, pinching her nipple and squeezing the swell of her breast. "Oh, Licinia, I feel left out."

Licinia bit her lip, torn between them. With her bound hands, she couldn't touch her love and she couldn't move towards her without moving away from Marcia and her fingers. Aemilia pulled Licinia's hair back away from her face, scrunching the long blonde strands up in her hand and using it to turn her head upwards into a kiss.

"Perhaps we can put these neglected lips to use," Aemilia murmured against them before glancing at Marcia. "Faster, little darling, faster."

Aemilia pulled her up further, forcing her to twist and clamber onto her knees, trying to keep her weight off of her bound hands. Balancing on her elbows, she leaned down, placing herself between Aemilia's thighs as she spread them, hiking up her robe to expose her cunt.

"Come on, girls, don't disappoint me."

Marcia sat up so she could still reach Licinia's cunt, her hand com-ing to rest on her back as she intuitively slipped a finger between her wet lips and inside her. Licinia pushed back against the heel of Marcia's hand, grinding against it until Marcia brought her thumb up to her clit. Aemilia made eye contact with her over Licinia's back, miming a short, sharp spank that Marcia hesitantly doled out.

"We wouldn't want you to lose focus, Licinia," Aemilia reminded her.

Licinia nodded, finding her balance again and pressing a kiss to the inside of Aemilia's thigh, her teeth grazing the firm flesh. Marcia's fingers pushed deep inside her and she couldn't hold herself back any longer. Tilting her head up, she closed her lips around Aemilia's clit, her tongue flicking over the nub until all she could taste was her lover's cunt, and all she could hear was her stifled moans as Aemilia threw her head back, one hand curling in Licinia's hair again.

"Harder, Marcia," Aemilia commanded for her and Licinia felt Marcia's fingertips clawing at her hip where all her focus, all her en-ergy was concentrated on the fingers curled deep inside her, working faster and pushing in and out with a force that made Licinia want to push back against them and match every pace.

The world around her faded down to nothing but Marcia and Ae-milia and what they were sharing, illuminated by Vesta's light. Un-able to keep up the deft movements of her tongue, she latched onto Aemilia's clit, sucking on it until Aemilia cried out and pulled her hair, her thighs pressing in tight around Licinia's shoulders as she came.

Almost before Licinia had a chance to catch her breath, Marcia pulled her upright onto her knees again, the hand that had left bruises on her hip winding around her front to cup her breast. Her fingers pressed sharply upwards, even deeper until they hit the sweet spot inside her, over and over. Marcia was desperate to make her come, fucking her frantically with her fingers, kissing and biting her neck and throat and pinching her nipple between her finger and her thumb until all together, it was enough to send her over the edge with Aemil-ia watching curiously from where she was sprawled in front of them.

For a moment, the whole world disappeared as pleasure took

over, dissipating her every thought into smoke and replacing them with tendrils of fire. For a moment, she truly saw Vesta and felt her blessing.

When she opened her eyes again, she was still bathed in warmth, from the devotion of her two girls and from the flames she had sworn to look after. She turned her head to kiss Marcia but this time it was not the chaste, questioning kiss of a friend, it was the kiss of a confirmed lover. She could taste herself on Marcia's tongue still and she didn't doubt Marcia could taste Aemilia on hers, like a triangle closing around them, a circle completed.

Licinia blushed and pulled away when she felt Aemilia's hand brushing back her hair but Aemilia shook her head. "I only wanted to see you together."

Licinia smiled, turning back to Marcia but not quite kissing her. "Poor love; we've barely rewarded her for her part. And she was so good."

Aemilia grinned, laying back on the dusty floor between them and running her hand up Marcia's thigh. "I think I know just the thing."

Licinia straddled Aemilia's body and Marcia followed her lead, with Aemilia's head positioned under her cunt. Licinia raised her bound hands to her mouth, pulling on the ribbon with teeth until it came loose. Sated for the moment, she was content to run her hands over Marcia's bronzed skin, pulling her robe over her head and taking in every inch of her. She trailed her fingertips over her soft skin then went over every place she'd touched again with her mouth, laying kisses on her lips and her chest, down to her navel and back up to her forehead until Marcia fell against her, body shaking, wracked with the force of what was likely her very first orgasm.

Licinia couldn't help but smile, her sheer happiness at saving this girl from a life untouched and unloved lighting up her whole face. She held her tight, whispering prayers of devotion to Vesta and stroking Marcia's gloriously thick brown hair. It was just like she imagined it, so full and heavy yet perfectly silken to the touch.

"We should get back soon," Licinia thought aloud to herself, her voice mired in sadness.

"Not yet," Aemilia assured her. "I have first watch. We can stay until dawn."

Marcia looked about them, as if for a short time she'd forgotten where they were and who they were, the promises they'd made to their goddess and their *Maxima*.

Licinia took her hand. "Do you want to stay?"

Marcia turned back to her and for the moment, she didn't answer. Licinia held her breath. She had wanted Marcia so badly and should be grateful to Vesta she'd gotten her the once, enjoyed her body and her attention, given her love in return but now, as once again they balanced on a knife edge, she realised maybe the once wouldn't be enough. She wanted her to become a part of them, as deeply involved as she and Aemilia were. She wanted her to love them.

The corners of Marcia's lips started to turn up in a smile, as she leaned in closer. "If you'll both have me."

"Oh, I assure you we will," Aemilia promised. "Repeatedly, every night."

Licinia couldn't help but smile at Aemilia's frankness. They would give their new girl everything she could ever want, yet it was she who was most grateful. She squeezed Marcia's hand in hers as Aemilia took the other. Kissing each of them in turn, she whispered, "Thank you."

Silence reigned for a while as they sat naked around the flames, hands joined in worship. It was Marcia who spoke first, eyes darting from Aemilia to Licinia and back again. "What happens if we get caught?"

"We'll die," Aemilia answered bluntly, not taking her eyes off the fire.

"Will Vesta disown us for breaking our scared vows to Her?" Marcia asked, true fear in her eyes now.

"No," Licinia said, squeezing her hand. "It is not Vesta we need to hide from. Vesta sees everything, She sees our love and our reverence; She will protect us from those who would hurt us, lie to us."

"Give me your hand," Aemilia said, holding her own over the fire.

Marcia reached out, wincing at the heat.

"O Vesta," Aemilia started and Licinia joined in, remembering the many times she too had needed this prayer. "If I have ever served you with unclean hands or impure thoughts, my hands and mind are yours to burn."

When the fire flickered but did not leap, Marcia pulled her hand back and looked at it, blinking slowly. A chill ran up Licinia's spine and she was sure she heard footsteps outside the door.

"Come on, little lamb, time to return to the herd," Aemilia said, reaching for her *infula*. The sun was not yet up, but Licinia trusted her judgement and took Marcia's robe in her hands.

"I'll take you," she offered, lifting the robe so she could slip it over Marcia's head before dressing herself.

The walk back was a quiet one and Marcia's hand was a constant warmth in her own. Tomorrow she would have more questions, about sex and about the vows that acted as a yoke around their necks, but for tonight, her curiosity was sated. At Marcia's door, she stopped, swallowing all the things she wanted to say to her for fear she wouldn't be able to leave.

"Goodnight, my love." She leaned in and kissed her softly, like every kiss goodnight she had promised her.

"Goodnight, Licinia," Marcia said back, letting go of her hand but pausing a second. "You really believe her, don't you?"

Licinia nodded. She'd often questioned her path in life and how to truly follow Vesta. She had to stray away from the words of their order but at the end of every day, she would rather sacrifice everything for love than sacrifice love itself. "I do."

"Then I do, too," Marcia decided, giving her one last kiss that lingered on Licinia's lips the same way her words would linger in her mind.

"O Vesta," Licinia whispered. "If I love you as I love Aemilia and Marcia, you would never have a more faithful servant. Now go, quickly."

Licinia closed the door. The sun had risen while they talked and shone down on her, making her heart beat wildly as she reached to smooth her hair, her robe, smooth away any sign she'd done anything other than dream the night away.

She barely made it to her bed before there was a harsh knock on her door. "Licinia, get up, girl. It is your turn at the fires."

Licinia closed her eyes as the door was pushed open, revealing their *Maxima*. A few moments more on Aemilia's lips or another second spent in Marcia's doorway and they surely would have been caught. But Vesta loved them still and for today, they were safe.

If you enjoyed this story, you can sign up for a free membership at
ForbiddenFiction and discuss it with other readers
and the author at the *Touched by Fire* story page
at http://forbiddenfiction.com/story/MP2-1.000240.

Hera's Punishment

Natasha Neil

Natasha Neil is a Los Angeles-based writer of novels, short stories and nonfiction. She lived in San Francisco, Japan and France before returning to her native Los Angeles where life is surprisingly easy and people are nicer than you would think—unless you're driving. Natasha has always found history in all of its forms fascinating, and is currently obsessed with uncovering untold truths in Persian, Greek and Roman history for use in her work. She finds the process of researching her subject matter nearly as enjoyable as writing about it. She is happily married to a spouse who is nothing like any of her characters.

Chapter 1
Binding the Lightning Striker

Long ago when the world was young, the gods grew tired of the rule of their king, Zeus. His brothers, Poseidon and Hades, resented his dominion of the sky, thinking both their realms inferior to his own. His wife Hera was weary of his many mortal and immortal lovers. So together the gods of Olympus conspired to bind the Lightning-Striker and usurp his power.

White-throated Hera went to golden-haired Aphrodite and begged the Goddess of Love and Beauty for a loan of her magic girdle. With the golden girdle taut around Hera's waist, she sought out her husband in their palace on Olympus.

Zeus was looking down into the woods of Arcadia. He had spied a beautiful dryad with voluptuous breasts and hips made to be gripped firmly. He was imagining how he would disguise himself as a cloud of mist and encircle her so Hera would not see. He could almost taste the dryad's silken skin, feel the moisture he would enrapture her with.

He sensed his wife Hera in the doorway and was suddenly aware of how he must look to her. He had lifted one of his muscular arms and was busy stroking his dark, pointed beard. His white *chiton*, trimmed with gold, shimmered like lightning. The sunlight itself kissed him as the dark hairs sprouting from his bulging arms and thighs caught the light. His golden crown glittered in his dark brown locks that fell in waves to his massive shoulders. He smiled to himself. He knew he was magnificent.

"What are you doing, Lord of the Skies?" Hera asked.

He turned to look upon his wife. She was the most beautiful of all the goddesses and the coldest. Her skin was as white as the moon.

Her light brown eyes always entranced him, even when burning with fury. Lithe and petite, Hera made up for her physical smallness with her tenacious anger.

She was wearing the peacock gown he had given her after one of their many fights. Fifty peacocks had been killed to make her garment, which shimmered with iridescence. The gown caressed her curves, and he felt the same dull ache of unfulfilled lust he always did when he looked upon her. Thoughts of throwing her down on the bed filled his mind, but she usually refused him. Instead he turned his gaze back out the window, to find a creature who would yield to him more easily.

"Just watching the mortals to see how they fare," he said.

But Hera surprised him by coming behind him to stand on tiptoes and kiss the back of his neck. He was distrustful of his wife's affection, but her full lips parted, and she pulled her peacock feathered gown over her head. She wore nothing but Aphrodite's glittering girdle, her own golden necklaces and peacock earrings. Zeus knew Aphrodite's girdle was enchanted and that his wife had come to seduce him, but this knowledge did little to help him. Released from her gown, her special fragrance of apples and amber wafted over the King of the Skies. His shaft grew hard and his eyes heavy-lidded.

"And, how do they fare?" Hera asked, turning away from him. Though she was small, her buttocks were rounded and full. They were irresistible to him. Every time he saw her behind, he yearned to cup the plump flesh in his hands.

Zeus sensed the danger, but like a dog after a piece of meat, he followed her to his golden couch.

"Wife," he said, sitting on his bed and reaching for her pendulous breasts, "what has come over you?"

She caught his hand with her two smaller ones, keeping it from her breasts. She gazed at his hand, which had thrown so many bolts of lightning, caressed countless women, and killed Titans and men alike.

"It has been too long, husband," she said, and pulled his hand between her thighs, trapping it there. She stood above him, stroking his neck and trailing her hands to the golden pin that kept his *chiton* clasped. He laughed at her attempt. No one but he could unclasp his lightning bolt pin. It was one of the many ways he protected himself.

139

He gripped her inner thigh with his captured hand and grasped her buttock with the other, teasing her crevice to distract her from his pin.

He pulled her toward him, onto his lap, ready to take her quickly, but then remembering one of their arguments, slowed his pace. He looked lustily at her pubis, the dark hair there glittering with gold. He began to tease her vulva, exploring her with his strong fingers, trying to draw her out. She was damp, but he wanted her to moisten for him before he took her.

Surprised by his hesitation, she urged him on, pushing him onto his back and straddling him. Her sex rode high on his belly, rubbing against the silken fabric. She put her hands next to his head, offering him her breast. His tongue lashed out at her hardened nipple, pulling it into his mouth. He knew his dark beard tickled her skin, but she paid it no mind as she struggled again to unclasp the pin on his *chiton*.

Seeing her distraction, he ran his hand over her haunches. He was unable to resist squeezing and kneading the flesh. She normally pushed his hands away, but today she allowed it. Feeling the fullness of her rump, he gave her buttocks a slap, savoring the sound and the hard sting he brought her. Since she did not protest, he slapped her again. She gasped but endured his hands and mouth.

Unable to remove his *chiton*, Hera began to pull the shimmering fabric up over his thighs. His hard cock, ravisher of so many goddesses, mortals and nymphs, stood waiting. She never touched him with her hands or mouth, but seemed eager to have him inside her.

The King of the Gods knew something was amiss, but he did not care. Perhaps it was Aphrodite's girdle, or simply how long it had been since she had last come to him. Looking at her erect nipples, her breasts pushed up by the golden girdle taut around her waist, he wanted to make her moan for him the way she had when their marriage had been young.

She moved to ease his cock into her, but he stopped her by slipping his finger into her glistening vulva. He gently stroked her until he caressed her bud with his thick fingers. He had recently learned how to touch her to kindle passion and was rewarded by feeling her moisten with desire.

"Queen of the Skies," he said, trying to sound amorous, but seeing the flame of anger in her eyes, he realized he had chosen his words foolishly. Their last argument had begun with her asking to be called the Queen of the Skies as he was King. She had asked for more power, and he had denied her, telling her to be content with simply being the Goddess of Marriage.

"Take off your *chiton*, husband, I want to feel you beneath me."

He looked up into her cold eyes and unclasped his lightning pin. She pulled his glittering garment over his broad shoulders, over his wild beard and held it wide so it did not tangle in his crown. The King of the Gods lay naked beneath his wife, and she smiled down upon him.

Zeus could see that despite the acrimony between them, his naked form aroused her still, and he could not fault her for it. He had arms stronger than any god, for he alone was able to wield lightning; a chest broad as the oak that was sacred to him. And his cock, well, he laughed to himself, it was heavenly.

And today she seemed to agree. She mounted him, and for the first time in centuries allowed herself to enjoy his oaken shaft impaling her. She did not usually come to his bed or desire to be on top, but today, all was changed. He moaned deep in his throat. He could easily finish with her quickly, but he wanted to take his time with her. Despite his mistakes, the Lord of the Skies wanted to please his wife.

"Wife," he said, "sister, Hera, what has come over you?"

She rode him harder, reaching down to pinch his wine-dark nipples. He shuddered and moaned, letting her ride him like an Amazon to war on a stallion.

"Perhaps," she said, slowing her thrusts and stroking his chest, "it is time for you to give me another child. The others have been so disappointing." She leaned forward, putting her hands next to his massive head, trapping his wild locks, and teasing his mouth with her nipple. "Perhaps it is Aphrodite's girdle." He sucked her nipple fiercely as she fed it to him and slowly pulled it out. She bent to him and bit his neck, hard.

Releasing his hair, she sat up straight upon him, his hands coming to her breasts. She leaned back, putting her hands behind her, between his legs. She felt the tenderness of his inner thighs as she pushed his legs apart and began to ride him hard again. Feeling the tightness of his sac, she slowed her rhythm.

"Keep yourself for me, husband. Do not spill your seed yet. Do you think you can do that for once?"

This was how it had always been, as soon as he felt tenderness for her, she insulted him. Electricity buzzed between his fingers and she pulled her breasts back. He flicked the extra energy away from her and took her by the hips, feeling her rock back and forth, harder and faster until it took all his strength not to come into his pleasure. He felt like begging her for mercy and was torn between longing and resentment, but before he could decide, the goddess came into her pleasure, arching her back and moaning. As the muscles of her inner walls squeezed his shaft tightly, he could resist no longer. He shuddered and spurted his seed deep inside her. They moved together, gripping each other fiercely, pushing into each other, wishing to be one. Their bodies glistening with golden sweat, the King and Queen of the Gods shared a moment of complete accord.

Unable to bear herself upright any longer, Hera collapsed upon her husband. His strong arms enfolded her, and he stroked her tiny waist for a moment, with only the golden mesh of the magic girdle between them.

"Wife," he whispered, "that was..." He thought for a moment to tell her he loved her, to apologize for his infidelities, to acknowledge the many times he had hurt her, but overcome by pleasure, Zeus-Lightning-Striker closed his eyes and fell into a deep sleep.

Hera lay still upon him, completely content for a moment. Slowly, she eased off him. She removed herself from his bed and unfastened Aphrodite's magic girdle. Silently she pulled her peacock feathered gown down over her head.

Hera went to the door and opened it. There stood the other Olympians: Hades, dark and foreboding, pale in the light of the golden sun, but smiling at what was to unfold; Poseidon Earth-Shaker, wild-haired like his brother and almost as strong; Apollo, God of Light and Truth, but in this case, ready to be a part of deceit. Hephaestus bore a lopsided grin and held the manacles he had made especially for his mother's husband; Ares stood in the shadows wearing his dark helm and holding his spear. Athena and Artemis had not been told, but Aphrodite stood smiling, as did Demeter who had never forgiven Zeus for allowing Hades to take Persephone as his wife. Hermes, the God of Ways, with his winged sandals and helmet, stood in the shadows, unable to resist a good scandal.

The Olympians silently surrounded their king. Hephaestus put the special cup-shaped manacles over Zeus' hands, and then the others all descended at the same time, tying him fast with magical rawhide thongs. He was slow to wake, but realizing his wrists were bound together, his eyes opened in rage and he struggled and kicked. Poseidon and Hades held him fast; each god caught one of his kicking feet with two hands and held them while Hephaestus tied his ankles together with a magical strip of rawhide. When it was done, the gods laughed to see their king bound naked and helpless.

Tied by a hundred knots, Zeus fought still, his muscles straining. Hera smiled to see her husband's eyes widen in shock, unable to believe that the magical thongs prevented him from changing his shape. This kind of betrayal by one god was no surprise, but by all of them! He shouted obscenities and threats, swore to kill them all, but with his hands manacled and his lightning bolts out of reach, he was powerless.

"You would do this to me?" he bellowed. "I am your elder! I am your king!"

Hades approached his captive brother. The richest of all the gods, owning every precious stone beneath the earth, the God of the Underworld was not known for speeches or for his smile. He reached out a strong, pale hand. His nails black around the edges, he stroked his brother's naked thigh. His hands were cold as night and his touch sent a shiver through the King of the Gods. The shock of being at the King of the Underworld's mercy hit Zeus hard. Hades inhaled as if he could smell his brother's fear.

"Cloud Gatherer, you always claim to be the eldest, but you are not. I was the first living born son of our mother, and you tricked me into ruling the darkest realm. I tire of my lands. Shades do not make good subjects. Why should you have all the power and all the fun? I rather thought you should take my place and live in my land. See how you like that. And I will take your place and rule the skies."

Zeus raised his brow at Hera, as if questioning her plan. She cursed him again for seeing that she had not thought this through. She had wanted only to see him bound, to be done with him, but she had not thought about where she would live once he was overthrown. She would still be his wife, and as such he could command her to live with him in Hades, but before she could speak, Poseidon interjected.

"What now? No, no, brother, I am to rule the skies. You can have dominion over the seas. It will be quite an improvement after the Land of the Dead."

"No," Aphrodite said, gently laying one hand on Poseidon and the other on Hades. Her ocean-blue eyes met Hera's and she handed the Goddess of Love and Beauty her magic girdle. Aphrodite tied it fast around her waist. The tight golden girdle pushed her alabaster breasts higher so they almost spilled out of her light-pink gown. Though she stood clothed, the gods could easily imagine her naked: waves of desire lapped at them. "My lords," she said, "I thought I would take back the seas, from whence I came. After all, I am the one who was foam born, should I not rule the oceans? Do you not feel the rise of the waves when you look upon me?"

Neither Hades nor Poseidon could reply. They gazed at the Goddess of Love through heavy-lidded eyes. Hades clenched his hands into fists over his thighs. Hera suspected from the way he held his body taut that he pictured Aphrodite in his dark palace, chained to his bed, begging him to ravish her. Hera shuddered, wishing she did not know her brother Hades so well.

Poseidon's pink tongue darted out of his mouth as he stared at Aphrodite and Hera had no doubt that he did indeed feel the rise of the waves, the pull of the tide and the tumultuous thrashing of the sea as he stared at her breasts, her girdle working its magic.

"No," Demeter said, breaking Aphrodite's spell and pinching the Lord of the Underworld. "Hades should have the skies." She had only supported this coup with the hope of freeing her daughter Persephone from the realm of the dead.

"Whoever rules the skies," Apollo said, "will share it with me, for I am the Lord of Light!"

"I will take the Underworld," Hephaestus said.

"If you do, I will not live there with you!" Aphrodite said.

"You don't live with me now, wife. But I suppose we could rule the seas together."

"Yes," the Goddess of Love and Beauty said, "so that's settled. We will take the seas."

The gods began to argue and threaten each other in earnest. Zeus began to laugh.

"You need me!" He thundered. "You need me to rule you and to unite you in hatred. Without me, you will do nothing but fight. It will come to war. I command that you free me! If you free me now, I will not punish you." His glowing eyes stared at each god in turn, settling last on his wife.

Hera saw Ares smile at his father's words. She knew war was why he had come. Demeter and Hades appeared uncertain. Apollo grimaced and Hera could see that Zeus' foolish son feared making yet another bad choice. Poseidon glared at Aphrodite. All knew how strongly the pull of the tide beat in his veins. His brow furrowed. Hera doubted he wanted to relinquish the seas.

"No!" Hera cried. "We will decide as you did to begin with—draw lots."

"Yes," Hades said, "only I will hold them."

Zeus laughed at Hades' suggestion. Zeus had held the reeds the last time, and Hades had never forgiven him for getting the skies. No one trusted Hades; it would not do for him to hold the reeds now.

As the gods argued, Hades and Poseidon almost coming to blows, Zeus noticed Hermes slip out. He would greatly reward the God of Ways if he were freed. Zeus tried anew to burst his bonds, but the rawhide thongs held him fast. Bound and naked, the King of the Gods refused to be humiliated as well. He would get out of this, and when he did, he would punish these traitors: his wife, his siblings and his sons. Even in his anger, he knew he would forgive Aphrodite after ravishing her in the violent waves. He would grind her against the wet sand as the waves crashed against them. He would not allow her to wear even her girdle... Tartarus take that girdle! He tried to think of a punishment for her, but every time he looked at her, he could only picture her naked body undulating in the foam.

Zeus focused on the others instead. He would punish Hades by returning him to his realm and forbidding him from seeing the light of day for centuries. The Lord of the Underworld was already miserable. Dashing his dreams of rising and then mocking him would be enough. And Demeter, she would suffer for Hades to go back to his lands. Apollo and Poseidon, he would make into slaves, yes! And to a mortal! Zeus laughed softly to himself, his eyes glowing with fire. Ares he would curse. Zeus had never liked his combative son. No one did. He would make Hephaestus his servant. The Smith God would make him anything he needed. And if Hephaestus disappointed him, Zeus would have him watch as he ravished Aphrodite. Despite his bonds, he smiled. He rather liked that idea. His mind turned to Hera, his traitorous wife, unfaithful sister, conniving queen. He would think of something exquisite for her.

Chapter 2
Zeus, Unbound

Zeus was taken from his reverie by a scream. It was Hera, shrieking. Thetis the Nereid stood before him with hundred-handed Briareus. For a moment the Olympians protested, but once the hundred-handed Titan set to work unknotting the rawhide thongs, they fled.

"Seize my queen!" Zeus commanded. As Hera turned to escape, four of the Titan's hands gripped her. She struggled and squirmed, trying to escape his hands, which manacled her wrists and ankles. Her eyes filled with terror and confusion as she tried to change her shape and found she could not.

"Your gown is charmed, dear wife. I had it sewn by the Fates especially for you. As long as you wear it, you will keep your current form." Zeus smiled to see the rage in Hera's eyes. Her helpless anger grew as the Titan held her fast and completed untying the King of the Heavens, finally removing the manacles Hephaestus had made.

Zeus sprang up, fury in his eyes. He held back from striking his wife, thinking instead of how he would savor her punishment later. He thanked Thetis, and Hermes, who stood behind her quietly smiling. He owed them both a boon.

He grabbed his *chiton*, slipped it on and clasped his lightning pin. Then he snatched up his lightning bolts and began hurling them at the other gods fleeing over the islands. He bellowed his rage over the land and seas. Destroying ships and temples, he roared and threatened his brothers and sons. If they did not return to face their punishment, he would destroy all their sacred lands, their cattle, their temples, their priests.

The gods dared not return to Olympus, but sought shelter in their sacred lands. Hades and Poseidon returned to their realms. Poseidon bore the worst of Zeus' rage, his open seas exposed to the Lightning-Striker's fury. Hades was safe under the earth, but Demeter's fields were easy targets for Zeus' bolts. The King of the Skies burned only a few before the Goddess of Harvest came to him begging forgiveness. Since she was the first, he forgave her easily and returned to punishing the lands of the other gods who had betrayed him.

While he threw bolts and sent out threats, Hera was held fast in Briareus' hands. When Zeus' rage had cooled a little, spent from throwing so many lightning bolts, he went to Hera. He had the Titan lift her so her beautiful feet dangled off the marble floor. He walked around her, savoring her helplessness, her silent rage and fear. Briareus held her away from his own body, as Zeus moved behind her. In her struggles, Hera's hair had become undone and fell wildly around her face. The King of the Gods lifted the silken tresses off her neck, caressing her tenderly.

She began to tremble, as if expecting him to strike her, but his anger had gone past fury and into a realm of calm calculation. He ran his hands over her body, stroking the peacock feathers on her gown. He lifted her breasts, teasing the nipples so they rose. His hands encircled her waist, his fingertips meeting over her belly.

"Why did you do it, wife?" he asked.

Hera kept her face passive, pressing her lips together tightly. It seemed her anger had also gone cold. It was not like her to keep quiet, for she was normally one to rage. But Zeus saw that she would hold her resolve for silence, so he began to pull her gown up to her calves, to her thighs and over her buttocks. Briareus tried to look away. Zeus surmised the Hundred-Handed One had not lain with a Titaness in some time.

"Go on, Briareus," Zeus said. "My queen has such a lovely ass. Why should I be the only one to enjoy it? I'm sure she offered herself to you in exchange for freedom. You might as well see what you've given up in the name of loyalty. Here, hold this." Zeus passed the Titan the hem of Hera's gown, the beautiful peacock feathers crushed and crumbled.

Hera bucked wildly, thrashing about in Briareus' vice-like grip, trying to make him drop her gown to cover her nakedness. Zeus knew the humiliation she felt for the hundred-handed giant to see her this way, her glittering pubis and white buttocks displayed like one of Aphrodite's sacred whores. She tried to kick at Briareus, at Zeus, but he only laughed and caught her foot in his hands. He unlaced her sandal. Laughing at her powerless anger, he dropped the sandal to the ground.

"Even if your foot struck me with all your force, dear wife, it would only feel like a feather." He plucked one from her gown, and slowly ran it along the sole of her foot. Zeus knew his wife was not normally ticklish, but trapped in her mortal form, her skin was sensitive and the bottom of her foot, normally well protected, was especially vulnerable. She squirmed in Briareus' hands as Zeus slowly stroked her insole with the peacock feather. He ran the feather back and forth along her foot until she bit her lip to avoid crying out.

Though Zeus enjoyed watching her struggle, his mind returned to her betrayal. His face turned dark. Storm clouds came into his eyes. He released her foot and dropped the feather, his eyes glowing with fire as he looked at her half naked body.

"Yes," the King of the Gods said, "a fine ass, but, Briareus, do you not think it could do with some color?"

The Hundred-Handed One said nothing as Zeus walked behind Hera and gripped her buttocks. Briareus held her gown with a different hand, to give the king more room and Zeus noticed how the Titan casually put one of his hands over his member. Zeus did not mind that the Hundred-Handed One was aroused by his wife. He could hardly blame him.

Zeus pulled back his hand and struck Hera's rump. She caught her breath, but did not say a word. He struck her again, hard and fast. He would make her beg his forgiveness. By the time he was done, she would swear it would never happen again. He reveled in feeling the supple flesh of her mortal form warm from his slaps. She would know his dominance and never defy him again. Her alabaster haunches changed to pink, and he continued striking her with the flat of his hand until her buttocks were crimson.

"Yes," Zeus said, "that is very satisfying. Briareus, do you not think that is better? Does she not have the loveliest ass on all of Olympus, perhaps even on Earth?"

Hera turned her head, glaring at her husband and the Titan who held her.

"What is it, wife? Do you feel betrayed that I would allow someone else to see you naked? Tell me you did not offer yourself to him."

Hera said nothing and Briareus' face reddened. He switched the hands that held the goddess, giving Zeus his answer. The King of the Gods could see that the Hundred-Handed One longed to stroke that red rump.

"Go on," Zeus said, "you can give her just a little pat. I would not normally allow another to touch my wife, but you deserve a little something."

Hera struggled in the Titan's grip, a low growl coming from her throat. Her eyes, piercing as daggers, stared at the Titan.

"My king," Briareus said cautiously, "I am here to serve you, but I must refuse your offer." He added two more hands to hold Hera steady. "My queen, please. I mean no disrespect. I am only a servant of the Lord of the Skies, nothing more."

Zeus laughed, thunder boomed over the gathering clouds.

"Ah," the King of the Gods said, "Briareus, the Hundred-Handed, I see how you have lived so long. You fear offending my wife, for if you do, she may well track you to the ends of the earth and have your head struck off. Remember this Hera, if I ever set you free, this Titan was wise and did you a kindness, though I will not."

Zeus stepped closer to his wife and stroked her buttocks, making her tremble at his touch. He knew then that a part of her enjoyed the torment as her anger and arousal combined. He pinched the burning flesh of her buttocks, squeezed her and struck her again. He was rewarded by a low moan deep in her throat. He wondered how long she could stay silent, how soon he could make her beg.

He wrapped his arm around her waist, pulling her enflamed buttocks to his hard cock. She pushed back against him, and he cupped her sex, probing her with his finger. She was wet with desire. After centuries together, perhaps he was finally beginning to understand his wife.

He wanted to take her then, fuck her hard while the Titan watched. He would thrust his cock into her anus, as if she were a man. And then when he recovered from the first time, he would take her as a woman, again from behind. But he remembered their argument about how he always pleased himself too quickly and decided this time, he would wait. This time, he would make her wait.

The Lightning-Striker moved his finger against her bud, making her shudder in anticipation. Then he withdrew. Her body stiffened in surprise as he told Briareus to drop her gown. Zeus stood behind her and breathed into her ear, biting the lobe gently. His shaft was hard against her as he whispered, "Wife, you remember Leto and Io? You remember how we fought after the births of Artemis and Apollo? After I gave birth to Athena and you to Hephaestus? Remember how I flogged you and struck you with my bolts? Well, that will be nothing compared to what I will do to you for this." He kissed her neck savagely and gripped her buttocks, but Hera did not say a word.

Zeus ordered the Titan to bind her wrists and lock her in an enchanted room with no windows. He left Briareus outside, to guard the door. He would let her suffer and worry over her fate.

In the throne room, Zeus drank nectar from a golden chalice. He would think of the best torment for his wife and while he did, the other gods would come to beg forgiveness.

Aphrodite came first, wearing her magic girdle and glistening with beauty. She knelt before Zeus' golden throne, her breasts heaving as she wept, claiming to have been coerced into betrayal by Hera and Hephaestus. The Goddess of Love and Beauty confessed to being fickle and foolish and pleaded for forgiveness. But she knew the price of betrayal. Despite his plans for her, he could not resist when she came to him on her knees and wrapped her arms around his calves, kissing his thighs and lifting his *chiton* with her teeth.

His shaft rose quickly. He did not have to wait long for her to open her mouth and envelop him. Her silken tongue caressed him fervently. He thrust his hands into her hair. Sinking his hands into her golden tresses to the roots, he pushed her down upon him. She took him completely then pulled back. She licked and caressed him, flicking her tongue over his tip delicately and then taking his cock to the back of her throat. No goddess had allowed him this and no mortal could withstand his fullness. She moved her head up and down over his member, taking him to the brink. He wanted to stop her. He planned to ravish her, to thrust himself inside her and make her beg for him. But he could not resist the urgency of her mouth on him. With an expert's finesse, she licked him from tip to stem and back again, then swirled her tongue over him, cupped his sac and enveloped him so completely, he came into his pleasure in a flash. She did not pull away, as he expected, but took his glittering fluid and swallowed.

The King of the Gods moaned and fell back in his throne, completely spent.

"Will you forgive me, Lord of the Skies?"

"Yes," he said, "but..." He had not even cupped her perfect breasts nor ploughed between her milky thighs. He had said yes too quickly, and her breasts hypnotized him still. She stroked his thigh and pulled down his *chiton*. As she leaned on the throne to rise, he gripped her hand.

"It will not happen again, Foam Born..."

"No, Lightning-Striker. It will not. But if Poseidon ever fails, I would be happy to rule the seas." She smiled and licked her red lips. They shared more than one secret now. The Goddess of Love and Beauty rose and turned around. Glimmering, she walked away. Zeus regretted not taking her from behind.

Poseidon and Apollo came next. The King of the Gods knew they would come; it was only a matter of how many of their temples he would destroy first.

The light behind Apollo's eyes was dark with defeat and shame. "Forgive me," the God of Light said, kneeling at his father's feet. But Poseidon made no such move.

"I am surprised at you, brother," Zeus said, ignoring his son. "I thought you loved your realm. I did not know you wished to take mine."

"It was folly," Poseidon admitted, his voice rough like sand upon skin. But he would not apologize.

"You will both be punished for this," the King of the Gods declared. "I will make you slaves—to a mortal." Seeing the shock on their faces, Zeus laughed aloud. He opened his hand and offered Poseidon a thick golden collar to put around his own neck.

"I will not," the Earth-Shaker said.

"If you do not, I will destroy every temple, every boat in the sea. The mortals will worship you no longer. They will make no sacrifices and you, dear brother, will be forgotten."

The God of the Seas snatched the golden collar from Zeus. With hate sparkling in his blue eyes, he fastened it around his bulging neck and clicked the lock shut. Zeus thought it very becoming on him.

Apollo's face had turned bitter and Zeus suspected his son was holding back golden tears.

"Don't worry, Lightbringer, I know you are more delicate." The collar he had had Hephaestus fashion for Apollo was a lighter gold, and the leash he would wear had a finer chain. Apollo took the collar and snapped it on his neck, wiping his eyes.

"You are to serve King Leomedon. You will build a great city for him. It is to be called Troy. The Fates say it will be known for all time. And just think, perhaps you will impress them so that they will build you temples. I know how you both long to be worshipped."

Neither his brother nor his son said a word as they left Olympus. Zeus smiled every time he thought of Poseidon wearing the collar. He was beginning to think his ordeal had almost been worth it.

Ares he cursed with ill favor. The God of War would fight, but he would seldom win. He would have no temples and few worshippers. Hephaestus was now his creature. The Smith God had to make Zeus whatever he bid. He had made the collars for Poseidon and Apollo and the golden cuffs that Zeus would now put on his treacherous wife.

Chapter 3
Queen of the Skies

The Queen of the Immortals did not struggle as Briareus brought her out, nor did she speak. She only stared defiantly at her husband. Zeus knew she expected him to take her forcefully, but he had chosen a different punishment, one she would not forget. He took her from Briareus and walked her to the edge of Olympus to the place where the clouds gather and turn pink as the sun rises and sets.

"Wife," he said, "sister, it has been too long since I have given you jewelry." He brought forth the golden cuffs. Her eyes grew wide. The cuffs were thick and strong and would hold her fast. She offered him her slender wrists, a light of defiance in her eyes, refusing to give him the pleasure of seeing her resist. He snapped the cuffs on, seeing the fear she tried to mask. He lifted her up into the clouds. Her feet struggled to find purchase but touched nothing but air.

Zeus attached the cuffs onto an invisible hook, leaving Hera dangling over the earth. He could see how she tried to keep her gaze calm as she stared down at the land below, but for one moment he saw the flash of terror behind her eyes. The skies were clear, all of Hellas stretched out before her, and Zeus smiled to himself, all of Hellas could see her as well.

"Wife, our wedding night lasted three hundred years. How long shall I leave you here? What is the appropriate punishment for trying to steal my throne? For conspiring with the other Olympians against me? How could I forgive this?" Floating next to her, he stroked the back of her neck. He waited for her tears, for her apology, for her promise it would never happen again, but she only glared at him with disdain.

It was as if she were giving him permission. He looked at her, hanging there and laughed. "You said you wanted to be Queen of the Skies, and now you are. I will leave you here until I am satisfied. And until I am, you can watch. I will not have to hide from your prying eyes any longer!"

He looked down to the woodlands of Arcadia where he had spied the beautiful dryad when Hera had first come to him. In a flash he was next to her tree. The dryad gave a cry of terror, but he gripped her wrists and pulled her to him.

"I am the King of the Gods, and you, sweet creature, will be mine."

"Please," she said, "it is an honor, Lord of the Skies, but I fear your wife. She will kill me."

Zeus kissed her throat, pulling off the gown of leaves she wore to cover her naked body. Her breasts were fuller than he had hoped for, her dark brown nipples big and hard. He took one into his mouth while caressing her thighs, slowly moving his hands toward the mossy green hair of her pubis. She trembled beneath his touch but did not resist as he gripped her buttocks, which he was disappointed to discover were slighter than he liked on females.

"You need not to worry about my wife, beauty. Give yourself to me and I will give you divine children."

He had intended to take her from behind, but now that he beheld how little meat she had on her bones, he decided to lie her down on the soft, dewy grass. He pulled her down and climbed atop her. She lay beneath him, her eyes big with fear.

"Mercy," she cried weakly, addressing the heavens.

Zeus' laughter boomed, shaking the ground and making the girl go pale.

"Who do you beg mercy from, sweet creature?"

She looked away from him, her moss green eyes filling with tears. Centuries ago, he would have enjoyed forcing himself on her, but now remembering Hera's complaints against him, and how much more enjoyable it was to truly seduce a woman, he had a different idea.

The dryad would not speak, so he spoke for her.

"Perhaps you have heard that the gods are brutal and rough? Do you beg mercy from some kindly goddess in hopes that she will turn you into a tree before I take you?" He stroked her green hued cheek, wiping away her sticky tears.

Remembering how Hera had chastised him for how he had hurt her the first time, he resolved to try something new.

"It is true that I am the ravisher of the world, but this time I will be gentle. And since my wife is occupied, we have plenty of time. I will take you slowly, little dryad." He kissed her neck, enjoying the woody-earthy smell of her. He stroked her nipples tenderly.

"No goddess will have mercy on you now," he whispered, "better you learn to enjoy it."

The dryad looked up into his eyes as if suddenly understanding. He could see her taking in his muscular form, his far-seeing eyes and the crown perched within the locks of his flowing black hair. Her panic seemed to be replaced with awe. He was the King of the Gods and he wanted her. He was the King of the Gods and he would have her. He bowed his massive head to her breast and tenderly licked her with his tongue, gently stroking her. She lay rigid under his mass and gradually began to relax, her taut limbs loosening as the wild look in her eyes was replaced with a sudden understanding of pleasure.

She seemed to like the way he suckled her breasts, so he worked at one then the other, feeling her gasp at the pleasure of it and shudder when his beard tickled her. He ran his hands over her waist and played with the mossy hair of her pubis. She tried to keep her legs firmly together, but by sucking her nipple while stroking her, he was able to make her yield to him and slowly her thighs parted, so he could delve his finger into her. It had been too long since he had turned an unwilling maiden to a willing one. And he was well rewarded when she began to ooze sap. When she was sticky and wet, he knew she was ready for him.

He inserted the head of his shaft into her opening. She was so tight. It had been too long since he had lain with a virgin. The dryad trembled, but Zeus stayed still.

"I will not take you by force," he said, reveling in the idea. "Go on, you move to me."

The nymph was hesitant at first, but encouraged by his hands, she arched her pelvis toward him. He lifted her thighs so her knees were bent, opening her to him more fully. Her fine brow rose in confusion and then understanding came as she stared into his eyes, offering herself to him.

"Go on," he said, taking her nipple between his fingers. She moved cautiously at first, wincing and then pushing up against him, she began to undulate beneath him, seeking to find pleasure she never knew existed. She moaned, and he thrust himself into her.

Zeus had never been so patient with a maiden. Feeling her taut skin against his shaft, opening for him, made him burrow into her. She gasped in pain as he broke her hymen, but her blood against his cock was too much for him, and he was only able to wait a moment before spurting his seed inside her.

The dryad cried out at the force of his ejaculation. Swooning between pleasure and pain, her body clenched and then lay still. For a moment he thought he had killed her, but she had merely fainted. As he rose, he felt a drop of rain and then another. He looked up into the skies, thinking of Hera watching him, how jealous she must be! To have taken the dryad so slowly was yet another victory against his wife.

He eyed the naked girl on the grass, his golden fluids leaking from her parted thighs. The rain fell harder. He would go find another nymph—no, perhaps a mortal would be better, a princess or queen. He would have to ask Hermes who the most beautiful mortal was these days—it was so hard to keep track. The rain on the grass looked slightly yellow and Zeus held out his hand to catch a drop. Smelling the pungent liquid in his hand, he realized it was not rain but a token of his wife's jealousy.

Rage filled him. Even bound, his wife insulted him still! Perhaps taking another woman was not the only way to stoke Hera's ire. Seeing the supine form of the naked dryad he had an even better idea. They both needed a bath now. Why not take one together in his palace?

Holding the girl in his arms like a child, he rose to Olympus. He stopped first in front of Hera dangling helplessly among the clouds.

"Wife, is there anything you want to say to me now?"

Hera glared at him and the girl. The dryad began to stir. She rubbed her eyes and opened one. Her dark brown hair, tinged with green, was undone and half covered her heavy breasts. The dryad looked at him with confusion as if trying to decipher what he could want from her now. She sniffed, confusion overcoming her lovely face. Then she turned her head and saw the Goddess of Marriage, her arms hooked above her head, her eyes ablaze. The tree nymph stifled a scream and fainted in fear.

Hera laughed and spoke for the first time. "Are you having fun, husband? Has this one won your heart for the moment?"

"Yes, I thought I would try taking her in our bed."

Her eyes narrowed to slits.

"Promise me, sister," he said, "that it won't happen again. Beg my forgiveness, wife."

Hera glowered. She was stubborn like Poseidon, like Hades and Demeter and like Zeus himself. She would rather hang in the sky than beg for anything.

"Go on," she said. "Enjoy your little whore. You both smell like piss anyway."

Zeus flew to his palace. He had his slaves bathe the girl and took a bath himself, trying to calm his anger. It had always been like this with Hera. Sometimes he thought he should never have forced her to marry him. He should have chosen Demeter or Hestia; his other sisters were more even-tempered, more docile and calm. They would never fight him like Hera did, nor would they ever bed him with the same burning passion. Demeter had some of the same anger, but she was too wounded whereas with Hera, her anger was a challenge for him to fight against.

Or perhaps he should have married a Titaness like Leto or Mnemosyne. He had loved Leto, but she had proven to be a coward. Pregnant with the twins, she had run from Hera's wrath. Had their places been reversed, Hera would have stood and fought. He had been angry at his jealous sister at the time, but in a way, he had also been proud. They had not even been married yet, and Hera's jealousy had been magnificent. Mnemosyne was a good mother, having borne all nine of the muses. She never would have incurred his rage the way Hera did. Her jealousy over his many affairs, would not have manifested into screaming fights. Her quiet nagging would have driven him to Tartarus.

His other lovers were a good respite from his angry wife, but none of the others had the same connection as he and Hera did, despite or perhaps because of their animosity. He thought back to how aroused she had been after he had beaten her. He had always suspected that their fights fueled her passion and in truth, he longed to go to her, but he was wounded that she had betrayed him so deeply. He would leave her there, hanging in the sky until she begged his forgiveness. He took the dryad to bed with him. He hoped it would be thrilling to take a mortal into his own chamber, but her fear and confusion were not as arousing without Hera to watch. He took her quickly and, not knowing what else to do with her, let her sleep next to him. She snored softly like the wind in the trees, and it kept him awake. But then he realized it was not the nymph that would not let him sleep, but a sound that only he could hear, his wife quietly weeping.

He was glad. Let her cry! She deserved it. She should have cried sooner. It should have been her tears of regret raining down on him. She should have asked him for mercy as soon as the Hundred-Handed One freed him. She should have gotten down on her knees like Aphrodite and begged his forgiveness with her mouth! Yet the sound of her tears grated on his ears and despite himself, his heart began to ache thinking of her misery. He had no regrets about the times he had struck her, or made her burn with jealousy. He felt no remorse for the women he bedded whom she then tormented, turned into trees or animals, or killed, but suddenly the thought of her hiding her golden tears from him as she dangled above the earth with only one sandal on made him long to comfort her.

When Hera saw Zeus hovering over the clouds, she wiped her eyes on her upper arm. He stroked her cheek, but she looked away, ashamed he should catch her crying. He wiped her eyes with his first finger and rubbed her lips with his thumb. She parted her lips slightly at his touch.

"Husband," she whispered, "brother." She had not known how long he would leave her. Seeing him with the dryad, slowing stroking her in the grass had infuriated Hera. But it had also renewed her passion. Zeus was hers. Her brother, her husband. He did not belong to anyone but her, and she hated him for not realizing it. But his punishment had worked as he had wished, raising a fear that he would abandon her and force her to watch him seduce nymphs, dryads, mortals and goddesses for as long as he liked.

But now, he had come for her. Feeling his gaze upon her, his thumb on her lips, the fire of her anger began to change to passion, as it always did.

He encircled her waist with his hands, lifting her slightly. He drew his lips to hers and kissed her. She allowed his tongue to delve into her mouth and kissed him back, pressing her body to his.

He gripped her tender buttocks, and she gasped at the pain and desire coursing through her. She did not know if he would release her, and she did not care. At that moment, she was only glad that he had come for her, that she had his complete attention.

"Promise me, wife."

She leaned forward, straining in her bonds to reach his ear. "I promise I will never again conspire to usurp your power, husband. I swear it by the River Styx." She nipped at his ear and added, "Now, if only you could promise to be faithful..."

He kissed her neck, biting her gently. "You do not really want that. Do you, wife? You do not really want all my attention, all the time. My need is too much for only one woman. You would hate me even more if I did not chase others, and I suspect sometimes that you enjoy the opportunity to rage."

She said nothing, for she could not deny it.

"Tell me," he said, "what would you have done if your coup had been successful? Where would you have gone? If Poseidon had the skies, Aphrodite and Hephaestus the seas, where would that leave you? Your place is by my side, as my wife. None of the others cherish you the way I do."

"Cherish me," she spat. "You humiliate me with every new conquest, rutting around like some randy goat, worse than Pan, fathering demi-gods on mere mortals, Olympians on Titanesses," her voice grew raw as she struggled, helpless in the sky, her only power her anger, "while I, I the Goddess of Marriage have born only disappointments." Her voice cracked and she wished to take the confession back, but it was too late, the true source of her anger had been exposed.

The King of the Gods stared at his wife in shock. After centuries together, tempestuous fights, years of animosity and passion, he was finally beginning to understand her.

He had not realized her deep disappointment in their offspring: Eileithyia, Goddess of Childbirth, Hebe, a mere servant, and Ares, the God of War, a bellicose fool, hungering for mortal blood. What were they compared to Leto's children, Artemis and Apollo, or even the muses? She had kept it from him. He had always thought her jealousy to be only for the women.

"I thought I was giving you something to do," he uttered in earnestness. "I thought it was a game between us, sister. Our game. Were you not jealous of the others before we were even wed?" he caressed her cheek, wiping away her tears.

She did not answer him with words but assented by pressing her cheek into his palm.

"Come now," he said. "Let us be honest. Do you not thrive on the challenge of catching me as I enjoy the challenge of escaping your watchful eyes? You have always loved me, Hera, as I have always loved you. Though my desires are too much for only one, my heart is not."

She did not answer his question, but her eyes softened. He knew that a part of her delighted in the acrimony between them, thrived on him tormenting her flesh after rending her heart.

"Sister," he said, "wife, it is you I always return to. It is you I chose to marry. You I desire. Let me give you another child, one to make you proud."

"I do not think it possible, husband," she smiled coyly, "but I'm willing to try. Release me."

"No," he said, "I want to take you here, above the world, as my queen, the Queen of the Skies."

He stroked her neck and placed his hands on the neckline of her dress. Slowly he began to rip the fabric. She moaned at the sound and the anticipation of his hands on her. Ripping her gown wide open, he took one breast in his hand and the other in his mouth, sucking her savagely, the way she liked.

She arched her back and gasped, but soon opened her eyes in discomfort.

"Zeus, I can't. They can all see us."

He caressed her breasts, enjoying her pale flesh in the moonlight, thinking of all he would do to her while she hung in the sky.

"Yes," he said. "The other Olympians can see what happens to anyone who attempts to usurp my throne. I should let them all watch." Her eyes began to harden at his words as her passion began to change again to anger. "But," he added, "since I wish for us to be reunited, not just in flesh, but in spirit," with a wave of his mighty hand, he summoned clouds to gather around them, making a soft chamber of seclusion, white in the moonlight.

"Is that more to your liking, wife?" But he did not wait for her answer, for he had decided to surprise her. Centuries ago, when he first had her, he had been too quick, thinking only of his own pleasure. Now he would appease her. He knelt on his cloud between her feet, and cupping her buttocks, still raw from his ministrations, drew her to him. He enjoyed seeing the shock in her eyes as he brought her mound to his mouth. Despite her disbelief, she parted her legs for him and let him explore her with his tongue.

The King of the Gods had never done such a thing before, and he enjoyed it more than he expected, but he was sure that his wife would be the only one he did this to. Still, he could tell from the small moans that escaped her lips that she appreciated his attempts.

Kneading her buttocks, he brought her closer, lashing her bud with his tongue until she let out a pleading sound. He licked her hard and she shuddered, pulling hard against the golden cuffs and coming into her pleasure.

"Husband," she moaned, "I did not know you could... that was...." Then recovering a bit, he saw the familiar spark of jealousy. "Have you..."

"No, wife," he said standing. "By the River Styx I have done that with no one else, will do that with no one else. But if you do not believe me, I can go, leave you here, alone in the clouds."

"No," she said. "Stay."

"You want me then?" he asked, a slight mocking tone in his voice. He would like nothing better than to make her beg him to take her.

But Hera did not say a word as she swung back, and using her momentum, lifted her legs, wrapping them around his middle. She entwined her ankles together at his back, her one sandal digging into his buttocks.

"You cannot escape me brother, we are bound together for eternity."

"Yes," Zeus said. Unable to wait a moment longer, he lifted his *chiton* with one hand. The moonlight glittered on his shaft, hard and thick as oak. He moved the extra fabric of her gown out of the way and they came together in one motion. He thrust himself into her as she rocked hard over him. She had never felt so good to him, silken and ripe, the perfect sheath for his sword. He gripped her buttocks with both hands, kneading the flesh and pushing himself deeper into her.

"Oh," she gasped, pushing against him, "Husband," she pulled against the golden cuffs, holding him taut between her thighs "brother," she whispered, "Zeus."

He pounded against her, harder than he ever could with a mortal, feeling the heat and desire within her mount until Hera arched her back and cried out, "Lord of the Skies! My king!" she shuddered against him, her sex sucking his shaft so hard he ejaculated like a bolt of lightning.

They held each other longer than usual. He, savoring the moment and she, uncertain of what he would do next.

"I should leave you here," he whispered. "It is what you deserve and then I will always know where you are."

"I promised, husband. Release me, my king."

He untangled himself from her and floated a moment, gazing at her. Dangling in the sky, the golden cuffs so large on her slender wrists, her beautiful peacock gown in tatters, and her body exposed in the moonlight. She was so small and helpless. He felt a strange sensation he could not recognize. It was new, a stirring in his heart, but it was neither desire nor rage. He thought again of her crying alone in the sky and realized the sensation was pity — for her, for being his wife, and for loving him.

He reached up and unhooked the golden cuffs. He held her in his arms and floated to the solid ground of Olympus.

"Thank you, husband," she said rubbing her wrists. She smiled at him, her face flushed from desire. With a complicit look in her eyes, she pulled off what was left of her gown and laughing, vanished.

The King of the Gods stood dazed. Not yet prepared to gather his wits, he stared at the emptiness where his wife had just stood. Then, hearing a scream from his palace, he realized what was to happen.

He materialized in his bedchamber. Hera had kept her mortal form. She had covered herself with a hastily thrown-on red gown that fell awkwardly across her breasts. The dryad cowered naked on the marble floor, prostrating herself at the goddess' feet, her eyes huge in fear. Kneeling on the ground with her buttocks in the air, Zeus saw that she did indeed have the ass of a boy. He watched his wife's keen eyes study her.

"Please," the nymph moaned, her voice shaking. "Protectress, have mercy. I beg you!"

Hera smiled seeing her husband's wild eyes, daring him to intervene.

"Mercy," the Goddess of Marriage said. "Yes, and protection." She lifted her white hand and shot a bolt of magic at the tree nymph. Zeus blinked, unable to see the girl at all. For a moment he thought his wife had killed her, just sent her straight to Tartarus. But he looked on the ground and saw a small creature, soft with a hard shell and strange eyes that roved around the room. The creature inched away from the immortals slowly, leaving a sticky trail behind.

"You took her so slowly, husband. So very slowly, this form seems fitting for her now. Pity, though. I shouldn't have offered mercy. It would be so satisfying to step on that and crush its shell. Oh, but..." she looked down at her feet and up in annoyance at her husband. The goddess snapped her fingers and her other sandal appeared on her foot. "That's better."

Hera stood up straight, power coming back into her eyes. Even though Zeus had just had her, he wanted her again. He half wished he had left her hanging in the sky.

"I will keep my promise to you, husband, but I am weary from your punishment. I think I shall take myself to Canathus for my annual bath to renew my virginity. Perhaps when I am ready to lose it, you can show me all you have learned." She looked down at the slow moving creature that a moment before had been a beautiful dryad.

"So slowly," Hera laughed. Then the Goddess of Marriage stared at her husband. Looking into his face in the way only she could, seeing what others did not.

"You need some nectar and ambrosia to bring the color back into your face, brother."

Zeus realized she was right. He was tired. Hera should be the one to look wan, to need nourishment, but she seemed pert and strong, as if taking his divine seed and transforming the dryad had given her energy enough.

She glanced again at the thing moving across the marble.

"You should have one of your slaves, Briareus perhaps, deliver her back to earth before someone steps on her." Hera began to laugh before adding, "But she could be carrying your divine child, Lightning-Striker, so perhaps you should keep her here where you can watch her."

He looked from the tiny creature on the floor to his wife in confusion. Hera grinned.

"Well, goodbye, husband. I'll see you when the fancy strikes me, but I'll be watching you. You know that." She disappeared.

Zeus stood in silence staring at the slow moving snail, frantically trying to move away from where the goddess had been. He picked the creature up by its hard shell and put it in his hand.

"I cannot change you back," he said, holding the once lovely dryad in his hand. Its cold, slimy body inched across his palm, still trying to escape. He began to laugh then. He would make sure his next conquest was a worthier challenge for his wife.

Notes: This myth was found in *The Greek Myths* by Robert Graves. This story is pretty consistent to Graves' version except for three parts: In Graves' story all the Olympians except Hestia were present at the coup, only Thetis the Nereid brought Briareus to Zeus' rescue, and Zeus attaches an anvil to each of Hera's ankles while she hangs in the sky, which just seemed like too much. The part about the dryad and the origin of the snail was invented by the author.

If you enjoyed this story, you can sign up for a free membership at
ForbiddenFiction.com and discuss it with other readers
and the author at the Hera's Punishment story page
at http://forbiddenfiction.com/story/NN1-1.000214.

Arena Breed

Konrad Hartmann

Konrad Hartmann writes action-oriented erotica and a bit of horror, seeking to offer exciting, cross-genre stories. Drawing on mythology, dreams, and the oddities of human experience, he explores the fringes of the imaginative world. Hartmann believes that we all have stories, and that the world will be better for the telling of them. Find his work in Forbidden Fiction's catalog, and scattered across the Web.

Chapter 1

Dying Well

Avitus peered through an opening in the arena wall and watched the fighters circle each other. The larger one, Hadrianus, lumbered about and tried to keep the smaller, but muscular and much faster Blasius, at a distance. Normally, the loser would be granted *missio*, the grace of losing honorably, and allowed to live. But Avitus knew the men hated each other. In the training yard, each swore to kill the other. Each swore to not raise a finger in surrender.

Hadrianus fought in the *murmillo* style, wearing a broad-brimmed helmet adorned with the image of a fish on its crest. His sword arm was covered by a *manica* arm-guard, consisting of layers of linen strips wrapped and bound with leather thongs so as to form a thick but flexible protection for the limb, with a leather piece protecting the hand and a leather cap for the shoulder. Loose thongs and strips of the linen material now hung in shreds. Small greaves, pieces of curved armor, covered his shins. Leg wraps, now blood-stained, further protected his lower legs. He bore a tall, oblong shield and a *gladius*, a straight, double-edged short sword.

Blasius fought as a *thraex*, a style different than that of the murmillo, favoring speed, His helmet crest bore a griffin decoration, the symbol of Nemesis. He also wore a *manica* on his arm, now crimson with Hadrianus' blood. Quilted wraps made his legs look as thick as small tree trunks. He carried a small round shield and short *sica* sword, the blade angled to enable its wielder to reach around an opponent's shield and armored parts.

The helmets covered the faces of both men with a grill, but Avitus did not wonder what their expressions might be. The way they moved told him everything. Hadrianus staggered, too tired to stop Blasius from lunging around his shield and raking his back with the curved sword. With each strike, Blasius' *manica* mopped up more of Hadrianus' blood. Blasius' attacks made Hadrianus lower his shield, up and down, left and right, struggling to block. Avitus also knew crushing headaches had plagued Hadrianus in the last weeks, and his performance reflected this; meanwhile Blasius had only grown stronger and faster.

Avitus counted them both as his friends, but now he tried to dissolve any feelings of affection. As he watched, he allowed their helmets to obscure their identities. It was not Hadrianus. It was the *murmillo*. It was not Blasius. It was the *thraex*.

As a *secutor*, Avitus would never have to fight either one. He almost always fought against a *retiarius*, a net fighter, and he counted none of this group as friends. When equipped for the fight, a *secutor* wore a heavy helmet, decorated with only a small ridge on its crest, the helmet's only openings two small eyeholes. The *secutor* fought with a *gladius* and a *scutum*, a large curved shield. A *manica* covered his sword arm. If the day came when he had to fight a friend, he would think of their combat idiosyncrasies and not their names.

The fighters paused, facing each other several yards away. The senior referee slowly stepped closer, his long staff ready, and Avitus expected him to stop the fight for a break to refresh the fighters. But as the referee began to lower his staff, Blasius launched himself towards Hadrianus.

The *murmillo* staggered and Avitus smiled, immediately recognizing the feint. The *thraex* swung his sword around for a killing plunge into Hadrianus' back.

The *murmillo* pivoted and caught Blasius' sword arm on his big shield. Hadrianus' feet churned the sand as he rammed his shield into the *thraex*. Blasius fell on his back, and Hadrianus dropped his shield onto the smaller man, kneeling on it. The crowd cheered with the sound of a thunderclap.

Blasius' heels hammered the sand as he tried to get up, his *sica* still in hand, but his arm pinned under the shield. With his small shield on the other arm, he flailed at Hadrianus' neck. Avitus knew he was trying to break the *murmillo's* collarbone, instead of trying to trap the sword arm as he should have. The mistake indicated panic.

The *murmillo* ended him quickly, jamming the *gladius* into the *thraex's* chest from the side, under the armpit, almost to the hilt, then twisting it back and forth until Blasius lay still.

Hadrianus patted his opponent's chest and Avitus wondered if the crowd noticed the gesture, before the *murmillo* stood and raised his *gladius* to the roaring amphitheater. At his feet, Blasius' blood puddled around him and soaked into the sand.

Avitus sighed.

"You died well, friend," he said quietly. "May your spirit travel well."

As the bearers came into the arena to carry Blasius away, Avitus happened to glance at an opening in the opposite side of the arena wall. Though shadowed by the afternoon sun, he could still see the large dark eyes burning into his, the eyes of Faustina, the *retiarius*. The *retiarii* fought with net, trident, and dagger. Wearing little armor, the fast net fighters were almost always matched against *secutores*.

"Carnuntum will remember today for a long time," Avitus heard a voice at his side. It was Felix, his *doctor*, the trainer for the *secutores*.

"They haven't seen a gladiator die in months. And Blasius a veteran at that. A waste. He would have given many more good fights," Avitus said.

"Yes, a waste. But it reminds us of who we are, doesn't it? From time to time, Carnuntum needs it. And the two of them could no longer stand to breathe the same air. But I also mean, they will remember Faustina's fight. Not only a left-handed net-fighter, but a woman. Does that bother you?" Felix asked.

"No. I don't care about the crowd," Avitus said, smiling. He gazed out into the arena.

"Hmm," Felix said, stepping close to Avitus. "Well, that isn't what I asked you, is it?"

"If she fights well, I don't doubt she will receive *missio*," Avitus said. He watched as a man dressed as Mercury came out with litter bearers and carried Blasius away. Slaves darted in, raking the sand smooth and filling in holes.

"Ah. If she fights well. And you? Three *secutores* versus three *retiarii*. And one single duel. Either way, the odds of you facing her in the arena are fair. The other net-men?" Felix shook his head, scowling. "Well, it won't be much of a fight. But Faustina?" He chuckled, staring at Avitus. "The rumors about her are true, you know. She has fought before. Fought a great deal. They're giving you 4-to-1 odds tonight, but that's because they're lumping her in with the other *retiarii*. They don't know how to make book on her. She ruins the odds. Take care tonight, Avitus."

Felix began to walk away.

"And where did you lay your coin, Felix?" Avitus called after him.

"On the *murmillo*. That was a clear wager," he said, walking away.

"Oh, no. Your fight? I wouldn't bet on your fight tonight. I like to have some idea of the outcome."

Avitus turned back to look through the aperture. The magistrate was handing Hadrianus the palm frond of victory, the big *murmillo's* helmet now off, revealing a pale but emotionless face. Behind them, Avitus saw Faustina's eyes still staring at him and a cool sweat broke out on his skin.

They trained you for two weeks, he thought, *and you fight tonight. Never have I seen someone come into the arena so quickly.*

Faustina arrived two weeks ago with two young men and one young woman, all four of them bearing a convict brand on the forehead, as did Avitus. Three of them bore the mark of "FUR," for *fure* or thief. But only Faustina bore that of false accuser, or *kalumniator,* the mark of "KAL" on her brow, as did Avitus.

On the same day Hadrianus killed Blasius, the three others would be en route to Rome for the midday executions at the Flavian amphitheater

But Faustina was sentenced to be a gladiator instead of being condemned. Avitus attributed this sentence to the fact that she was a woman, thus providing a large draw for the events. But for such a short training period? She must have fought before, unless this was simply a ruse meant to bring in spectators. And her brand looked no less fresh than that of the others.

But then they would have matched her with the other female convict, or even any convict, Avitus reasoned. Such a match would provide much more of a show. And why would they condemn Zari, the other convict woman, to death but spare Faustina? No. He would pay attention to Felix's warning.

It all felt odd. Carnuntum itself felt odd to Avitus of late. When he was a child, Rome seemed like a place that must be a day's travel away. Now it seemed as far away as Egypt.

And it felt odd that condemned convicts were left at the *ludus*, the school and housing for the gladiators. That night, when the *contubernium*, the unit of eight legionaries, dropped them off, a silence fell across the school. The gladiators, confined to their cells upon the arrival of the condemned convicts, heard the soldiers give quiet instructions to Crispus the *lanista*, the manager of the *ludus*.

While the men and the girl wore dingy white garments, Faustina wore a blue *palla*, the shawl-like garment covering her head. The *palla* draped over a red *stola*, an article resembling a sleeved long dress. Even these loose garments failed to cover her sumptuous curves. Dark eyes blazed within an almond-colored face, reflecting the torches and lamps illuminating the yard. Were it not for the chains and forehead brand, Avitus would never have taken her for a slave, let alone a convict. While the others stood with slumped shoulders, Faustina stood erect, her chin raised, defiant.

Avitus watched as they led her away, and a murmur broke out as the gladiators saw her taken to a cell in the *retiarius* section. Hoots and cat-calls rose from the cells, growing louder and louder until the lead guard struck an iron bell, and they fell back to a murmur.

The other three convicts were separated and led away at the same moment. The first man was taken to the *murmillo* section. The second man began to drag his feet, but the guards prodded him on towards the *thraex* section. Avitus swallowed the bitter memory of his own first night at the *ludus*, and knew what awaited the men.

When the guards walked the girl towards the *secutor* section, she stared at the ground. Avitus heard giddy laughter from the neighboring cells and rapping on the walls. Avitus' cellmate had recently been sent on to Rome, and as the only cell with one occupant, Avitus heart pounded as he heard the bolt slide in his door.

He stepped back and sat down on his bed. The door swung open and the guard removed the girl's manacles. She hesitated at the door and the guard placed his hand on her back, pushing her slowly inside. The door shut behind her and Avitus heard the heavy bolt shoot home. She stood with her back pressed against the door, her eyes wide and staring at Avitus in the light of a small lamp.

"You're Persian, I think," he said.

She nodded. Unlike the other female convict, she was slender and short. Her long hair hung in her face.

"You speak Latin, then?" he asked.

She nodded again.

"What is your name?" he asked.

"Nona," she said.

"That doesn't sound very Persian."

She looked down at the floor, shivering. *Shivering not only from the cold April night*, Avitus thought.

"Zari," she said, clutching her thin *stola* around her shoulders.

Avitus looked at the spot where his cellmate's bed had rested until last week. He looked back at Zari as he moved to the far end of the bed.

"Are you hungry?" He asked, motioning to the bread laying on the table next to the lamp.

Zari looked at him and slowly picked up the bread, taking one bite and then another, until she had soon devoured the small loaf. She picked up the pitcher of watered wine and drank deeply, all the time never sitting down.

Avitus stood up and undressed, unfastening his tunic and loincloth and hanging them on the wall. He looked over and saw Zari, her back pressed against the door again, again swaddling herself in her *stola*.

"If you want to sleep, I won't fuck you," he said, climbing under his thick blanket. The rapping against the wall resumed until he banged the base of his fist against it. "But what my comrades do tomorrow, I can't say."

Avitus did want her, wanted to feel her slender form beneath him and her sweet breath in his mouth. He wanted to be with her and fall asleep with her in his arms. But it was more pride that he could have other women in Carnuntum, that he did not need to rape a condemned convict. That was the sport of old men and weaklings, those who could no longer catch the eye of an interested spectator.

Zari extinguished the lamp and Avitus saw her as a ghostly form draped in white in the dark cell. The form moved closer, and he felt her lay next to him on the bed, still dressed. He felt his cock stiffen as her shoulder touched his arm. He laid still, listening to her soft breathing.

"When will I die?" she asked.

"A fortnight? A month? It all depends on when the caravan reaches Rome," Avitus said. "You are all *noxii*?" The *noxii* held no hope of survival, most of them perishing in the jaws of predators.

"I am. And the men. Not Faustina. She fights," Zari said. "So. In a fortnight, perhaps I die. How?"

"Is it easier to know?" Avitus asked. "There are a number of possibilities. Why spend time thinking about it?"

"You do not know who you will fight? Are you a *retiarius*?" she asked.

Avitus snorted.

"I am a *secutor*," he said.

"Then you fight *retiarii*. You always know what you will face. Would you want to not know?"

"A lion, probably. Or it could be a bear. Or dogs. Leopards. Or, a bull. But it will probably be a lion. Maybe a few of them."

He heard her quietly sobbing next to him and he put his arm around her.

"Cry now," Avitus said. "But do not cry when they bring the beast into the arena. Run towards him and shout at him. It will anger him and he will strike you down quickly. If you run, he may play with you and slowly kill you."

Zari cried louder now, and Avitus held her tighter now, feeling her thigh press against his erection.

"Pray to Hercules. Or pray to Nemesis if you wish. How well you die is your only choice left," he said. He leaned down and kissed her on the forehead, feeling the raised letters of the scar on his lips.

He felt Zari's hand sliding down his body, lingering over his own scars in its descent, until her soft grip closed around his penis, stroking him. She lifted her face to his and he felt her tongue flicker over his lips before intertwining with his, and he tasted her tears as they ran.

Avitus reached between her legs and lifted up her garments. He pulled her leg to the side, sliding his calloused hand along her smooth inner thighs, up between her legs. He trailed his fingertips through the short curls along her labia, slipping between the folds and wetting them with the dew from her cunt before sliding them up to circle the nub of her clit. She breathed harder now, squeezing his prick in her hand.

He slid his middle finger inside of her, resting his thumb on her fleshy nub while he hooked his finger and rubbed back and forth. Zari sighed, her hips moving into a slow roll as Avitus slid in a second finger.

She held onto his hand, pressing it harder against herself and whimpering. She reached down, caressing herself, pressing her lips against his fingers. Her body stiffened and she tightened around his hand. He heard her gasping through clenched teeth, until her breathing slowed and she collapsed.

Avitus felt her limp body become rigid, and she jumped from the bed. He heard the table knocked to the floor and the pitcher shatter. He heard things being thrown, shattered, and spilled.

He jumped up and clutched the flailing white form. She reached back and clawed at him in the dark, her nails digging furrows into his neck and scalp. He grabbed her arms from behind as she kicked wildly. He twisted her arms up behind her back, hoping to subdue her with pain, but she only kicked harder, punting his belongings against the wall and across the floor, kicking his shins. He gripped both of her slender wrists with one hand while he grabbed a supple belt from the wall, wrapping it around them and fastening it tightly.

One hand in her hair and one on her wrists, he forced Zari face down on the bed, her knees on the floor. He pinned her with his weight, feeling her linen-covered bottom against his erection as he managed to light what little fuel remained in his cracked lamp.

Debris littered the floor. She had smashed, thrown, or kicked everything within her reach. Avitus found a leather thong and forced Zari's ankles together, binding them tightly. She hissed and spat and cursed at him, and he knew he had to be inside of her now. He felt his scalp and neck, and his hands came away bloody. Now, she was only an opponent to be subdued, defeated. He felt his body moving without thinking, without having to direct it.

He grabbed the hems of her *stola* and *palla* and wrenched them up over her back, revealing her soft clenched buttocks.

He knelt behind her, his penis like heated iron now as he slid back his foreskin, and pushed between her legs, the angry head of his cock prodding against her lips. Zari clenched every muscle, now pulling away from him, now twisting and pushing back to deny him entry.

His skull throbbing, Avitus smeared his fingers with oil from the floor and drove them into the cleft of her ass. Her anus clenched as he drove his finger into it, jabbing it in and out as she squealed in rage. *This kindness was more than I received my first night here*, he thought.

Avitus pulled out his finger and took her small ass cheeks in each hand, pulling them apart to reveal her sphincter. He took his erection and set his glans against the tiny hole, pressing slowly but never stopping, relishing the tightness, feeling the muscle twitch around his shaft as he went in further and further, gripping her by the shoulders now as she cried out and and the other *secutores* pounded on the walls. Soon he was all the way inside her, listening to her gasp, crushing her body beneath his, sliding all the way out only to plunge all the way home, again and again. His girth stretched her asshole into a tight band around his shaft, squeezing him, seeming to flutter at times. He smelled her fear and her rage and her pain and her sweat. The orgasm rose within him and roared, pulsing through him, shaking his body as he pounded into her, jetting his scum deep into her bowels.

He slid out and stood over her, dizzy, his cock erect and reddened. Zari laid perfectly still now. He watched a last drop of come fall from the tip of his penis onto the small of her back, trickling down into the cleft of her ass.

Zari lifted her head and slowly looked over her shoulder at him.

"I will die well," she said to him, grinning defiantly through tears.

Chapter 2
The Arena

Faustina inhaled deeply, held her breath, and exhaled slowly through her nose. Her *doctor*, Albus, checked the fastenings of the *manica* on her right arm and of the one piece of armor on her right shoulder. Albus massaged her neck and shoulders and then let her run in place as they stood in the corridor. Faustina honed the points of her trident one last time and did the same to her *quadrens*, a dagger consisting of four, foot-long spikes extending from the guard instead of the usual dagger blade. She tucked one of the prongs of the *quadrens* into her belt, adjusted her tunic, and checked the net-cord tied to her left wrist. Braids held her thick black hair tight and high on her head. Bouncing from one bare foot to the other, she stopped moving only long enough for Albus to give her water.

Faustina's stomach churned. She felt hot, though it was a cool evening. Everything on her skin felt prickly. She smelled her own sweat, pungent with anxiety. She made her face rigid and looked for any reaction from Albus.

Albus was the first good trainer Faustina ever had, she thought, wishing he had always been her doctor. As the *retiarii* wore no helmet, they could not hide their expressions from their opponent or from the crowd. Albus constantly reminded his fighters that as *retiarii* wore no helmet, they must wear no emotion, save that which they wished their opponents to see.

"Avitus is an actor," Albus whispered. "Remember that. If he looks tired or weak, it is just for show, just to bring you in for the *gladius*. You must be a new net-fighter, one he hasn't fought before. Being left-handed isn't enough. You must move like water. Make him react to you, always moving, always striking. Do not expect him to tire. Do not expect anything from him."

The horns of the musicians bellowed.

"Go now," Albus said. "And show Carnuntum how the East fights."

Faustina set her face and rounded the corner. As the *secutor* appeared in the hallway, she did not acknowledge him, nor did his stride change. His polished helmet covered his head completely, save for two small eye holes. Muscles rippled like river water over his body, and he carried his *gladius* and *scutum*, the curved and heavy rectangular shield painted with a roaring lion, almost carelessly.

So you are Avitus, she thought. *Did you even see me through your little eye-holes? How do you wear that bucket and even see?*

They walked side by side to the gate, Faustina peripherally observing the bulky form next to her. As always before a fight, she pushed down the urge to face him, to attack. His proximity quickened her pulse and tightened her muscles.

The guard at the arena gate smirked at them. Faustina stood still next to Avitus, waiting to be announced, her stomach twitching. When the guard opened his mouth as though to speak, Faustina stared at him, calculating how she could best punch her trident through his eye sockets. The guard closed his mouth again and slowly looked towards the arena, placing his hand on the door.

Faustina heard their names announced from the podium, the accented voice strange to her ears. The guard slammed the door open and Faustina felt herself walking out, propelled by her feet as though riding a horse. A mixture of cat-calls and cheers thundered down from the oval of the amphitheater as she raised the trident in her right hand, vaguely aware of Avitus doing the same with his *gladius*. They passed each other as they circled the arena, and then the horns blew again and she stopped to salute the magistrate serving as editor for the event. At the next sounding, she took her place opposite him and prayed quietly to Nemesis.

Nemesis, guide my hand and let me strike true.
Let me see my enemy's weakness. Let my enemy feel my strength.
Let me not falter, and if I fall, let me perish with weapon in hand.

Faustina felt a coolness over her body and felt the air warp around her. Despite the torchlight, she felt more than saw the stars and moon above her. She felt her body tighten like a bowstring as she stood, her right foot forward, net clenched in her left hand as it held the back of the trident, her right hand forward on the trident shaft. She held the trident pointed towards Avitus' feet.

Avitus faced her, the top of his *scutum* even with his eye-holes, his *gladius* held almost behind him.

Faustina felt herself moving as the horns blew, moving backwards as the *secutor* charged her. The man's feet churned the dirt. This was not a man, this was a bull. His speed surprised her as his blade lunged towards her lower abdomen. She swiveled, still moving backwards, and swept the *gladius* aside with her trident, then jabbing into his arm through the *manica*. Stepping to the right to break Avitus' forward momentum, she saw a moment when she was in his blind spot, beyond the eye holes of his helmet.

On Avitus' right-side, his sword-side, Faustina whipped her net, bundled together like a flail, using the weights to wrap it around the neck flange of his helmet. It was a trick that worked many times before. She would snag the neck flange, the *secutor* would lift his sword to cut the net cord, and she would stab him in the ribs, with a good chance of at least one prong penetrating the lung.

But Avitus made no attempt to cut himself free and Faustina now found herself tethered to him by the wrist cord. She choked up her grip on the trident, but the rope occupied her left hand, forcing her to wield the trident one-handed. The *secutor* lunged at her like a machine as she tried to block awkwardly with the trident. She felt a punch right above the crease of groin and thigh, and she knew she was now cut, the strike aimed at an artery.

Faustina now stabbed at his wrist and forearm, and knew she was striking the flesh beneath the linen of the *manica*, but he did not slow his attack. She felt another bite, this time at her waist. She pulled backwards, hoping to unbalance Avitus with the net, but he only leaned backward himself and left a line of fire across the top of her breasts with a horizontal slash.

Faustina felt herself falling backwards, but rolled to one knee. She was free of the cord now, but her body ached with the wounds and she dared not look down as she felt the blood wetting her tunic. Avitus paused and threw the net aside, apparently waiting for Faustina to raise a finger. Faustina grinned, though the arena tilted in her vision. She was not sure if the roar in her ears was the crowd or if she was passing out. But she stood and leaned on her trident, feigning a yawn of boredom, and now knew she heard the applause and laughter of the crowd.

She regretted her taunt as Avitus suddenly appeared before her. She felt hands pushing down on her shoulders from behind. She fell to her knees, regaining her sense in time to lift the trident. She held the prongs sideways and the tips slid past the *secutor's* shield, stabbing into his belly before he checked his charge. When he stepped backwards, Faustina realized the wounds were shallow. She cursed herself for not thrusting, but lurched to her feet and kept the trident in the space past the shield. If she would fall, she would fall plunging holes into the *secutor*. She stabbed into one pectoral, twisting and tearing the skin before he moved back. He knocked the trident down with his sword arm, but Faustina stabbed into his thigh.

As she stabbed, she saw Avitus' shield fall away, realizing too late he was now grabbing the trident shaft with his shield hand before she could back away. She felt the weapon wrenched from her hands and thrown aside. She blocked a *gladius* thrust with the *manica* on her right arm, but still felt the bite. With no time to run, Faustina pulled the *quadrens* from her belt, the hilt sticky with her blood, and thrust at the *secutor's* groin.

Avitus blocked the weapon, the blade of his *gladius* wedged between the prongs of the *quadrens*. He forced the weapon to the ground as Faustina held onto it. She watched as his bare foot stomped on her hand.

Hold onto it. You die if you let go, she told herself.

She freed the weapon, but saw all but one of the prongs were broken off. She launched her arm forward, striking, an animal in her death throes. Avitus staggered backwards, the hilt of the *quadrens* projecting sideways from the left eye hole of his helmet. The breath vapor pouring out from the holes made him look monstrous. Faustina could not tell if it was a mortal wound or if it was only lodged between helmet and face.

Faustina staggered over to her trident and picked it up, turning in time to see Avitus wrench the *quadrens* from his helmet and throw it aside. He bellowed, a voice of rage and pain resonating inside the helmet, and charged again. Faustina screamed, running towards him. She felt weak but he had no shield now. She had a chance if she could stay on her feet.

She felt something hit her chest and looked down to see the referee's staff restraining her. He was screaming at her, his face red, something about ignoring a command to halt. Looking over at Avitus, she saw him similarly restrained by the assistant referee. She set the butt of her trident on the ground and leaned on it, struggling to stand up, refusing to fall.

She saw everything else through a fog. The officials came out. *Missio. Missio.* She was being granted *missio.* But she hadn't yielded. Avitus was receiving *missio.* He hadn't yielded either. She was being cheated. She could have won, but it was being taken from her. She would not go as champion in her next fight. She dared to look down at her blood-soaked tunic. Dirt stuck to the rivulets of blood on her legs.

Will I die? she wondered. *Am I already dead?*

She looked at Avitus as he took off his helmet. The remnants of a ruined eye filled his right eye socket. He turned a pain-filled left eye to look at her, nodding to her. She stared back, and he did not look away until she nodded back. Somewhere, the crowd roared. The sound seemed to vibrate inside her skull. The arena spun for a moment, then she found herself laying in the sand. She had fallen. She stared up at the waning moon and let darkness overtake her.

Faustina writhed in the bed, opening her eyes to stare puzzled at the ceiling, then closing them again. In dream, she watched as the *secutor* charged. She felt hands pushing down on her shoulders again as she fell to one knee. She looked around. Both senior and junior referees stood nowhere near. The *secutor* stopped and backed away. She now lay on a bed in the middle of the arena, the sky dark. She looked up at the amphitheater and found the seats empty. The arena began to spin, or the amphitheater spun around her. Torches flared to life, lit by unseen hands, and she realized it was the bed that spun as the torches formed a ring of flame with the movement. The arena grew brighter and brighter.

Still on the spinning bed, Faustina found herself awakening in a strange room, ornately painted and decorated, and brilliantly lit by oil lamps and candles. It felt warm. No, hot. Very hot. Was it summer? No, it was still spring. The room slowed now, soon only shaking instead of spinning. She felt pain and looked down to see bandages on various parts of her body. She plucked at the one on her arm, trying to lift it and see the wound beneath. A soft hand grasped hers and she looked to see a doe-eyed young woman who smiled sadly and shook her head. The woman lifted a cup and trickled cold water into Faustina's mouth. Faustina swallowed and closed her eyes. *If only the room wasn't so hot. It feels like an oven*, she thought.

She felt a cord on her left wrist and realized she'd been sleeping. Someone was putting something in her right hand. Her trident. Was it time? A new match already? The fight with Avitus. She had not finished it. She must fight him again.

Faustina opened her eyes in time to see the *secutor* approach the bed. He wore the helmet, but he looked smaller now, carrying no shield and naked except for a broad belt, an erection and a *gladius* jutting towards her as he approached. A piece of uncut amber hung on a gold chain from his neck. There was a second *secutor*, as well, this one female, soft and full-breasted, and wearing only helmet, belt, and a necklace similar to the man's.

Faustina needed to get up, needed to fight, though she did not understand the reason why they were in a room and not the arena. She tried to rise, but fell back on the bed, dropping the trident and hearing it clatter on the floor. Her head throbbing, she reached for her *quadrens*, but it was gone and she was naked. She tried to gather up the net. She cast it at the male as he approached, but there were no weights on it and it fluttered to the floor.

The woman stooped and gathered up the net. Faustina tried to yank it away from her but the woman was too strong. The female *secutor* spread the net over Faustina, holding her down with it. Faustina struggled, but found the net only pulled tighter. She felt sweat drench her body and now the room felt cold.

Hands pulled her legs apart, and Faustina thought to kick too late. The male *secutor* knelt between her legs, his hand stroking her vulva, his finger penetrating her, his thumb rubbing her clit too hard. The pounding in her head felt better when she closed her eyes.

Pain forced her eyes open again. The bronze of the helmet rested against her face and she looked in to see two brown eyes staring back at her. *Not Avitus*, she realized. The weight of the helmet hurt her, but the coolness of the metal felt good. From inside, she heard the hollow echo of his breathing. The aching came from the *secutor's* weight resting upon her wounds. She grunted with pain and the *secutor* rubbed against them harder. Faustina gritted her teeth and realized his penis was thrusting in and out of her. She focused on the feel of his cock inside her. She had to keep sliding her concentration from her wounds back to the sensations inside her pussy. The net still covered her, but the man reached up and squeezed her breasts, and she welcomed the pinching of her nipples as a diversion. The wound above and to the side of her groin hurt worst of all. Faustina looked up to see the female *secutor* kneeling on the bed beside her, fingering herself as her breasts bounced.

A moan rang inside the man's helmet and Faustina felt him thrust deep into her. She felt his cock throb as it pulsed inside, and then he slid out and off of her. She gasped with relief. The net was pulled from her head, but she looked to see the woman's bottom as it descended to her face. Faustina growled with rage as she turned her face aside, trapped between two thighs. She felt the wet softness of the woman's sex on her cheek, rubbing on her.

For a moment, she clenched her teeth, ready to bite this woman. As a *gladiatrix*, slave, and convict, Faustina knew what it was to have her body used by others. This she accepted as a chore in most cases. Sometimes it gave her pleasure. Sometimes it disgusted her. But rare were the times when someone defiled her mouth.

"The *retiarius* does not submit, my love," Faustina heard the woman say, the voice muffled in her ears.

"No *missio!*" she heard the man cry out. Pain stabbed through the wound near her groin.

"Submit!" the woman yelled, her voice metallic in her helmet. She bounced on top of Faustina's face. The pain in her wound grew agonizing. She felt a finger probe it. Sweat poured anew from Faustina's brow. She tried to push the woman off, but her arms felt like willows. The female *secutor* twisted Faustina's hair, pulling her face into her musky pudenda.

Faustina forced her tongue out, haltingly. It made contact with the women's folds and she tasted the salty tang of her cunt. The woman sighed and sank down, holding her labia open as she pressed down against Faustina's mouth. The intense pain in her wound stopped, leaving only a dull throb, pleasant in comparison.

Keep the pain away, Faustina told herself. She drove her tongue deeper into the woman. *This is nothing. Only a game. There is nothing but doing this and stopping the pain. The faster you pleasure her, the sooner this ends. No! There is no 'her.' There is only this cunt. Connected to nothing. Only this. Lick it. Suck it. There is only this. Nothing else. This is not you. This is not her. You enjoy this. You like this. This is someone doing it to you.*

Faustina let the room, the bed, and the woman fall away as she lapped. She flexed her tongue as far as it would go, deeper, sliding out and sucking at the lips, and then plunging back in. The pussy twitched and bounced on her mouth. It slid forward onto her chin, and she wiggled the tip of her tongue against a puckered anus, tasting and smelling dirt and sweat, buttocks enclosing her face. She heard a woman moaning, the sound hollow. The cunt slid backward again and her tongue slid into the wet slit. Faustina stabbed her tongue towards the inside front of it, probing its piss hole. The pussy mashed down on her, suffocating her, her nose inside the wet slit, inhaling her scent. It slid back further and Faustina sucked at the long, fat clit resting on her lip. A woman cried out and hands squeezed Faustina's breasts, nails digging into them.

The cunt lifted from her. Faustina looked up to see the female *secutor* squatting over her face.

The helmeted head tilted down to look at her. A voice rang out from within the helmet.

"Keep. Your precious mouth. Open."

Chapter 3
Joining the Stable

Avitus sat in his chair and watched as Paula squatted over Faustina's mouth. He set his face, aware that Paula's husband Gratianus was watching his reaction. The *secutor* helmet hid Gratianus' expression, but the man hopped from foot to foot, masturbating and cheering Paula on.

The exhibition sickened Avitus, mainly the mockery of the *secutore* and the *retiarii*. He wanted to kill Paula and Gratianus. But instead he could only watch, staring as a stream of golden piss squirted from Paula's cunt into the mouth of the *gladiatrix*. Faustina retched, spitting up some of the urine, but when she turned away Gratianus stepped forward and poked his finger into the wound above her groin. Faustina righted her face again and opened her mouth, swallowing the last trickles of urine pouring in. An involuntary quiver twitched through Avitus as he watched and he reminded himself this was wrong.

Gratianus clapped as Paula dismounted from Faustina's face. Paula made a mock bow before Avitus, and then Gratianus laughed and did the same. The pair took off their helmets. Gratianus grinned. Avitus realized the man's face was considered handsome, but it held the suggestion of a rat in expression.

Paula's red-dyed hair rested in a hairnet. Dispute his disgust, Avitus admired her form. She was soft without being flabby, like some of Carnuntum's best prostitutes, her breasts full without sagging. But in her expression, Avitus saw not a rat but a snake. The vaguely reptilian cast of her face alarmed him as much as it intrigued him. On the bed behind them, Avitus saw Faustina laying on the bed, defeated in her fever and too weak to clean herself of the piss soaking into her hair and pillow.

"You are not entertained?" Gratianus asked, sarcasm staining his voice.

"But we thought to amuse the gladiator himself for a change!" Paula said. "You who entertain others so well deserve to see a match from time to time."

"Your remaining eye still works, does it not?" Gratianus asked. "Why do you not clap? You still have two hands. I said, clap!"

Avitus raised his hands, mechanically, and beat his palms together. The couple laughed, gathering their *gladii* and walking out of the room.

It had been two days since Avitus learned he and Faustina would be sent to the villa. He dreaded the visit. He hated Gratianus, though he barely knew him. Rumors circulated wildly about him, including many stories of prostitutes and visitors never seen again. None of these stories involved the nobles, but for an actor or a servant, perhaps few would question their disappearance too closely. And maybe, Avitus thought, a gladiator still under sentence could simply be reported as a runaway.

"Sir, I wish to decline the invitation," Avitus said to Crispus, the *lanista*. Avitus stood in Crispus' office, while Crispus wrote at his table.

Crispus set down his pen and looked up at Avitus. Avitus saw the man's face soften for half a second before turning to stone.

"Decline?" Crispus said, his voice almost a whisper.

"Yes, sir," Avitus said.

Crispus stared at him without speaking or moving, then said,

"One of the most powerful and wealthy men in Carnuntum sends you a personal invitation to recover at his estate. And you wish to decline."

"Yes, sir," Avitus said. His thigh ached from the inflamed puncture wounds.

Crispus cleared his throat and folded his hands in front of him on his desk. He stood up and walked slowly to the door, opening it and looking casually left and right before closing it again. He stood next to Avitus and spoke quietly, not facing him.

"My best fighter, no, my two best fighters have received invitations to recuperate at a most important man's home. I will speak frankly with you, Avitus. By turning down this invitation, you would insult Gratianus. Your insulting of Gratianus would be seen as my insulting Gratianus. There are persons of influence involved in this matter. The politics of hospitality often supersede one's own desires. That bears true for a gladiator. And it bears true for a *lanista*.

"You belong to this school, and the school, and I, belong to Rome. The Emperor's Rome. Faustina has already been sent to Gratianus. I cannot emphasize enough how ill-advised a refusal of Gratianus' hospitality would be at this time. The only help I can render you is this advice. Reconsider long and hard your choice to decline. That is my final word on the subject."

Crispus walked to his table without another look at Avitus. He sat down and began writing.

"You may go. And have your bandages changed," Crispus said, his voice strained.

"Yes, sir," Avitus said. His hand shook as he opened and closed the door on the way out. He walked away from Crispus' office, blood pounding in his ears. He was still adjusting to seeing with only one eye, and he felt dizzy as he stomped along the way. He didn't know where he wanted to go, but he walked toward the sound of the drill yard, towards the sound of Felix's rasping voice barking out commands.

Avitus rounded a corner and saw Felix holding something too flexible to be a rod, and too rigid to be a whip. Rows of *secutores*, each wearing an extra heavy training helmet, sprinted back and forth between two lines on the ground about ten yards apart. The men threw themselves along as Felix screamed at them to charge. Those too slow, or who fell, Felix stepped forward and struck with his whip rod. Most of the men bore at least one fresh red stripe on their sweating, dirty bodies.

Felix looked over at Avitus, and whistled to an assistant doctor, who ran to Felix's side. Felix handed the man the whip rod and pointed to the *secutores*. The assistant took over the sprint drills as Felix walked up to Avitus.

"You look like dogshit, boy," Felix said. "Change your bandages before you turn green."

"How long will they keep me at Gratianus' villa?" Avitus asked.

Felix looked away and shrugged.

"I don't know," he said.

"Well, has this happened before? That gladiators had to recover there?" Avitus asked.

"A couple years ago," Felix said. "A few gladiators were guests for a week. No one still at the *ludus*."

"What did they say?" Avitus asked. "I've heard what the whores say about Gratianus. And Paula."

"Well, then you've already heard it," Felix said, rubbing the back of his neck. "What can I say? They are a pair of rich fucking degenerates. Have fun. Fuck. Make the best of it."

"Crispus warned me not to decline the invitation," Avitus said.

"Decline, eh? Avitus. Gratianus is a friend of Diocletian, or at least a friend of an important friend. You and Faustina, you're a favor. Do you think Crispus has any say in this?" Felix shook his head and laughed without humor, and spat in the dirt. "No. Gratianus did something for somebody in Rome. What, I don't know."

Felix stared off in the distance. He smiled suddenly, his face a mask but for the toothy grin forced onto it. He slapped Avitus on the shoulder. "You're looking at it all wrong. You'll go there, probably hump his wife raw, and come back to the arena fresh as springtime. See you in a few weeks, Avitus." He grabbed Avitus' hand, squeezed it, and walked away, his back stiff.

"And change your fucking bandages!" he called back over his shoulder.

Avitus watched as Felix took the whip rod, dismissed the assistant, and resumed screaming at the *secutores*.

Now into his third day at the villa, Avitus waited in his room, laying on the bed. The humiliation of Faustina the other day had confirmed his fears. From different prostitutes, Avitus heard stories about the house he hoped were exaggerations. He never expected to be sent there, didn't know he *could* be sent there. True, as a successful fighter, he received and accepted many invitations for dinners and parties. He'd even been a party guest at this villa. The luxury impressed him but the quality of the hosts did not. Gratianus behaved like most of the retired officers, one with an undistinguished career, owing his fortune to intrigue and birth more than achievement.

And now Avitus found himself a prisoner through virtue of politics. Though so far he had suffered little but boredom, he dreaded the days to come and looked forward to returning to the amphitheater. He saw little of his hosts. He wondered if Faustina still lived. His hand strayed towards the bandage covering his right eye socket.

He was down to one eye. Fighting as a *secutor*, his helmet impaired his line of sight even with two eyes. What would happen next? This changed everything. He would need to retrain entirely. Perhaps he should train in a new style, he thought. And what? Begin as a novice *murmillo* with one eye? If he would fight with this limitation, would it not be better to use the style he knew and excelled in?

The door opened and Paula stepped inside, her red hair pinned up, her *palla* gleaming white. The amber chunk hanging from her necklace caught the light and cast orange rays across her bosom. An enormous hound stood at her side, its short fur black and shining in the sunlight streaming in through the window. The dog's shoulder reached Paula's hip, its muscles rippling under its slightly loose skin. Avitus thought of the girl Zari and wondered what became of her. The dog ignored him and sniffed around the room. Avitus recognized the breed as one similar to a type used by the army. He'd been told the breed was sometimes used in the Flavian amphitheater in Rome. The head of the massive beast seemed larger than Avitus' head.

"You look well, Avitus," Paula said, approaching him and checking his bandages. "You must forgive us for being such poor hosts. But we have been extremely busy. I hope the servants have treated you well?"

Avitus nodded. Paula's lip curled.

"This must be quite a change for you. Not training. Not fighting. Doing nothing but lounging and eating. You must be bored," she asked. The dog exhaled loudly and sat next to Paula. She stroked his head without having to bend over.

"No, ma'am," Avitus said. Admitting boredom seemed unwise to him.

"Good. All the same, I thought I might impose on your reverie by asking you to visit the garden with me."

"Of course," Avitus said, standing up.

"Come then. Gratianus is already waiting for us."

Avitus walked next to the dog, who walked next to Paula. They walked down several halls toward the rear of the building. Though having learned almost nothing of art, Avitus marveled at the paintings and mosaics on the walls. Scenes of gladiators gave way to sylvan scenes. As they went further, human figures reappeared, the scenes beginning as erotic and becoming increasingly bizarre. Centaurs and satyrs impaled women on their gargantuan penises. Pairs of women pleasured themselves with the opposite ends of snakes.

The last hallway emptied onto a tiled circle outside, surrounded by trees. Gratianus sat on a chair, while a naked young woman knelt on the tiles to both his left and right, while a third knelt on the tiles before him. Unlike the dogs, each girl wore a collar and leash, the lanyard ends of the latter casually hung from the wrist of Gratianus. Next to him sat an empty chair. The center of the area was untiled, green grass growing in a circle of about two yards in diameter. Two more dogs, similar to the first, paced aimlessly about the area, casually approaching their comrade as he arrived with Paula.

Paula walked over and sat in the empty chair. One of the dogs sniffed Avitus loudly, slowly circling him. He extended his hand, letting the dog smell it, but when he tried to pet her, she pulled her head back and growled, her sound deep and resonant. Avitus placed his hands on his hips and ignored her after that.

Gratianus and Paula spoke to each other quietly, occasionally glancing at Avitus and giggling. None of the slave girls, as he assumed them to be, met his eyes, and instead stared at the ground, shifting uncomfortably on the tiles. Avitus let himself start to shut down. In times of imprisonment, he learned to still his mind. It took years of practice, to think of nothing, no feelings, no reaction, but to remain alert to danger. He looked up at the sky, watching the clouds move.

"Avitus!" he snapped back into the moment when he heard Gratianus call his name. "Avitus, come here, will you? Instead of standing like a tree waiting to drop its leaves. Come here."

Avitus approached and stood rigidly before the couple.

"Avitus, I don't suppose you know anything of animal husbandry, do you? Now I don't mean to speak of a man marrying his horse, you see," Gratianus said as Paula tittered. "I mean, the breeding of animals."

"No, sir," Avitus answered. "I don't suppose I know anything about the topic."

"You weren't a farmer before you were a gladiator? What did you do?"

"I...," Avitus started to speak.

"Never mind. I don't actually care," Gratianus said, waving his hand. "But you know nothing of animal husbandry. And I admit, I know little of it myself. But, my dear Paula here knows a bit. She actually knows a great deal about breeding livestock." He lifted one foot and set his sandal in the middle of the girl's back before him. She flinched, her brown hair spilling over her face, but she remained still, except for the rocking motion as Gratianus jiggled his foot.

The girl suddenly lifted her green eyes and stared at Avitus. He met her gaze but did not hold it for long, not wanting Gratianus and Paula to witness the contact. In her eyes, he saw she was taking a chance and knew she only did so because her back was turned to her masters. He wondered if those who never knew slavery understood how to speak this way, to talk with nothing but the eyes. He realized Gratianus was still speaking.

"Horses and dogs, mostly. She's skilled enough that the Legion even buys breeding stock from her. Yes, indeed. But she does, from time to time, experiment with other species, don't you, dear?"

"I do, I do," Paula said, reaching down to pet the chestnut hair of the girl next to her. This one also flinched at her touch.

Avitus tried to take everything in, how the girls reacted, what the masters said, and more importantly, the sound of their voice, the way they moved, and the look on their faces. Avitus tried to feign boredom and recognized the couple doing the same thing. But where Avitus tried to mask alarm, the couple masked excitement. A tang of anticipation wafted through the air. He smelled it there in the garden, the same way he smelled it surging from the crowd in the amphitheater.

"You see, Avitus," Paula said, standing up and taking the green-eyed girl's leash from Gratianus. "As I breed the finest dogs in Carnuntum, if not all of Petronell, I intend to breed the finest gladiators. The next generation of fighters will not be broken miners and crippled prisoners. They will be beautiful beasts of combat, like my lovely hounds. Like my handsome Avitus. Come." Paula walked the girl over to the grassy circle in the center of the area, the girl walking on hands and feet. She looked too comfortable doing it, Avitus thought, as though she had been trained, her shapely bottom thrust high in the air. "Fours," Paula said as they reached the grass, and the girl got on hands and knees, facing the chairs. "I think you know what to do, Avitus."

Avitus stared at the scene before him. The girl's beauty stunned him. She looked like she came from one of the tribes north of Carnuntum, her movements feral, her limbs well-formed. A cord of smooth muscle ran down either side of her spine, her back narrowing sharply to a wasp-waist. Her firm buttocks swelled and parted, revealing the fleshy lips of her pussy seeming to sprout from the soft frame of chestnut-colored hair.

Yet his audience unnerved him. Paula and Gratianus leered at him from their chairs as the two girls cast furtive glances.

"Go on," Paula said, motioning Avitus toward the girl with a gesture and a look, her eyebrows raised. When Avitus hesitated, Paula jumped to her feet and stamped her foot. She grabbed the two other leashes from her husband and walked quickly towards Avitus, a leash looped over each wrist. Neither of the girls were as nimble as the green-eyed one, and they struggled to keep up. Paula's eyes blazed as she grabbed Avitus' tunic and yanked it upwards.

Avitus took hold of the garment and pulled it off, less humiliated by stripping than being stripped. He felt cold iron against his belly and froze. Paula smirked, a small dagger now in her hand, and cut the loincloth from him. The proximity of the blade to his genitals did little to engorge his cock as it hung flaccidly. Paula grabbed his organ with her free hand, squeezing it.

"Do tell me you find this attractive," she said motioning to the green-eyed girl's ass.

"Is our little gladiator not up to the challenge?" Gratianus called out, tittering.

"No fear, my love. These beasts just need a little help from time to time," Paula said. The blade disappeared again under her *palla* and she grabbed the curly locks of the nearest girl, lifting her to kneel before Avitus. "Suck!" she said, and the girl docilely opened her mouth, her eyes closed, and dipped her head to take his soft prick inside.

Avitus tried to ignore Gratianus and Paula, as would ignore the spectators in the amphitheater. The girl's cheeks sucked in and out as she pulled at him with her mouth, her cheekbones high and delicate. He felt himself begin to stiffen. Paula grabbed the girl's hair again and forced her head back and forward roughly. The girl grabbed onto Avitus' thighs, trying not to fall over. He felt her tongue scrubbing his shaft and concentrated on the pleasure, trying to ignore Paula's barking voice. His face stung as an open palm smacked against it, and felt his dick sliding out of the warm mouth.

"I said fuck! Now!" Paula yelled in his face, pointing at the crouching girl on the grass. Avitus stepped forward and knelt behind her. The girl twitched her hips. His head felt hot as he parted her lips with his fingers, the flesh warm and slippery. He eased the head of his cock between them and the girl cooed softly as he penetrated her. He focused on the warm grip of her cunt around his shaft as he sank deeper, trying to ignore the pain of the puncture wounds on his thigh. He gripped her hips, pumping harder and faster. Sliding his hands down to her ass, he held onto her cheeks now, listening to her groans. He leaned forward, setting his knuckles on the ground, then reached up with one hand to feel her firm breasts as they swayed. As he stroked one nipple, she whimpered. He slid his hand down her belly, into the soft patch of curls between her legs.

"Breeding, not pleasure, Avitus," Paula said, squatting next to them. She grabbed his arm and pulled it until his now clenched fist rested on the ground again.

Avitus stared forward, pumping into the girl, feeling her push back against him, her pussy wet and tight. In the corner of his vision, he saw Paula touch one of the other girls, and in a moment, a slippery finger slid between his buttocks and rested on his perineum, massaging him. Another finger pressed against his rectum until it slid inside.

He felt himself coming without warning. He lifted himself up again, clenching the girl's ass in his hands as he pulled himself deep into her, grunting, letting all the pain dissolve into the white heat of the orgasm flashing through his brain.

"Good boy!" he heard Paula say, and the girl was suddenly pulled away from him. Avitus saw the delicate girl thrust to the ground before him. "On your back," Paula said. The new girl lay down on her back, her dark eyes wide, frowning as her legs were pulled open by her mistress. Her curly locks haloed around her head.

Paula clenched Avitus' wet cock as it started to soften, pumping vigorously and forcing it rigid once more. Avitus felt himself sweating as Paula pulled him by it. She spit on the girl's vagina, rubbing her saliva into it as she pulled Avitus down and pressed his prick against it. He lay down on top of the girl, working himself into her slit. She felt almost too tight, and he wondered what was wrong. He felt a foot on his ass, pushing down.

Trying to penetrate, he suddenly realized the girl was a virgin. The thought bothered him, for he had never been with a virgin. But he did remember his own first unwelcome penetration. He remembered the pain and in that moment, he realized all of his life had been spent giving and receiving pain. There was no avoiding giving and receiving it. One could only bear it well. One could only deal it well. Running from it only made it last longer.

Avitus plunged his cock into the girl in a slow, steady push, closing his eyes as he heard the girl mewl beneath him. He fucked her with neither sadism nor callousness, but accepted her pain. Right now it was her agony, but perhaps tomorrow it would be his. Better to grasp it, embrace it. He held her small breasts as his flesh slapped against hers, listening to her grunt with each thrust. She held onto his wounded arm, but he welcomed the ache of her fingers pressing against the unhealed gouge, feeling somehow closer to her for it. In his ear, one of the dogs sniffed him.

"What a good boy," he heard Paula say, not knowing whether she was talking to the dog or to him.

Chapter 4
The Amber Road

Faustina felt the wine spread a pleasant numbness through her mind. In the string of bad days spent at the villa, it had been an exceptionally bad day. Now she found herself, along with Avitus, guests of honor presented at the dinner party of Gratianus and Paula. Three musicians played their strings in the corner, ignored and frequently drowned out by the guests. Granted the privilege of place on one of the couches around the table, Faustina gazed back coolly at the hard looks of those seated on simple chairs. In their faces, she saw jealousy mixed with contempt. Three of Paula's dogs wandered about the room, eating bones and scraps from the floor.

Faustina gazed across the dining room table from her couch and found Avitus staring back at her. Like her, he rested belly down, his chest propped by the cushion. He now wore an eye patch over his right socket, and a wide leather bracer over each wrist. To his right, a middle-aged man spoke loudly to Gratianus, who lay on the center couch in the horseshoe arrangement of couches. The man gestured towards Avitus and slapped him on the shoulder from time to time between plucking dormice from the dish before him. He seemed to inhale the flesh and cast the bones on the floor in one movement.

On the other side of Avitus rested a small and young fair-haired woman named Iulia. It took Faustina a moment to realize Iulia was speaking to Avitus, her lips barely moving. Her ribboned garment resembled that of the other women in the room, but her copious amber jewelry spoke of exotic and distinctly un-Roman elements. Faustina watched as Avitus inclined his head, apparently listening to her. Iulia sometimes punctuated her speech by touching Avitus' hands.

When Faustina saw her walk earlier in the evening, she noticed the girl possessed a slight limp, a feature that neither slowed Iulia's gait nor failed to impart a strange charm to her mannerisms.

Faustina felt her stomach twitch, a small pain in her side. She drained her cup and refilled it. Faustina watched as Paula, seated on the center couch, darted glances at the pair. But whereas Paula's face seemed otherwise calm and happy, Gratianus looked visibly distracted, answering the loud man who sought his attention, but frowning at Iulia. One of the black dogs paced around Paula's couch.

"You met my daughter earlier this evening, yes?" the amber merchant, Aelius, said to Faustina from his place next to her on the couch, on her left. Faustina stared at him in surprise, for he spoke in fluent Persian. He smiled behind his long gray beard, his weathered skin crinkling. His eyes looked mad, pupils dilated. Like his daughter, he wore an excessive amount of amber jewelry. Faustina noticed, in contrast, neither Gratianus nor Paula wore their usual amber pendants.

"Your Persian is excellent," Faustina replied in the same language. She glanced across the room as she heard Avitus guffaw.

"Thank you. I hoped you would understand it, and your master and mistress over there trying to read our lips would not."

Faustina laughed and nodded. She could feel the couple's eyes upon her now.

"Without looking down," Aelius said, reaching for a thrush from a platter on the table, "you will find a tiny shard under your cushion."

Faustina fidgeted in her place and slid her hand under the cushion. She felt a sliver of something hard but not metallic, and needle-sharp, less than an inch long. She watched Aelius curiously as he ate the thrush. He spoke between bites.

"Keep it near you always. When the time comes, slide it into your skin, like a splinter."

"When what time comes?" Faustina asked, tucking it inside her leather bracer and reaching for her cup. Paula had given her the bracers earlier that day. They covered the rope-burns on her wrists.

"A time of desperation. When you absolutely must slay one who needs slaying. You will know the time. Laugh now," he said.

"What?" Faustina asked.

"Laugh as if I told you a very funny joke," Aelius said, draining his cup.

Faustina forced a laugh.

"Good enough," Aelius said. "And when your enemy is finished, run towards the Pole star. You will find us there. Now act as if I just told you something ridiculous."

Faustina sighed and shook her head, chuckling.

"Perhaps you did," she said. She realized she was slurring her words.

"Perhaps I did," he said. "Or perhaps not. Drink less wine in the days to come."

"Why?" Faustina asked. She had been drinking more wine in the past few days, nursing her wounds between her hosts' increasingly taxing demands.

"Because it is making you weak and foolish. And you need to see clearly. You need your strength. Suffering is not new to you. You've always known it. It's made you stronger. Faster. Smarter. But this luxury?" Aelius said, holding up a snail, plucking it from its shell and eating it. "This luxury you haven't known. And it will kill you. It tricks you. It tells you to avoid facing the pain with one more drink. One more concoction. One more nap on silk pillows. But the drink fades and you wake up from your slumber. And the suffering returns. And you experience it the same way you did the first time. Over and over again. No. Endure instead, Faustina. Your time will come."

Faustina drained her cup and sneered at Aelius. She felt the hand of the man to her right sliding his hand up her thigh, stopping at the tuck of her buttock.

"Endure?" Faustina said, still speaking Persian. "Ah. I shall endure. Tell me, Aelius, have you ever drank piss? Ever had an eel inserted into your body?" She was speaking louder now, and those around them were becoming quieter. "Ever felt a stallion come in your face? No? Never? Well I could tell you more about these things. More than I wish I could. And do you know why? Do you know why I get to experience these lovely experiences, Aelius? Well, it's because I am an honored guest! An honored guest of Diocletian's most honored shit-heel in all of Carnuntum!"

"Ah, Faustina!" she heard Gratianus say. "Would you grace us with your speech in a civilized tongue?"

"Would you have it so, sir?" Faustina hissed in Latin.

"I would," Gratianus said, raising one eyebrow and crossing his arms. "Especially your thoughts on our beloved emperor, since you appear to be on that subject." Silence hung in the room, the guests staring and the musicians pretending to adjust their instruments.

"I've nothing to say about the emperor," Faustina said, checking herself but gritting her teeth. "Only about you," she said, rising to her knees and pointing at Gratianus. "And you," she said, pointing at Paula. "Tell me, Gratianus, when last did you see combat? Did you ever watch it from a hill, perhaps? Did your soft hand ever shake that of a soldier? Did you listen to his stories, remembering them in detail so you could claim them as your own during these soft dinner parties?" Gratianus glared at her, fists shaking, clenched. "And you, Paula? How many senators have you sucked to attain your current position of Queen to the King of Sycophants? Were the two of you the only rotten fish left in the bottom of Carnuntum's aristocratic barrel?" Paula's face reddened and she stared at her husband, her burning eyes demanding retribution.

"Ah, these Persians and wine," Gratianus said, pressing his face into a grimace and presenting it as a smile. "They mix poorly. And unlike my wife's hounds, they forget how to conduct themselves in public. I'm afraid your face gives you away." Gratianus ran his fingers over his forehead, smiling in mockery of her brand. "You're simply a lying slut with a net, misusing her short-lived fame." Faustina now saw the villa's guards appearing in the doorways, silently filtering into the room in surprising numbers.

Faustina let herself fall forward onto the table as her hand grabbed a knife. She rose and threw it in one motion. The room tilted in her vision, and she cursed the wine now as the knife passed over Gratianus' head, clattering against the marble wall. She saw movement towards her from the corner of her eye, and drove her elbow backwards, feeling teeth break as a guard stumbled backwards, cursing and spitting blood.

The dogs were almost upon her now.

"Hold!" she heard Paula call out. Only for hearing this word did Faustina pause. Had Paula given no command, she assumed the dogs would have attacked to kill. And no sooner had she paused than hands gripped her arms. She felt her legs kicked out from beneath her, until they too were held. As the guards carried her from the room, she watched the scene upside down as her head hung. Aelius and Iulia were gone. Avitus watched, his chin in his hand, with no expression. When she passed the sneering face of Paula, Faustina spat, the projectile landing in the woman's hair. Stars crackled in Faustina's vision.

Faustina became conscious as she felt her *palla* pulled from her, and when she felt her undergarments being unwrapped, she tried to kick. Her body arched with the movement, but the hands held her leg firmly. She looked around at the circle of guards holding her, leering over her. By the torches in the undecorated walls, she knew this was what the house called the Inner Room.

She felt herself spinning, turned, and lowered face-down to lay naked on her belly. The cool stone felt good at first, as Faustina pressed her throbbing forehead against its surface. But almost immediately, it chilled her. She felt her limbs jerked, manacles clamping down on wrists and ankles. Her bracers mercifully protected her wrists from further damage, but the iron bit into her ankles. Chains connected to four of the dozens of rings bolted into the floor pulled her limbs out, forcing her body into an X.

It would be worse now, she thought. Whatever relief from her situation vanished when she threw the knife at Gratianus. She'd humiliated him in public, and was overheard speaking about Diocletian shortly before her outburst. Maybe, she would be sent to Rome to fight with no weapons against animals. Or maybe she would be made to disappear as a runaway. She would have been wise to remain silent as Avitus, she thought. He understood the wretched people of Carnuntum.

What had Aelius given her? A poison needle of sorts? She tried to reach it but could not bend her wrist enough. She would use it. It was time for an end. If she couldn't die in the arena, she would at least claim this last measure of control. It was time to use every moment, every opportunity.

Faustina raised her head, testing her range of motion. Above her, the guards leered. She lowered her head and paused to collect her strength. Flexing her neck, she whipped her head up and slammed her forehead into the floor. Faustina crumbled, unconscious, to the floor.

She awoke and tasted metal. Something pulled at each corner of her mouth, forcing her to grimace. Touching the pieces with her tongue, they felt like dull hooks, not piercing the flesh but pulling her lips back. There was something bound around her head, the binding running from the mouth hooks around to the back of her head. Someone crouched before her and she looked up to see Gratianus grinning down at her. He had one hand behind her head, clutching the binding. When he tugged it, the hooks pulled painfully at her mouth. He reached with his other hand and touched her forehead, then held up his hand. It was bloody. As she looked at his hand, she saw Paula now stood behind her husband.

"There," he said. "You see. We had to take measures to prevent you from hurting yourself. These," Gratianus said, making Faustina wince as he pulled and the hooks tugged her mouth. "These are to keep you from beating your brains out on the floor. And this room is to keep you from getting in trouble with friends of the Emperor. I do, after all, have a responsibility to you as my guest. As a man of influence, I am here to help."

Chapter 5
Wolfmarked

Faustina tried to take in every detail. If he came close enough to her jaws, she would allow her cheeks to be torn if it meant getting her teeth into him. If he tried to use her mouth she would bite off anything she could.

"You look like one of the wolves we sometimes trap. Right before we allow Paula's hounds to tear them apart. But listen. I cannot hold your harness all day. So I have another means of keeping your head up." Gratianus reached around with his free hand and showed her a thin chain, apparently running to her head harness. At the end of the chain was fastened an almost circular bronze hook, perhaps three inches in diameter. "We have this," Gratianus said. "I'll admit it isn't sharp, but you'll notice it's fairly thin and hammered flat. Trust me when I say this will hurt you if you pull against this. Your asshole will start at your waist if you don't keep still." Paula tittered behind him.

Faustina's mind teetered, half of it testing every limb, every restraint, quickly searching for a way out. The other half of her mind began to shut down, began to view her body as a thing separate from herself. The hooks yanked her mouth back, the metal hard against her gums. She felt herself tilting her head back to avoid the flesh tearing.

She felt something wrap around each knee, something that felt like leather bands. She watched as two guards each ran a rope across the floor, each running their rope through a ring in the floor. Then she winced as she felt someone's knee pressed into each of her calves.

"Faustina!" Gratianus hissed. And no sooner were the knees lifted from her calves than the ropes were pulled tight, dragged her knees up under her. The irons remained on her ankles, but there was no tension on them. She tried to kick but the hands were on her legs again, forcing them into a frog-like position, splaying out to the sides. Unable to turn and look, Faustina felt her knees and ankles secured to floor rings in this position.

The hooks tugged at the corners of her mouth again, but now she also felt a cold metal point poking into her rectum. She sucked in her breath.

The greatest pain now rested in Faustina's neck as she strained to keep her head back. She tested the hooks, stopping before they tore. She realized she had the tiniest movement available, in order to relieve the tension in her neck. She began to abstract the pain, letting it happen to her body, watching it happen to her body. She focused on sounds and smells in the room. She focused on the smell of coals burning. Her head throbbed, and she thought of the day she had received the KAL brand on her forehead.

"Look, Gratianus, she's already used to it. These Persians know their place if only you keep them properly," Paula said. She loomed over Faustina, and Faustina sucked in air as she felt the hooks pull at her mouth and anus. Rage welled up within her, but she pushed it down, letting it turn to cold liquid inside herself. *Feel nothing. Show nothing.* "Is it ready, yet?" Paula asked.

"Yes, I believe so. Not white, but orange will do, won't it?" Gratianus said.

"Quite so," Paula said. "Bring it here."

Faustina's eyes scanned the room, her heart pounding harder. The smell of smoke increased as guards carried a brazier and set it on a table against the wall. Above the table, a long, funnel-shaped copper shaft extended to the wall, apparently covering a window. One guard methodically worked a lever back and forth, and the wisps of smoke began traveling up into the funnel. Faustina felt herself breathing harder now. Behind the smoke, she smelled her own sweat, pungent with fear. She worked her wrist back and forth, hoping to drive the shard into her skin.

Paula approached and squatted in front of her, a set of iron rods in her hands. Each iron ended in a letter.

"Can you read, Faustina? Yes? Maybe you can tell me what this spells?" Paula's eyes sparkled and a small twitch moved her cheek.

"P.A.U.L.A. I think you know how this works," Paula said, tracing letters on her own forehead. "Well, let's start with P." Paula stood up and handed the irons to a guard. "You've done this, before, I know, but it's a novelty to me."

Faustina felt herself going numb as she remembered the day of her own conviction. Already a slave, she had told of the murders committed by her owner. She remembered the way the sky spun in her vision when the brand touched her face. It had been one brand with all three letters that time.

And now her body cartwheeled through pain. She spasmed at the burning in her back, lurched back at the pain in her mouth and anus. Her body twitched and shook beyond her control. She heard someone shrieking and smelled burning flesh, but she focused only on moving her way through her dance of agony. She shut out everything else, accepting the pain and pulling it outside, only to welcome it back again, over and over again. Darkness fell like a curtain in her vision, only to be wrenched free by pain. The faces of Paula and Gratianus danced in her vision, grinning, leering, spitting.

And then she lay face down on the floor. The tension was gone between her asshole and mouth. Her back throbbed with the pain of a burn, making the pain in her orifices feel almost insignificant. She lay on the floor, gasping as though washed up and thrown from a violent surf. The room became black.

When Faustina opened her eyes again, there was light, confusing her since the torches were gone. She looked up to see two fine-boned white feet walking towards her, the figure limping slightly. The person squatted down in front of her. Iulia. Iulia touched her wrists and Faustina realized the manacles were gone now. Iulia held the tiny shard between thumb and forefinger, and held it before Faustina's eyes.

"They will find this when they take off your bracers. Hide it in your teeth. Open your mouth," Iulia said, gently tapping Faustina's swollen lips.

"Poison?" Faustina asked.

Iulia cocked her head and squinted.

"No," she said. She held out the shard, and Faustina opened her mouth. The girl slid her fingers in, and Faustina felt her pressing the shard in between her back teeth. When she finished, the shard rested somehow molded into place. Iulia smiled with her white teeth and stroked Faustina's cheek. She sat down cross-legged before Faustina and reached for her arms.

Faustina crawled forward, every muscle quivering in pain. Her back burned with fire. Iulia guided her, until Faustina lay draped across the smaller woman's lap.

"Not much longer now," Iulia whispered in her ear. She stroked Faustina's hair. Faustina felt the pain rise up inside, every branding, every beating, every unwelcome penetration of her life, welling up and spilling over. She wept with loud jagged sobs as Iulia held her, rocking back and forth. She flinched as Iulia touched her back, but where the soft fingers touched her, the fire in her skin cooled and faded.

Iulia held her tightly and stood, carrying her in her arms. It seemed absurd to be carried by such a small woman, Faustina thought. But Iulia seemed to have no trouble doing so, though she walked with her familiar limp. Iulia carried her towards the wall, but instead of feeling the hard marble, they passed through it into the cool night air. Faustina looked down and saw they no longer walked on the ground, but above it. As Iulia walked they moved faster and faster, ascending into the sky. Faustina laughed, euphoric to be free from the villa, the night whipping past her in a blur.

They descended, finally, in the hills north of Carnuntum, before a huge oak tree, massive in the light of the waning crescent moon. A gray-bearded man stood before it, crouching to strike sparks to a small pile of wood. Iulia set Faustina down, standing next to her as the sticks kindled into flame. Aelius smiled and sat down on a stone. He motioned for Faustina to come closer, to sit next to him.

"Not much longer now," Aelius said as Faustina sat down on the stone.

"What?" Faustina asked.

Aelius produced a bundle of cloth and unwrapped it, revealing a thin sheet of lead.

"Do you wish for justice, Faustina?" he asked.

"I do," she said.

Aelius pulled an iron, stylus-like tool from his sleeve. Picking up a small wooden tablet, he flattened out the lead sheet on it. Faustina felt a hand on her hand and turned to see Iulia. The girl smiled as she flattened out Faustina's hand, as though studying the lines on her palms. Iulia's hand fluttered, and Faustina saw blood running from her own palm. Iulia then grasped her father's wrist, and Faustina now saw the small blade in her hand as Iulia made a cut on the man's forearm. Dazed, Faustina examined the fine cut on her palm, but then Iulia took her wrist and placed her palm against the wound on her father.

"Hold tight. Do not let go," Iulia whispered in her ear. "Think of justice. Think of vengeance." Faustina felt an urge to please Iulia, and she gripped the man's arm. Faustina thought of Nemesis, and remembered the feel of hands on her shoulders, guiding her to avoid a death blow from Avitus. She thought of Nemesis flying above her now, sword and scourge in hand, soaring towards the villa. For the first time in weeks, Faustina felt strong again, felt glad to be alive.

Aelius stared into the fire, his face slack. His hand dragged the stylus across the lead sheet, and soon the image of Nemesis took shape, wings outspread like a bird of prey, sword and scourge raised high. He now scrawled words on the sheets, a strange mixture of Latin, Greek, Persian, and other languages Faustina did not know. Aelius spoke, and his words were a mixture of the languages, the word sometimes spoken in a language different than that written,

"Honor to the divine Nemesis. I complain to you winged justice-bringer that we have suffered grievously at the hands of Gratianus and Paula. The pair have inflicted countless sufferings upon Faustina and another, Avitus. Gratianus and Paula have stolen the burning stones from my order and broken oath with us. I would ask the genius of your divinity that the guilty pair suffer a doom wrought by their own perversions. I would ask that you provide vengeance to us, the aggrieved, and that you would guide this retribution past the couple's own safeguards, and that their evil be their own undoing. With fervent prayers, I ask your divinity that our petition may bring satisfaction to us by your righteousness.

"Give me your palm, Faustina."

Faustina released his arm. Aelius guided her palm to the surface of the lead sheet and smeared their mixed blood across it. He then folded the sheet three times. He produced a nail, and with this he pierced the folded sheet nine times. He moved a stone, revealing a hole just small enough for the folded tablet to pass as he dropped it inside. Faustina could not see how deep the hole was before Aelius covered it again with the stone. He turned and smiled at her, and she felt herself lifted again.

Faustina turned to look at Iulia as they ascended, Aelius and the tiny fire disappearing below them. With a shock, Faustina realized they were traveling towards the villa again. She squirmed in Iulia's arms, kicking free only to feel herself free-falling through the night air. As the ground rushed up towards her, it grew darker and darker, until, looking up, she could no longer see the stars.

She blinked, and seeing torchlight, realized she was awake. She felt the restraints again on her limbs and the cold floor, but her back no longer burned. She looked at her palm, and the dried blood smeared over a thin cut.

Chapter 6
Camilla

Avitus' confinement began with his first thoughts of freedom. For the first weeks at the villa, he complied with the wishes of Paula and Gratianus and accepted his role of stud in their stable. Focusing only on the flesh of the women, he concentrated on the pleasure of the experience. He became a dull thing, a machine powering a collection of nerves. The girls were also things to him, they had to be, because if they were something else, he would have to realize he spent every day coercing his seed into the wombs of unwilling women, rape after rape, interspersed with an occasional willing female. But aside from the few noblewomen seeking novelty, were any of them willing, or only acting to please their masters? Only one convinced Avitus of her enthusiasm without doubt, and that was Camilla, the green-eyed girl he met in the beginning of his visit.

He thought of her often, and he was pleased by Paula's enthusiasm for him to breed with Camilla, for it meant she would be the first brought to him each day. They found each other in the evening, and spoke whenever they could. She was indeed from the north, and spoke often of her tribe. Avitus found himself worrying about her in a way he knew to be unwise. Yet he also wondered about his own well-being, for he had not seen Faustina in the week since her ill-advised dinner party outburst. He assumed her to be dead.

"Have you seen Faustina?" Avitus whispered to Camilla one night as they sat in an alcove. Camilla looked both ways down the hallway.

"No," she whispered. "She may be dead. Or she may be..."

"May be what?" Avitus asked.

"She may be in the cellar with the others. That's where Paula keeps them, you know."

"The girls?" Avitus asked.

Camilla nodded.

"Stalls. Like animals," she said.

"But you have a room on this floor," Avitus said.

"Aye. That I do," she said, a sad smile on her face. "It appears I have favored pet status with our master and mistress." She looked away.

"How long have you been here?" he asked.

"A week longer than you. Long enough to know I don't want to go to the cellar."

"Let's run," Avitus said, hearing the words tumble from his mouth. He felt giddy, hearing himself.

"Where?" Camilla said, half-smiling, half-frowning.

"To your people," Avitus said.

"My people sold me, and would sell me again," she said, quietly laughing. "We have nowhere to go, Avitus. Where would you go that Gratianus wouldn't have you looked for?"

"We could go to one of the other tribes," Avitus said.

"You've never lived outside of Rome's reach, Avitus. You don't understand," Camilla said, taking his hand. "They would kill you and fuck me to death. If you're not one of them, you don't stand a chance. You have no tribe. Neither do I anymore. Stop struggling. This is what we have. Accept it. Believe me, it could be much worse in Carnuntum. Or in this house. Don't be a fool like Faustina. I love you. I want you to survive."

Avitus felt the little sphere of amber, tucked away in a hidden pocket he had sewn into his tunic. He stared at Camilla for a moment. Could he trust her, he wondered? He reached into the pocket and pulled it out, holding it in his open palm. In the light from the hallway lamps, something dark seemed to move about inside the sphere, but when Avitus held it up before his eyes, it became clear. He looked at Camilla. Her eyes narrowed.

"Iulia gave this to me," Avitus said, whispering quietly. "Do you know what it is?"

Camilla's face looked slack. She shook her head, no.

"She gave this to me, and she told me something strange. She told me that one day, I would need to kill someone. And when that time comes, I am to swallow this. And when the deed is done, I am to run to the Pole star, and meet her and her father."

Camilla stared at him, her lip quivering. She grabbed his hand and closed it around the amber ball.

"Do *not* let them find this on you," she said, barely audible, her hand shaking.

"But you will come with me?" Avitus said.

Camilla stood up and stared at him, as though wavering. She reached down and took the amber piece from his hand.

"Open your mouth," she whispered. "Hide it like this." She reached into his mouth and pressed the sphere against his back teeth. Avitus felt the amber soften and mold itself into his teeth.

"I cannot come with you," Camilla said. She turned and sprinted down the hallway, the balls of her feet padding softly on the marble floor.

Avitus did not sleep that night. He lay in bed, wondering about Camilla and her reaction to what he told her. He wondered what happened to Faustina. The woman nearly killed him in the arena, and perhaps destroyed his career, but now? She was plucked from Carnuntum before she could reap the rewards of fame. She was magnificent, tiger-like in her movements. Her eyes blazed like black fire. And now perhaps, that fire had been snuffed out in the plush expanses of the villa. They were nothing now, lions stuffed into cages, deprived of even the dignity of a death in the arena.

And what of Camilla? Was she loyal to Gratianus and Paula after all? Would she betray him? Would she tell them of the amber given to him by Iulia? Her response gnawed at him. Why would she not leave with him? As he thought about it, he realized part of what she said was true. He did not know how to survive outside of Carnuntum. For his entire life, he had been kept by others, whether as slave, convict, or gladiator. He slept in quarters provided by someone else, ate food given to him, and fought fights arranged by others. And until Iulia gave him that damned amber sphere, the thought of running to the forest never occurred to him.

No wonder Camilla refused his request. Iulia's words were madness. What was this foolish prophecy, and why had he believed it? It was just a game played by the idiot daughter of a merchant, just to amuse herself at his expense.

By the time he'd finished breakfast, Avitus decided he would tell Camilla how ridiculous the idea was. He would even pretend it had all been a joke. He would deride the amber merchant's daughter, and they would laugh together.

His heart leaped when the door to his room opened. He had grown accustomed to being observed by Paula or by one of her assistants during the breeding sessions, and he looked forward to the first session, which was always with Camilla. When Paula entered not with Camilla, but with a new girl, his heart sunk. The girl stared at the floor and twisted a strand of hair tight around her finger. Her eyes looked red, swollen, and moist. She seemed to cower, while Paula entered proudly, her hair tied up high in a net. The chunk of amber hung from her necklace, shining rays of refracted and colored sunlight, one of them resting on the girl and seeming to pin her in place. Paula smiled broadly.

"Undress," she told the girl.

"But where is Camilla, ma'am?," Avitus asked. His chest felt tight and he badly wanted to see her.

The muscles of Paula's face flickered for a moment and then froze, mask-like, into a jubilant smile.

"Have you not heard then, my stallion? Why, Camilla is the first of our stock to be with child! Her cycle is long overdue," she said.

Avitus felt the room shake a little. The young woman next to Camilla now stood naked, her body willowy. Avitus cleared his throat.

"Will I see her today?" he asked.

"But why would you?" Paula asked. She disguised her delight poorly, gloating underneath her feigned confusion. Avitus wanted to choke her. "She has been bred. Why plant seed on a growing tree?" She pushed the girl slowly towards Avitus. "Present yourself to him."

"My lady, I wish to see Camilla first," Avitus said.

"Avitus, you will do as I say. Now. If you would be so kind. Impregnate this one," she said. She took Avitus by the arm and pulled towards the bed. He yanked his arm away from her. The girl lowered herself to lay on the bed, staring nervously between Paula and Avitus.

Paula stepped back and stared at Avitus, her brows lowered. She walked slowly backward, and when she reached the door, she smirked and clapped her hands.

The entrance of the villa guards did not surprise Avitus, but their number did. Paula slipped from the room as the dogs and guards streaming into the room. The girl cowered against the wall, but as Avitus picked up a chair, she wasted little time in flipping up the mattress to cover herself for protection. The guards carried only clubs and nets, and no swords or spears. The first two men fell quickly as Avitus swung the chair with sweeping blows. It felt good to have a fight, to feel his blood pumping and his opponents crumpling before him.

It was the dogs who changed the balance of the fight, their ivory jaws clamping into one calf and then the other. Avitus fought, trying to fend off the dogs, the guards landing blow after blow with their clubs, often striking from his blind side. He became dizzy and dropped the chair. He threw one arm around the neck of the nearest guard, the room a swirl of shouting and barking, flailing clubs and snapping jaws. Avitus wrested the club from the man's hand, slamming the end of the weapon into the guard's face until the room tilted in his vision. A bell rang in his ears and darkness flickered in his vision.

He was on the floor now, hands, nets, and teeth restraining each limb. As he felt himself lifted and carried, he looked at the ruin of his room. Four of the guards lay on the floor, most of them not moving. From behind the mattress, the girl's eyes peered at him. One slender hand rose, palm out towards him. Avitus smiled and tasted copper as blood trickled into his mouth.

Avitus awoke to coldness on his face. He opened his eye and saw Paula's face. She held a wet sponge in her hand and used it to wash him. His first thought was to grab her, but he could move neither hand nor foot. He looked around and saw he lay on some kind of rack, tilted at forty-five degrees from the floor. He felt a plank underneath, and another piece served as a footrest to bear his weight. Clamps held his ankles together, his legs extended straight, while other clamps held his wrists, his arms extended at forty-five degrees from his body. He was naked and could see a number of fresh bruises on his body, his calves lightly bandaged.

Avitus felt calm. In fact, he felt very little. He let Paula ladle watered wine into his mouth and enjoyed the crisp coolness in his throat. She smiled and looked across the room. Avitus followed her gaze, and saw the girl from his room, still naked, standing on the other side. Another nude young woman sat on a low bench, her eyes almost closed as she stared at the floor, hugging herself, her thick blond hair framing her face.

"They are for you, my gladiator," Paula said. "You will make them big with child, and give me more warriors. I have to tie you down, for you love the fight more than the fucking. What is it? Must you see blood to become excited?" Paula's eyes widened, her pupils expanding, and Avitus felt like a snake crawled through his belly. She leaned close to his ear. "I like it," she whispered. "I like to see the blood. I like to see men bleed. It's when they're at their best. The moment when their essence is leaving them, pouring out of their body, readying them for death, that is when they are truly alive. I can take as much, or as little, of your life from you as I want. I can take as much seed from your loins as I wish. I can take as much blood from you as I wish."

She leaned in very close now, gripping his head by the hair, tight, twisting his hair around her fingers. "I like the blood, Avitus." Avitus snarled as pain shot through his ear. He bellowed with rage as he realized her teeth were locked onto the cartilage of his ear. Insane laughter rattled out between her clenched teeth, until with a final sheet of pain, she stood up again, spitting the top of his ear into his face. It bounced off his forehead and onto the floor. She stared down at him, leering with blood-stained teeth and eyes not of the waking world.

She darted over to a table against the wall. Avitus glanced at the other women and saw terror masked by flat expressions. Paula returned to his side, an iron carding comb in one hand. The other hand held two bronze needles between thumb and forefinger. The carding comb consisted of a wooden handle widening out to a head like a brush, but instead of bristles it bore iron nails. Used to comb wool, Avitus had also seen its work on human flesh.

"Any sons of mine will grow to hate and kill scum like you," Avitus said. "I will die today, but the gods will see to your punishment."

Paula giggled like a madwoman.

"But you won't die today! No, I shall not give up my lovely pet, with his lovely milk and his lovely, lovely blood!" she said, her voice rising and falling unevenly. She tittered as she set down the comb and, pinching one of his nipples, jabbed a bronze needle through it. Avitus set his teeth, staring at the ceiling, and when he felt the needle stabbing through his other nipple, he steeled himself to not flinch. But when she twisted the needles back and forth, a gasp shot out of his mouth and Paula cackled.

She stepped back and wrenched off her own palla, her breasts heaving as she panted with excitement. Picking up the iron comb, she climbed onto him, straddling him, rubbing her wet pussy against his flaccid penis.

Chapter 7

Resurrection

"Fuck me!" she hissed, raking the comb over his shoulder. It felt like fire laid across his skin. "Fuck me!" she hissed, and now the comb raked across his chest. Again and again, the tool tore its way across his torso, as Paula jammed and ground her pelvis against him. Avitus clenched his teeth as he felt the comb catch on the pin in one of his nipples, feeling as much as seeing the white flash of pain as it tore out. He felt Paula working his cock into her vagina, shocked he could somehow be erect.

The wet pull of her hole gave a pleasure in parallel to the pain blazing across his skin. By focusing on the slick friction of her cunt, he felt some of the energy fade from the pain. Paula bounced on top of him, still occasionally raking him with the comb, but distracted by the sex. He could identify her orgasms only by the clenching of her internal muscles, for her expression masked all normal forms as she spluttered and spat. She leaned forward and rested her face against his shoulder. He felt her tongue lapping at the blood, and he was grateful at the cessation of the carding comb's attack.

When she sat up again, he knew his respite was at an end. He was surprised at how much blood covered her face. Crocodile-like, she grinned and this time carefully slipped the shaft of the remaining needle through the teeth of the carding comb.

"Your blood, your life, all mine," she cackled, snapping her wrist and tearing out the needle. Avitus groaned, the pain now all blending together, his mind confused by the feeling in his penis.

"Now, little bitch," Paula said, climbing off and dropping the carding comb with a chuckle. Blood was smeared across her face, breasts and hands. She turned to the girl from the room, her gaze changing from fire to iron. The girl walked over to the bench and set one foot on it, opening her shaking legs. The blond-haired girl turned with a rigid expression and stuck out her tongue, lapping mechanically at the smooth folds of the other girl's labia, spitting into her slit and working the saliva in with her fingers.

"Now," Paula said again, and both girls approached Avitus on the rack. Avitus stared at them, feeling as though he was not in the room but only observing them. His skin ached, and he almost laughed at the thought that part of his ear was gone. He wondered how much more of his body Carnuntum could take. The blond lowered her head and he watched as she sucked his softening cock into her mouth. He groaned with pleasure as the suction stretched his organ, but somehow he felt like two different people, both Avitus and someone observing Avitus. When his penis did not harden fast enough, Paula snapped the girl's bottom with a short strap, and the blond sucked with renewed vigor.

"Enough," Paula said, and the girl backed away, leaving Avitus' prick to bob in the air. "Now," Paula said, and the dark haired girl climbed over Avitus, straddling him. She bent her knees slightly and lowered herself, holding his cock with circled thumb and forefinger, aiming it inside. She lowered onto it, gingerly at first, until Paula's strap flickered against her, then grunted as she took it all the way in. She leaned her hands on the rack and stared at Avitus with her empty eyes, pumping her hips up and down like a machine. It bothered him, the way she stared and so he closed his eyes and focused on the wet pumping, allowing himself to feel only inside her until he came. He regretted looking into her eyes as he felt the white burn leaving his body.

Before his erection had time to soften, Paula goaded the blond onto him, who bounced hard on his pelvis with an erratic rhythm, eventually milking a second orgasm from him. Paula fed him wine, cheese, and mushrooms from her blood-stained fingers then, before a third girl mounted him later, clumsily jerking her hips and whimpering. Paula lashed her, heckling her with criticisms. When Avitus came, without pleasure and looking into the girl's sobbing face, it was because the whip had forced her into a spasm with each strike.

By the fourth girl, Avitus began to hate them, hate the way they sobbed and writhed on top of him, weeping as they stopped to suck him hard again. What did they have to complain of? Did they bleed, too? The rack seemed to sway and he demanded frequent drafts of wine, which Paula, laughing, supplied. The girl on top of him straddled him facing in the opposite direction, her muscular ass slapping against his hips as Paula's small lash flickered against her sweaty back.

"You can't even make him come?!" Paula barked at the girl. "Use this!" Paula, sneering at Avitus and letting him see it, placed a bulbous iron rod in the girl's hand, an object about the size of a dagger handle.

"I don't understand," the girl whined.

Paula grabbed the girl's hair, pulling her head close to her lips as though Paula wished to whisper in her ear. But Paula did not whisper.

"Stick it in his ass!" she hissed.

The fluids wetting his crotch did little to ease the pain as the girl, still astride him, pressed the device between his legs, pressing down on one testicle momentarily. Avitus spread his legs as much as he was able to, if only to shorten the process. Paula continued to lash and shout at the girl, and in her fear she jammed the tool against his anus, finally pushing it in at an angle.

"Wiggle it!" Paula shouted.

The girl jammed it back and forth, until Avitus felt himself convulse and come, like a painful reflex. He allowed himself to groan, lest Paula should fail to notice his orgasm.

Avitus closed his eye. He must have dozed, for he felt himself wake up to shrill laughter, coming from the girl on top. Her back laced with thin red lines, she turned her head to look back at him. He did not recognize her at first, for the blood covering her face. But when she turned further, he saw from the remaining half of her face it was Zari, the other half rent by tooth and claw. Her one eye fixed upon him as she reached back with a lacerated arm to lean on his belly.

"I died well, Avitus," she said, coughing blood. "By Hercules, I did not cry. I died well for you."

Needles of pain stabbed through his limbs as the guards lifted Avitus from the rack. They lifted him to his feet as they fitted manacles and leg irons. His legs throbbed as he stepped from foot to foot, but he was happy to be off the rack and did not ask where they were leading him. He gulped the watered wine given to him and even thanked them.

He walked, dizzy as they led him down a flight of marble stairs. It felt cool down there, even cold. He almost fell down the steps, stopped only by the guards' hands. When they came to a door, one guard unlocked it and stepped back.

"Go in," the guard said, his face pale. An acrid smell leaked from the door.

Avitus chuckled and pushed against the door. As he walked in, he felt a hand shove his back and heard the door slam behind him, the lock snapping shut. He looked across the room to see Camilla on tiptoes, her wrists fastened to chains suspended from the ceiling. Her naked body glistened with sweat, her long hair plastered to her face. She whimpered, lifting one foot at a time to relieve the pain. Avitus had seen people suspended enough to know her arms were already injured, if not ruined, from the way she hung.

He lurched towards her, forgetting his leg irons. He saw the floor rising up to meet him and put his hands up in time to break his fall. He looked up and noticed Gratianus and Paula each sitting on a chair to either side of Camilla, each with a massive black dog. Gratianus held a spear, Paula, a *flagrum*, its twelve straps flickering in the air as she bounced the handle of the scourge on her knee. He heard the tips, likely embedded with glass, bone, and metal, rattle against the floor.

A brazier, the source of the acrid smell, burned against the far wall behind the couple. Gratianus and Paula looked at each other, grinned, and stood up. Avitus felt his stomach squirm as he watched them approach the brazier. He struggled to his feet, feeling an urgency to do something, but he knew not what. Gratianus turned and sneered, pressing the tip of his spear against Camilla's belly, dimpling it.

"Stay," Gratianus called to Avitus.

Avitus stopped. Gratianus leered at him, making Camilla twitch as he poked her with the spear, just hard enough to make tiny wounds. Behind Gratianus, Avitus saw Paula drop the *flagrum* and open a wooden box. Paula took a number of metal objects out of the box, each the same size, about as large as a woman's fist and roughly square. They looked hollow and formed of iron sheets bent into cubes. Distracted by Camilla's suffering, he lost count of the cubes as Paula placed them gently on the floor in what may have been a pattern. He realized she was chanting or reciting something, though he could not make out the words.

When somewhere between ten and fifteen of the cubes lay on the floor, Paula pushed the box aside and squatted before the cubes, something small in her left hand. She lifted her face to the ceiling and a low drone climbed out of her lungs and into the air. She held the tone for a long minute, and then with a bark, clutched one of the cubes and tossed it across the floor. As it landed, it made a long clang, like a discordantly tuned bell, and he heard the sound repeated. When she threw another cube and he heard the sound echoed, he realized the noise came from Paula's mouth. She dashed forward, and with a piece of charcoal drew a strange symbol midway between the two cubes.

Again and again she threw the cubes, echoing the sounds in a way that made Avitus' skin twitch. Each time, she made a mark on the floor between the last two cubes thrown. When one cube struck another, the jarring sound coiled his stomach with nausea. That which burned in the brazier smelled worse now, but instead of producing smoke, a shimmering distortion rose from the device. It looked much the same as air quivering over an intense heat, but it took up too much space, thought Avitus. And it seemed to move away from the brazier, towards Paula. Gratianus tittered, hopping from foot to foot and snapping his head back and forth to look at Avitus, Camilla, and Paula.

The haze moved over Paula. Caught in the middle of singing out a metallic echo, her voice rose to a shriek and she leaped to her feet, her body convulsing without falling down. Avitus saw her as though she were a mirage, her form wiggling. She crouched down and snatched up the *flagrum* from the floor. She stood hunched over, her face distorted by the shimmering but also by a feral rage. She suddenly appeared to notice Camilla and sprinted towards her.

Gratianus darted backward, his giggling now shrill and idiotic. Avitus started forward as the first stroke of the *flagrum* hit Camilla's back. The girl convulsed as though struck by lightning, her feet flailing through the air. Paula drew the *flagrum* back, flicking blood across

Gratianus as he danced.

Gratianus started as he saw Avitus approach. He charged with his spear, feinting and tangling the spear in Avitus' leg irons, tripping him. Avitus fell to the floor, cursing his failure to spot the ploy. He felt a cord around his neck and realized Gratianus sat on his back. Every struggle brought blackness to his vision, and after one black-out, he looked up at Camilla.

The girl hung limply from the wrist chains, no longer struggling to stand, her feet trailing in a pool of blood, the pool growing from her dripping form. Severe lacerations marked the front of her body in places, and Avitus knew the back of her was far worse. Paula stood next to her, panting and sweat-drenched, staring at the girl and at the *flagrum* in her hand.

"So sorry about the girl, Avitus," he heard Gratianus say, still feeling the cord about his neck. "But there's nothing we can do about it now."

Avitus stared at the floor. It felt so cold in the room, impossibly cold. His ears rang and he felt himself shaking.

"Well," Paula said, catching her breath. "There is one way. And I would be willing to let him try, just to see it happen. How much do you love Camilla, Avitus? Do you love her enough to bring her back?" Paula stood up straight and walked over to the wall. She grasped a wooden wheel and turned it. The chains clattered through their brackets, dropping Camilla to fall wetly on her back.

"What do you mean?" Avitus wheezed.

"Can you *fuck* her?" Gratianus said.

"If you truly love her," Paula said. "And can summon the energy to spend yourself inside her, I can bring her back. I swear it."

"She's dead," Avitus sobbed.

"But only just," Paula said. "Here in the villa, Gratianus and I have the power to grant death *and* life. Yet, even we will be powerless to help you if too much time passes. As her blood cools, she will become rigid and her spirit will travel too far to recall it. But it is as you wish. It becomes tedious to explain what you cannot understand, and it becomes decreasingly relevant to do so."

Avitus felt the cord removed from his neck and Gratianus' weight lifted from his back. Gratianus walked forward and joined Paula, his hand on her back as they walked to the chairs.

"The guards will be here soon. Use your time as you wish," Gratianus called out.

Avitus started to stand.

"Crawl!" Gratianus barked.

Avitus lowered himself and crawled forward on knees and elbows, approaching Camilla. He crawled through the cooling pool of blood. He pictured Camilla laughing, smiling. He wanted to see her smile, if only one more time and decided he would do anything to make that happen. He tugged his loincloth free, dropping it into the blood as he climbed between her legs. Numbly, he was surprised to find himself erect as he pushed inside of her, quickly and deeply. She still felt warm. He pumped, vaguely aware of the snickering from Paula and Gratianus as he kissed her lips. Camilla's body slid on the wet floor as he thrust into her. He thought of the first time he saw her. He thought of what could have been, of their child, of an escape to the north. When he came he closed his eyes and saw her laughing again.

The orgasm fell from him like a curtain. Camilla's dead green eyes stared up at him, and his ears rang with the laughter of Paula and Gratianus. His tongue probed the piece of amber lodged in his tooth. It fell onto his tongue, almost like a living thing, and he swallowed it. He would kill them now. He would kill them both.

He tried to rise, but slipped in the blood and fell onto Camilla. More laughter, louder now. He slid off of her, his vision red with rage as he crawled towards the couple. He vaguely heard footsteps approaching him before the hood fell over his head, a noose around his neck, and hands on every limb.

Chapter 8
The Hounds

A dream, a foolish dream, Faustina thought. There would be no escape, no curse brought down upon the heads of her captors. Her hand had been cut in her torments, and a frivolous spirit must have woven this into a dream for her. If the amber merchant and his daughter could have saved her, and if they did remove her from this place, then why was she still here? It was nonsense. Nemesis would not save her now. She felt the cold floor underneath her body, her limbs cramping with thirst and the chill. *I will die here. All that remains for me is to kill anyone who falls within reach. One life, Nemesis. Let me take one life with me and I will happily die.*

Faustina immediately spotted the weaker of the guards when they arrived and opened her restraints. She felt the blood course into her limbs again as they lifted her, yet she let herself hang limp. When they fed her watered wine, she forced herself to be sick as they dragged her along the hallway, much to the guards' complaints.

There were three guards, two dragging her and one walking behind. Faustina noticed two of them, the one behind her and the one on her right, watching her. The one on the right pretended he was dropping her, perhaps checking her for a reflexive action. She barely resisted the attempt, but managed to sag towards the floor. The guards laughed then, groping her naked breasts and buttocks, probing her as they walked. But the guard on her left barely looked at her, apparently distracted and irritated by the others.

They stopped at a door and the guard following them stepped forward, unlocking the door. He pushed it open and turned, calling out to another guard down the hall.

Faustina felt the hilt of the weak guard's *pugio*, the broad-bladed dagger in her hand before she thought about grabbing it. In one movement, she drew it and severed the windpipe of the guard on the right. She spun, not stopping to look, and thrust the *pugio* into the lower abdomen of the weak guard, driving him into the room with both the dagger thrust and her shoulder.

Inside the room, she spun once more, shouldering the door closed and barring it shut. She turned to face the guard in the room with her. The man clutched the dagger, still embedded in his belly. Faustina heard a ragged laughter and realized it was her own. There was a rack of sorts in the center of the room, almost like a milking stand for goats. The man gasped and tried to keep the stand between himself and Faustina, but she quickly circled it and plucked the *pugio* from his belly.

She kicked his knee and he fell face-down on the floor. She heard him weeping as she knelt on his back. A strange warmth filled her. She could kill him instantly, as she had done before in the arena. A quick thrust to the base of the neck would end him. But for the first time in her life, it wasn't just about the win. It wasn't just about an order to kill. It was the giddy pleasure she now felt that surprised her. She wanted this to last. She heard the pounding on the door. They would soon break through the door. But she wanted the pleasure of making the man suffer.

Faustina felt herself drool a bit as she slowly sunk the *pugio* into the guard's kidney. He squealed with agony, and she with laughter. She looked up in time to see the door splinter, a guard kicking the door in, axe in hand. He stood still, his face flexing as though trying to comprehend what he saw.

Faustina raised the *pugio*, and with a shriek of joy sunk it into her victim's other kidney before she was knocked to the floor.

Faustina felt herself tumbling, as though in a crashing surf of kicking feet and leather straps, agony alternating with blackness. She sometimes looked up to see the room spinning with angry, shouting faces before falling again into darkness.

She opened her eyes again after the beating stopped. Broken blood vessels cast little threads over her vision. She felt herself lifted, the floor passing beneath her. Was Iulia with her again? She wondered until she felt herself dropped upon the wooden stand in the center of the room. She felt a guard holding each of her limbs, strapping them in place so her belly rested on a raised plank. Straps around ankles and knees secured her spread lower legs against the floor of the stand. Other straps fastened her forearms by the wrists and elbows. Faustina screamed in anger as the guards swiveled into place a vertical wooden bar against each side of her neck. The bars latched together at the top, preventing her from moving her neck. The belly-plank prevented her from moving forward, and now the neck bars stopped her from pulling backwards. She looked down and saw droplets of blood pattered on the floor, dripping from her nose and unknown cuts on her face or head.

"The most ill-behaved of all your bitches, Paula!" Faustina heard Gratianus say as he entered the room, but she could not turn to see him. "And she appears to be barren, no good even for breeding. Why do you keep such a dangerous and useless creature in your stable?"

"Ah, my dear husband!" Paula said, following him into the room. "Have you no mercy for poor beasts? This is a fine Persian bitch." Faustina snarled as she felt a hand slap her buttock hard. "But you cannot expect such a thing to come to Carnuntum with a civilized heart."

Three dogs walked on the floor in front of Faustina. One approached her, sniffed, and began licking the blood from her face while another licked the floor. A fear crept into her mind, but she pushed it back, unwilling even to identify it. She let herself enjoy her face being licked. It was like having a pet, and the one kind affection she experienced in weeks of torment.

"Mercy kills the innocent. Ask the guards about their fallen comrade. Ask them about mercy," Gratianus said.

"It is all a matter of understanding the creature," Paula said, the couple still standing behind Faustina. Faustina stiffened as she felt greasy fingers press gently but insistently into her cunt, into her anus. It was the mockery of tenderness that bothered her the most, the soft circling of a fingertip on her clitoris. Her body reacted against her will. The dogs paced in front of her, panting. She closed her eyes so she would not count more than the four she already noticed. She felt fingers making soft circles around her nipples, stroking the nubs as they hardened. *Focus*, she told herself. *Just feel the pleasure. Don't think. Just feel.*

The fingers stopped. Paula stepped in front of her, and Faustina's blood chilled as she saw the leash in the woman's hand.

"You see, Gratianus," Paula said, her face twitching, leering as she stared at Faustina. "You need to know the beast at hand." She lifted her fingers to her nose and sniffed. She walked over to the nearest dog and let it sniff her hand, its long pink tongue licking her fingers. Paula fastened the leash on the dog. "You say she is useless. Barren. But do you breed a lion with a house cat? No. You breed horses. With horses. Lions. With lions. Dogs." She showed all of her teeth to Faustina in one smile, and then slowly walked the dog around behind the rack.

"No," Faustina said, her voice hoarse. "No no no. You cunt. I'll cut you to ribbons. Let me *out!*"

"Dogs. With. Bitches! Hup!" Paula said.

"No! No! No!" Faustina shouted, groaning with the effort of pulling against her restraints. The fear in the back of her mind was revealing itself and nothing she could do would stop it.

Faustina felt the furry weight of the hound on her back. She tensed every muscle, the rack rattling and shaking as she fought, but holding her fast. The dog's toenails raked her flanks and she grunted with disgust as the moist organ squirmed into her vagina. She felt herself shaking uncontrollably as the cock sunk deeper and deeper into her, forming what felt like a hard knot inside her. The dog panted, wheezing through its nose. Again, Faustina felt a finger stroke her clit.

"No," she sobbed. The finger flickered against the nub. Faustina tried to push down the reflex rising inside her, tried to ignore the warm rub of the knot inside her, but the heat rippled out from beneath the finger. Faustina felt herself falling, letting go of something deep inside. It wasn't enough to just think of it as something being done to her body, though that had been her escape in the past. It was that she had to give in or go mad. And so she let the rush pulse through her, embracing it, enjoying it. She heard herself crying out as she felt the pulse inside. She felt the dog grunting, and in a few moments the knot inside her shrank and the dog dismounted her.

Faustina maintained her grasp on her mind for the duration of the second dog, her attention entrenched in the pure physical sensation, letting herself go and reaching orgasm without resistance as Paula stimulated her while the dog fucked her. Any intellectual activity, any thoughts of what was actually happening, where she was, who she was, all of these she locked far away.

But during the third hound, as her focus drifted down through a haze, something flashed before her. She looked up, and in the cold reflection of a large mirror placed before her, she saw herself as Gratianus held the mirror, giggling. Battered and bruised, hair clinging to her face with sweat and blood, it was not her dishevelment that made the blackness rise from her stomach, the cold self-loathing spreading through her body. It was the first second she looked in the mirror, and saw an expression of ecstasy on the face of the wretch within, mounted by a slavering beast.

This was the end. Someone had to die, and if it could not be Paula or Gratianus, it had to be her. Was this not what Aelius and Iulia had meant by the amber shard? The merchant told her she would know the time, when she would absolutely need to slay one who needs slaying. It would be her. The amber came away easily as she probed her tooth with her tongue. She felt it changing shape, reverting to its sharpened form. As she pressed it with her tongue, it slid easily into the skin of her inner cheek. She felt a sharp sting, like that of a bee, and then it was gone, embedded.

A cacophony filled her ears, every dog baying suddenly and frantically, the one on top of her scratching her back as it scrambled off, hurting her as he withdrew. The animals raced around the room, knocking the polished mirror over to rattle on the floor. They leaped at the walls, as though trying to reach something, running into each other, snapping at one another. The barking and howling echoed back and forth across the room.

Paula and Gratianus cursed, screaming at the dogs and trying to subdue them. All efforts to re-interest them in Faustina failed. Faustina did not know how long it went on. She no longer listened or watched, but felt an icy chill spread throughout her body. She waited for her heart to stop, waited for the darkness to cloak her vision. And when the end did not come, she screamed and screamed in the midst of the barking and did not stop until her voice left her and her sight fell into dreams of falling.

She awoke in dim light. She heard voices, females, the buzz of excited whispers rising steadily to talking, calling out, until a male voice screamed at them to be silent. There were bars in front of her, and heavy wooden plank walls to one side and stone wall on the other, with more planks above to form the ceiling. She lay on straw on a dirt floor, in a cell, just too small for her to stand or to stretch out. The bars faced a wall, with what looked like a walkway between it and the cell.

The whispers started again, rising in volume until once again, the screamed command for silence barked out. Faustina listened in the silent moments, and could now hear the sounds of struggle and violence from the villa above. And with each silent moment, the conflict seemed to come closer. Again, the murmur of the voices grew.

"Shut up, you--!" the man shouted, but this time, Faustina heard the wrenching and shattering of wood, and the man's voice turned into a shriek of terror. She heard a sound of something wet being slapped against a wall. A storm of screaming female voices filled the air. The noise swelled, approaching her cell. She heard the sound of cage doors opening, and looked about for anything to use as a weapon as she crouched in her cell, naked and empty-handed. She lay on her back and started kicking the wooden cell wall, trying to dislodge a plank.

A figure appeared in front of the bars and Faustina rolled to the far side of the cell, reflexively moving to one aching knee and bracing to fight. But as she focused on the person, her stomach revolted and she fought against the urge to retch. It was the girl, Camilla, but something horrible had happened to her. Caked in dirt and dried blood from head to foot, she crouched before the cell bars, holding a long bloodstained bundle in her arms. Her hair stuck to her face in spots, plastered by a crimson crust. Her eyes glittered like two lumps of polished coal, all pupil. She tottered slightly in a way that reminded Faustina of a puppet. This was not Camilla, she thought, but a blood demon, something her grandmother spoke of.

"Faustina," the demon said. "I mean you no harm." The creature spoke in Persian. "Your time has come," she said, unlocking her cell door. "I merely offer you a choice." The demon held up her bundle and smiled, her teeth stained with blood not yet dry. She let the bundle's covering fall away. A trident and a *quadrens* clattered to the floor, followed by a bundled net, and the pieces of a *retiarius's* armor.

"If you wish, accompany me as I collect a debt from one Gratianus and one Paula. The final pleasure will not be yours, but I offer you the opportunity to witness their disposition, and, perhaps, bid them farewell. Or you may simply fight your way out on your own. You already know where to run. Do as you wish, but Gratianus' friends will look and find you should you take any direction but the Pole Star."

Faustina saw her hand shaking as it pushed open the cell door. The creature stepped back, giving her room to climb out and stand with her back to the wall. Faustina tensed herself, ready to grab a weapon should the blood demon attack.

"You were sent by Aelius?" Faustina asked, hearing her own voice crack.

The figure of Camilla smiled.

"In a manner of speaking," she said.

"You are a demon?" Faustina asked, spotting the corpse of the guard at the end of the corridor, blood smeared on the wall behind him. The cell doors all stood ajar, the girls all having fled.

"Tonight, some will call me such," the thing said, chuckling hoarsely.

"Demon you may be," Faustina said, picking up a tunic and belt from the pile and dressing herself. "But I cannot leave this place until I know the end of two other demons." Faustina picked up the shoulder armor and placed it on her right shoulder. Unlike the last one she used, the *manica* arm-guard was of chain mail, something she knew and used only far to the east. She pulled it over her right arm and smiled, the metal cool on her skin. "It all fits too perfectly, and that is strange," she said.

"And you do not run from me," the thing said. "That too would be strange, were it not for the loathing you must satisfy. I, too, know loathing, and that hunger must be sated."

Faustina heard herself laugh quietly as she tucked two prongs of the *quadrens* in her belt and picked up the trident and net. Simultaneously calm and coiled, she felt the old feeling she had before every big fight. Her mind took note of every injury in her body, calculating her strengths and weaknesses. Sound became crisper. Vision became clearer. She followed the demon down the walkway, abstractedly studying the ruins of Camilla's back.

"The *flagrum*," Faustina said. "That is the only thing I know to make such wounds."

"Indeed," the demon said as they walked past the dead guard. The shape of Camilla crouched and plucked the spear from his hands. The man's crushed head hung at a strange angle. "Ready?" she asked, her hand on the latch of the door. "They wait without."

Faustina held the trident mid-shaft in her right hand. In her left, she let the weighted net hang bundled together like a flail. She tensed, took her stance, and nodded, standing behind the demon.

Camilla's form threw the door open and darted into the corridor, spearing the throat of a wide-eyed guard as he thrust his spear into her abdomen.

Faustina did not stop to watch but moved to the demon's left flank, snapping the weights of her net into the face of a guard. He seemed so slow as she drove her trident past the man's spear, easily penetrating his chest, passive meat before her weapon. There were more guards behind the first pair. At her side, the thing attacked the men like an animal and Faustina felt herself splashed with blood as guards fell before the onslaught. Faustina's heart pounded, driving her trident reflexively into man after man, the smell of blood and fear soaking her nostrils. The men ran now, and Faustina raced behind her terrible ally as they pursued them, drunk with bloodlust. They ran over the bodies of those they killed, but also other bodies already present, men with pale eyes and skin like Camilla, armed and dressed like the guards.

The pursued men turned a corner and a hand grabbed Faustina's tunic, stopping her short. She wheeled to face the Camilla-demon who held her, Faustina's bare feet sliding in blood. The thing grinned at her.

"There is one other who may wish to join the hunt," she leered at Faustina. "Your comrade, Avitus."

Chapter 9
The North Star

Silence hung in the dark air. If Avitus did not sleep, he let his mind sink into a numb, gray void. He lay on the wooden rack, as inert as his thoughts. *Do not think. Do not imagine. But most of all, do not remember.* When he slept, he dreamed he was a gladiator, a *secutor*, his feet churning warm, summer sand in the arena. In the dream, the amphitheater stands stood empty. But every so often, he heard the sounds of combat and realized he fought an opponent. His foes seemed mechanical and unable to fight back. They stood still while he gutted them or slit their throats. And when each new opponent arrived, the body of the last was already gone.

The sun grew brighter after the last fight. Two figures approached him, but now he could not move his arms. The light grew even brighter, the arena turning into the room within Gratianus' villa. But the figures approaching were not gladiators. What were they? It took time for Avitus to focus his eye upon them, but when he did, he recoiled, pulling at his restraints.

Lamiae. Blood-drinkers, the monstrosities who fed on life. The word rose heavily from his memory. One looked like Faustina, and her eyes burned with black fire. One looked like Camilla, and her eyes burned with green ice. Blood covered the naked form of Camilla, and Faustina stood equally soaked, wearing a crimson tunic along with her sparse *retiarius* armor.

"What is this?" Avitus heard himself croak. "Camilla."

Camilla shook her head with a crooked smile. She held a rectangular bundle in her arms.

"Sorry, friend," her voice rasped. "Not exactly, but I'm afraid I need to borrow her shell for the evening. Camilla is no more. Think of it simply as a similarity in appearance. A robe discarded may be worn by another."

Avitus felt a numbness in his chest and waited for his own scream, which never came. He saw Faustina look at the girl and frown.

Avitus let the feelings slip away from him. This would be a new game of Paula and Gratianus, but he knew not what. The restraints were falling from his limbs as Faustina bent over them. Should he kill these creatures who pretended to be his loved ones? His loved ones? He loved Camilla, but did he love Faustina? He realized he did. He was free now and the women were pulling him to his feet.

"Avitus!" Camilla clutched his face and shook him, too strong for a small woman. He stared down into her blood-caked face. She seemed wrong somehow, as though her face were not her own. "Avitus! Will you join us? We go to find Paula and Gratianus. Would you see their end?"

"Aye," he chuckled, trying to comprehend the dead face of the girl. "That I would."

"Then you will see, but it will not be your hand that ends them," Camilla growled. She shoved the bundle into his arms.

Avitus smiled, knowing exactly what was wrapped within. He set it down on the floor and slowly unwrapped it. He first took out the greave and fastened it onto his leg. Outside in the corridor, he heard the sounds of fights starting and ending. He worked faster, Faustina helping him into his linen *manica* armguard. The dried blood covering him crackled and flaked as he flexed.

"Can you still fight?" Faustina asked, nodding towards his bloody torso.

"Aye. What is this?" Avitus asked, pointing at Faustina's chain mail *manica*. He had never seen such a thing on a *retiarius*.

"It's what the true *retiarii* wear," Faustina grinned at him. Beneath the blood, Avitus could still see the ravages of the past weeks. Her face looked hard, swollen with bruising, tense with unrelieved pain. But in the terrible intensity of her stare, he saw something that made him wonder about the night of their fight. Was this the same woman?

He looked at Camilla. Camilla was certainly not the same woman. She was a thing of death now, horrifying in her malevolence. But as Camilla appeared transformed in death, Faustina throbbed with an overwhelming life. Looking upon this gladiator now, he knew he would never survive a second fight with her. He knew he looked upon the core of her being, the inner flame. It chilled him and boiled his blood in the same moment.

He felt the confusion sliding away from his mind. He knew where he was and who he was. It was time to get ready to die well. It was time to kill and perish and there was no difference between the two. As he pulled his helmet over his head, and lifted shield and *gladius*, the metal seemed to merge with his body. He felt his heart pump like the hooves of a horse.

"Now," Camilla said. "Now the real game begins. Now we find your most gracious hosts. Out in the villa, a raid takes place. The raiders know to not attack you. Please extend the same courtesy and do not pursue them. We kill any guard in our way. When we have Paula and Gratianus..."

"Run to the North Star. The tree," Avitus said, facing the door, balancing sword and shield in his grip.

"Indeed," Camilla said, chuckling, throwing open the door.

Avitus uncoiled his muscles as he sprang into the corridor, hitting two villa guards running. He drove his *gladius* into the first man's throat. Still charging forward, he pinned the second man to the wall with his shield and saw Faustina's *quadrens* dart behind the man's ear, sinking deep. The guard's eyes stared into Avitus' helmet, fading in death. Avitus stepped back and let him crumple to the floor.

Avitus turned to see the hallway blocked with guards, three rows of three men each, spears ready in a miniature phalanx. He held his shield and felt the cold hand of Camilla shove him forward.

"First row!" the creature barked in his ear. He saw the front row of men hesitate, and so he charged.

Too late, he realized his error. The front row of men dropped to one knee and readied their spears as the second row thrust forward. He stopped several with his shield but saw the rest lancing towards his chest. Before he had time to recoil, one of the men in the second row tumbled forward, his head wrapped in a net. The man was pulled forward, falling upon the shoulders of the front row.

Avitus took a step, dropped to one knee, and stepped again, holding his shield high as he stabbed at the forms struggling to rise. He saw a form dart past him as Camilla's form plunged into the chaos, ignoring spear thrusts. He saw her back, shredded from the *flagrum*. Avitus stabbed into the men, frenzied, his *gladius* competing with Faustina's trident, iron and bronze serpent fangs driven by reflex and instinct. His sword stopped when the last movement in the flesh pile ceased. He looked up in time to see Camilla locking her teeth into the last guard's face while snapping his neck.

At the end of the corridor, he glimpsed two robed figures running into a room. Camilla tossed aside the still twitching form of the guard and darted down the hallway. As the door almost closed behind the figures, Camilla threw herself through the air like a partially-flayed leopard, disappearing into the room.

Avitus sprinted down the hallway towards the door, Faustina's hot breath on his back. His shield held before him and *gladius* ready to stab upwards, he raced into the room, checked by Camilla's cold outstretched arm. A panel hung open in the far wall, and he saw the face of Gratianus turn to him and titter before disappearing into the passageway.

Avitus no sooner lunged forward than the iron-like arm of Camilla locked around his throat. From the corner of his eye, he saw Faustina likewise restrained, her eyes bearing all the rage of a tormented lioness as she plunged her *quadrens* over and over into Camilla's unbleeding form. His thoughts tumbled. Kill Camilla? It was not her. Camilla was dead. This was just another trick. He reversed his grip on his *gladius* and stabbed at the girl's pale leg, but a mist already covered his vision as he choked in the headlock. He was no longer sure if he stabbed Camilla, Faustina, himself, or the air.

He found himself on his knees now, empty handed, but with the arm still locked about his throat, loose enough to allow him to breathe now. He saw Faustina next to him, her face contorted with emotion, while the naked and tattered form of Camilla crouched between them, holding both gladiators. The handle of Faustina's *quadrens* stuck out, embedded in Camilla's chest.

A metallic taste soured the air, and before him he saw both Paula and Gratianus backing up towards him, both of them now back in the room. An orange light shone from the passageway in the wall, and the pair seemed to be retreating from it. Something flashed through the air, and Avitus now saw the *quadrens* bury its prongs in the shoulder of Gratianus. He heard Faustina bark laughter as the man looked back in pain.

Paula and Gratianus retreated to a far wall, each of them holding a *flagrum* before them as the light from the passageway waxed brighter. Something was tossed out of the opening to clatter and clang on the floor. Avitus recognized it as something like the small iron cubes used by Paula. Gratianus and his wife started at the sound. Another clattered and rang across the floor, soon followed by seven more in quick succession.

Avitus heard the snuffling of dogs and watched as the green eyes of one of Paula's immense black hounds appeared at the entrance.

"Come!" Paula called, her voice quavering, but the dog did not respond. It walked into the room, heedless of its master, followed by eight more.

"Come! Come! Come!" Paula yelled, over and over again, each time striking the floor with her *flagrum*, each time more shrill, her voice edged in panic.

The light grew brighter still, and in a moment, its source appeared. A guard appeared, his head hanging from a broken neck, his features twisted with mirth. In his hands, he held an amber globe, pulsing with the orange light, something writhing within it.

"You are well, Father?" the guard said, turning his body so his eyes could look at Camilla. The bend of his neck distorted his voice.

"Fairly well. Until these gladiators destroy this form completely, yes," Camilla said, chuckling.

A babble rose from Paula's mouth. She spoke incoherently, none of the sounds resembling anything Avitus knew as words. She waved one hand in the air, her eyes wide. Gratianus stared without expression, reaching back and grimacing as he tugged the *quadrens* out of his shoulder. He stared at it for a moment, then whipped his arm through the air towards Faustina. Avitus felt Camilla twitch and heard metal clattering onto the floor behind the trio.

Avitus looked at the amber dangling from the chain on Gratianus' neck. It glowed now, casting its orange light upward into the wearer's face. Paula wore a similar piece, and it glowed as well. Gratianus seemed to notice Paula's necklace first. His face twitched and he reached out, clutching it. He yanked it, breaking the chain, pulling Paula's neck down with the effort. She did not cease her babbling, but only grew louder, staring at the bauble with rolling eyes. Gratianus tore his own piece free, and threw both necklaces at Camilla.

"Take your fucking trinkets!" Gratianus screamed. "Do you think you can carry on without me? The trade stops without me! Carnuntum will close to the Amber Road without me! Do you think Diocletian's people will not come for you?"

Camilla laughed. The sound rumbled through the cold breast at Avitus' ear. He heard an audible puncture in her lung.

"If I was willing to come tonight without permission from anyone," she said, "then I would have come long ago. Truly, do you trust your own status to account for the ease with which you were permitted to pluck gladiators from the Imperial stable? Not just any gladiators, but these two? Your confidence eclipses your worth, my boy."

Gratianus' face slackened, his shoulders sagging. He stared at Camilla, and suddenly, as though in pain, he screamed and began swinging his *flagrum* into the ranks of the black hounds.

Avitus saw the guard raise the orb high and throw it down to the floor. It crackled as it shattered, bursting into hundreds of glowing fragments. Bitterness flooded Avitus' mouth and he felt himself gag with the taste. He saw Faustina likewise overtaken. Everything in the room took on an outline somehow both crisp and liquid, and tendrils of smoke rose from some of the luminescent pieces. Avitus renewed his struggles as he watched the tendrils move towards the dogs, wrapping around them, seeming to slide into their panting mouths.

Avitus did not then know if the room shook or if he himself convulsed. He saw Gratianus and Paula recoil, pressing their backs to the wall. The dogs twitched, their backs seeming to arch, legs growing longer and disproportionate. Some of them stood on two legs now, their forelegs thickening into arms, paws distending into misshapen, clawed hands. Avitus' feet churned the floor uselessly as he watched the hounds turn into hunchbacked monstrosities. Their jaws slavered and echoing growls almost resembling words bounced throughout the room.

The beasts bounded towards their former owners, ignoring the feverish strokes of the *flagrum* landed upon them. Their hands clutched Gratianus and Paula, lifting them in the air, their talons piercing their limbs. Nausea washed Avitus' stomach as he saw slimy red members jutting from the loins of each creature. And though he felt horror, he also heard laughter spilling from his lips as he watched tunic and *pella* torn away from his captors.

He saw Gratianus held horizontally, turned face down and held in midair as his kicking legs were parted. As one of the beasts thrust into Gratianus' rectum, Avitus heard the man scream with a mixture of outrage and pain seasoned with terror. Avitus heard himself laughing, his voice hysterical. While sodomizing Gratianus, the hound-demon's claws cut strips of skin away from his back. Paula, likewise, hung mid-air from the claws of her pets. While two of the creatures reduced her breasts to ribbons, another penetrated her rectum. Claws and teeth worked continually at the screaming pair, the floor soon becoming littered with severed extremities.

"They will lose interest in these two once their hearts stop beating," Camilla cried to Avitus and Faustina, yelling to be heard over the din. "And you won't wish to be the next object of interest. You know where to run."

Avitus fell to the floor as Camilla released him. He looked at Faustina, startled at the grin twisting her face. She nodded to him as they picked up their weapons and ran for the door.

Avitus sucked in the cool night air, letting it drench his lungs. He realized he had not seen the night sky outside of Carnuntum for years, nor had he ever gone this far north of the city. He and Faustina heard no signs of pursuit, yet they drove themselves on, not daring to stop. His legs burned. His stomach churned with hunger and a throbbing lanced through his head. Which was the North Star? He was not certain, but followed Faustina who did seem to know.

Something thumped ahead of him in the darkened trees, and he dropped to one knee. At Faustina's insistence, he discarded both shield and helmet at the villa. During their run, he was grateful for the advice. Too heavy and cumbersome, he would have ditched both items and left further clues to their route. Still, they made no effort to cover their tracks, and any effort to do so would be futile if pursuers used hounds. Avitus shuddered at what those hounds might be.

The pair reckoned their only hope to be putting distance between themselves and the city as quickly as possible. But now, with only his *gladius* for protection, Avitus sorely missed his shield and helmet. He remained on one knee so he might be less visible, so he might provide less of a target, but mainly because it cooled the fire in his legs for a few seconds. A few yards away, Faustina crouched, almost invisible in the shadows, her net draped over her face. Unlike himself, she retained all of her gear.

Avitus heard more thumping, and a slender form led a tall, white horse into a clearing ahead of them. The person looked female, and Avitus recognized the limp of Iulia. He exhaled his breath, and the girl turned at the sound, smiling in the moonlight. She waved him forward. He stood up, his legs cramping as he walked forward.

As he entered the clearing, Avitus saw two more horses, Aelius stroking one of them. He thought of Camilla as he saw the old man, and suppressed a gag. Aelius smiled at him. Avitus looked back and saw Faustina close behind him, trident held alarmingly ready. He checked his arm as he reflexively reacted to the stance. Faustina smiled at him.

"Why are there only three horses?" Avitus asked aloud, adjusting his grip and stepping away from Faustina. His chest began to pound as he watched Iulia scamper up a tree and climb out onto a limb, a pale creature in the moonlight, her white *palla* making her ghost-like. He felt himself placing his feet for a fight.

"Have you ever ridden a horse?" Iulia called down from the tree.

"No," Avitus said, scanning the tree line for enemies while keeping Faustina in his limited line of sight. So this was it. Having freed Faustina, they would now kill him or leave him behind. If they didn't kill him, he would have to kill himself before Carnuntum's troops found him.

"Then you'll ride with me," Iulia said. She stood up on the tree limb and made a clucking sound. The white horse walked beneath her. Iulia squatted, gripped the branch, and lowered herself to stand on the horse's saddle, sliding down until she sat on it. She stared at

Avitus and patted the horse's back behind the saddle. "You may sit here if you put your little knife away," she said.

Avitus heard Faustina and Aelius chuckling as he pulled himself up behind the girl, gripping the back horns of the saddle. By the time he was seated, he saw the other two already sat astride their mounts. Too tired to feel embarrassed, he watched as Faustina rode up next him. She leaned towards him. Without thinking about it, he reached out and traced the white scars of the letters on her forehead. KAL.

"I suppose no one will believe this, either," Faustina said, smiling. She held his hand.

"Faustina doesn't sound very Persian," Avitus said.

"Farnaz," she said.

Avitus leaned towards her and their mouths met, the *retiarius's* lips impossibly soft as they kissed. He heard Iulia cluck her tongue again, and the horse pulled away, Farnaz slipping from him. He held onto Iulia's slender hips as they rode, feeling her silently giggle. He watched Farnaz, regal astride her horse, trident still in her hand, and realized he looked upon her true form for the first time.

If you enjoyed this story, you can sign up for a free membership at ForbiddenFiction and discuss it with other readers and the author at the *Arena Breed* story page at http://forbiddenfiction.com/story/KH1-1.0001YY.

Hunting Artemis

Annabeth Leong

Annabeth Leong has written erotica of many flavors. She loves shoes, stockings, cooking, and excellent bass lines. Forbidden Fiction publishes many of her dark erotica titles.

Find her online at annabethleong.blogspot.com
or on Twitter @AnnabethLeong.

Chapter 1
Forbidden Glimpses of the Goddess

The day I came to Delos, as a girl of ten, to dedicate myself to Artemis, my mentor took me out beside the stable before the ceremony. Most of her advice washed past me. I had eyes only for the barren earth around the temple, the gleam of forest beyond, and the girls in white who whispered and giggled and peered at the newcomer.

I do remember one thing she said: "We run so hard and shoot so sure, Nikia, not only for love of the goddess and the hunt, but also because we must take revenge for all we sacrifice."

A dry, brown woman, she had skin the gray-brown color of a nut husk. I glanced up and found unexpected heat in her eyes. She cackled and thumped me on the shoulder, making me buckle under the strength of her arm.

"When the fire between your legs awakens, you'll call my words wise," she said.

Ten years passed before I did—when Theron came. On the first day of autumn, I went with the temple's delegation to greet him. Theron sat foremost in a fleet of smaller boats dropped into the water from the decks of his black ship. The sun glinted off the hard curves of his muscles as he steered toward shore with great sweeps of the oars. I couldn't make out his features from where I stood, but my body thrilled at his perfect, manly geometry. Even in the noonday heat, his brown hair gleamed with a touch of moonlight. I wondered if the goddess' fingers had recently touched his brow and brushed back his thick curls.

He disembarked with his hound at his heels, and as the high priestess spoke a welcome, I went to him and knelt in the sand, holding the ritual cup before me. He smelled of leaves and rain, as if fresh from the hunt. I tried to fix my eyes on one of his sleek calves, but they wandered up and mapped the lines of his thighs. I wondered what lay between his legs. Theron took the cup from my hands without a glance at me, without the slightest brush of flesh to flesh. He drank to the goddess' honor, his tall, lean body upright and quivering faintly with devotion. His bright brown eyes and pointed nose gave his pretty, noble face a hungry look. I breathed him in, imagining my body falling against him and my hands winding around the places my eyes had been.

Theron stepped past me and spoke the next words in the ritual.

I asked Eurydice about him at dinner, but my friend had little to say. "He is some great follower of Artemis from Thessaly. He brought a dozen steeds with him as a gift to the temple." She shrugged, whipped her black hair off her thin shoulders and looked at me suspiciously.

I tried to keep my voice light. "How long will he stay?"

"How long do any of these travelers stay? They come by the sun and leave by the moon. Who knows?"

Theron entered, and I snapped my mouth shut, swallowing what I planned to say. A hush fell over the room, reminding me I wasn't the only woman in awe of him. I smiled at Eurydice, and spent the rest of the meal focusing on the arch leading up to the white ceiling, and the carvings on the pillars around the hall. I could do without her curiosity.

My charade aside, I noticed every movement of his hands, and every change in the tilt of his head. I wished I sat beside him. I lingered after dinner rather than retire to the room I shared with Eurydice. When the moon rose above the forest trees, he crept to the stable. I wandered in after him with my bow slung over my back.

Theron's black-eared hound raced in circles at his feet. His fine black horse edged sideways as he saddled it. I watched him reassure it with strong, sure fingers and wished he caressed me instead. Theron narrowed his eyes and looked at me.

"Do you go alone on a midnight hunt?" I said, fingering my bow.

He turned away and mounted without a word, but I stopped him with a hand on the horse's neck. I knew better than to touch Theron. "Let me ride beside you," I said. "My duties multiply, and I do not often hunt."

"The ritual hunts are not the same as the real thing." He nodded. "I won't wait long."

I grinned, chose my horse, and saddled her in a rush before he had time to change his mind. When I returned, Theron gave another short nod and headed for the forest. Though I tried to hunt, I cared nothing for the flash of deer between the trees. I raced after the rich, male scent of him, strong and big enough to fill the forest. I could have followed him with my eyes closed, and yet I did not want to. I felt grateful for every moment he rode ahead of me, leaving me free to stare at his elbow, the tip of his ear, or the start of his spine above his shirt. In my heart, I feared Artemis would judge me for paying more attention to a man than to the chase.

Finally, the familiar rhythms of the hunt took over, and I found myself sighting and stalking deer. Theron, however, blundered on despite the silvery animal bodies, never touched his weapons, and made no particular effort to ride quietly. After the third time he startled my quarry, I turned on him, surprised at the anger in my voice. "What is it you're seeking here?"

His guilty eyes met mine. His brash confidence had fallen away, and beneath the veneer, he seemed haunted and harried. With an urge to lay my hand over his, I pressed my horse forward, but he pulled his mount into shadows illuminated only by the barest dusting of moonlight.

I went on the attack. "You're not really on a hunt, and it's clear you're not in this to be alone with me."

Theron swallowed. "It's the goddess," he said, his deep voice full of shame. "I dreamed of her the night before we landed at Delos. I must ride every night seeking Artemis."

"You know as well as I that Artemis will suffer the touch of no man." I didn't really mind his heresy, but I wanted to shame him as punishment for ignoring me.

His head snapped up, then dropped a moment later. "Then there's only one thing left to do."

He cleared his throat, dug his heels into his steed, and bolted off into the forest, so suddenly my horse shied. I collected her and tore after him, keeping my body low to avoid being flung from the saddle by a low-hanging branch.

Caught up in the chase, I felt his speed, as the lingering howl of his heart's desire joined with mine in longing. The leaves whipping about my face became his hair, the wind tearing at my clothes became his hands, and the horse between my legs, his body. I closed my eyes. His distinct scent seemed to spread through the forest. I breathed him in, bucking against the saddle and riding ever wilder. Surpassing him in speed, only the moon watched me.

When the mare and I tired, I fell against her neck, crazy for the touch of a lover. Theron, not yet spent, charged past me, crested the hill beyond, and hurtled down the other side like lightning. His horse's hooves ripped over the ground like thunder. His hound, staying abreast of his wild ride, yipped an otherworldly challenge to the night.

We tell a story among the girls of the temple about a man named Actaeon, a Theban prince and hunter. One day, he followed his quarry into a vale on Mount Cithaeron. As soon as Actaeon entered the vale, his animals went strange. His horse balked at some unseen thing and threw him, and his hounds lost the scent of the quarry, circling Actaeon in confusion before wandering away into the undergrowth.

Actaeon scarcely knew why he had come to that place. The air intoxicated him, and he walked on as though dreaming.

After an hour, he heard water nearby, and followed the sound to a hidden pool. Before stepping out into the clearing around the water, he froze at the sight of a woman bathing there. Tall and powerful, she stood in the center of the pool, snatching handfuls of water and sluicing her bare skin. Her short hair curled tightly about her head, and dark eyes burned from her face. Actaeon became entranced by the glow of her skin and the patch of dark curls between her strong thighs. He could not tear his eyes from her large nipples, covering half the surface of the small breasts perched atop her muscled chest.

And though we imagine the goddess Artemis does not wish to be described thus, we do it all the same, lingering on every beauty Actaeon saw. In hushed tones we talk about how Artemis stepped out of the pool and sunned herself on the rocks at the edge, running her hands over her face and neck. Before Actaeon's astonished eyes, the goddess teased her nipples, pulling and pinching them until her sharp breathing filled the clearing. Her pink tongue licked the edges of her mouth as she gasped and trailed her right hand down her belly and between her legs. Slowly, she spread her cunt and slid one long finger into the opening. The goddess writhed upon the rock as she stuffed her sex with more fingers, reveling in her private ecstasy.

Her muscles rippled gloriously, bunching in her sides as her body strained toward satisfaction. She exhausted herself before achieving bliss, however, and uncurled her body and rested on the rock, one hand still cupping her sex. Breathing hard, she turned her head to the side and saw Actaeon in his hiding place. The prince's hand pumped his straining cock. In truth, it took all his control not to charge into the clearing and take her into his arms. Artemis snatched her hands away from her cunt and leapt to her feet, turning a furious gaze upon him.

Ignoring his stammered apology with a wave of her hand, she turned Actaeon into a stag, and as the creature wobbled away on its new feet, she set his own hounds upon him.

Seeing no sign of Theron again, I dismounted and walked my mare back to the stable. I prayed, begging the goddess to forgive him for what he wanted from her, and to forgive me for what I wanted from him. I tried to placate her with hymns, and even accused Aphrodite of plotting against us.

Nearing the stable, I spoke the truth of my heart into the night. "Lady of the hunt, I don't know if I am fit to be in your service. If there is something you would have from me, take it and release me."

At breakfast in the morning, Theron sat with eyes blackened and shadowed by the night's ride. I would come to know the look well, for every night he went riding after the goddess, and every night I followed him until my horse could no longer run. And though he rarely looked at me, our kinship grew.

Autumn faded and winter threatened every evening. The leaves fell and crunched sharply underfoot. The wind traded claws for teeth, biting ever deeper during the midnight rides I took in pursuit of Theron. The naked trees struck obscene poses against the sky, digging into the earth with fisted roots and spreading their branches apart like pairs of legs.

Theron hadn't eaten in days. The endless hunt had wasted him, wearing thin the beauty of his face. The hard man beneath attracted me even more than before.

A hand closed over my shoulder as I crept behind him one night. "Nikia," Eurydice said. "What are you doing?"

"I go riding at night."

"So I hear. They say it's him you ride." She jerked her chin toward the stable, where I knew Theron would be saddling his horse.

Would he notice my absence? Or had I been creating a bond that only mattered to me?

Eurydice misunderstood the blush in my face. "It's true, then," she said.

I flashed a smile. "Eurydice, any fool can see he cares only about the goddess."

"And what about you?"

"I see nothing but him."

Her hand clutched mine. "Walk with me."

We walked behind the stables, in the direction opposite Theron's nightly ride. The trees thinned until the shore appeared and the pale beach beyond it. Barely in sight, the mast of Theron's black ship poked up into the darkness. We stepped onto the beach. She darted ahead on bare feet, but my shoes gathered sand until I stopped to remove them.

"They say they built the temple here in Delos because this is the place where Leto birthed Artemis, and where Artemis in turn played midwife for her twin brother Apollo," Eurydice said in a tiresome, pious voice.

"I know the story," I said.

She silenced me with a sharp slash of her white hand through the night. "On her birthday nights, when the moon is dark, they say Artemis comes to bathe here in honor of her mother." To my surprise, Eurydice cast her robes aside and stepped toward the chilly water. She gasped as the first of the waves reached her feet, but pressed onward until they slapped her knees, her thighs, then between her legs. Her body glowed, framed by the ocean, and her nipples stood dark and hard against her breasts when she beckoned to me. I shed my clothes and obeyed, allowing her to take me in her arms.

"We are like the goddess," Eurydice said. "Strong and brave. Forget that man." She bathed me as she spoke, scooping up water and smoothing it over my skin, holding me up against the force of the crashing tide. Her touch, though innocent, ignited a fire between my legs. I shivered as my flesh awakened beneath her chaste, teasing fingers. She ran her hands through my hair and over my face, her fingers fluttering against my eyelids, lips, and nostrils. She drew light circles over my back, but did not touch me any of the places where I most wanted to be touched. I clung to her and pressed my breasts against her breasts, sliding so her thigh slipped between my legs. Nearly sobbing from the tension, I pressed against her thigh and she allowed it. Soon I crashed against it, even as the waves crashed against me, until the breath shuddered out of me in a long spasm.

Eurydice kissed me on the forehead as the pulsing between my legs continued. "Forget him," she said again and patted me on the shoulder blade.

Confused, I moved to kiss her on the lips, but she stepped back as the water churned and filled the space between us. Without her body against mine, I trembled.

She waded back to shore and retrieved her clothing, wrapping it around her body as if nothing had happened. I longed to lie down at the edge of the waves and press my fist between my thighs, but I climbed up after her and collected my own clothes. From the look on her face, she thought she had saved me from my lust for Theron. She didn't know that the relief bursting forth like a long-held breath transformed back to desire the moment I breathed in again. He would have understood. Nothing could replace him for me, just as nothing could replace the goddess for him.

Chapter 2
Sacrifices Made for Artemis

Eurydice caught me going after Theron every night for a week. Each time, she took me to the ocean. Finally, my shaming need and her indifference became unbearable. The next night I didn't go out, but lay in my bed and pretended to sleep.

When the moon reached its height, I could stand no more. I went to the stable and took a fresh horse, hoping to catch the second part of Theron's nightly ride.

Flashes of silver peeked out between the trees, but tonight I would not stop to watch the deer. I rode on carelessly, sparing no glance to anything but the trail before my eyes. My guts tangled and twisted as I pictured Theron's face. In my dreams, he smiled when I approached and pulled me into his arms. Awake, I imagined him sneering, sending me back to my bed alone.

I passed beyond the area that I had traveled well with him, and the path before me grew rockier. I slowed for fear of harming the horse. A stone's throw ahead, between two slender trunks, silver flashed again, then stayed and glowed. It was no deer.

Catching my breath, I followed Artemis' beckoning finger, cursing myself for allowing thoughts of Theron to blind me. I knew not why she called to me, her unworthy servant, but I followed, wondering if she planned to punish me or banish me from her temple. I saw only the curving finger, the strong hand, and the well-muscled forearm used to handling a bow. She led me into the forest's darkest heart where the smell of animals crowded thick and close upon my senses. The moon failed to reach this place, and I had to trust the finger to lead me on a path my horse could manage.

The smell of sex, sharp and wild as the sea, spiraled up my nose, making my body throb. My horse shied and threw me into the bushes. I walked on, following the silver glow without reservation. A hound—the tilt of its black ears familiar to me—burst from the undergrowth, whining at my heels and running ahead to guide me. I followed, not understanding the dog's urgency.

A long time later, I heard water nearby, followed the sound, and crept up to a hidden pool. Before stepping out into the clearing there, I froze. The fog lifted from my brain, and I saw Theron, a deep wound in his gut leaking into the pool, staining the water with a thick red swirl. I rushed to his side while his hound whimpered and licked its master's forehead. I dared not look into Theron's face, for fear I'd collapse into useless sobs.

I gathered him in my arms, pressed my hand against his neck, and prayed life still flowed in him. A breath, weak but warm, fluttered the hair beside my face, and I cried aloud. I wrapped a rough bandage around his wound, tearing my attention from the feel of his soft skin. His distinct scent had been polluted by the acrid stench of blood and pain. I needed a horse. I could barely lift him, much less carry him back to the temple.

His horse, the fine steed from Thessaly, stepped into the clearing then, and I did not pause to question why. It came easily at my call. I coaxed it to kneel so I could roll the man into the saddle. After a struggle, I let the horse rise again and climbed up behind Theron.

I held him on the long ride back to the temple, my desire for him pushed to the back of my mind. I didn't cry. Instead, my eyes felt drier than seven deserts. If he died in my arms, I might be free at last, and so would he. I spent the next hours regretting the thought.

Daylight loomed on the horizon by the time we returned, and the sun's rays scattered gloriously over the land. I saw only how pale Theron looked in that exuberant light. Though he breathed and sometimes mumbled, his mind lay somewhere far away. At the last bare stretch from the tree line to the temple, the horse and I wanted to break into a run, but I held us back since it seemed Theron could not withstand it.

From a distance, the priestesses ran, bringing aid. I gave Theron over to their care and stumbled numbly to the room I shared with

Eurydice. They could ask their questions later. For now, I would let them tend to him.

The sun streamed through the windows of the room, striking me in the face with light as pitiless as the heel of a palm. I'd never been in my room this time of day before.

Eurydice sat beside me. She took my hand and began to relay a strange story. "A bird came into the high priestess's window late at night. The creature made such a nuisance and racket of itself that, still half-asleep, the high priestess took her hunting knife and killed it. But the bird's death cry rang with the voice of prophecy, and the priestess got up at once, carried its body out into the courtyard, and sliced it open to see what message the gods had written within.

"At the sight of its entrails, the high priestess entered a trance. She saw Artemis bathing alone, with none of her maidens present to attend to her. Ares, god of war, stalked the goddess of the hunt, hoping to slake his lust. The priestess saw a warrior sacrificing himself for the goddess, and a maiden sacrificing herself for the warrior."

I stirred and shook off Eurydice's hand. "I've never heard this story."

"It's the story they're telling about you."

"What's this talk of sacrifice? Is Theron—"

"Alive, and they sing your praises for saving him."

Her expression resigned, Eurydice's fine features hardened. She knew those nights in the ocean hadn't abated my longing for Theron at all. I smiled, an offering of peace, and to my relief, she returned it. "Do they plan to ask me why I was out there?"

"You were led by the goddess," Eurydice said and winked at me. "It won't stop the young girls from talking, but nothing does."

"I have to see him."

"Artemis appeared to the priestesses in a vision," Eurydice said with a smirk. "You, and you alone, are to tend to him. And when he is well, you are to leave Delos forever."

"Banished?"

She nodded and watched my face for a reaction. It should have destroyed me to think of leaving the island that had been my home for half my life. Instead, I felt exhilarated. I'd loved hunting night after night, but the thought of the wide world before me, free of vows, made my heart soar more than any midnight ride could. I kissed Eurydice on the cheek to say goodbye, and her answering sigh made me wonder if I had read her wrong on our nights together. It didn't matter now. I went to him.

Pale and weak, Theron tossed in anxious sleep. Though rest healed me, it left him untouched. The healers assured me he would live, but most of winter would be over before he recovered.

They left me alone with him, no questions asked. I soon got over the shock and began to come to terms with the realities of his body, which needed to be fed, washed, lifted, and turned. I saw his every ugliness and scar. I saw his face by evening light, by morning light, by noon light, and in the darkness. Sleeping in the corner of his room, I never spoke except to murmur to him or pray to Artemis.

What spell had controlled me through autumn? At the time, I'd thought I loved Theron, but now my feverish longing faded as I attended to his care day after day. When the healthy Theron spoke, walked, and hunted, I dreamed about his body. Now, with his body in my charge, I dreamed of the man. I wanted to see expression in his face. I wanted to see his lips curve into a smile or a frown. I still marveled at his body, but what obsessed me now were the memories of his wild laughing as he charged through the woods. I would stare for hours at his features, trying to tease out the history of his life. Childhood play, I imagined, left as its mark the old scar on his elbow. A badly-made sandal shaped his crooked second toe, I decided. Love, to me, meant knowing every inch of him, and at the same time knowing him to be a mystery.

Desire no longer drove me. I waited for him patiently, trusting he would one day return.

Theron's eyes opened one day in late winter as I dressed the wound on his familiar body. He caught my wrist.

"Nikia," he said.

I answered with a smile.

"How long have you been here?"

"Most of a season."

"And the goddess?"

"She led me to you."

Theron shook his head. "Ares tore me in half. His body blazed so I couldn't see him. I couldn't do anything to protect Artemis."

"What you did must have been enough."

I tried to calm myself by turning my attention back to the routines I had built around his inert form. I couldn't. Meeting his eyes and hearing his voice restored my desire, and my anger at his obsession with Artemis. I blushed as I ran my hands over the wound, averting my eyes from the bare skin of his stomach and the trail of fur leading down below. He caught my hand again. "She wanted me there, watching her," Theron said. "I would never have dared to be there without her knowledge."

White-hot jealousy crowded out my vision, and rage as deep as the ancient anger of the Titans pounded through me. I went on with my work, trying and failing to lock him out of my heart.

Theron grew stronger every day, and I knew I would soon leave Delos. Tendrils of spring peered around doorways like timid little girls. The sun, which had sneered down on us like a cold and distant monarch through winter, turned to gentler pursuits, taking an interest in tracking soft shadows over sloping meadows and wind-blown beaches.

I took Theron outside. Obeying the order of the goddess, everyone hid from us. "What is her plan for us?" he said into the eerie silence. I shrugged, avoiding the thought of losing him.

"Will you stay on Delos?" I said. My face gave more meaning than my words.

"Yes," he said. "I'm sorry, Nikia."

I shrugged again. It would never satisfy me for him to submit to my caress as Eurydice had done. I'd had months to resign myself to this.

The priestess came one evening. "The temple will prepare a boat for you in the morning," she said.

I did not speak of this to Theron. I cooked his evening meal, waving off his attempts to help. At the end of the meal he took my hand and pressed it to his cheek. I stared at him, heart pounding in my chest.

Emptiness woke me in the middle of the night. I couldn't smell him. Remembering autumn, I pressed the sleep from my eyes with my fist and got up to follow him to the stable. He waited there with two of his fine black horses saddled. He tossed me the reins of the mare. "You'll need to be able to keep up with me tonight," Theron said.

I nodded, feeling self-conscious. We mounted, and our horses rushed from the stable as if from the starting gates of the games at Olympus. We raced faster than the first horses rushing up to shore from sea foam under the whip of Poseidon. The magnificent horses of Achaean heroes, which pulled bright and deadly chariots behind them as they thundered toward Trojan enemies, could not have caught us. The moon witnessed our ride, our horses as sure on the night trails as at the height of noonday, and the forest sounds fading to a whisper as we gave ourselves over to the thrill of speed.

We came once again to Artemis's secret place in the heart of the forest. Intoxicated by the heady scent of the goddess's body, we dismounted just outside the clearing. Theron took my hand before we passed through the undergrowth and onto the wet brown earth beside the pool.

She appeared then, her body deadly and glorious. She wore nothing but bow and hunting knife. Her eyes flashed at our intertwined hands. I pulled away from Theron, but she stopped me with a gesture. "I won't be jealous," Artemis said, her voice large as battle but soft as a flower. Theron fell to his knees, pulling me with him.

"Rise and come here," she said to me. When I obeyed, she took me in her arms. The pleasure of her touch pounded through me, too strong for my body. "I will know the touch of no man," Artemis purred. "But my Theron deserves some reward. Give him this for me." She bent her head and kissed me full on the mouth, her sweet tongue pressing my lips open and slipping into me. I would have fallen, except the goddess held me up and pushed me into Theron's waiting arms.

Trembling, I wound both arms around his neck, letting him support my weight. He shook, too. Even in the full presence and terror of Artemis, I smelled Theron's body and longed for him. I gave him her kiss, and a little of mine, too.

His eyes on the goddess, he caught his breath, still holding me, and said, "If the goddess will accept it, I would have you repay her this in turn from me." Theron loosened my robe and let it drop from my shoulders and into the mud. He picked me up and wrapped my legs around his waist, then lifted my breasts to his lips, kissing and sucking on the nipples. I groaned and ground against him, my blood thudding in my ears. *At last.* I didn't mind being a vessel for her, as long as he touched me that way. When he set me on the ground again, I turned back to Artemis in a daze. Her eyes flashed, but she nodded her permission, and I took her nipples in my mouth one after the other, nibbling them gently as Theron had nibbled mine, trying to transmit to the goddess every nuance of the lips and teeth I had dreamed of for so many nights.

I ferried caresses between them for what felt like hours. I trailed kisses down his chest for her, ending by dragging teasing fingers up both his thighs. For him, I pressed my lips to the insides of her elbows, the flesh behind each knee, and the place where her neck met her shoulder. I vibrated with the touch of mortal and immortal alike, until my mind thrummed with pleasure and power. My fingers explored Artemis's sex, as Theron had explored mine. When I didn't think I could walk another step, Artemis made me lie down in the earth beside the pool and beckoned Theron closer.

"Look at me but do not touch," she said, this time to him. The goddess looked down at me then. "Do you give yourself to me and him?" she asked. I swallowed hard and nodded. Artemis settled her sex over my face, her scent going straight to my head. I gripped her thighs with both my hands and opened my mouth wide to her, letting my nose press into her opening as I suckled the hard nub between her legs. She gasped and laid her hands over mine, squeezing. Theron probed the wetness between my legs, then replaced his fingers with his long, hard cock. The sensation as the two consummated their love through me filled me more than to the brim. I forgot myself as man and goddess gasped above me.

I think the orgasm started in Artemis, but it passed from her into my mouth and down my body, until I shuddered and rolled my hips up to meet Theron's thrusts. Then it caught hold of him, too, and he clawed at my hips at his own release. Almost before Theron finished pouring out his seed, Artemis disappeared, leaving us alone in each other's arms, and yet not lonely.

We fell asleep at once, exhausted by the force of her immortal presence. I had no dreams, only the sensation of his warm arms around me, holding me up even in the land of sleep.

The light of the next morning's sun brushed against us like feathers. I opened my eyes to Theron. I feared he would be disgusted by me, since I no longer served as channel for the goddess. But he stroked my hair as he woke and smiled into my gaze, meeting my lips with a kiss meant only for me. "We are much the same, the two of us," he said.

If you enjoyed this story, you can sign up for a free membership at
ForbiddenFiction and discuss it with other readers
and the author at the *Hunting Artemis* story page
at http://forbiddenfiction.com/story/AL1-1.000228.

About the Publisher

 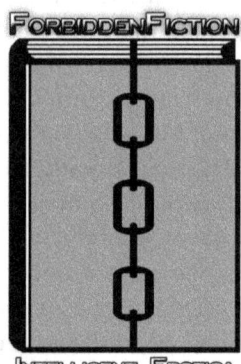

ForbiddenFiction.com is a publisher devoted to writing that breaks the boundaries of original erotic fiction. Our stories combine intense sexuality with quality writing. Stories at ForbiddenFiction.com not only arouse readers through sensations, but also engage them emotionally and mentally through storytelling as well-crafted as the sex is hot.

ForbiddenFiction.com is also designed to be a social reading environment. You'll have fun even if just reading the latest post each day, yet you will have the chance for so much more. Readers and authors can be part of ongoing discussions of specific works and individual authors as well as more general topics.

Sign up for a FREE Membership today at ForbiddenFiction.com.